BLAIR'S
ATTIC

BLAIR'S ATTIC

Joseph C. Lincoln
Freeman Lincoln

COACHWHIP PUBLICATIONS
GREENVILLE, OHIO

Blair's Attic, by Joseph C. Lincoln and Freeman Lincoln
© 2025 Coachwhip Publications edition

Cover: *Shipwreck off Nantucket*, by William Bradford

First published 1929
Joseph C. Lincoln, 1870-1944
J. Freeman Lincoln, 1900-1962
CoachwhipBooks.com

ISBN 1-61646-612-X
ISBN-13 978-1-61646-612-1

PART ONE

Which Deals with the Wreck of the Bark,
"Pride of the Fleet," in December, 1883,
and the Happenings of the Period
Immediately Following It.

Recorded by
Iantha Beasley Hallett

I

When Mr. Thornton and Marian made me understand
they honestly wanted me to write out the first part of this
story—history—whatever you mind to call it—I was real
kind of tickled, as you might say. All my life I've been a
great reader. I read "The Mysteries of Udolpho" when I
was a ten-year-old child and I can remember dreaming
about it and screeching right out in my sleep and waking
up all hands in the house, including my father, poor suffering soul, who had nervous dyspepsia and was all of a
twitter till four o'clock next morning.

And ever since then I've read and read. Jonas Jones, he
vows I have wore out the steps of the Orham Public Library
cruising in and out with books. And, which is one of the
queer things about a business that is full of nothing but
queer things from the time when the *Pride of the Fleet* came
ashore in December, 1883, till last August in this year of
our Lord A.D. 1927, the kind of stories and books I have
always loved best to read is them where something secret
and mysterious and blood-curdling is always happening
and you don't know why nor wherefore it did happen until
the very end and then you find out it happened all different from what you thought it did. There is a whole shelf
down there to the library filled with what Etta Small—she
is the librarian—calls "mystery stories." I bet you I have

read every one of them stories three times over and Etta always lays out every new one that comes in so as I can have it first. She is real nice that way, Etta is.

But never in all my born days until I was eighteen year old did I so much as dream that I should be mixed up in a real honest and true mystery myself, let alone being asked to write down my part of it. And now, this minute, as I begin to think of what did happen there, at the beginning, forty and more year ago, and all that has happened since, I declare I can feel the shivers run up and down my back same as they run so many, many times while it all was going on. Reading about a mystery is all very well, but living in the middle of one is—well, all I can say is that I wonder I am living.

But there, I must get going, I suppose, because the very last words Mr. Thornton said to me was, "Don't spread it out too much, Iantha," says he. "Begin quick and keep moving." And Jonas Jones, who don't know one single thing, except by hearsay, of what happened away back in them old days, though I must allow he has been a lot mixed up in them that have happened lately, had to put in his word.

"Iantha," he says, "get her under way fast and crowd her the whole voyage. If you write same as you talk you ought to have a full sail breeze from port to port."

Well, be that as it may, and I shall not bemean myself by wasting time on his sauce, I realize I must begin somewhere and so I will.

> "Iantha Beasley Hallett is my name,
>   Humble is my station.
> Wellmouth is my dwelling place,
>   And Christ is my salvation."

That is how I used to write it in my Fourth Reader when I was a girl in school and it is just as true now—

except the Wellmouth part—as it was then. My father,
Octavius Ginn Hallett, died when I was going on seventeen, less than eight years after I scart him almost into his
grave by screeching out of "The Mysteries of Udolpho,"
same as I have already put down. Mother was left in our
little six-room house down to Wellmouth Neck, with half
a dozen children—one to every room as you might say—
and almost no money. I was the oldest one of the six and
says I, "I will go to work and earn my own living, for as
the Good Book tells us, 'Yet is their strength labor and
sorrow, for it is soon cut off and we fly away.'" (Psalm xc,
verse x.)

Well, having set out to do a thing it did not take me
long to do it, that being always my way. The man who
drove our butcher cart told me that the man who drove the
Harniss baker wagon had told him that old Captain Freeland Blair, who lived in East Orham, was in need of somebody to be extra hired help for the woman who kept house
for him. So, unbeknownst even to mother, I took the next
morning's train to Orham Center, walked from there to
East Orham and the Blair place, made my bid for the job
and got it. I crossed the threshold of the Blair house in
June, 1881—if you can call a back woodshed doorsill a
threshold—and I have never uncrossed it, to stay out per-
manent, I mean, since that hour. For over a year and a half
I done dishes and scrubbed and made beds and was a sort
of first mate and crew put together for Eliza Tidditt, the
widow woman who had been there so long. Then she got
too feeble and rickety—not wishing to say cranky—to put
up with any longer and, after she and Captain Freeland
had a big row about nothing in particular, he discharged
her or she resigned, whichever it was depending on whose
story you happened to be listening to. I think now, knowing what I do, that the captain wanted to get rid of her.
He was already beginning to act queer and nervous and to

have his praying fits and glum spells. Not the way he had them later, but some. And I should not wonder, too, if he was figuring on saving money, for her wages was naturally higher than he would have to pay me just starting in.

At any rate, after she had gone I took over her work and mine and began to keep house for the Blairs. I little thought, when I moved my trunk and things from the little dingy, dark room leading off the unfinished attic in the ell to the more pleasant one in the back of the house, that that very room was going to be my sleeping and resting and reading place for the rest of my life. But I have done the Blair housework for forty-four years now and I presume likely I can keep on doing it, if I want to, till I am called above. One thing I will say and that is that, so far anyhow, I have never set down and whined for anybody to help me do it. I was brought up to use my hands ever since I was old enough to stand on my feet, pretty nigh. I have had scares enough, and a plaguy sight more than enough, in this room and in this house, mercy knows, but it was never the prospect of hard work that frightened me.

Mr. Thornton tells me to be sure and say something about where the Blair house is and what it is like, because that will help him and the rest when they come to tell their part. Well then, it is a great, long, low, white-clap-boarded house, standing away off by itself on the road folks call Nickerson's Road, which leads from East Orham village, a mile or so to the eastward, and winds along the shore of Herring Creek and on past the inlet we call the Salt Pond, over and between little hills spattered with bayberry and beach-plum bushes, with splotches of pitch pine hither and yon, till it comes out again on the main road to Orham Center which bears about five miles east of south—Orham Center does, I mean, not the road.

The house was built by Captain Ezekiel Blair, Captain Freeland's grandfather, but it has been added on to and changed around some since. It sets north and south, its east side—that is the back—towards the ocean and its front to the road. It is a good ways from that road, too, and there are silver-leaf trees and lilac and snowball and syringa bushes and a flower garden in the big front yard. There is a brick walk leading to the front gate from the big white front door and a gravel one from the kitchen door, which is on the land side of the house. Then there is another path still, which makes three altogether, and that twists around the corner of the one-story woodshed ell to the woodshed door on the side towards the Creek and the beach.

Reading this over after I have wrote it, it comes acrost me that nowadays there is one more path, which makes four. It goes around the south end of the house to the porch and from that porch there is a door into the parlor. But in Captain Freeland's day, the time I am telling about, that door was just another window and there was not any porch. Aunt Becky had that porch put on and the door cut through a long spell afterwards, when she was in charge.

The house is only two stories high—except the woodshed part, which is just one—but it makes up for it by its length and width. Jethro Gould used to say it was all "spraddled out," if you know what that means. Abreast the end of the woodshed, and about fifty feet from it, is a good-sized barn and there used to be pigpens and a henhouse and hen yard the other side of that. The barn faces the road, of course, and there is a gravel driveway from it to the road. The gate to that drive is not a gate at all, but just two stone posts with an iron chain between them. So it was when I first saw it and so it is to this day.

Inside the house is as big and spraddly as it is out. When I first began to write this it was my idea to tell about how it was laid out and about where the rooms was and how you got to them and all like that. But, my soul!

it took me one whole afternoon to tell about the front hall
and parlor—they call it the living room now—and by the
end of the next afternoon I was so mixed up myself, let
alone the mix-up in the mess I had written, that nobody
on earth could have told whether I or they was in the cel-
lar or up on the roof. So I gave it up and you will have to
do the best you can imagining the layout for yourselves.

There is just one word, though, that I must call your
attention to afore I leave off about the house and begin
about the folks in it, and that word is "doors." I do honestly and truly believe that there never was a house built
with so many doors in it as this one. It is just shot full of
doors, as you might say. There is not scarcely a room, nor
a hallway nor nothing downstairs and up, that you can't
get in and out of two or three ways if you have mind to.
Jonas Jones vows it is the best house to play hide and hoot
in that ever *he* see.

Now about who was living there when I came and right
afterwards. Captain Freeland Blair was there, of course.
He was born and brought up in this house, same as his
father was afore him, and he used to come home to it when
he was on shore leave from voyages, for, like most Ostable
County folks, he went away to sea when he was young and
got to be captain of a square-rigged vessel when he was
not much more than twenty. When he was thirty-five, or
some such matter, he give up seafaring and went into the
ship chandlering trade on Commercial Street in Boston.
He done well at it and, when—along in the 'seventies it
was—he retired from business altogether and come back to
East Orham to live in the house that had been his grandfather's and father's afore him, he was accounted well-
off and already one of the township's substantial folks.
He was selectman for eight or nine year, director in the
Orham Bank, and one spell there was talk of running him
for representative up to the Boston State House. He was

along about sixty when I went to work for him, though he looked and acted lots older. He was a widower and had been for a long time, for his wife—she was one of the Wellmouth Bassetts—died afore he quit square-rigging and he never married again.

The only other souls drawing breath of life on the place at that time, after Eliza Tidditt went—leaving out the cat and cow and horse and hens and me, of course—was Jethro Gould and little Mary Blair. Jethro was a dried-up little man, with the back of his neck all sunburnt and cracked acrost with wrinkles. He—this Jethro, I mean—was a sort of odd-job man around the place. He tended garden and took care of the horse and cow and hens and chopped wood and shoveled snow and emptied ashes and built fires and mowed grass and whitewashed fences and pruned trees and the land knows what all.

"The only thing I ain't been called on to do around here yet, Anthy," says he to me one day, "is beat down the price of huckleberries when the Portygees come peddling 'em. I can't do that because they can't talk much English and I can't talk no Portygee. If I could do that," he says, "I would make myself solid with the old man. Anybody that can save him a couple of cents these days is fixed for life."

"Why don't you learn Portygee?" says I. "It must be lovely to have the gift of tongues. I wish I had it."

He shook his head at me as if he was surprised.

"If I had the gift of one tongue like yours," he says, "seems to me I would not hanker for any more—unless I wanted to talk in my sleep."

I understood what he meant, of course. The poor thing stuttered something awful when *he* talked.

"You could study Portygee in your spare time, remember," I told him.

He looked at me, more solemn than ever. "Thank you, Anthy," he says. "I'll remember that by and by maybe; but first I'll have to go back over the last seven or eight year and try and remember when I had any spare time."

He was a real good-hearted man, Jethro Gould was. He has been dead for years and years, but, as I think of him now I can see him and hear him stutter just as plain as day. I hope and trust he is free from his inflictions where he has gone. I am real sure he is; somehow I can not imagine a stuttering spirit.

Mary Blair—she was just a little girl going on nine when I came to work there—was Captain Freeland's niece. He was her lawful appointed guardian. She was his brother Oscar's child. This Oscar Blair lived in Chicago and his wife, Mary's mother, died when their baby was born. Then, along about 1874 it was, Oscar Blair was killed in a railroad accident and poor little Mary was left alone. There was a few relations, all Western folks and not much account, on the mother's side and one nigh one, besides Captain Freeland, on the father's. This one was a sister, Miss Rebecca Blair, who was fifteen years younger than Freeland and twelve younger than Oscar, and was a single woman teaching school out somewheres in Ohio. I had never laid eyes on Aunt Becky at the time I am telling about, although later on I came to know her as well as I know myself.

There was, so I have picked up from what I have heard, a good deal of question about who was to have the orphan and her money, for it was calculated that Oscar must have left considerable. His will, when it came to probate, settled all that. Outside of a few bequests scattered around here and there he had left all he had to his daughter—pretty close to a hundred thousand it was—and he had left her and it in charge of his brother Freeland with a letter begging him to be Mary's guardian and take care of her.

There was a tremendous row, particularly among them grasping out-West relations, but Freeland stood to his guns and would not give up the child nor the trust. He fetched her on home with him and he, with Eliza Tidditt and Jethro Gould to help, set out to bring up the poor forlorn little thing. They was not, nary one of them, fitted for the job, according to my notion, but I give in that they done pretty well with it, for Mary was a nice, well-mannered girl as ever I see when I come there and got acquainted with her. I was not very long learning to love her and she to love and trust me. For the matter of that, we have loved and trusted each other ever since.

Jethro Gould had one of the rooms in that ell over the kitchen. It was the one with the window toward the road and nighest the back stairs and the hallway. When I first arrived I was put in the little room off the attic and next his, at the very end of the house, but when Eliza got her walking papers—that was about February in '83—Captain Freeland had me move into the nice room I have got now. From my windows you can look for miles and miles, across the Creek, which is awful narrow right here and can be waded at low tide, acrost the half mile of white sand beach, with the surf always pounding it, and from there out to the very edge of nothing, where the water and sky come together.

Next to this room—my room—was Mary's, that is it was hers forty years ago. It is a bright, sunshiny room, with a big closet and a window fronting the sea same as mine. And next to that was Captain Freeland's own room, over the parlor and two-thirds as big. Beyond him in the hallway towards the front was another spare room and acrost the hall from my door was the biggest spare room of all—the company room, we used to call it. Mr. Samuel Gregg had that room for his, years and years afterwards, but there was nobody in it then.

1 had not been working in my new place very long afore I began to notice that Captain Freeland Blair was a

queer-acting, nervous sort of man. Even then, and it got worse and worse as time went on, he was liable to be kind and easy-going half the time and jumpy and fretful the other half. He would joke and laugh with Mary, or with Eliza Tidditt and me, at breakfast and then at dinner be glum and set in his chair without speaking hardly a word and eating scarcely nothing. Eliza used to declare that he did not use to be this way at all. She said the change had come on in the last couple of year and that she, for one, was not going to put up with it much longer.

She had a lot to say about it.

"There has something gone wrong with him," says she. "He used to be the nicest, unfaultfindingest body a person could ask to work for, and now see how he acts and talks. He is worried half to death about something. Don't tell me different, because I know. I have been married in my time and I can tell when it is a man's stomach that is torment-ing him, and when it is his head. Why, my own sainted Darius used to—"

And so on for half an hour. When she got going about her husband, who by everybody else's account was a poor stick and died from drinking a whole quart of cherry rum on a bet one Fourth of July night, there was no stopping her.

But it was plain enough, even to me, who had not known him so very long, that Captain Freeland Blair was anything but happy and contented. Jethro Gould and me used to have a lot of talks about him. Jethro had worked there some longer than Eliza had and he told me a lot.

It was Jethro's notion that money matters was behind it all.

"He never used to pinch and scrimp the way he does now," says Jethro. "Used to be free-handed and liberal, buy what he craved in reason and never count the cost. Nowadays he won't even buy the Boston *Advertiser* because that is three cents and he can get the *Record* for one."

This particular talk of ours was later on, after Eliza had gone and things was worse than they had been in her day.

"Sometimes I calculate," Jethro went along, "that maybe he has made bad investments or such matter. There was a long spell there when he used to watch the stock market pages in the *Advertiser,* turn to them the minute he grabbed the paper, and more than once I have seen him take a look and then groan and chuck the paper down as if it had bit him."

"He is terrible anxious to get ahold of the letters and mail soon as you fetch them from the post-office," says I. "Have you noticed that?"

He grunted. "A blind man that was deef and dumb would notice it," he says. "And that spell when he had eye trouble and the doctor wouldn't let him read, he would ask me to look over the letters and see if there was one with a foreign stamp on it. There was not and there hasn't been since, because I have been curious enough to watch out for it."

"He hasn't got any folks in foreign parts, has he?" says I.

"Not as I know of," says he. "The only friend or acquaintance I can think of who is overseas just now is George Crossley and I can't imagine why Captain Freeland should be so dreadful anxious to hear from him. Of course him and George are pretty close friends. There was a spell when he was George's father, as you might say."

"His *father!*" I sang out. "Now what on earth do you mean by that, Jethro Gould? Who is this Crossley one?"

Well, he told me and it took a dreadful sight of telling. Boiled down and with the scum skimmed off it amounted to something like this: Seems that away back when Captain Freeland was in command of one of his first ships he picked up a boy on one of the Liverpool docks. This boy— George Crossley his name was—was a poor thing who did not even know who his pa and ma were, or whether or

not he ever had any, far as that goes. He had been left in
a basket, or a wash boiler or something, at the door of
a foundling asylum when he was a tiny baby, and what
schooling and bringing up he had had since was hardly
worth mentioning, I judge. At any rate, he had run off
from where he was working and when Captain Freeland
found him on that dock he was half starved and so miserable that the captain took pity on him and made him cabin
boy on board his vessel. I was not so surprised to hear this
part for I had known of two or three cases of New England
skippers doing things like it.

At any rate, this George Crossley come to America with
Freeland Blair and during the voyage the captain took a
great notion to him. According to Jethro he arranged for
the boy to go to school in Boston and, by and by when
he got old enough, they went more voyages together, and
Freeland learned him navigation and pretty soon he was a
first mate and then a sea captain himself. He never married and, not having any relations on this side of the ocean
and none that he knew about on the other, he stayed as
devoted to Captain Freeland as he could have been to a
regular father. After Blair had retired from ship chandlering and was living here in East Orham Captain Crossley
never missed a time ashore that he did not come down to
spend a few days in this house. He was commanding the
bark *Pride of the Fleet* now, according to Jethro, and was in
the East India and China trade for a firm of Boston men,
running long voyages that kept him away for a year or so
at a stretch.

"So him and Captain Freeland write back and forth
regular, do they?" says I.

"Why, no," says he, "they don't. The old man ain't much
of hand to write letters and never was since I have known
him. And lately, since he had that spell with his eyes,

about all the writing he does, I guess, is to scribble in his log-book—diary—whatever you call it."

"He does that regular enough," I says. "I see him at that diary every evening right after supper."

"Yes, I know. I calculate he got in the habit of keeping log when he went to sea. Him and George see each other when Crossley is in port, but I don't calculate they write to each other none to speak of."

"Then what makes you think Captain Freeland expects a letter from him now?" I wanted to know.

"Because he is the only likely one in foreign parts, that is why. And, besides, the last time Crossley was here, early last January it was—you was away that week, Anthy; your mother was sick, don't you remember?—him and Freeland was terrible interested and secret about something or other. They was shut up together in the setting-room for hours on end, so Eliza told me—it was just before she left—and if she so much as dared to open a door without knocking the old man give her pepper for doing it. And after Crossley went he was all tittered up and excited for weeks."

"Well, he is that now," says I.

"Yes, but it is a different kind of excitement. Then he was more good-natured and jolly than I had seen him for months, almost like what he used to be when I first knew him. Now anybody can see he is way down in the dumps again."

"Has he had any letters at all from this Crossley man since he has been away this time?" I asked.

"No," says Jethro, "nary one that I have seen and I fetch over the mail every day. Far as that goes I don't hardly understand why he would expect one. The *Pride of the Fleet* runs her trips pretty regular and she must be homeward bound long afore this. It is all funny enough. Maybe George Crossley hasn't anything to do with it, after all."

We had another talk a week or so after that.

"Jethro," says I to him, "has Captain Freeland always been a religious man?"

He laughed. "About as religious as the average run of sailors, I guess," he says. "He goes to the Baptist meeting-house over to the village of a Sunday fairly regular, but I never calculated he let his piousness interfere with his meals. I have heard him cuss a tramp out of this yard so thorough you could pretty nigh smell the brimstone. Why? What makes you ask that?"

"Well," says I, "I went by his bedroom door the other night after he had turned in, or I thought he had, and the door was a little ways open and there he was on his knees, praying. Praying out loud and hard he was, too. The lamp on the bureau was shining right on his face and I could see the sweat standing out in big drops on his forehead. It kind of gave me the creeps to see, it was so lonesome and awful like."

Jethro rubbed his chin. "I want to know!" says he. "Humph! What was he praying about—anything 'special? Could you hear, Anthy?"

"I heard a little as I went by. Nigh as I could make out he was asking the Almighty to give him some chance or other. 'Just this one more chance, oh, Lord, I beseech thee,' I heard him begging. 'Don't—oh, don't take away this one hope from a poor, miserable sinner who is trying to make up for his wickedness.' That is what I heard, and I don't like it, Jethro: I don't like it."

All Jethro said was "Humph" again, but I could see that he did not like it any better than I did.

Well, more weeks went by and it got to be November, cold and raw weather, with lots of wind and driving rain that beat and splashed against the windows of my bedroom at night and made me almost homesick, which is a disease I am not much troubled with as a general thing. It was not

all homesickness that troubled me neither. There was a
kind of something hanging about or in or over this house,
even then, that gave me gooseflesh. I had just been reading
some perfectly lovely horrible stories by a man name of
Poe. It was on the shelf in the sitting-room, the book was,
and I took it up to my own room to read after I turned
in. I have always had a habit of reading myself to sleep, as
you might say, but all *that* book ever done to me was scare
me wide awake. One story in it was about a house with a
curse onto it. With that wind a-howling and the windows
rattling and that old man, as I knew perfectly well, a-pray-
ing his head off on his knees in the room at the other end
of the hallway—well, I leave it to anybody if it was not
natural to begin to wonder if there was not a curse on the
very house I was in that minute. I began to think there
was and I have thought so many and many a night since. I
ain't real sure there is not, even now when Marian and Mr.
Thornton think they have settled everything. It may break
out again, that curse may. It died down for forty odd year
and then turned loose, worse than ever. Who knows what
it may do in years to come?

Captain Freeland's actions by this time was enough to
scare anybody, even if they had not been reading that Poe
book. He would go for whole days without speaking to
Jethro or me. As for the way he acted towards little Mary,
that was the queerest of all. Sometimes he could not seem
to bear her in his sight, would get up and go out of the
room when she came into it. And then again, sometimes he
would grab her up and all but cry tears down on her hair, a
kind of sickening sight that was, because you do not naturally figure on seeing a big, red-faced man cry. Mary, poor
child, did not know what to make of it, and no wonder.

He was not healthy, neither in mind nor body, that was
the reason of course. It got to be what you might call a
toss-up with Jethro Gould and me whether he would be

took down sick or go crazy; seemed as if he was bound to do one or the other. It was the sickness that beat out in the race finally. One morning, along early in December it was—when I went to tell him breakfast was ready, there he was in a high fever and not fit to lift his head from the pillow.

He would have lifted it though, if I had let him. He would have lifted himself right out of that bed, sick as he was, if I had not shoved him back into it again and talked to him like a Dutch uncle. I did not tell him what I was going to do, but I sent Jethro off with the horse and buggy for Doctor Palmer, who was practicing in Orham Center in them days. The doctor came a-flying—the poor old horse was all of a lather when Jethro drove him into the yard—and he—the doctor I mean, not the horse—put his foot right down on Captain Freeland's stirring from that bed for a week at least.

"What ails him, Doctor?" says I. "Has he got anything catching?"

He looked at me kind of funny.

"Suppose he has?" says he. "You are not going to desert the ship, are you, Iantha?"

It was my turn to look at him.

"What do you calculate I be—a rat?" says I, pretty sharp and snappish, for such talk made me mad. "I only asked about the catching part so as to know whether Mary ought to stay here or not. You ought to be ashamed of yourself to say such things to me, Doctor Palmer."

He patted my shoulder. "I am," says he. "I knew better when I said it. No, it is not anything catching. It is—well, I can't make out just what it is, yet. Has he got anything on his mind that frets him, do you know?"

I said if he had I did not know what it was—which, you will notice, was the living truth. Then the doctor was all for my getting in a hired nurse woman to help take care of

him. Worried as I was I could not help smiling, for, knowing Freeland Blair, it struck me funny.

"You tell him that," says I, "and see what happens. He
wouldn't have a nurse any more than he would have the
very Old Harry. For one thing, nurses cost money and, for
another, he will say it is not necessary, which it isn't."

So we did not hire any nurse woman. I had my hands
full, though, for that week, not to mention them that come
right on top of it. Captain Freeland was fussy and cranky
as all get out, and it took one grown person to keep him
where he ought to be. All the time he wanted to know if
he was dying.

"Am I going to die?" he kept asking. "Did that damn
doctor tell you I was going to die?"

(Excuse me for putting that word in, but I have had my
orders to stick right by the truth in this writing of mine,
and it was what he *did* say.)

I lost my patience finally. "No, he never," I told him.
"He said 'No such luck.' There! does that satisfy you, you
foolish critter?"

He stared at me for a minute or so, not being quite sure,
I judged, whether I was joking or not. Then he grinned. It
was the first time I had seen him show even the one-sided
symptoms of a grin for six months, I guess.

"You would have made an A1 first mate, Iantha," he
says. "Well, well, all right! Clear out now and leave me
alone."

So I done it, and glad of the chance, and the next time
I stopped by his door he was talking to himself—half crying and half praying it sounded like.

Well, between taking care of him and looking out for
Mary, getting her up and off to school and all that, and
cooking meals and trying to keep house generally, I was so
tired when night come that I could not even read more of
them Poe horrors and I was crazy to finish the one I was

in the middle of. Captain Freeland did not get any worse, in fact the doctor seemed to figure he was a little better. And then came the first of the two terrible storms and the night I have been setting out to get to since the telling of the very first page.

II

If you should ask any East Orham folks of my age or older
if they remember the two big gales in December, 1883, I
am sure you not get no for an answer. They all remember
them and sometimes they talk about them, even at this
late day. We are pretty used to gales and storms on this
coast, for scarcely a winter passes that we do not have a
northeaster that is a regular twister. That is why there are
so few big trees along our village main road and why the
Baptist meeting-house has not got any steeple. It had one
in the beginning and, after that was blowed down, it had
another. After *that* went the Baptists got kind of discouraged. Seemed as if the Almighty did not care much for
steeples, on that particular meeting-house anyhow, so they
have never put up a third one.

But, of all the storms and gales I have seen and lived
through I do honest and truly believe them two that
December was the very worst. And the first was worse
than the second. That morning Jethro came back into the
kitchen, after having been into the front hall where the
ship barometer hung, and was shaking his head. I was just
going to the back yard to hang out the clothes, for with
the extra sheets and bed things from Captain Freeland's
sickroom I had an especial big wash.

"Where are you heading for, Anthy?" says he.

25

I told him and he kind of laughed.

"All right," he says. "Only I wouldn't let them stay out too long unless you hanker to have them blown over the Hog's Back lightship. The glass is falling as if somebody had tied a cod sinker on to the bottom of it. If we ain't in for a living gale of wind by noon I miss my guess. It is thickening up to the no'theast already, black as my hat."

His hat was an old brown thing, faded pretty nigh red, and I told him so, but he was right just the same. I had a regular fight to get them clothes off the line even at eleven o'clock and I declare I did think one spell that me and the best bedspread would fly up and over the edge of the bank and down into Herring Creek together. By noon it was screeching right out and beginning to rain besides. I had Jethro hitch up the horse and drive to the schoolhouse to fetch Mary home. It was a good thing I did, for the poor little soul would either have been blown out to sea or drowned by the downpour if she had tried to navigate on foot.

By supper time the storm had settled down to business and the noise outside was frightful to hear. The silverleafs in the front yard was whipping and thrashing—there was five of them then and we lost two that night—and the water was beating in around the sash of the windows on the ocean side till I used up about every spare towel I had to keep it from soaking the carpets. The way those gusts of wind yelled when they went by the corners of the roof I shall never forget till I die. I was almost scared, and it takes considerable storm to scare me, and even Jethro was nervous. He kept jamming his nose against the kitchen windows, though it was so pitch black he could not see much, and I could hear him muttering to himself.

"There will be wicked doings along these shoals this night, Anthy," says he. "The life-savers will have their hands full, I am afraid."

Then he would take another long look out of the window to where, away off down the outer beach, you could just see the lights of the Orham life-saving station winking—that is, provided you could see anything at all, which was seldom.

Odd enough little Mary was the least upset of any of us. She seemed to think the noise and hullaboo was a kind of show put on to liven things up. One time when the back chimney fetched a grunt and a tremble that we could feel away down in the kitchen, she laughed right out loud to see me jump clear of my chair. When her bedtime come I took her up and put her in my bed in my room.

"You may not need company, young lady," says I to myself, "but *I* do and you and me will sleep together this night."

Every once in a while, of course, I would run up to the front bedroom to see how Captain Freeland was getting along. What I saw every time I got there did not help me any. He was all of a shake, his eyes shining and his limbs a-twitching as if he had the Saint Vitus. The last cruise I made to that room I do declare if he was not out of bed and kneeling by one of the east windows, with his hands around his face to shut out the lamp light. I flew at him like a setting-hen at a cat.

Says I, "What in heavens and earth are you trying to do? Get pneumonia along with the rest of your troubles? You come right along with me this minute."

I shall never forget how he looked when he turned around. His chin was quivering and his eyes rolling in his head.

"Is there—is there any trouble alongshore?" he sang out, stuttering almost as bad as Jethro. "Is there—is there? You tell me, woman!"

As a general thing I object to being hailed "woman," but there was too many real important things just then for that to bother me.

"No, of course there isn't," I snapped at him. "Are you coming back to your bed, like a Christian, or shall I fetch Jethro to help tow you there?"

He stood up, holding on to a chair back to steady himself.

"I—I guess I have been dreaming," he says, drawing a long breath. "I dreamed she—she was off there and—and— Oh, my Lord A'mighty!"

The way things turned out this was as nigh a prophecy as I am liable to run acrost in my lifetime, but I did not realize nor pay attention then.

"Never mind about *her,* whoever she is," I ordered. "You stop your profane swearing and get right back into that bed. March!"

Well, between us, I pushing and he trying to walk, he made out to cross the room and I tucked him in.

"Now you stay there, where you belong," says I. "It is time for your medicine and don't you move till I fetch it."

Doctor Palmer had left me some sleeping pills which I was to give him according to what the doctor called my "discretion." I judged it was discretion time that minute, if ever, and I put two of them in his tumbler of water. He drank it down, never suspecting nothing, and I planted myself in the rocking chair to wait till they took effect. I did not have to wait so very long. In twenty minutes or so he was dozing peaceful and I turned the lamp down and tiptoed out and along the hall to my own room. Little Mary was sleeping as sound as if the Old Scratch's own fandango was not being danced on the roof over her head.

It was a long time afore *I* got to sleep, though. First off I tried to read a spell in that Poe book, hoping it might soothe me down, as you might say. But reading that outrageous horribleness was like trying to soothe a mosquito bite with red pepper. I put the book away in less than three minutes, left my lamp burning—on that night and after reading that book I would not have blowed it out for a million dollars—and snuggled in beside Mary. And long afterwards, the land knows how long, I did drop off, finally.

What woke me up was a steady "knock—knock" at the door of the bedroom. I hopped up like a kernel of corn in a popper.

"What is it? *Who* is it?" I whispered. I had to scream when I whispered, on account of the storm racket, which was worse than ever, if such is possible. The answer come prompt and if I never was glad to hear a stutter afore I was glad to hear that one.

"It is me—Jethro. I am going out. Don't be scared if I don't get back for quite a spell."

I jerked the door open a crack and peeked out at him.

"Going out!" I hollered. "Going out—this night! My land of love! Is all *hands* in this house struck loony?"

hie was rigged up in oilskins and rubber boots and a sou'wester and he had a lighted lantern in his hand.

"There is a vessel ashore on the beach right abreast this house," he says. "Look out of your window and you can see the lights. I'm going."

And he went. I turned and run across to the window. Sure enough, there, not more than half a mile off, was lights moving on the beach and, only a little further be- yond that beach, was two or three more lights swinging and bowing and whisking in circles, a sight to set your flesh crawling if you realized, as I did only too well, what they were and what they meant.

I put my clothes on again—thank goodness Mary had not waked up, but was sleeping the way nobody but a child can sleep—wrapped myself in a quilt and all night long I set in a chair by the window. I could see nothing but the lights moving and moving, but once in a great while, when there was a jiffy of lull in the storm noises and I risked lifting the window a crack, I could hear faint hollering over on the beach.

Morning came finally, and a sickly gray light with it. It was still all black clouds and pouring rain but the wind had eased down ever so little and I began to hope that the worst of the business was over. I could make out the outer beach now and the group of life-savers and other folks moving there and, in between the sheets of rain, I could begin to see the wreck itself. The first thing that struck me was how nigh to the shore she was laying. I have seen wrecks enough on this coast in my day and time, but never, afore nor since, have I seen a big vessel so drove in over the shoals. She was almost up to the inside line of the breakers.

A square-rigged craft she was, keeled away down on her side, and when the big waves went driving past her the white water would fly half way up to her mastheads. Looking at her then you could not dare hope that a single soul aboard her had been saved.

Yet when Jethro came in—about half-past seven it was—he had better news to tell than I expected. The second mate and two of the crew was lost—they went overboard when she first struck—but everybody else had been took off in the breeches buoy.

"It was her being drove in so close that was responsible for that," says Jethro, between the big swallows of boiling hot coffee that I made for him. "She hit first away off on the outer bar, but them great rollers hoisted her up and kept flinging her in, further and further. At last she was where they could shoot a line across her and rig up the buoy. A mercy too, for they never could have launched the life boat in such a sea."

The poor half-frozen creatures who had been dragged ashore were at the life-saving station. They were all right, or would be pretty soon, all but the first mate whose

name, so Jethro said, was Burke. He was in a bad way
with concussion of the brains and two broken ribs and
the land knows what all besides. A heavy block from one
of the masts had fell on him and he was unconscious and
liable to be for weeks and weeks, even if he ever did pull
through which was doubtful, so Doctor Palmer was afraid.
The crew—a brave, cool-headed crowd they must have
been—had packed him into the breeches buoy, tied him
fast with a line, and sent him ashore like a bundle of old
clothes. He would be took up to a hospital in Boston that
very day, according to Jethro's tell.

"But the captain?" says I. "You have not said anything
about the captain?"

He was rubbing his chin and looking at me kind of
strange, so as I thought.

"The captain?" says he. "Yes, the captain. . . . Well,
Anthy, I have not told you the queerest thing about this
wreck. She is a bark, bound from Hong Kong to Boston,
and her name—well, her name is *Pride of the Fleet.*"

For just a second that name did not mean anything to
me—but then it did—my soul, yes! I remembered what he
had told me.

"Pride of the Fleet!" I sang out. "Why, Jethro Gould! She
was that George Crossley's ship, wasn't she? That George
Crossley that you said was—was pretty nigh like a son to
Captain Freeland. . . . Oh! *Oh!* And was he—"

He did not let me finish. "George Crossley is dead,"
he says solemn. "He was not drowned, either. He died—of
Java fever, they calculate it was—about a fortnight ago
and they buried him at sea. He was half sick afore they
left port, so the cook says. The cook was one of the saved
ones."

Well, at first I was too upset to think straight at all.
Somehow the idea that the very vessel commanded by the
very man him and I had talked about, and whose letter

Captain Freeland had been expecting and asking about every day, should be cast away right at the back door, as you might say, of Freeland Blair's own house was too staggering to let me think of anything else. It did not seem as if it could be so; seemed like something you read about in a book.

But when I said that very thing to Jethro he did not seem to think it was so very outrageous strange, after all.

"It struck me funny at the beginning," says he, "but it ain't, really. She was heading in around the tip of the Cape for Boston harbor and she was on the course that all vessels from across take to that harbor. I can remember a dozen others bound the same way that have piled up on these shoals. It just happened so, that is all. . . . But I snum I don't know how the old man will take it! He thought a sight of George Crossley."

I was commencing to get my thinker to working by this time and I spoke up prompt.

"He must not know it," I declared, sharp. "Not until he is well again, anyhow. You and me must keep it from him until then and we must not let the doctor or anybody else tell him, neither. Why—why, it might fetch a stroke of palsy on to him."

He agreed that was so and that I was right.

"You leave it to me, Anthy," says he. "If he asks me I am going to lie. You never heard me lie when I really set my mind to it, have you?"

I sniffed. "I have heard you when I thought you was doing a fairly good job," I said, sarcastic.

He grinned. "Them times was just for fun, to keep me in practice. This lie will be the genuine article, with hand-knit lace on the edges. You leave it to me, Anthy Hallett."

Well, he had his chance that very forenoon. When I fetched Captain Freeland his eggs and toast-bread at ten o'clock—the blessed sleeping pills had kept him quiet until almost then—there he was out of bed and staring through the window at that wreck. He was shaking from head to foot. He swung around at me as if he was on a pivot.

"What craft is that?" he sang out, pointing. "What is her name?"

Thank the eternal goodness, Jethro had followed me up and was right at my heels.

"Morning, Captain," says he, cheerful. "That craft? Oh, she is the bark *Snowball,* from Glasgow, with a load of all sorts. Run in close, didn't she. Everybody saved, that is a comfort."

Captain Freeland stared at him for what seemed a whole minute, without speaking, breathing so hard you could hear him way acrost the room.

"What's that? What was her name?" he asked, when that minute was over.

"Snowball," says Jethro, smiling and easy.

"You are sure? Who commanded her?"

It did look to me as if Jethro had not just expected that. He kind of choked up and coughed.

"Why—er—now let me see," says he. "I did have that name. It was Captain—er—er—Hog—er— Hogbloom— seems as if that was it."

"Hog—*what?*" sang out Captain Freeland—and no wonder; I should thought he would!

Jethro laughed. "Why no, it wasn't that," says he. "No, no, course it wasn't: it was Hoggins—no, Higgins. That was it—James G. Higgins. He is a Bangor man, I believe."

Well, that seemed to pacify Captain Blair some. Anyhow he let me lead him back to bed again and I left him nibbling at his toast-bread. Jethro was waiting for me in the kitchen.

"Well, Anthy," says he, proud as Punch, "do I rate A.B. as a liar, or don't I?"

I looked him over. "You did for about half a minute," I told him. "That *Snowball* name was good enough and so was Glasgow; but Hogbloom! My mercy sakes! If I could not think up anything better than that I would have labeled him Smith and let it go."

He could not help showing he was a little mite ashamed. "To tell you the truth," says he, "I *was* kind of caught aback with my canvas flapping. Funny, for I had that skipper's name all thought up. You see, I fixed first to call him Captain Blossom—I used to know a fellow named Blossom once—and then I changed it to Hogg, because I know a Captain Hogg and he does hail from Bangor. But when the old man snapped that question out at me I sort of lost my bearings and mixed the two of them up. It comes from tackling too many lies at once. Look out you don't try it, Anthy."

"Humph!" says I; "I don't propose to tackle any, if I can help it. *You* look out and remember his name is Higgins now. Don't forget and call him Pigbud next time, that is all."

The strangest part about that first storm was that it died out almost as quick as it started up. By the next morning the sun was shining and, except for the big surf rolling in, it was almost a flat calm. The forenoon train brought one of the owners of the *Pride of the Fleet* down from Boston and the undertaker's—no, I mean the underwriter's—agent along with him. The poor old bark was so far in on the shoals that they see right off there was no chance of saving her, but they did hope to salvage part of the cargo.

They took the things from the cabins and forecastle that very day and we could see them being piled up on the shore, chairs, tables, sea-chests—all sorts of the like of that. They got everything that could be lifted on to that beach and late that afternoon the underwriter man came to the house. He wanted to talk with Captain Blair, but that I would *not* allow, so he had to get along with talking to me. What he wanted to know was if that furniture and such on the beach could not be carted up and put in our barn. The glass was falling again, so he said, and they was afraid there might be another storm in the wake of the first one.

I could not see any reason for saying no and neither could Jethro, so the *Pride of the Fleet* stuff was put in the barn. There was quite a pile of it altogether. And the very morning after that the second storm struck and lasted three whole days. When it was over the *Pride of the Fleet* had been smashed to pieces and chunks of her was scattered from West Orham Point to Trumet Neck. So that settled the salving of the cargo.

A day or so later Jethro and me had two more visitors. One of them was that Boston owner—his name was Bliss—and the other was Judge Saunders, from Orham. The judge was Captain Freeland's lawyer when the captain had any lawyering to be done. They had come to see him— Freeland, I mean—but when I explained that he was not allowed to see anybody they decided I would do instead.

It seemed—this was what Judge Saunders told me and Jethro—that amongst the stuff fetched ashore from the *Pride of the Fleet's* cabin was a folding writing desk that had belonged to Captain Crossley. He having died, and this Mr. Bliss being one of the owners he sailed for, Mr. Bliss took it on himself to open that desk and look over what was in it. And one of the very first papers they found was George Crossley's will. He had wrote it out himself, and the first mate—the Burke one, who was hurt and had been took to the Boston hospital—had signed his name as witness. It was short but to the point, so the judge told us. Captain Crossley had left everything he owned to his friend and benefactor Freeland Blair, of East Orham, Mass. Every single last thing.

Judge Saunders went on to say that, nigh as he could make out, there was not a great deal of any account. A few hundred dollars in a Boston savings bank and the stuff belonging to Crossley that was in his stateroom and in the cabin of the *Pride of the Fleet,* that was all. But there was a good deal more than you would expect in that cabin and stateroom and Crossley had left a memorandum list of it.

"Mr. Bliss here tells me," went on the judge, "that Captain Crossley had commanded that bark for ten years or more and she was the only real home he had, he being a bachelor. Consequently he had that cabin crowded full of tables and chairs and pictures and ornaments he had picked up in foreign ports. From what I hear it must have looked more like a small museum than the cabin of a sailing vessel. That is so, isn't it, Mr. Bliss?"

The Bliss man smiled and said yes indeed, it was so.

"We were very fond of Crossley," says he. "He was one of our smartest skippers and we let him do about as he pleased. We used to joke him about that cabin and his stateroom and tell him we could not see how he could pick his way through the junk there was in it. Well, all of it— the junk, I mean—was taken ashore after the wreck, and now it is stored in Captain Blair's own barn, so—"

"So," says Judge Saunders, breaking in, "it has come to the place where it belongs, for the will, though it is pretty informal, seems to be binding enough, and there is nobody to dispute it, anyhow. What we came here to-day for was to tell Captain Blair of his windfall and then, if there was no objection, check over the goods in the barn according to Crossley's list. His personal property we will leave right there and whatever else there may be we will have taken away."

I could not see why that was not all right and Jethro could not either, and so said, so done. The judge and Mr. Bliss went out to the barn with the list and Jethro went with them. There was not any real excuse for his going— except just curiosity, but that was always excuse enough for Jethro Gould. He come back again, after a spell, all foamed up with what he had seen.

"You never laid eyes on such a queer mess of odds and ends as that Crossley man owned, Anthy," he says, stuttering out his words like a bunch of firecrackers popping. "Let alone the three funny, outlandish carved chairs and the two writing tables, there is a clock with all sorts of carving cut on the case, and two or three images, heathen idols I guess likely they be, and a sea-chest, and a ship painting in a frame, and a cast iron elephant, and a carved Chinee little chest of drawers like, and some Chinee pictures, and the model of a Chinee junk craft, and a brass spittoon all painted up with flowers, and a—oh, I don't know what all. I don't wonder that Judge Saunders calculated that cabin must have looked like a dime museum."

"Is any of it good for anything?" says I. I never have had, then nor since, much use for knickknacks and such. Dust collectors, I call them.

"Not according to my figuring," he says. "That spittoon is kind of pretty to look at, and they always come handy; but I would not give a hoot for the balance and I don't believe Freeland will neither."

"Think it will be safe to leave the stuff out there in the barn?" I asked. "I see by the *Item* that there has been one shut-up house and a couple of fish shanties broke into lately."

He laughed. "That was over to the Center," he says, "and there was nothing stole but a couple of clam hoes and an anchor and such stuff. Some of the Point gang is responsible, so the constable thinks. I don't believe anybody will take the trouble to come way down here after none of that trash. I would not take the heft of it acrost the road without being paid wages."

So we left it in the barn, awaiting the time when we could tell Captain Freeland the whole yarn. He was getting some better and was able to come down stairs noon-times for dinner. And then—a week come that Saturday forenoon it was—the letter arrived and that night I had the first of my shivering fits. After that I had them thick and fast.

We was at dinner, the three of us—Captain Freeland, Mary and me—when Jethro come into the dining-room. He had been up to the post-office, same as he always did. It was baking day and I had dinner ready a little ahead of time. I thought Jethro looked sort of funny when he opened the door and saw the captain setting there at the table. But he could not back out, for Freeland had seen him and seen the paper and letter he was carrying.

"Is that the mail?" he asks, quick. "Give it to me."

Well, there was nothing to do but obey orders, so Jethro handed over the paper and the letter. He looked at me the second after he did it and I knew something was up by the look in his eyes. And a jiffy afterwards something *was* up. Captain Freeland had not paid any attention to the paper—that week's *Item* it was—and he let it fall on the floor. But he grabbed the letter, a big fat one, took one look at the envelope and jumped to his feet with a—a gurgle is the only word I can think of that fits the noise he made.

I jumped too, you better believe. He was white as a piece of paper.

"What is it? What is the matter?" I sung out. "Are you took sick, Captain? . . . Where you going?"

His chair had fell over backwards when he got up, but he did not so much as touch it. He was headed for the door leading to the hallway.

"Where are you going?" I asked again. "Don't you want your dinner?"

He answered then, if you can call it an answer.

"No," says he, and almost run out of the room. I looked at Jethro and he at me. I suppose Mary, poor child, was looking at both of us, but we did not pay attention to her.

"What was that letter, Jethro Gould?" I wanted to know. "Was it—?"

He nodded his head. "I guess it was," he says. "The postmark was all blurred up, but it had a couple of foreign stamps on it. I don't doubt a mite it was the one he has been expecting so long. . . . Whew! It must be something pretty important. You saw how he acted when he got a glimpse of the envelope."

"I saw," says I. "But—but, Jethro—it could not be from Captain Crossley, for he is dead and gone."

"He might have wrote it afore he died, don't you think?" he stuttered out.

"If he wrote it at all I should think probable it was afore he died," I said, pretty snappish. "Why in the world you ever handed it over I don't see. . . . Oh, well, yes, I do; you could not help it, of course. Finish your dinner, Mary. I must run up and see to your uncle."

But her uncle did not want to be seen to. His bedroom door was shut and locked and he ordered me to clear out when I touched the knob. All that afternoon he stayed in that room and would not let me nor nobody even nigh him. But when I went up at six o'clock, with his tray of supper, his door was wide open and he was sitting in the rocker. I was some relieved, I tell you!

"Well, Captain Freeland," says I. "Feeling better, I hope?"

He managed to pump up a smile, such as it was.

"I am all right now," says he. "I had a—a kind of bad spell at dinner time. Indigestion I suppose it was."

"Oh!" says I. "Was that it? Jethro and me was afraid you might have had bad news. In that letter you got, I mean."

He looked at me, innocent as a baby in arms.

"Letter?" says he. "Oh, yes, yes, of course! No, that letter did not amount to anything. It was just a note from an old sea captain friend of mine, name of Bangs. His ship was at—at Havre and he dropped me a line from there. . . . Well, how about some supper? I am commencing to feel pretty sharp set."

Maybe so, but I noticed, later on, when I went up again to get the tray, that hardly a thing on it had been touched. However, he went to bed peaceful enough and I began to wonder if Jethro and I might not have been off the track altogether and that his funny actions that noon was an indigestion spell, after all.

And that very night something happened that set me off on another shivering fit.

III

I went to my own room pretty early, but I set up late
reading a new book that Jethro had got for me from the
library. I was right in the middle of an exciting part; the
poor young woman the story was about was promised to
marry a lord who, so anybody but her poor old ninny of a
father—I did lose patience with *him!*—could see was a perfectly awful kind of man, and I could not bear to lay the
book down until she was clear of that part of her troubles,
although, of course, I knew there would be more a-com-
ing. Well, she got clear finally and I did what that kind
of books calls "heave a sigh of relief" and commenced to
think about getting ready for bed. When I looked at the
clock on the mantel-piece I decided I better not waste
time thinking, for it was half past twelve. I undressed in
a hurry and blew out the light. Then, same as I generally
do, I went to the window and took a sort of observation of
outdoors before turning in.

The window I looked out of this time was the one at
the back end of the house and from it you can see around
the end of the woodshed ell and on to the barn. It was one
of those half and half moonlight nights, all bright and
shiny one minute and clouds blowing across the moon and
darkening it all up the next. When I first looked out it was
one of those dark spells, but a few seconds later the cloud

slid by and the back yard lit up so that every little bush and weed cast a sharp shadow. And while I was looking at them shadows, all so clear cut and blue-black and still, I saw another one, a big one, and it was not still at all. It was the shadow of a man and it came around the back corner of the barn, stopped for a second, and then, careful and slinky as a cat creeping up on a mouse, turned and slid back again. The upper part of the shadow was uneven and hunched up, as if the person it belonged to had something in his arms.

While I stood there, holding back the edge of the window shade and peeking out, that plaguy moon went behind a cloud once more. I did not hang around waiting for it to shine again, you better believe. My heart was somewheres up next to my palate, judging by the way it felt, but I managed to swallow it down, jumped for the closet where my wrapper hung, pawed around till I got it, put it on somehow—that wrapper was supposed to have only two sleeves but that night seems as if it had no less than twenty —and ran out and down the hall to the door of Jethro's room—not the door opening off of the back stairs landing, but the next one, that at the very end of the hallway.

And while I was running—it is funny, isn't it, how quick you can think without meaning to?—it come acrost me: "Are you making a fool of yourself, Iantha Hallett? How do you know but that may be Jethro himself out there, coming home late from lodge meeting or something?"

It was not though. Just one jiffy of listening outside Jethro's door settled that. He was in that room and sound asleep, if noise meant anything. I pounded on the door, pounding soft, so as not to wake up Mary nor Captain Freeland.

"Jethro! Jethro!" I whispered through the panel. "Get up! there is somebody breaking into our barn."

He was out of bed and out of that room in less than a half minute, I do verily believe. Lucky it was pitch dark in the hallway, for I am sure I was not dressed up for inspection and I rather guess he was considerable less so. "What is it?" he wanted to know and I told him what I had seen.

"Wait a jiffy, Anthy," says he. "Don't be scared. I'll fix that rooster, whoever he is."

Back into the room he flew and I could hear him digging around, getting some clothes on, I judged. Out he came again, clear tear.

"You go back to your room and keep cool, Anthy," says he. "There is nothing to worry about. I'll fix him."

He left me and tore along the hall, through the other door and down the back stairs. First I started to run after him, then I decided not to. I had no notion of letting him, or a burglar either, see me as I was that minute. I ran to my room, lit the lamp, fixed that wrapper a little more as if a decent person was wearing it, stuck my feet into slippers and, carrying the lamp—I remember my hand was trembling so that the chimney rattled like all possessed—I scampered down to the kitchen after him. He was not there, of course. The back door was wide open and the freezing cold air was pouring in, but freezing to death was the least of my frets just then.

I went to the door and looked out. I could not see a thing, for the moon was under another cloud, a thick one this time. And I could not hear anything either. For a whole year I stood there—I will not take a second off that year even now—and then I heard him coming back. At least I *hoped* it was him. If it had been anybody else—but it was not.

He was barefooted and he had his trousers on over his nightshirt—even then I remember being thankful he was presentable that much—and he had the shotgun which always hung in the kitchen, in his hand. He was calm as could be. You would hardly thought there was anything the matter.

"Hello, Anthy!" he hailed, stopping to shut the door behind him. "What be you trying to do—take the fresh air cure? It is fresh all right! B-r-r-r."

Frightened as I was, the sight of him, so self-possessed and grinning, made me brace up. He should not realize how I had been feeling, if I could help it.

"Well, you told me to keep cool, didn't you?" says I. And then, for I could not make believe any longer. "Oh, Jethro! Who was it? Was there truly anybody?"

He nodded. "There had been somebody," says he. "But he got away afore I showed up. The door nighest the pig-pen was open—been pried open, nigh as I could make out by the feel. Where is the lantern?"

"My suffering heavens!" I screamed. "You ain't going back there, are you?"

"Certain I am. And I am going to stay there on watch till morning. If that Point gang think they can catch me napping they are liable to find out their mistake. I'll make it plain to 'em with a dose of duck shot. Come! find that lantern for me, will you, while I put on a pair of boots. This ain't no night to go barefoot."

Yes, sir-ee, just as calm and everyday as that! A fine, spunky common-sense man Jethro Gould was, poor departed soul, even if he did stutter.

Well, he found his boots and I got him the lantern and out to the barn he went to stand watch till morning. I watched too, from my bedroom window, but nothing happened. At half past five I went down to get breakfast and he came in and we talked it over.

"The fellow you see was one of them no-account Point loafers, most likely," he says. "Though for that matter, all Orham knows of the wreck stuff being stored in our barn.

But I have made up my mind to one thing, Anthy, and that is that it had not ought to stay in that barn any longer. Can't you and I manage to bring it into the house sometime to-day? You can carry one end of a table, can't you? You look pretty husky."

"I am husky enough for that much, I guess likely. But where on earth can we put it? We shall have to be awful careful and not let Captain Freeland catch us. He would ask all sorts of questions and I am certain sure he is in no condition yet to have the news of George Crossley's death broke to him."

He realized that too, but he had an answer ready. He believed him and me, after Mary had gone to school and while Freeland was supposed to be taking the forenoon nap the doctor ordered, could lug the things from the barn through the kitchen, up the back stairs, and store them in the little back room that opened off his own room and the unfinished attic.

"The old man never comes to this end of the house," says he.

Well, it was a fine plan and I agreed it was, but like a whole lot of fine plans in this mortal world, it talked better than it worked. First place, Captain Freeland was contrary as an off ox that forenoon and would not even try to take a nap. Every time I tiptoed up to his room he was setting at his desk over in the corner, with his elbows on that desk and his head in his hands, studying and studying, it seemed so, at some papers or other. And every single time he would yell at me clear out and 'tend to my own affairs. Finally, I got desperate and put another sleeping pill in his tea at dinner. That did the trick and about one o'clock I peeked in and he was laying on the sofa sound asleep. So I passed the word to Jethro and we started bringing the things in right away. It was a back-breaking job, too, some of it, but I was a strapping, healthy girl in those days.

What surprised me though—Jethro had talked enough about it but I had not realized—was how much trash and truck that George Crossley had been in the habit of carting around the world with him. Outlandish things! Some of those heathen idols and the ugly graven images cut out on the boxes and knickknacks gave me the all-overs to look at. We toted up the small stuff first, the light things that were easy to handle. The heavy ones we left to the last. About the heaviest of all was Captain Crossley's own sea chest. It was a fine one—Jethro said the finest ever he saw—made out of hard wood all painted up and with his name lettered on the side of it. It was packed full of his clothes, of course, and weighed something terrible.

Getting that chest acrost the back yard and up the back stairs was a tussle. We had to stop and rest every few minutes and we both of us was all out of breath afore we finally got far as the second floor. And, just as we were getting there I declare if Jethro did not catch his foot on the top step and his end of the chest went "Whang!" against the wall, striking it so hard I expected to see the plaster tumble off.

"There!" says I. "If *that* don't wake up Captain Freeland then the trumpet of Judgment won't do more than make him turn over in his grave."

But of course his room was away off at the end of the front hallway and its door and the door leading from the back stairs was both shut. So, after listening a while, we tackled the chest again. We had got it through the attic and was just ready to set it down in the little room beyond when that landing door was jerked open. Jethro says "Godfreys mighty!" and let go of his end of the chest. I let go of mine too and swung around.

There, right astern, stood Captain Freeland Blair himself, staring at us. . . . Whew! I can see him now!

I said he was staring at us, didn't I? Well, that is wrong. He was not paying attention to us at all, he was staring at that sea chest. And on the broad side of it, in two inch letters was "George H. Crossley. Bark *Pride of the Fleet.* Boston, U. S. A." The frying pan was upset for certain and the fat in the fire!

Jethro, as usual, was the cool one. He told me afterwards that he was as took back as I was, but he did not show it.

"Well, well, Captain," he said, "what are you doing out in the fo'castle? This is moving day for Anthy and me. I am helping her clean house."

Captain Freeland did not answer nor as much as lift his eyes to look at him; all he was looking at was that sea chest.

"What is that?" he sang out, pointing. "What—what is it?"

"That?" says Jethro. "Oh, that is just something Anthy wanted me to help put up attic here out of her way."

"What is it?" sang out Freeland again, his voice jumping up high and shrill, like a woman's. "My—my God, it is *his!* Where—"

He stopped short. He was staring over our shoulders into the little room where all that *Pride of the Fleet* truck was piled around. He took another step forward and looked and looked. Then he gave a kind of gasp, grabbed hold of his shirt collar as if he was choking, staggered and then fell—no, sort of slid—down on to the floor in a heap.

For a minute we both thought he was dead, I guess; I am sure I did. But he was not, and, somehow or other, we contrived to half carry, half drag him through that long hallway and lay him on the bed in his room.

"Now go for Doctor Palmer!" says I to Jethro. But Captain Freeland heard us and he riz right up in bed.

"No!" he ordered and, weak as he was, he almost yelled it. "No! I don't want a doctor. I want to know about that chest and those other things out yonder. They are George Crossley's, I know it. What are they doing here? Where did they come from? Where is he? . . . Tell me—if you don't I—I swear I'll choke it out of you."

He was climbing out—to commence the choking, I judged. Jethro pushed him back, firm but gentle. Him and I looked at each other.

"Well, Anthy," says he, "I should say that making a clean breast was the only way out of this mess. What do you think?"

I shook my head. "It can't be any worse than not doing it," I gave in. "There, there, Captain Freeland! You just put your head down on that pillow case and Jethro and me will tell you every last thing."

He did not believe us at first, but, after a spell of coaxing and begging and bullying, we got him so he would lay still and let us talk. Then, between us, each taking turns sort of, we told him about the wreck and about Captain Crossley's dying at sea and the will and his belongings being brought to the house. The only bit we left out was about the barn being broke into. That we did not mention. What was the use?

He let us tell it, only groaning and muttering every once in a while. I could not make out much of the mutterings, and Jethro could not either, but there was one thing we both heard and it was queer enough. He broke out with it right in the middle of the story. It was like a prayer—only it wasn't.

"Oh, isn't there *no* balm in Gilead?" he screamed all of a sudden. "What is the matter with you, God? Isn't there the promise written out that you will forgive the sinner that repenteth and save him from hell fire? Haven't I been in hell for years? What more do you want that you take away my only chance? They call you a loving and merciful father! Merciful! Do you call this mercy?"

We calmed him down somehow and he heard the rest. Then he shut his eyes and laid there, breathing hard. But when Jethro got up to tiptoe out and fetch the doctor he stopped him.

"Wait!" says he. "Stay where you are, both of you. Was all of his—of George's property brought up here? Is it all here now? Don't you dare lie to me; you hear!"

Of course we told him it was, so far as we knew. Then he wanted to know what Judge Saunders and the Bliss man had said when they came with the will.

"Go get Saunders. Go get him now—this minute. I must see him."

So Jethro went out to harness up and notify the judge, but I knew he would fetch the doctor first.

He did, of course, and Doctor Palmer was sober enough about the state his patient was in. He gave orders that he must stay in bed and not be allowed to worry and get excited.

"He is a sick man, Iantha," say the doctor to me. "He has got what amounts to an incurable disease and has had it for a good while. He does not know it and I have not told anybody else, but I am telling you and Gould now so you will realize how serious his condition is. I was more scared than I let on when he had the other upset, but this one makes it a whole lot worse. If he keeps in bed for a while and has absolute rest of mind and body he may pick up and live for months. If he doesn't—well, he will go out like a candle. That's the plain truth."

Judge Saunders came that evening and Captain Freeland *would* see him, nothing I could say would put it off. The judge did not stay but a little while—I saw to that—and after he had gone Freeland had me in and asked me a lot more questions. Did I know any more than Saunders knew about how long George had been sick and how long was it after the ship left port afore he died, and was he rational and conscious when he did die, and all like that.

"I can't tell you, Captain Freeland," I said. "The only person who was with him when he died, nigh as can find out, was his first mate, Mr. Burke, and the last word from him was that *he* was in a dying condition up there to Boston."

When I went to him next morning he did not look as if he had slept much and breakfast did not interest him a mite. I gave him a good talking to. All the good that did was for him to tell me to go to Jericho—or a place even further off—and mind my own business. No woman was going to order him around, if he knew it.

"This one is," says I, "and she is doing it now. And, unless you mind and behave, I will get a hired nurse in here whether you want her or not. I mean that if I ever meant anything!"

That shut him up for a time. The pow-wow ended by his promising to stay in that bed and act sensible.

All that day and the next he kept to that promise and the doctor, every time he came, looked more contented and hopeful.

The morning of the third day the captain called after me as I was leaving the room with his breakfast tray. "Iantha," says he, "you will do a little favor for me if I ask you, won't you?"

"Of course I will, if it isn't the kind of favor that is against doctor's orders."

"Darn the doctor! He is a fuss-budget old woman! Take those things downstairs and then come back here and I'll tell you what I want."

So, after I had carried the tray down, I did come back, but I brought Jethro with me.

"Now then, Captain Freeland," said I, "what is the favor you want done?"

He started off on a long rigamarole about how much George Crossley and him had been to each other and what an awful shock George's taking away was and all like that.

It was pitiful to hear and yet, somehow, I could not help feeling that this was not what was really on his mind. He kept repeating and going back to say the same things over and over and I thought he never would come to the point. Finally, though, he did, and it was not such a dreadful important point, after all; not nigh what you might have expected.

"All these days and nights," he said, "I have been laying here thinking about the poor fellow, and grieving for him, and last night it came over me that I should like to have something that belonged to him—something personal, you know—here in this room where I can see it all the time. I wonder if you or Jethro will not bring me something like that from the back attic. You will, won't you? I know it sounds kind of foolish, but it would please me a lot."

"Why, my soul! of course we will!" I says, thankful enough to be able to say yes so easy. "Was *that* all the favor you wanted to ask? We will fetch in anything you say."

"His writing desk is there," suggested Jethro. "Of course Judge Saunders and Mr. Bliss opened that and went through the papers in it, but—"

No, no, it was not the writing desk he wanted. "I have seen all there was in that desk," he cut in, impatient. Then, as if he realized we must think that sounded kind of funny, he went on to explain. "That desk is not exactly what I had in mind," he says. "You can fetch the desk too, if you want to—yes, maybe you better—but what I would like to have you find and bring to me, if it is there, is a Chinese cabinet, little chest of drawers like. I bought that cabinet myself in Shanghai years ago and I gave it to George for a present. He carried it every voyage he made. I know it is there with the rest of the things. It must be! It has got to be! Go find it. . . . Well? Why don't you go?"

He was commencing to get excited, and his fingers to twitch and his eyes to shine. When you are dealing with a sick man the easiest way is to pacify him, provided the pacifying is as simple as this looked to be.

"Go get it—quick!" says I to Jethro; but he had started for the storeroom already. In a few minutes back he came with the cabinet thing in his arms. I had noticed it and spoke about it when we lugged the stuff in from the barn. A person who had seen it once was not liable to forget it. It was about two foot and a half long, maybe, and two foot high. The outside was some sort of hard, foreign wood and the inside part was made of that smelly camphor wood same as used to be used to make moth-proof boxes out of. There were three little doors in a row acrost the top and three drawers underneath with little ivory knobs to them. It was old—you could tell that to look at it—and was 'graved all over with the ugliest carvings you ever laid eyes on. Anywhere you looked there was wicked horrid faces peeking at you and hands with long claw fingers a-clutching. It set up on four little carved feet. It made me think of one of them Poe stories worked in wood.

I should have hated to sleep in the same room with the outrageous thing, but old Captain Freeland's face lit up when he saw Jethro bringing it in as if it was a bouquet of roses, which it certainly did not look like—or smell like either.

"That's it! That's it!" says he, eager. "I knew it was there! Good! Good!"

"Where will I put it, Captain?" asked Jethro. "Over on the floor in the corner yonder?"

No sir-ee, that would not do at all. There was a little low wooden bench, a footstool, in the room and that must be put right alongside the bed and the thing set on it. Captain Freeland reached out and patted it, actually patted those awful carvings as if he loved them. He happened to catch me looking at him when he did it.

"Pretty, isn't it, Iantha?" he asked, smiling kind of embarrassed and foolish like, as you might say.

"Pretty!" I sang out. "My soul!"

He laughed, or tried to. "It reminds me of George more than anything else in the world," he says. "Every time I look at it I shall think of him. . . . Well, there, there!" getting fretful again. "Go away both of you. Shut the door when you go out. I am tired; maybe I can get the nap that fool doctor is always preaching about."

When Jethro and me got down to the kitchen I spoke what was in my mind.

"It is pitiful, isn't it, Jethro," I said. "He must have loved this George Crossley dear, and that is a fact. But I am honestly afraid his brains are getting as sick as the rest of him. Nobody with a healthy set of brains would pick out *that* thing to remind them of somebody they cared for. I should hate to have it remind anybody of *me.*"

Jethro rubbed his chin. "Yes, Anthy," he says, "that is funny, but it ain't the funniest thing about this business. Why, if the old man wanted that cabinet in his room didn't he order us to find it and fetch it to him? He is the boss aboard here, isn't he? I have never noticed him being bashful about giving orders. Why on earth did he back and fill and talk about our doing him a favor? And trouble himself to make all them long-winded explanations? Now what is behind it all? What is he up to? Something he is ashamed of, or afraid we may find out or suspicion? Why did he want that heathen Chinee box right alongside his bed?"

"Why, he told us that part—over and over again, Jethro. It was a present he gave, himself, to Captain George, and so, I suppose—"

"Yes, yes—sure! . . . Well, so long, Anthy; I am going out to the barn. The jibboom and foretopmast of the *Pride of the Fleet* are down yonder on the beach. In case he takes a notion to have *them* toted up and laid on his pillow you can give me a hail."

For the rest of the day nothing out of the common happened. Captain Freeland kept his room door shut tight and once, when I opened it without knocking, he could not have blown me up much worse if I had called him what, just then, I felt like calling him. When I looked in, the drawers from that cabinet thing was spread around in on the bed and I declare to man if he was not sitting up, with his legs out from under the covers, peeking in the cubby-hole behind one of the little doors. Before I had much more than opened my mouth he blared at me like a foghorn. By the Lord Harry, wasn't it possible for a man to have any privacy in his own house! Get out! And so forth and so on, hollering and swearing like a wild creature.

I went out; it seemed the only sane thing to do just then. But, as I said to Jethro, his actions convinced me that matters was bound to end mighty soon and in one of two ways. "Either he will hop in and out of that bed till he drops down dead from exercise," said I, "or he will go raving distracted and die of *that*. Why—oh, why, did Doctor Palmer pick this day, of all times, to go to Wapatomac in! He won't be here till tomorrow."

I declare it does seem, as I look back now, as if the gift of prophecy descended on me when I spoke those words. (So far as that goes, I verily believe that gift has descended on to me more than once since and you will see what I mean when you come to read what Mr. Thornton writes, which, of course, is neither here nor there just now.) For that very night the end *did* come—or, if not the end of the end, the beginning of it, certain.

I went to my room and to bed pretty early, intending to get a good night's rest if I could; but, after an hour or two of tossing and tumbling, thinking and thinking and worrying and worrying, at last, being sick and tired of my own troubles, I decided I might as well tackle somebody else's. So I got up, lit the lamp, put on my wrapper and set down in the rocker to read some more about that girl in the book. That pesky lord of hers was after her again and he had hired a gang of cut-throats to carry her off and marry her by main strength—of course it was the lord who was to do the marrying, not the cut-throats. The more I read the more harrowing and scary things in that story got and I kept on, not paying any attention to time at all.

It must have been almost one o'clock when, just as on the night the *Pride of the Fleet* came ashore, there was a knock on my door. And when, just as I did that night, I opened the door and peeked out, there was Jethro Gould standing in the hallway. He was dressed, for, as it happened, he had been out to Odd Fellows' meeting; he was what folks call a "joiner," Jethro was, and belonged to land knows how many societies.

"What—" I began; but he made a quick sign for me to hush.

"I judged you was up," he whispered. "I saw your window was lighted when I come across to the kitchen door. Come with me, there's something going on out back here."

Well, naturally, when he said that all I could think of was that there was more robbers around.

"Oh, my soul's mercy!" I moaned, all of a tremble. "Oh, Jethro, have you got the gun?"

"Gun!" says he. "What— No, no! I don't calculate we'll need any gun. Say, Anthy, was the old man abed and asleep when you left him?"

"Eh? . . . Why, yes; least he looked asleep. Why?"

"Sshh! Come along with me. And don't make a sound."

He led the way down that pitch dark hall and I followed him, my knees wabbling and my heart pounding like a bass drum. Between being all harrowed up by that book and then routed out this way in the middle of the night, I vow it seemed as if every hair I had—and I had a good many more then than I have got now—was unkinking and standing up straight. What kept my curlpapers from coming off *I* don't know.

He stopped at the very end of the hall at the door of his bedroom. That door was shut, but he opened it gentle.

"Look!" says he.

I looked, but the room was black as the hallway and at first I could not make out what he meant. Then I saw. At the far end of his room, beyond the bed, was the door opening into that little storeroom where him and I had put the stuff from the wreck. And under that door a bright strip of light was shining.

"Listen!" he whispered, his mouth right close to my ear.

I listened, and behind that door and in that storeroom I could hear faint noises, little rustles and once in a while a sort of shuffle. Somebody was in there—somebody with a lamp or a lantern.

I think I was just going to scream and I guess he heard me draw in breath to do it with, for he clapped his hand over my mouth, jerked me back into the hall and pulled his bedroom door shut again.

"Sshh!" he whispers, savage. "Be still!"

I could not do anything *but* be still, long as he kept that hand over my mouth, but, soon as he took it away, I spoke.

"Oh, Jethro," I whispered, grabbing hold of him, "it *is* another robber! It is—it is!"

"Sshh! No, it ain't either. Don't you understand yet? It is—"

He did not get any further, for that second there was a noise, or a whole set of noises, from behind his door and in the room beyond. First a kind of rumble, then a thump, then more thumps like things falling, then a smash of glass, and then a groan.

Jethro let go of me—or I let go of him—or both—
yanked his door open and flew across to the door at the
other side. He grabbed the knob and tugged at it, but it
did not budge.

"Damnation!" he swore. "It is locked! Captain Freeland! Captain Freeland, is that you? Are you hurt?"

There was not any answer; nothing but another faint
groan.

"The other door from the hallway!" I sang out. "Go in
that way, Jethro! Quick!"

But that hallway door, when we got to it, was locked
too, and on the inside. Jethro was bracing himself to smash
it in, when a new notion—almost the first sensible one I
had had that night—flashed to me.

"The back stairs!" says I. "We can come up the back
stairs! Hurry! Oh, hurry!"

He got my idea almost as soon as I said it. Along the front
hallway he raced, and I after him, down the front stairs,
through the sitting-room to the back stairs landing and up
them stairs two steps at a time. He had the advantage of
me, for a flannel wrapper is not the best rig to run in—but I
bet you I was not more than two foot astern all the way.

There was nobody in the landing at the top of those
stairs, nor nobody in the unfinished attic. But we did not
linger by the way. Acrost that attic and into that storeroom we bolted, and what we saw when we got there kept
us busy for the next few minutes, you had better believe.

It was as empty as the attic, so far as any humans but
us was concerned, but somebody had been there, there was
no doubt of that. When Jethro and I carried those wreck
things to that room we had piled some of them one on
top of the other against the north wall. Now a half dozen
of those things were all scattered on the floor—the noise
of them tumbling down was part of what we had heard—
Captain George Crossley's sea chest was open, its lid was

tipped back and his clothes and belongings all hove around hither and yon. And—and this was what we both jumped for first—a kerosene lamp lay beside it, smashed to bits, with the blazing oil running all around.

I am thankful enough that Jethro Gould was with me then. If he had not been the whole house would have burned down flat, I guess. He could always be depended on to keep his head. He tore out to the trunks in the other attic and in a jiffy he was back again with an armful of quilts and blankets. Between us we smothered that fire in almost no time. When it was out for certain, and the room was pitch black again, he grabbed my arm.

"Now then, Anthy," says he, "where is he? Where has he gone?"

I rushed over to the door opening to Jethro's room, the one we had found locked. Well, it was locked yet. (We found the key on the floor a day or two afterwards, but we was too flustered to find it then.)

"Down the back stairs again," ordered Jethro, but when we got to the landing at the head of those stairs we did not need to go down them. The door from the landing out to the front hallway—the one Jethro had been just going to smash open—was unlocked and on the jar now. Whoever had been in that storeroom must have gone out that way while we was galloping through the lower rooms.

We did not stop to ask whys and wherefores. A second after I found that door was unlocked I was on my way to Captain Freeland's room. I always, since first sickness, had kept a turned-down lamp burning on the little walnut stand around the bend of the front hallway. It was there now. I grabbed it up and rushed into his room, expecting to find—well, I did not know what.

And I declare to man if he was not there in his bed, looking at me kind of dazed and numb, as if I had just woke him up!

"For—for heaven sakes, Freeland Blair," I gasped, too upset and paralyzed with surprise to remember even to call him "Captain." "For heaven sakes, wasn't—wasn't it *you* in that back attic?"

His answer was so faint and feeble that it was as much as I could do to hear it.

"No," says he. And then, a second later and louder and more emphatic, "No" again.

I flopped down in the rocker, the lamp in my hand. If it was not him, who on earth was it?

But cool-headed old Jethro walked over to the bed and put his hand on Freeland's forehead. Then he turned and held up that hand for me to see. The palm of it was shiny, dripping wet with sweat.

Captain Freeland had not told the truth, of course. It *was* him who had been in that storeroom. But why had he sneaked out there at one o'clock in the morning? And, even after doing such a crazy thing, what need was there to lie about it?

IV

Those were the questions Jethro and me asked each other afterwards—but not that night or morning. Just then we had something else to do. Captain Freeland had laid perfectly still after saying "No" to me. Now, as I was hanging over him, he lifted his head from the pillow, started to speak, made a funny noise in his throat, and fell back.

Jethro bent down to listen. "He is breathing, Anthy," he said to me. "He has fainted or had a stroke or something. Get some water—yes, and the hartshorn bottle. Hurry!"

"I will attend to that part. You harness up and go for the doctor, quick as the Lord will let you. If Palmer isn't home yet get the other one, the one from Harniss."

He was gone afore I could turn around. And he was back inside of an hour and with him Doctor Palmer—who had got home from Wapatomac earlier than he expected. Captain Freeland had not stirred nor made a sound. I had been bathing his forehead with cold water, holding the bottle of hartshorn under his nose, rubbing his poor cold hands—doing everything I could think of, but I could not bring him to. The doctor took charge when he came, but he did not have any better luck. He was solemn and shook his head when we asked him if it was very bad. When he heard what we had to tell of the goings on that night he looked more solemn still.

"It is the finish, I am afraid," he said. "Well, I have been expecting it."

I kept Mary home from school that forenoon. I thought it was my duty, and yet afterwards I wished I had not. About two o'clock Captain Freeland came to himself for a short spell. He was rational, too, for just those few minutes, and when he saw us all—the doctor and me and Mary and Jethro—standing around him in that room, his thick eyebrows drawed together and he looked from one to the other.

"What is all this?" he whispered—he was too weak to talk loud: "What are all hands in here for?"

"There, there, Captain Freeland Blair," says Doctor Palmer. "It is all right. Don't excite yourself."

He did not pay any attention. "What are you all here for?" he wanted to know again. "Why is that child crying? . . . Look here, Palmer, you don't think I am going to die, do you?"

"No, no. Of course I don't! Just take it easy now and—"

"Shut up! If you think I am dying you are mistaken. I can't die—I won't die yet! You hear me—I won't! I have got things to do first—God A'mighty, yes! Don't let me go, Palmer! You keep me here, you understand! I tell you you have got to! I—I—"

Weak as he was, he was fighting to sit up in bed. Poor Mary was close to hysterics. I hurried her out of the room and downstairs, where I put in my time trying to comfort her. Ten minutes or so later Jethro came down. One look at his face and I knew what had happened.

"Oh!" I gasped. "Is it—?"

He nodded. "Yes," he says. . . . "Well, Mary, what do you say to a ride? I have got to go over to the Center and I had just as soon have company. Get your things on and we'll start."

Captain Freeland Blair's funeral was one of the biggest I have ever seen in Orham anywhere. The minister—he was one of the smartest young preachers we ever had in the East Orham meeting-house—said the loveliest things about the deceased departed. He just flowed eloquence, like turning on a faucet. If I was sure such things would be said over me when my time comes, I should be reconciled, pretty nigh. And the procession of buggies and carryalls to the Orham Center cemetery was a regular parade, it was so long.

Thinks I to myself, "Captain Freeland, if looking down and seeing this I know you are a proud soul this minute."

Which showed how much *I* knew about it!

But I knew more afore many days had passed. Miss Rebecca Blair, Freeland's younger sister from out in Ohio, the one I told about at the beginning when I was talking about all the Blairs—she came on for the funeral, of course, and was going to stay a spell, at least until the will was read and the estate settled up.

What weighed heaviest on my mind was what would become of Mary. Somebody would have to take charge of her, of course. I would have undertook the job and glad of the chance, for already she and I was what you might call devoted to each other, but it was not likely she would be turned over to a hired girl, which was about all I was in them days.

Well, Judge Saunders, who was what I understand they call executioner of Freeland Blair's affairs, got the will from the captain's box in the Orham bank safe and when he read it out it was no more than all hands had expected. It was not a new will, having been drawed some years afore, and it left almost everything to his niece, Mary Blair. Aunt Becky, his sister, come in for five thousand and there was a hundred or so for the East Orham church society and two hundred to Jethro Gould and the like of that. But, as I say, the heft of the property, including this house and land, was to be Mary's in trust till she come of age.

And, so it was wrote in the will, Rebecca Blair was to take on that trust, drawing regular wages from the estate so long as she had charge of Mary and her money.

I was betwixt and between in my feelings when Judge Saunders told me this. I was glad in a way, for already— judging from what I had seen of Aunt Becky—I had decided she was a capable, kind-hearted woman, even if she was straight up and down and schoolmarmy and sot in her ways. But the idea that Mary was to be took clear out West to live and that I was not likely ever to see her again, was a hard shock to me. I went up to my room and cried after I heard the news.

They were tears wasted though, for afore any arrangements at all were made, the big surprise came. Judge Saunders drove over to the house one evening and him and Miss Rebecca were shut up in the parlor for hours on end. I was sitting reading by the stove in the kitchen, for it was a piercing cold night, and when I heard him go out and slam the front door I thought I would make sure Aunt Becky had locked it after him. That lock was an old one, old as the house, and sometimes it did not catch unless you knew just how to turn it.

When I got to the front hall the lamp had not been put out and Aunt Becky herself was still standing by the foot of the stairs. The minute I set eyes on her face I knew something had happened, for she was white as the driven snow.

"Why—why, Miss Rebecca!" says I. "What—"

She just put up her hand to stop me.

"Don't, Iantha!" says she. "Please don't—now! Good-night."

She went up the stairs, slow, and holding on to the bal-
usters, and left me standing staring after her.

She said nothing about this to me, nor I to her of
course, the next morning when we met, but, after dinner she called me and Jethro into the sitting-room. There,
with the door shut, she told us dreadful news. No wonder
that session of hers with the judge had left her white-faced
and shook. No wonder I had guessed something was wrong
the second I looked at her. What she had to tell us was
about as awful and shameful as a thing could be.

Freeland Blair, the man the whole town had respected
and figured to be rich, and was jealous of according—the
very man over whose coffin the minister had said such
beautiful words—was not rich at all. Not only had he got
rid of practically all his own money, but he used every cent
of Mary's hundred thousand—wasted it, as nigh as could
be found out, gambling in stocks and such. So far as de-
serving respect—well, he was what they call an embezzler,
which, I judge, is the name they give to a thief who steals
a lot of money instead of a little.

"I am telling you this, Iantha," said Miss Rebecca, "you
and Jethro, because you are almost as much members of
this family as I am. And, besides, I am sure that what I tell
you will go no further."

We told her it would not—that is, Jethro did; I was too
upset to speak just then. But I spoke as soon as I could.
All I could think of was that poor, dear little girl of mine.

"Do you mean—" I asked her, "that Mary won't be well-
off at all? That, instead of being what folks call an heiress,
she is just—just—"

"Just a poor orphan, with nothing of her own but this
house and land and, perhaps, one or two thousand when
the bills are paid and the estate is settled. Yes, Iantha, that
is what I do mean; I am afraid there isn't any doubt of it."

Good old Jethro had something to say and he said it.

"Look here, Miss Blair," says he, "if that two hundred the old man left me will help along you put it in with the rest of what Mary's got coming to her. I don't need it. Fact is, I wouldn't know what to do with it, anyway. All my life I have been used to scratching along without a cent and it ain't safe for a man as old as I be to risk changing his habits. You count my two hundred in with Mary's and say nothing to nobody."

"And, Miss Rebecca," I put in, "if this place has got to be sold and Mary has not got anywhere to go you let her come with me. She can live with Ma and the rest of us over there in Wellmouth. There is so many of our tribe in that house already that one more won't make a mite of difference. Seems as if I could not bear to have her took to one of them orphans' homes. I have read terrible stories about such kind of places in books."

The answer she made I have never forgot. Many and many a time in the years to come, when she was old and cranky and had tried me till I was on the point of losing patience altogether, I would think of what she said that day to me and Jethro and bite my tongue and choke back my temper.

"Thank you, Iantha," said she. "And you too, Jethro. You are dear, good people, both of you. I— I—" She stopped a second, being, I rather guess, as nigh to breaking down as I was, which was plenty nigh enough. "I thank you, for Mary's sake—indeed I do," she went on, "and I know you mean exactly what you say. But Mary's future is settled; I settled it myself last night. I am not rich, but I am not exactly poor either. I am a single woman. I have saved some money and made a little more by good investments. I have taught school since I was seventeen and I am getting tired of it. I love this old house; I lived in it when I was young and I shall be quite contented to stay in it until I die. I have decided to break up my home out West, move my things to East Orham and live here with Mary. Between the little she may have and what I have put by we should be able to get along quite comfortably. And, of course, I shall count on your staying with us, just as you did with Freeland. I hope you will be willing to do that. Will you?"

Of course we said we would, and did not need time to consider, neither. And so, inside of another couple of months, the furniture belonging to Aunt Becky, a whole freight car full of it, was brought on and moved in and the old Blair house had a new boss. And she *was* boss too, from the very beginning; and when she died—she lived to be ninety—she was bossing with her last breath. Fair and square and honest as the day as long, but sure of her own mind and intending to have her own way—that was Aunt Becky Blair, peace to her.

To show what I mean: The house, every last room of it, was crowded with furniture already, for three generations of Blairs, all sea captains, had lived and died in it and they had brought home lots of things from foreign parts. When Aunt Becky's carful was added to the lot it looked to me as if there was not going to be space to move, scarcely. But Aunt Becky settled that, right off.

She, with Jethro and me at her heels, marched through one room after the other, she giving orders and us jumping to the whistle like foremast hands. This and that and t'other was to be moved up attic out of the way.

Jethro shook his head. "That attic is going to be so cram jam full," says he, "that the sides of the house will begin to bulge if we ain't careful. Seemed to me I heard the clapboards cracking last time I was up there."

Aunt Becky said "Nonsense!" but she and us went up to the attic to look. When she got as far as the little back storeroom she had questions to ask.

"What are all these odds and ends in here?" she wanted to know. We told her they were the things that had come off the wreck, them belonging to George Crossley. She knew about them afore but she had forgotten, I suppose.

"I don't calculate they are much account," says Jethro. "We could sell them to the junk man, I suppose, if you had rather had their room than their company."

I could not help put in my oar. To tell the truth, I would have been only too glad to see the last of them images and heathen contraptions. You remember, maybe, what I wrote about commencing to be afraid there might be a curse on this house, same as on the one in the Poe story. Well, by now I was pretty close to believing that the curse, if there was one, was on that wicked, outlandish stuff in that room. It had come from nobody knew where and, as soon as it came, our troubles started. Nobody can call me superstitious, and Marian and Mr. Thornton can laugh all they want to. For the matter of that, poor Mr. Samuel Gregg laughed later on, and now where is he?

So, when Jethro said that about selling those wreck things I spoke right up.

"Yes, why not sell them, Miss Rebecca?" says I. "It will be good riddance to bad rubbish, in my opinion."

But, as we learned when we come to know her better, if there was one streak stronger than another in Aunt Becky's make-up it was that of always keeping things. She kept everything, every old letter and bill and bank check and Christmas card—no matter how rubbishy it was she put it away and kept it. Jethro used to say she was a regular crow for hoarding up trash. So she shook her head.

"No," says she. "I guess we won't bother the junk man, not for the present anyhow. Iantha, you and I will go through that sea chest and the table drawers and such. I, for one, hate to touch the things—it seems like searching a dead man—but," with a sort of shiver, "it must be done, of course. . . . Poor Freeland! . . . Oh, well! let's get at it."

So we got at it, she and I, and we took out all Captain Crossley's clothes and the like of that and some she gave away and some she sold. When we finished the chest and every drawer and cubby hole in the lot was empty.

"Now," says she, with another shiver, "you and Jethro push all those things back against the wall there and put what we bring up from downstairs in front of it."

So that we did and piled the downstairs furniture in front. And never again, not for more than forty years, was the things at the back of the storeroom disturbed—never once.

The Chinese cabinet was put in with the rest. I saw to that. Aunt Becky, I was happy to say, made no objections.

"What is that ghastly thing?" she asked, pointing to the cabinet where it set on the foot bench in what had been her brother's room. I told her a little about it.

"It is ugly as sin," says she. "Wait until I look through it and then have Jethro take it away."

I did not wait for Jethro; I took it to the attic myself and I never came out of a place quicker than I did out of that one after I left it there. I could feel them carved claw hands clutching at my skirts, or seemed as if I could.

Of course Jethro and me had a lot of talks about Captain Freeland's queer actions those days afore he died. A good part of his reasons for them, such as his scrimping so with money, was plain enough now, but some was in a thick fog even yet. As Jethro said, it was easy to understand what set him to praying and asking for the Lord's forgiveness; he had stole his poor little niece's property and no wonder it weighed on his conscience, to say nothing of the fear of being found out any minute. But what had he been up to in that storeroom? He was looking for something—that seemed certain, but what on earth could it be?

"It was something to do with George Crossley," Jethro said. "It must have been. You remember how he acted when the foreign letter come. I have always suspicioned that was from Captain George. If you and me could read that letter, Anthy, we might know a whole lot more than we know now."

"Well, we are not liable to read it," I told him. "My opinion is that letter was burned up. The stove in his room was half full of burned paper; I found it so the day he died. I should not wonder at all if he had put in hours burning up his private letters and things. Probably he did it that very evening afore he crept out to paw over George's sea chest. What *do* you calculate he was hunting in that chest for?"

"Maybe the same thing he hoped might be in the Chinee cabinet."

"But there was nothing in it. Miss Rebecca went through every drawer and cubby-hole in that cabinet. I saw her, myself, and they was every one empty."

"Yes, yes; but you can bet the old man had been through them first. Did he find what he was hunting for—there or in the sea chest? And, whether he did or not, what was it anyhow? There is the conundrum. A lawyer paper or some sort of business agreement between him and Crossley, perhaps. That seems the most likely, but we don't know."

"No," I agreed, "we do not, and we never will now."

"If he did find it he probably burned it up with his other papers. If he did not find it—"

I cut in sharp. "Whether he did or did not is not my concern, Jethro Gould, and, if you will my advice, you will stop trying to make it yours. You heard Miss Rebecca's orders. If she should ever catch you prying and peeking into her affairs—well—"

I did not finish and I did not need to. Already we had seen enough of Aunt Becky Blair to realize that with her orders was orders. He grinned.

"You needn't worry," says he. "I know which side my bread is buttered. But, Anthy, there is one other little chance—a slim one, I grant you, but kind of interesting, just the same. How do we know all that wreck stuff was ever put in that back room?"

"How do we know! Why, you and me put it there ourselves, every last thing. And Judge Saunders and Mr. Bliss checked it over from George Crossley's own list. You know they did."

"Right enough, so far as it goes. But the checking was done out in the barn and done afore that barn was broke into by the Point gang thief, or whoever he was. You told me, the night when you caught a glimpse of him or his shadow, that it looked to you as if he had something in his arms. He might have carried a few odds and ends away with him—it is possible he did. . . . Oh, well! we could never tell without that list Judge Saunders has, or had, and that is none of our concerns, neither. But, just for fun, suppose this fellow did get away with a few things and suppose this paper, or what not, that Freeland was hunting for was in one of them? . . . Eh?"

I shut him up. "Jethro Gould," says I, "you stop where you are. Do you want to go crazy and die like poor Captain Freeland? Stop your guessing and riddling this minute. You let sleeping dogs lie."

He laughed. "That is good sense, Anthy," says he. "They can sleep, for all of me. I should like to know how much they are lying; but, as you say, it is probable you nor I never will know now."

One more queer thing happened before the conundrums connected with the *Pride of the Fleet* faded away for years and years. Aunt Becky had been living with us a while when she got a letter. It was from a nurse in that Boston hospital, where the Burke man, Captain Crossley's first mate, had been took. Seems that this Mr. Burke had laid in that hospital up to a few days afore this letter was mailed and then died.

Most of this long time he had been unconscious or out of his head, but a short spell afore he passed away he came to himself and asked his nurse to write the letter. It was addressed to Captain Freeland, for neither him nor the nurse knew of the captain's death.

It was about a message that George Crossley, the very day *he* died aboard his bark *Pride of the Fleet,* had give to his first mate to carry to Freeland Blair. Crossley, although he had been sick and getting steadily worse ever since the ship left Hong Kong, had not seemed to realize, or would not let himself realize until then, that he would not live to reach Boston. When, at last, he was forced to realize it, he was so weak that he could not say much, but the little he did say he seemed, according to Mr. Burke, to think was awful important. And he charged Burke to go to East Orham himself and tell Captain Freeland the message by word of mouth.

"'You tell him,'" says Mr. Burke, repeating to the nurse what Crossley had told him, "'that everything went off just as we hoped it would. He knows that from the letter, but you better tell him again. And tell him that I have left everything to him in my will and that he is to read my letter again and bear in mind that I say to him, "Look for one foot one hand."'"

That was the main part of the message, according to Burke, so the nurse wrote, and Captain Crossley had made his mate say it over and over so as not to forget. "One foot one hand." Mr. Burke was to remember that part above everything else. Captain Freeland would understand—or guess pretty quick—what it meant.

Well, Mr. Burke's own accident, which turned out fatal finally, stopped his going to East Orham with the message, of course, but, during his one spell of consciousness, he was so earnest and seemed so anxious to have his captain's last wish carried out that he made the nurse promise to write to Captain Freeland immediate. And so she had done it.

"He made me put it down on paper then and there," the nurse said in her letter. "He was of course, very near the end, and it may be that this 'message' was only a memory of some dream he had had in his delirium. However, I have kept my promise to the poor fellow."

Aunt Becky showed the letter to Jethro and me next day after it came.

"Now what on earth do you make of it?" she wanted to know. "'One foot one hand!' It sounds like the ravings of a Bedlamite. Have you a ghost of an idea as to what it might mean?"

I had not, for one. And Jethro, although he rubbed his chin and shook his head considerable, was obliged to own up that he could not see any sense to it.

"Maybe if we had that letter Captain Crossley mentioned to Mr. Burke, the one he wrote to your brother, Miss Rebecca," says he, "we might put two and two together and take some sort of an observation. I am pretty sure that letter was the one Captain Freeland got a few days after the wreck. Now if you could find it—"

But Aunt Becky did not wait for him to get through.

"Goodness gracious!" she snapped, "do you suppose I need you to remind me of that? I can't find that letter anywhere. I spent all last evening hunting through the few papers and letters my brother left. It is not among those. I imagine he burned it; he seems to have burned almost everything."

So, although we talked a while longer, we were no further ahead than when we started. It ended by Aunt Becky stuffing the nurse's letter back in the envelope and vowing she was not going to let it bother her another minute.

"I have enough on my mind," she declared, "without spending my time fretting over a sick man's craziness. I am going to throw this thing into the fire and forget it."

That was what she said, but I know mighty well she never would throw it in the fire. Being her, nine chances to one she would put it away and keep it forever, same as she kept everything else.

"'One foot one hand!'" says Jethro, after we two were alone together. "Humph! There is another sleeping dog for you, Anthy. And if you could tell me what *he* is lying about I might be able to tell you a lot of things."

V

Well, this stint that Marian and Mr. Thornton set for me is pretty nigh done. Goodness knows there is enough more I might write if I had leave to do it. Crowding the heft of a lifetime onto a few sheets of paper is going to be a job, but every day I have my orders to "Keep it short—keep it short, Iantha," so short I suppose it will somehow have to be.

The weeks following Captain Freeland's death and Aunt Becky's taking charge got to be months and the months years, same as they do in this fleeting show of a world we live in. Mary grew up and got to be a young woman. When she was twenty-two she married Franklin Fisher, the Wellmouth high school teacher, and he took her away to Worcester, where he had a fine job offered him. A few years after that they had a daughter, Marian, born to them, and all through the winter me and Aunt Becky, left alone in this big house—for Jethro Gould passed to his reward, of pneumonia, in 1897—put in our time looking forward to summer when the young folks and the baby would be down spending vacation.

Aunt Becky got older and more sot and cranky, as was natural, and probably I got the same way, although I hope not—the cranky part, I mean; getting older is the common lot and can not be helped. (You can help showing all your age and acting it, though, and that I have tried to do.)

The porch was built on off the front parlor in 1907—seems to me it was—and the bathroom at the head of the front stairs a year or so afterwards. Otherwise the old Blair house was kept just about so. In 1912 Mary's husband passed away—lung trouble, he had had it for a long spell—and Aunt Becky was hoping, as I am sure I was, that Mary and little Marian would come to live with us. But no, the Worcester school committee, or whatever they call it in cities, offered Mary a nice position teaching and she took it and stayed in their home up there. We saw them summers and Christmas and Easter vacations and that was all. Then, when Marian was eighteen, and had graduated from boarding school, she was possessed to earn her own living—girls have willful notions nowadays and grown folks indulge them in them—so she went to Boston all on her own hook and took a position as secretary in a big wool concern. Mary stayed in Worcester, teaching.

Then me—Aunt Becky and I, I mean—were lonesomer than ever, for Marian had only two weeks' vacation and her Sundays and holidays she spent with her mother in Worcester. I suppose likely it was that lonesomeness that led Aunt Becky into taking a boarder and lodger; it must have been that, for she did not need the money certain—not the way she and I lived. Queer, isn't it, how nigh in money matters some folks get in their old age. Miss Rebecca Blair up to the day of her death took solid comfort in adding up grocery bills and making sure the store folks was not cheating her.

Our boarder's name was Samuel Gregg and he was a single man, or a widower—I do not think anybody in Orham was just sure which, although if he had a wife he never talked about her. He was a round-faced, bald-headed, stubby little man, and, as a usual thing, easy to please and good company. Most of the time—he had a few grumpy spells—he was moony and cheerful, chatting away and eating anything—I was just going to say everything—set afore him; he had a tremendous appetite. He had money enough so he did not have to work and—for fun, I imagine—he was writing a book about ships and salt water matters. For a spell after he came to Orham he lived at the Ocean View House, but Aunt Becky heard him give a lecture about old shipping times, in the East Orham meeting-house vestry and—maybe because he mentioned the Blairs as one of our oldest seafaring families—she took a shine to him. One day she made proclamation to me that he was going to lodge and board with us regular.

"He will be the sort of company you and I ought to have, Iantha," says she. "He is a gentleman and a scholar. He can talk about something besides how the hens are laying and how outrageous the neighbors behave."

So far as that was concerned we had not kept hens for ever so long and the nighest neighbor was Jonas Jones, who was, and is, about as fine a neighbor as you could find anywheres; in spite of his forever teasing me, pretending I am his "best girl" and such foolishness. His furniture painting shop and the place where he sleeps—he takes his meals down in the village—is a good ways off by the road, but not half so far by the short cut acrost the fields and in those times, same as now, he was always stopping in to talk with us and ask if there was not some errands he could do when he went to the village. But you will hear enough about Jonas Jones pretty soon, so I must not bother with him now. It was Samuel Gregg, our boarder, I started to tell about.

Mr. Gregg, I mean—moved into the spare room, the big one opening off the back upstairs hall opposite my bedroom. He had to be careful of his health—his heart was leaky, or something like that—so he did not go out much, but put in his time doing puzzles out of the newspaper, or playing solitaire with cards. He played chess whenever he could get somebody to play it with him, which was not very often except in summer. Then Mr. Harvey Blodgett, the rich man from New York who built the bungalow cottage on the road a mile to the northeastward of us, used to come in and them two would set for hours staring at the chessboard and saying nothing. A poor idea of a good time according to my notion.

One more thing Mr. Gregg loved, besides chess and puzzles and tobacco and strong tea, was antiques. Mr. Blodgett was an antique loon too and the way that pair would go into fits over a crippled chair or a nicked glass candlestick was perfectly ridiculous. They spent a lot of time at Miller Jenkins's antique shop in the village and Mr. Gregg would come back from one of those cruises all excited and saying, "Bless my soul! Bless my soul!" over and over. I read once in a book—I forget now what one it was—about an English earl or count or something who was forever singing out to have his soul blessed, but I never heard a body in real life do it but Samuel Gregg. Far as that goes, he always talked like a book, scarcely ever used a short word when he could use a long one.

It was over some chess game or other that him and Mr. Blodgett had the spat that broke off their friendship. There was no sense to it and it was too bad, for it left Mr. Gregg all alone with hardly a real chum in the whole of Orham. It made me feel sorry for him, it did so.

But I did not have a great deal of time to be sorry over his little no account trouble because soon afterwards—last fall, the fall of 1926 it was—a real trouble came. Aunt Becky had not been feeling just right for a couple of days and when, on the morning of the third day, I went up to her room to see what she wanted for breakfast, there she was dead in bed, poor old soul. She had passed away in her sleep, peaceful as a lamb.

Well, she was in her ninetieth year and it was to be expected any time, of course; but somehow you never do expect those things and when they come they are a dreadful shock. Thinks I, "Iantha Hallett, now you are alone in the world for sure!" My own brothers and sisters, them left alive, were married off and scattered all around and it was only once in a while that I as much as had letters from them. So, when the thought came to me that more than likely this house would be sold and I would be turned out to go to the Lord knows where, my heart just let go all holts and dropped down into my slippers.

But it need not have, as it turned out. Aunt Becky had left some money and the house and land was Mary's anyhow, under her Uncle Freeland's will. So Mary decided she could afford to quit school teaching and live in East Orham, which is not so far from Boston that Marian could not spend Sundays with her just as she had in Worcester. As for me I was to stay right along and keep house.

"It would not be home without you, Iantha," says Mary; and Marian said the same thing. And Mr. Gregg was to stay, too; he had come to be almost settled a part of the establishment as I was.

So there was more moving in and changing around. Mary and Mr. Gregg and me lived along peaceful and contented through last winter and in May Marian came down unexpected making the announcements that she was through with her wool business and wasn't going to do a thing but play until September. She was going to have the whole summer in this dear old ark of a house and what a good time she meant to have!

"Oh, I am going to do lots and lots of things!" she vowed and declared. "You will see, Iantha! No, mother is not to have any part in doing them, either. I have my plans for her, too."

Just what those plans were she would not tell us right off, but they came out in a week or so. She was happy and excited as a ten-year-old and I could not quite make out why—that is, I could not until I began to notice how many letters she was getting. I will not go as far as to say there was one every day, but there was at least three a week, all postmarked Boston and in the same handwriting. Unless I was more mistook than I believed I was it was not female handwriting either.

One day Mary got me alone in the kitchen and told me what was what. It was not so much more than I had guessed already. I am a single woman—although that is nobody's fault but mine, for I have had chances enough—but, single or double, I *hope* I am not a born fool.

Marian, so her mother told me, was engaged to a young man by the name of William Thornton. She had met him up to Boston and—well, the rest of it had come along in the way of nature. Mary was reasonably contented about it—that is, as contented as a mother can be when some-body is figuring on taking her only child away from her. She—Mary, I mean—had met this Thornton young fellow three or four times and she liked him very much indeed.

"Of course, Iantha," says she, "they are not planning to be married yet awhile, for he is just finishing his course in business college and Marian wants to earn and save a little more. He is a nice boy I am sure; but you will have a chance to judge him yourself, for he is coming down here soon to spend at least a part of the summer with us."

I said that was just lovely, and I meant it. The idea of our little Marian getting married seemed—well, I could scarcely make it seem at all and it did make me feel as if I must be upwards of a hundred and fifty—but I was all tingled up at the news. I do love romance and always did. Thinks I, "Won't it be splendid to have them two young things lovering around and have to be careful and keep out of their way and all like that!"

But, my soul! When I thought that I did not realize how this world has changed since I was a girl. Judging by what I have seen since a love affair between young folks nowadays is about as romantic as a—as a coal hod. Marian Fisher and her beau may think the world of each other, and I am sure they do, but you never would guess it. By the way they act and talk to each other—when a third party is around anyhow—you would think he was a brother and she a sister—a step-sister at that. I never in my life! . . . But there! What is not my business I do not meddle with. Which has always been my motto.

Mary had something else to say to me besides telling about the engagement. Seems that some of her husband's folks—they were Fishers, too, and they lived in Buffalo, New York State—had been trying for a long spell to coax her to come up there and make them a long visit. And now, so she said, Marian was possessed and determined that her mother should go.

"There is, in one way, no reason why I should not go," said Mary to me. "I should have a wonderful time, I am sure, and the change would do me good. But do you honestly think, Iantha, that it would be right for me to go and leave William and Marian here—unchaperoned, as I suppose it might be called. You know this town as well, or better, than I do and—well, people do talk."

I bristled right up. "They will talk anyhow, some of them," says I. "Doesn't the Bible tell us about, 'Busybodies, speaking things which they ought not.' Let them talk! They won't do it when I am round. As for the rest of it— Mr. Samuel Gregg will be right here in the house, won't he; although I grant you he is so absent-minded most of the time that he can't see a thing till he falls over it. But never mind him: I shall be here and there is nothing the matter with my eyesight. If there was anything going on that—but there, Mary Fisher, you know Marian and you know there won't be. She is not that kind. . . . What does she say about it, herself?"

Mary could not help laughing. "She says, 'Mother, don't be so hopelessly old-fashioned!' And I suppose old-fashioned is exactly what I am."

"So am I and I thank the Lord for it. . . . You go along and have your good time and visit, Mary."

So she went and no sooner had Marian come back from the depot in her little automobile than she commenced to put those other precious "plans" of hers into work. I shall not say much about them, because they are not really in my part of this history. It will be enough if I just say that what they amounted to was undoing most of what her Great-Aunt Rebecca had done when *she* first came. Nigh as I could make out that girl was calculating to put the downstairs furniture and fixings in the attic and the attic stuff downstairs again.

"Oh, I tell you, Iantha," says she, her eyes shining, "I am going to have a perfectly great time! Mr. Gregg is going to help me; you know he worships antiques, just as I do, and he is a very good judge of values. He says he is sure we can sell almost all we do not want to keep and for good prices, too. I have always known that that attic and the little back storeroom were full of wonderful old things. I— Why, what on earth is the matter? Why do you look at me like that?"

I do not know how I was looking but I do know how I felt. When she mentioned that back storeroom one of them cold crawly shivers that I had not had for forty years ran right up my backbone.

"Oh, Marian!" I begged her. "Don't touch those things in that back storeroom. Whatever else you do, don't disturb *them*. It'll fetch bad luck, I know it."

She just stared at me. Then she burst out laughing. "Iantha," says she, "how can you be so ridiculous!"

I opened my mouth to answer and then I shut it again. What was the use? And yet that minute, with those shivers crawling up and down my spine bone, I was surer than ever that there was a curse laid on those things from that wrecked bark. That was what I thought and what I knew; and yet all I said was: "Humph! As I understand it this young Thornton man of yours is expected here to-morrow forenoon. How do you think he will like having to pitch right in and help lug dusty, dirty old furniture up and down stairs?"

She laughed again. "Oh, he'll love it," said she. "He'd better, anyhow!"

There! . . . That is the end, so far as my part of this writing is concerned. It was not the end of my part in the awfulness. No, indeed! It was only the beginning. I was mixed up in that from start to finish. And, if you read along—as I presume likely you will, even though I have not been asked to set it down—you will see whether I was right or not about that curse and the bad luck and all. *I* say I was. Marian and Mary and Mr. Thornton seem to figure that I was not—not more than halfway right, anyhow. All I say to that is: "We are not dead yet."

That is what I say to them and I have not heard them make any satisfactory answer.

The Scripture says (Isaiah xxx—verse viii), "Now go, write it before them in a table and note it in a book."

That is what I have done, and tried to do it truthful and to the best of my capabilities. And so I lay down my pen, signing this, as I most generally sign my letters.

Faithfully yours,
Iantha B. Hallett.

PART TWO

The Story of the Unusual Events Which Took
Place at the Old Blair House in East Orham
During the Summer of 1927.

Told by
William Todd Thornton

I

Iantha has passed me the torch with the earnest exhortation to keep it burning, to carry it on, and to hold it high. She had passed it, I fear, with some slight feeling of misgiving, for she has a very natural pride in accomplishment and trembles lest the fine fibre of her work may suffer at my younger and much ruder hands.

"Mr. Thornton," said Iantha tensely, her bright eyes snapping behind her glasses, "there's only one thing I want to say before you go on with this writin' we're doin' and that is this: Don't you worry about the excitin' parts. There's enough of them, gracious knows, what with screamings and midnight alarums and excursions, to set a body's teeth on edge. They're all right in their place, and their place is plenty, but they ain't enough." She shook her head vigorously. "No, sir-ee, they are not! There's one thing this story of ours must have, and if it don't have it we might as well heave the whole thing overboard, because nobody—or next to nobody—will read it."

"Yes, Iantha?" I was all attention.

"Romance!" Iantha pounced on the word triumphantly, with sharp emphasis on the first syllable. "Romance! What it ought to have is moonlight, them foreign birds—what are they?—Oh, yes, nightingales—and roses. That's what it should have to make all hands crazy to get a-hold of it.

It can't have all of them, perhaps, but it has just got to have some, or we are wastin' our time."

"Oh." I winked covertly at Marian and shook my head. "I see what you mean, Iantha, and I agree with you on principle, but there's one big kick. This story of ours is based on fact. Where can we find this romance you want without stretching the truth?"

"Where can we find it?" Iantha, in her indignation, pointed a quavering finger at me. "Ain't you and Marian engaged to be married? Haven't you been engaged all through this awful summer? Ain't you suffered together, and been scart to death together? Haven't you met violence and destruction together?" Her contempt was withering. "And you ask me where we can find it!"

"I'm sorry." I was properly subdued. "You may be sure I shall mention that Marian and I were engaged before all this trouble started."

"That isn't all I want! I tell you we ought to have a hero and a heroine and some real love-makin'. Yes—and kisses." She was defiant. "There never was a story worth while without *them* in it, was there? Considerin' that you two treat each other like almost perfect strangers, I shouldn't be surprised if you *would* have to 'stretch the truth' as you call it, so as to fetch in a little romance, and if so be, then stretch it—it won't do any harm." She was grim. "If you was real reckless you might even go so far as to hint you was good-lookin'. But perhaps that would be *too* much to ask."

Marian had the bad taste to show amusement at this unkind thrust.

Romance, it seems, must be part of my story. If Iantha is to be satisfied I am not to be permitted even a small amount of decent reticence. "I'll give you moonlight," I promised her reluctantly at last, "and perhaps I can ring in a couple of roses. I am, however, a little leery of those nightingales you crave, Iantha. They aren't very thick in this part of New England."

It was romance, strangely enough, which was directly responsible for my having a part in this story at all. If it had not been for that disturbing emotional experience known as "falling in love" I should have spent this last summer upon the shores of Lake Michigan where I have always lived, and where my greatest mental discomfort would have been caused by the missing of a two-foot putt.

I met Marian Fisher, however, during the winter of my second and last year at the Harvard Business School. She was employed as the secretary of some busy vice-president in Boston, and she lived with another girl in a small apartment on Beacon Hill.

We saw quite a bit of each other during the winter and early spring, and by the time the first buds were appearing on the historic elms of Cambridge I was in a more or less pitiable condition. My appetite had almost entirely disappeared, I was a subject to long fits of abstraction, and work seemed impossible.

There was only one thing to be done about the situation and I did it. One evening in May I sent Marian a large bunch of roses as a warning of what was about to happen, and then took her out for a stroll along the river. It was a beautiful moonlight night, and the water was very pretty, if I remember correctly.

After a number of false starts I was finally able to say what I had to say, and to my complete amazement Marian did not seem to find the idea altogether objectionable. I went home in a daze from which I have not, even yet, entirely recovered.

(I hope Iantha is satisfied with the love story. It contains almost all the elements she desires, and it happens to be true—all except the part about the roses. The thought

of sending roses did not occur to me, although it undoubtedly would have been a very good idea.)

It is almost impossible to explain the potent spell
which Marian Fisher, without the slightest effort on her
part, is able to cast over me. Marian is capable, and I have
an abiding distrust of capable girls. They belong, I have
always felt, to the class which haughtily regards the world
through thick, horn-rimmed glasses, and which is addic-
ted to good stout "sensible" shoes. They hold business
positions of some little importance, take delight in airing
their well-considered views upon eugenics or politics, and
always dismiss the masculine sex with a sniff of amused
contempt.

Marian is none of these. She wears no glasses of any
description, although I have always suspected her dark
eyes would welcome their aid. Her shoes, far from being
sensible, are the most ridiculous little contrivances of this
or that fragile material upon which have ever been privi-
leged to gaze. She never discusses eugenics, and she says
that the subject of politics both confuses and annoys her.
She does not observe workings of my poor male mind with
evident commiseration. She seems, to the contrary, to
respect its labored creakings.

In company with the rest of her enlightened generation,
Marian attempts to assume a very practical and slightly
cynical outlook upon life. She insists, so she tells me, that
a spade must be called a spade, and yet I have a strong
suspicion that she believes in Santa Claus and in the de-
sirability of regarding a new moon over the right shoulder.
She is entirely too pleasing to the eye and too delightfully
inconsistent in behavior to be classed as capable, and yet
that is exactly the way she must be classed. I do not understand it, and I do not pretend to understand it. I merely
offer my most humble thanks to whatever gods there be,
and let it go at that.

I had labored under the delusion that being engaged to Marian would alleviate my distressing mental condition, but I found to my dismay that it merely intensified it. June was approaching at an indecent rate of speed and so, too, was our inevitable separation. If, and when, I graduated from business school I was expected to depart for home. It was patently impossible to take Marian with me, for my expected salary would not permit even one person to starve with any degree of gentility.

Fate is, at times, a kindly power. Marian's vice-president was suddenly captivated with the idea that he had labored long enough in the interests of his business, and he proceeded to retire permanently to his estate at Prout's Neck. Marian joined the army of the unemployed, and almost simultaneously I received a letter from my father in Chicago in which he very generously offered to finance me in whatever kind of a summer vacation my fancy might dictate.

"You had better take advantage of this opportunity," he wrote me with some humor, "for you won't have another for a long, long time."

There is no doubt of the fact that I followed his advice, but at the same time I feel justified in pointing out that I showed every consideration for his pocketbook.

Marian and I decided that she was to return to her mother's home in East Orham for the summer and that I was to visit her there. We determined to have three glorious months of golf, swimming, sailing, and the like. In the fall, rested and eager for the fray, I was to go to Chicago and my work. Marian was to accept another position in Boston which would occupy her until my financial condition provided some slight excuse for matrimony.

The plans were excellent, and to a certain extent they materialized. We had our three months at East Orham. Whether they were lazy months, whether they were occupied in the innocent diversions of outdoor sport, whether they left us rested and eager for the fray is another question. We had them, at any rate.

Marian departed for East Orham just before the period of my final examinations, and left me with no refuge but my books. I turned to them, and with the further aid of large quantities of black coffee was able to assimilate enough last-minute information to save me from disgrace. I learned, one bright morning in June, that I was considered fit to assume any responsibility, from the leadership of a large corporation to the mere presidency of some modest banking institution. I received the assurance with a loud shout of delight and, grasping my suitcase in one hand and my golf clubs in the other, I dashed for the South Station and the train for East Orham. In the back of my head, I admit, was the thought that it would be nice to see Marian again.

That thought sustained me throughout the journey. As the train puffed its leisurely way through mile after mile of thick, scrub pine growth I pictured our meeting. I would swing down from the car into the crowd on the East Orham platform and stand smiling, for a moment, in the midst of the confusion. Then someone would call my name, a handkerchief would flutter, and a familiar figure would come running toward me.

The intimate details of the grand climax would be both tender and appealing.

So vivid became the scene in my mind that I was unable to restrain myself when, after an age of waiting, the conductor shoved his head into the far end of the car and announced my destination. I clutched my belongings to my bosom and darted out upon the platform. There was a breath of cool, salt air; another breath of soft-coal smoke and cinders; a glimpse of rolling country with a flash of the sea beyond; a final protesting lurch as the old wooden cars rounded a curve, and then, all at once, we were there.

I squared my shoulders, tweaked my tie in anticipation, and staggered down the steps to receive a rude shock. There was no crowd upon the East Orham platform. A number of men lounged easily in the floorway of the weather-beaten wooden structure that seemed to serve as the station. Another man in overalls trundled a handtruck in the direction of the baggage car. The conductor was assisting an old lady to alight from the coach ahead.

There were no shouts of greeting and no signs of Marian.

I suppose I was slightly stunned. I stood there, at any rate, with my mouth slightly and unattractively agape until the train had departed. Then I blinked my eyes and came to the realization that I was being regarded with evident interest by the group in the station doorway.

"Is there," I began uncertainly; "that is, can I get a taxi?"

Most of my audience laughed for no apparent reason, but I got an answer at last. "I don't know as you'd exactly call it a taxi," replied one of their number, pointing a long, lean finger, "but Lem Small there has got somethin' that might make out to get you somewheres, if it ain't too far. Where are you aimin' to go?"

"To Mrs. Mary Fisher's house. I think they call it the old Blair place."

"So?" My informant shrugged and looked about him reflectively. "Well, that's a pretty long haul for Lem's gas ruin, but if you want to get there, and ain't too much of a hurry, you might chance it. Hold on, though!" he added, pointing again but in the opposite direction. "Guess you won't have to, after all. That's the Fisher flivver over there, and if I ain't mistaken, Sammy Gregg is asleep behind the wheel. Wake him up gentle, because he's a dangerous feller!"

I mumbled my thanks and made off to rouse the dangerous Sammy. He did not appear particularly vicious as I first saw him, crouched on the driver's seat of the little car. He was a short, fat, middle-aged man with steel-rimmed glasses. A brown felt hat, small out of all proportion to the tremendous head upon which it rested, gave him a wistful and almost laughable appearance. If I had known then what I know now about him—if I could have foreseen that morning when Jonas Jones, his face white under the tan, was to beckon to me from the dining-room door—I might have looked more closely at Samuel Gregg. I was, however, disturbed and exasperated at Marian's non-appearance, and I had thought for little else.

Mr. Gregg was not asleep. He was pondering deeply over a small slip of paper, and he looked up at me with pale unseeing blue eyes when I tapped him on the shoulder. "My Second," he repeated dreamily and to my great astonishment, "is one who waits, and waits, and wonders why."

I had not the remotest idea what he was talking about, nor did I greatly care; my annoyance was rising. "Perhaps," I replied, with sarcasm, "you are referring to me. My name is Thornton."

The name seemed to rouse him from his trance. He had muttered, "Bless my soul!," had hopped down to the ground, shaken my hand, and placed my baggage in the back seat before I was fully aware of what he was about. He moved with remarkable agility for one of his great weight.

"I hope you'll forgive me, Mr. Thornton," he was saying as he ushered me to my place beside him and started the motor. "I do hope you'll forgive me! I had no idea that the train was in. I have a habit of losing myself in complete concentration."

He pulled down the throttle, stepped on the reverse pedal, and swept in a wide backward circle out into the station yard without taking his eyes from my face. I steeled myself for the inevitable crash but it did not come. The flivver lurched to a sickening stop and then leaped forward. Mr. Gregg was still talking with great animation.

"Are you interested in puzzles? I was doing a puzzle—a very baffling charade. 'My First' I solved very easily, but 'My Second' is another proposition altogether. 'My Second is one who waits, and waits, and wonders why.' What do you make of that, Mr. Thornton?"

"Why, nothing, I suppose." I was bewildered.

"Puzzles are a boon to the world." I do not think he had heard me. "They offer mental exercise and the freedom from the humdrum things of life which complete concentration alone can bring. Like chess." Once more he turned his gaze upon me. "Do you play chess, Mr. Thornton?"

"Yes." I sighed as we slithered around a sharp curve, narrowly missing a telegraph pole. "A little."

My admission seemed to please Samuel Gregg greatly. He would have discoursed upon the glories of chess all the way to the Blair homestead had I not interrupted him. There were certain things on my mind. "How is Marian?" I inquired with some misgivings.

"Marian?" The new train of thought seemed to confuse him momentarily. "Eh? Marian? Oh, yes, yes, of course! Marian is in splendid health. She is a splendid girl. She is at present occupied in sorting and classifying a collection of antiques which she—she and I, that is—found in the attic—a really remarkable collection of antiques. Are you interested in antiques, Mr. Thornton?"

"Not particularly." I am afraid I was abrupt. "So that was why she didn't meet me at the station!"

"Too bad!" Mr. Gregg ignored the last half of my speech and was bemoaning my lack of interest in what was evidently another hobby of his. "Antiques are a mirror of the past. I love them. If I may say so I rank them on a level with puzzles and chess. I anticipate great pleasure in helping Marian identify her newly found treasures. There are three chairs—" he leaned toward me and whispered hoarsely in my ear—"there are three chairs that I suspect of being genuine Sheraton!

So it went on all through the rest of the trip. Samuel Gregg indulged in an animated and uninterrupted monologue concerning antiques and puzzles, with plenty of chess thrown in for seasoning. He drove the flivver, meanwhile, with a magnificent abandon that inspired almost as much admiration as terror. He did not come to grief, it seemed to me, solely because the possibility of grief never occurred to him.

We rattled through the narrow main street of East Orham, past what I came to know later as the Post Office and Miller Jenkins' antique shop, and out into the country beyond. The road wound down through the warm pines to the edge of the sea, which sparkled, deeply blue, to the far horizon. It was beautiful, I suppose, but at that time I paid no more attention to it than I paid to the smooth flow of my companion's words. My sense of self-importance had received a rude blow and I was entirely occupied in sympathizing with myself.

All at once Samuel Gregg tugged the steering wheel violently to the left. We darted, with undiminished speed at right angles across the road, grazed a stone post on the far side, and lurched drunkenly up a narrow gravel drive to the house.

I received a hazy impression of thick shrubbery and tall trees, with a long, rambling white-frame building in the background. Then I was urged to earth, my baggage was extricated from the back seat, and I bustled across the lawn to the front door.

Iantha Hallett was waiting for us in the dim light of the hallway.

Beyond saying that she is a slim, wiry little gray-haired woman whose black eyes sparkle restlessly behind her glasses, and whose quick smile is a thing of warmth and understanding, I shall attempt no description of Iantha Hallett. Iantha in her narrative has described herself with a vividness that would put any poor words of mine to shame. She has spirit, dry humor, sympathy and a vigorous imagination, the latter inspired and encouraged by the kind of literature she loves to read. She has been my friend since the very beginning, and will remain so, I hope, until the end.

She welcomed me to East Orham with a sincerity that left no room for doubt, though I felt that I could detect a faint hint of indignation in her manner. "Well now, we are real glad to see you, Mr. Thornton," she said briskly in conclusion, and her chin came up in a manner which was to become so familiar. "Some of us may be a little mite funny in our way of showin' it, but young women are different from what they was in my day, and probably you know that and can make allowances."

I thought that I understood her meaning and was about to reply when she turned to the momentarily silenced Mr. Gregg. "And now if you wouldn't mind fetchin' along Mr. Thornton's things," she suggested. "we'll show him where he's going to be put. After ridin' all that time on those awful steam-cars, poor soul, he'd probably like a little rest and quiet."

My room was a large square one on the second floor. It had a big four-posted bed in one corner and a large mahogany bureau against the opposite wall. There were a number of small hooked rugs scattered about the gray-painted floor. The light poured in cheerfully from windows on the west and south.

Iantha inspected it critically. "It ain't exactly one of them marble halls you read about," she observed, "but there has lots of nice folks slept in it, just the same."

I assured her that I should be more than comfortable, and she turned away with a little nod. "Dinner won't be for another hour yet," she informed me, "so you'll have time to fix up or take a nap, or do whatever you've a mind to. That is—" she regarded me sharply—"that is, unless you'd like to say hello to Marian first."

"I think I'd like to." I made an elaborate and unsuccessful attempt to be casual. "I'd like to, if she isn't too busy."

"Busy!" Iantha sniffed. "She isn't busy, unless you call messin' around with a lot of old second-hand trash that is no good and would be better off left alone, bein' busy. If it was me I wouldn't be kept so busy that I couldn't meet my—couldn't meet a friend at the train; but, however, that ain't my affairs, so be it as it may." She shrugged. "I presume likely we'll find her in the unfinished attic and buried out of sight by her precious antiques."

The word seemed to restore his vocal powers to Gregg. "Yes!" He grasped me by the arm and almost dragged me to the door. "You must see those three chairs! If those chairs aren't Sheraton Mr. Thornton, then I am very much mistaken."

"You have no idea," I informed him solemnly as we hurried down the hall with Iantha bringing up the rear, "how anxious I am to see those chairs!"

We opened a door which led past the top of the back stairs to the rear portion of the house, and crossed another narrow corridor to the storeroom. This apartment was piled with old trunks, wooden boxes, and decrepit furniture to such an extent that the light from its two windows was almost altogether shut out. I could see no trace of Marian in the gloom, and had come to the conclusion that she was, indeed, buried beneath her treasures, when all at once a muffled but cheerful voice called out a greeting.

Iantha grunted. "She is in the next room, I guess, though I should think there was enough junk in this one to drive anybody crazy. Go right on in, Mr. Thornton."

I took her advice, and in the smaller but equally jumbled adjoining chamber I found Marian. She waved me an airy welcome from the top of a pile boxes upon which she was standing. "Hello, there! she remarked casually, as though I had just returned from an errand to the corner drug store. "Did you have a good trip?"

I am very seldom annoyed with Marian. I think I may honestly say that I am practically never annoyed with Marian. This time, however, I was filled with just and righteous indignation. "The trip," I retorted gently, "was splendid, but my enthusiastic and even boisterous reception at its conclusion has moved me as I have never before been moved."

Marian smiled. "Do you detect," she inquired of Iantha who was behind me, "any faint note of irony in the young man's words?"

Iantha's chin came up. "Not knowin' what it is—I don't," she replied tartly. "But if he is mad I ain't surprised at it and I don't blame him. Some things are just a little *too* much, that's all *I* have to say."

"Really all? I'm glad." Marian climbed down from her perch and looked at Gregg, who seemed completely bewildered. "And what have you to say, Mr. Gregg? Will you join in the general hymn of hate or will you admit I had matters of pressing importance to attend to? Will you be kind enough to explain to these people that I am in the very midst of making a fortune?"

Mr. Gregg seemed incapable of explaining or admitting anything. He merely rubbed his bald head. Iantha was still vocal. "If you're goin' to make your fortune out of this claptrap," she remarked with a contemptuous wave of the hand that included both storerooms, "then Martin Kelly, the junk man, ought to be richer than the whole Standard Oil by this time. It beats me how some folks can get all het up over rubbish!"

"Rubbish!" The word seemed to rouse Gregg from his lethargy. He reached out a plump hand and pointed at three chairs which were ranged side by side against the wall. "Look at those, Mr. Thornton—just look at those!"

Marian was no less excited. She grasped my arm and shook it. "Yes, Bill," she commanded earnestly. "Just look at those! What do you think they are?"

I was still bitter. I admit I was still a trifle bitter. I regarded the three chairs thoughtfully for a time and then nodded my head. "I think," I said slowly, "yes, I am almost positive that those are chairs."

Marian sighed, dropped my arm, and shook her head at Gregg. "I'm afraid," she said sadly, "that Mr. Thornton is a wit. Not only that, but Iantha is busily poisoning his mind. We shall have to take him into the secret or there'll be no living in the house with him."

They took me into the secret.

It appeared that Marian, in a casual inspection of the storerooms, had discovered what she believed to be a valuable old mahogany writing desk. She appealed to Gregg as an authority and he confirmed her opinion. The desk was, undoubtedly, a find, and could be sold to almost any antique dealer at an impressive figure.

The hunt was on. Marian and Gregg spent day after day in the musty storerooms. They unearthed, and uncovered, and unpacked. They exclaimed, and marveled, and crooned with delight. In addition to the writing desk, they discovered tables, chairs, and sundry old furniture the value of which, according to the infallible Gregg, was nothing less than startling.

I was interested in spite of myself. "What are you going to do with them all?"

"Sell what we can of them!" There was a bright spot of color in each of Marian's cheeks. "Mr. Gregg knows their value and he is going to sell them for me to antique dealers.

They're worth money, do you understand? Actual cash money!"

Yes. Money was one thing I really had no difficulty in understanding, and I also had a keen realization how welcome it would be to Marian and her mother.

"Of course," Marian shrugged, "there are some things that are hardly worth selling, even though they are interesting. Those things I am going to scatter about this house. Take this little fellow, for example. I found him this very morning when I might have been frittering away my time meeting you at the train!"

She picked up and held out for my inspection a bit of statuary about twelve inches high. It was a grotesque and particularly evil conception of Buddha which had been carved from a block of some dark wood.

"Won't it brighten your declining hours," she demanded, "to have this little beauty staring at you from the living-room mantel?"

I don't know what my reply might have been, for at that moment Iantha interrupted. She had listened to the preceding talk with what she plainly hoped was an air of lofty and dignified disinterest. Now, however, all pretense of disinterest vanished.

"What!" she cried, sharply. "Do you mean you are cal'latin' to *keep* that heathen image and set it up in our livin'-room? Don't you do it, Marian Fisher! The idea, after what I've told you so many times!"

"Oh, Iantha! Please! Don't be idiotic! What will Mr. Thornton think of you?"

"I can't help what he thinks. If you are a sensible girl you'll let everything in this back room stay right where it is. If you won't do that, if touch it you must, then sell it. Get rid of it! Oh, Marian, please! My nerves ain't what they used to be—"

Marian interrupted. "Hush, hush, Iantha!" she broke in, laughing. Then, turning to me; "Don't be alarmed, Bill. She isn't insane, she is merely superstitious, that is all."

"Superstitious!" Iantha repeated the word with scorn. "There isn't a superstitious bone in my head, and you know it. How can you talk so! Was it superstitiousness that made your Great Uncle Freeland drop down dead in this very room?"

"Wait a minute, Iantha. He did not drop down dead in this room. He died in his own room and in his own bed. You have told me about that five hundred times at least."

"Maybe so. If you went through what I went through them days and nights I guess likely you'd tell it. Well, he didn't actually do his dyin' in here, I give in; but he had been here and laid hands on the stuff that was took off the *Pride of the Fleet* and the curse got him. He might have been alive—" I think Iantha was about to say "yet," but instead she pulled up short and finished with "for a long spell, if he hadn't started that curse again! And now you want to start it! I never heard such wicked foolishness. I only wish your mother was here; she'd back me up, I know she would."

To say that I was astonished by this outburst would be to understate my feelings. Marian saw the expression on my face and laughed again. Before she could speak, however, Samuel Gregg came forward from where he had been caressing the Sheraton chairs. He, too, appeared surprised.

"Why—why, bless my soul!" he exclaimed. "What is all this, Iantha? *Pride of the Fleet?* That was the ship that was wrecked here forty or fifty years ago, wasn't it? But—but a curse? What on earth do you mean by a curse?"

Marian held up a warning hand. "Wait, wait, Mr. Gregg," she ordered. "Is it possible that you have lived in this house all this while and haven't heard Iantha's pet story? I have heard it ever since I was a little girl. I supposed she had told it to everybody."

"I guess likely I know when to keep my mouth shut to outsiders about family concerns," cut in Iantha, tartly. Gregg, who scented a puzzle, I think, paid no heed.

"She has told me about the wreck," he went on, addressing Marian. "Yes, and Captain Blair's death I seem to remember. But a curse—no, I am sure she has never said anything about a curse. Now that is very interesting. Isn't it, Mr. Thornton?"

"Interesting and spooky," said I. "You never told me you owned a family curse, Marian."

Marian was plainly out of patience.

"It is all nonsense, of course," she declared. "Iantha reads so much about ghosts and curses that perhaps it is no wonder she believes in them. Don't start her on that subject now or we shan't have any dinner."

She put an arm about Miss Hallett's shoulder.

"There, there, Iantha dear," she said, soothingly. "We won't wake any sleeping curses, I promise you. We intend to sell all these things, if we can. Now don't worry. Curse!"

Iantha's agitation seemed to subside. She smiled, rather shamefacedly. "I guess likely you must think I'm cracked in the head, Mr. Thornton, but the sight that idol thing Marian was wavin' around brought it back to me. . . . Oh, well! I've said my say. I must be goin' right down to the kitchen or everything in or on the cookstove will be burnt to a chip."

Samuel Gregg would not let her go. He had a number of questions to ask and he asked them. Iantha answered the first two or three patiently enough, but then she turned on her heel.

"I can't stop another second," she declared. "I've got my work to do. Oh, yes!" as if the thought had suddenly occurred to her, "that reminds me. Speakin' of work, didn't you promise to fix that woodshed door latch for me this mornin', Mr. Gregg?"

The fat little man shrugged his shoulders. "That can wait until later just as well as not," he replied, testily. "I am interested in this—er—curse or whatever it is. You say it is connected, in some mysterious way, with the articles stored in this back room, those brought ashore from the wreck. Now what makes you think—"

Iantha did not let him finish. "I do hope, Mr. Gregg," she observed, with a casual irrelevance, "that you don't care much about that chess problem stayin' just so, the one you had laid out on the board in the library. It just run acrost my mind that the window was open and, with the wind blowin' so, I am afraid most of the pieces are on the floor by this time."

Samuel started as though he had been pricked by a pin and hastened from the room, muttering, "Bless my soul!" over and over under his breath.

Iantha's lip twitched. "That window hasn't been open all day," she informed us, "and there's nothing in the world wrong with his precious chess problem, so far as I know. I figured probably you two had just as soon have him out of the way." Her smile broadened. "I have been young myself in my time, and I know a thing or two about it." She nodded emphatically. "Now if you can get along without *me*—and shouldn't wonder if you could without much strain—I'll go, too."

When she had departed, Marian looked up at me. "Did you ever in your life?" she inquired with a little smile, "hear anything so utterly silly?"

I caught her by the hand and made her face me. "Since you ask my opinion," I replied slowly, observing with interest a tiny smudge of black on the tip of her impertinent nose, "I'll say that, to me, it didn't exactly sound so darn dumb!"

II

We had our noonday meal in the big, pleasant dining room that overlooked the sea. Iantha termed it dinner because of the hour of the day, but I later came to learn that any repast cooked and served by her hands might well be placed in the same category. She believed that food, hot food, and plenty of food was necessary to a happy existence, and she certainly extended herself to make us happy.

She continued to bustle in from the kitchen bearing gifts until my eyes were as round as saucers and my feeble city appetite entirely put to rout. Each new offering was clapped upon the table to the tune of some deprecating remark. "I haven't the slightest notion," she declared, eyeing coldly a plate of delicious hot bread, "what happened to these biscuits. I put enough bakin' powder in 'em, gracious knows, to rise up the dead, but they're as flat as upset tomb stones, and just about as tasty, I shouldn't wonder."

Samuel Gregg ate with astonishing speed and unflagging enthusiasm. His conversation was as spirited as it was disjointed. He asked no more about the "curse," but he was greatly excited about the antiques in the attic and it was evident that the pressing need for nourishment alone could keep him from them for any appreciable length of time.

He bounced to his feet before his last bite of chocolate cake had had time to reach its logical destination. "There is much to be accomplished," he assured us solemnly, his huge bald head cocked slightly to one side. "Very much remains to be done. Shall we betake ourselves to the treasure cave?"

"I'm afraid not." Marian, to my great relief, smiled and shook her head. "Bill has hardly had time to draw a deep breath and he'd probably prefer to draw it in the open air than in that dusty attic. I think I'll take him for a walk, just to lull his suspicions before I put him to work."

"Of course, of course! Bless my soul!" Gregg covered any disappointment he may have felt in a profusion of apologies for his thoughtlessness. He assured us that our presence was unnecessary and that he could carry on very well by himself. He almost thrust us bodily from the room in his newly discovered eagerness to be rid of us.

It was very pleasant on the beach. The sand was warm and white underfoot and the ocean a shining, unruffled vastness. Our only companions were the seagulls which swept screaming overhead and the flocks of tiny little sandpipers which scuttled busily ahead of us along the water's edge.

We walked slowly toward the life-saving station to the northward and we said some of the things that were in our minds to say. I do not remember exactly what they were, but I know that they seemed very important at the time. Marian finally asked me whether I thought I should be happy in my new summer home.

I looked down at her with the wind ruffling the dark hair across her forehead, and made the only possible reply. "I don't see," I returned with some emotion, "how I could be anything else."

"Don't be silly." Marian always flushed when I made remarks of that nature and she always told me not to be silly. I have a sneaking suspicion, however, that she rather enjoyed them. "I mean," she continued on this occasion, "how do you like East Orham, and the house, and Iantha, and Mr. Gregg?"

I laughed. "When I first saw Mr. Gregg," I confessed, "I thought he had wandered away from some local institution. He was muttering something that didn't make any sense to me, but I found out later it was only a puzzle. Is he often that way?"

"He's always that way." She nodded reminiscently. "If it isn't a puzzle it's chess, and if it isn't chess it's antiques. He's a man of violent enthusiasms but he's really awfully nice most of the time. He's been boarding at the house for five or six years and he's almost like one of the family. He seems fond of us all. He loses patience with Iantha sometimes, but he likes her, I am sure."

"I can't hate him for that." I smiled. "Iantha seems to be a great number."

"Iantha is splendid! She's been with us since mother was a very little girl and she'll never go away until she dies. She is almost as close to mother, I think, as I am."

"She seems to have a lively imagination," I remarked. "What was all that she was spouting in the attic? About the curse, I mean."

"Oh,—that?" Marian shrugged and smiled. "Iantha's chief amusement is reading the most harrowing, blood-curdling stories that she can get her hands on. She has read so many of the crazy things that, as I told her, she almost believes things like that happen in real life. This idea of a curse is stuck so firmly in her head, anyhow, that nothing will get it out."

"What's it all about?"

"I'll get Iantha to tell you, herself. When she gets through you'll be ready to jump if a board creaks."

It was late in the afternoon when we got back to the house but two or three hours still remained before supper. "You can read," Marian informed me, "or you can take a nap if you feel like it. I really haven't very much excitement to offer."

I looked at her attentively. "You wouldn't be interested, I suppose," I suggested casually, "in doing any more work in the attic."

Marian came over and took me by the lapels of my coat. "You're a nice boy, Bill," she told me, looking up in the way that I seem to find so disturbing. "I really can't understand how you happen to be such a very nice boy. I'm dying, as a matter of fact, to get at those things, but I don't want you to think that that's all you are going to do all summer."

I was weakened by that time beyond all resistance. "Nonsense!" I said heartily. "I'm as much interested in the darn antiques as you are."

She refused to let go of my lapels. "I promise you," she pleaded, "that it won't take long. I just want to sort the things over and to sell what I can. Mother and I need the money so very badly. Besides that, I want to fix this house up a little. This horrible old black-walnut furniture gets on my nerves, and there's no reason why it should stay here with all that beautiful stuff in the storerooms."

I kissed her, just by way of allaying her fears, and turned to the door. "We shall waste no time," I informed her, "in joining the redoubtable Mr. Gregg."

The redoubtable Mr. Gregg was not difficult to join. We found him in the same room I had found Marian a morning, and he was kneeling in a manner of reverence before a small chest in one corner. He glanced at us absently as we came in. "Marian," he remarked without any greeting whatsoever, "I wonder if you have yet had the pleasure and opportunity of observing this truly remarkable Chinese cabinet. I think you will grant me that it is unique."

We peered over his shoulder at the cabinet. It was a funny little box with a number of doors and as many drawers, but what caught the attention and held it, was the profusion of grotesque carved figures and faces which decorated its entire surface. They leered at the beholder with an evil, wooden intentness.

Marian shuddered. "It's unique all right. Gives me a bad case of the creeps. Where do you suppose it ever came from in the beginning?"

"China." Gregg nodded thoughtfully. "Not a doubt in the world of its Chinese origin." He regarded her hopefully. "You won't want to sell this, of course."

"Won't I, though!" Marian laughed. "I'll sell it as quick as a wink if I can find anybody feeble enough in the head to buy it. It may be unique and all that, but I freely admit that I don't like its face."

Gregg sighed. "I am sure there won't be any trouble about selling it. Harvey Blodgett looked at it this afternoon and is very much interested. He's coming back again."

"Harvey Blodgett? Who is he?" I asked.

"A summer resident." Gregg pointed vaguely to the northward. "He has a cottage on the bluff there, and he is greatly interested in old things. His ideas concerning them are—er—ridiculous at times. He and I disagreed sharply on one occasion. However, I sank my personal resentment for the moment and invited him here first because I thought he might pay better prices than the dealers."

"Really?" Marian was excited. "That was awfully good of you: Did he see anything he liked—anything besides the cabinet, I mean?"

Samuel Gregg struggled to his feet and nodded triumphantly. "Blodgett not only saw some things that he liked but he purchased one settee, one mahogany clock, and three assorted tables." The little man was fairly swollen with pride. "I am glad to report that my afternoon has not been entirely in vain."

I have every reason to believe that if it had not been for the restraining influence of my presence, Marian would have kissed him. She made, as a matter of fact, serious gestures in that direction, "Isn't it wonderful?" she demanded of me at last, "Isn't it perfectly great? Didn't I tell you we'd all be rich?"

I answered all three questions in the affirmative and was properly enthusiastic during the period of mutual congratulation. Then, quite heartlessly, I was put to work.

Most of the time I lugged. I lugged heavy articles downstairs and I lugged even heavier articles upstairs. I pushed bulky couches from here to there so that Marian could observe the effect, and then I pushed them back again when she decided that the effect was not to her liking. I hung pictures, and distributed knick-knacks and made myself useful.

I left Marian in the attic at last, and descended to the living room with a small model of a Chinese junk, the placing of which had been left, foolishly, to my discretion. My powers of decision were not all that they might have been and I had stood for some time in the center of the carpet with the junk under one arm, when all at once my revery was broken by the sound of a diminutive and apologetic cough.

I whirled about, nearly dropping the precious model, and saw a man standing against the wall just inside the hall door. He was clutching an ancient straw hat tightly in both hands and he coughed again nervously as I stared at him.

"—I beg your pardon," he was saying in a flat, faded voice which sounded as though it might disappear altogether at any moment, "Don't know as I'd ought to have come in so sort of quiet—and sudden like. Made you jump, didn't it. I didn't know there was anybody here."

"Perfectly all right." I laughed in relief, "I must be smoking too many cigarettes or something."

He did not answer me, nor did he look at me. His grasp on the straw hat was such that the brim bent dangerously under the strain and his gaze roved aimlessly in any direction but mine.

Upon studying him I decided that I had never seen a more nondescript individual. He was not light or dark, tall or short, fat or thin. His hair and eyes were of an indeterminate color, and his clothing was totally without character. He gave me a feeling of insecurity; a feeling that if I looked away for an instant he might disappear into thin air. He coughed delicately, once more, as a contribution to the proceedings.

"Well," I said brightly, when it seemed that something must be said, "is there anything I can do for you? My name is Thornton. I'm a guest here."

"Oh." His gaze stole swiftly past me and came to rest on a distant corner of the room. "No," he observed with great caution, "I don't know's I'd say there was exactly anything you could do for me."

We seemed to be against a blank wall again so I tried another tack. "Would you mind telling me your name?"

I could see that he was not totally in favor of the idea, for he gave me the information grudgingly. "My name?" he said slowly. "Oh, my name's Jenkins. Is Miss Marian to home?"

"Yes." I was glad to be on the trail of what he wanted at last. "Do you want to see her?"

"Oh, no!" The idea seemed to startle him considerably. "Oh, no, I don't want to see her."

"I understand." In spite of myself my exasperation was increasing. "You just wanted to know she was in, so that if any one asked you about it, you could give him accurate information! Is that it?"

"I—I guess so." He twitched the hat. "I suppose Iantha Hallett ain't home—or Sam Gregg?"

"Yes," I replied patiently, "they're both here. If you want Iantha I can get her in a moment."

"No, no!" he said hastily, "I don't want nothing with Iantha."

I wagged a finger at him. "Then I'll just bet you're hunting for Mr. Gregg!"

He writhed, blushed, and gazed earnestly out of the nearest window. "Well—" he admitted with great hesitancy, "If you're sure he ain't busy, or anything."

"No, indeed!" I grasped Mr. Jenkins firmly by the arm and almost shoved him from the room ahead of me. "He isn't busy and I'm sure he's just crazy to see you."

Samuel Gregg, as a matter of fact, was much crazier to see him than I had anticipated. He grasped Mr. Jenkins' shrinking right hand and pumped it up and down with great affability. He inquired anxiously as to the state of Mr. Jenkins' health. He contorted his fat face at Marian and me in a manner which indicated that our presence was no longer desired.

We caught the hint and departed hastily down the backstairs.

"That's Miller Jenkins!" whispered Marian excitedly. "He may buy something. He's an antique dealer!"

"Oh!" I was beginning to understand. "So that's what he is."

"Yes. He has a shop in the village and he does quite a large business during the summer."

"I see." I looked at her. "Do you happen to know," I inquired tentatively, "whether or not he has anything particular on his conscience?"

"On his conscience! What on earth are you talking about?"

"I'm not quite sure," I shrugged. "It just occurred to me that perhaps he might recently have murdered his wife or beaten up some feeble old man with an ax handle. He had that manner."

Marian laughed. "I see what you mean. His manner is peculiar. He always acts sort of hunted—as though he were afraid of something."

"Afraid of something!" I sniffed with some contempt. "I'll bet he's afraid to take a deep breath, and I'll also bet that if he did take one, he'd be afraid to admit it."

"What of it?" Marian was soothing. "As long as he isn't afraid to buy something, he suits me."

I had no great hopes that Miller Jenkins would ever be able to bring himself to take so positive a step to buy something, but it was soon apparent that I had misjudged him. Samuel Gregg, after an hour's interval, bounced into the library rubbing his hands.

"The esteemed Mr. Jenkins," he announced cheerfully, "has departed." Of course he said "departed" instead of "gone." He seemed to love the taste of syllables.

"Really?" said Marian. "I didn't see him go."

Gregg chuckled. "Miller Jenkins is one of those persons whom one never catches in the act of coming or going. He materializes from nowhere and he vanishes into nothing. A truly remarkable individual. Yes—remarkable is the word."

My respect for Mr. Gregg's judgment was increasing rapidly. "Was he interested in any of the antiques?" I inquired skeptically. "Or did he discuss with you the question of disarmament?"

"Yes," said Marian more pointedly. "Did he buy anything?"

Gregg answered my question first. "With the exception of three items," he informed us solemnly, "Miller Jenkins was interested in everything in the storerooms. He showed no curiosity concerning the Sheraton chairs, the maple chest of drawers, or the mahogany writing desk. The remainder of the goods he examined with great care."

"What did he buy?" Marian demanded impatiently.

"That's easy," I laughed. "He bought, of course, the writing desk, the chest of drawers, and the Sheraton chairs. What else would he buy?"

"Mr. Thornton is perfectly right." Samuel Gregg bowed deeply in my direction. "He is a man of perception and he realizes that Miller Jenkins has a genius for circumlocution. Jenkins is, if I may say so, a master of indirection."

Marian was tremendously happy about the sales of the day. She seized pencil and paper and added at least three times the various amounts to be received so as to be sure that the total was correct. She inquired anxiously as to the prospect of further profits. "Do you think," she asked Gregg, "that there is a chance of our selling anything else?"

He nodded thoughtfully. "I have every expectation of continued success. Blodgett assured me that he would return for another inspection, and Miller Jenkins led me to believe that his first visit would not be his last. Then, too, Jonas Jones is coming to see us in the morning."

"Oh, good!" Marian smiled at me delightedly. "Just wait till you see Jonas, Bill. He's simply splendid!"

"What is he?" I demanded suspiciously. "Another antique dealer?"

"In a way—yes."

I shuddered. "Well, then, if you'll pardon me, I think I'll be busy in the barn when Mr. Jones arrives. I've had enough of antique dealers to last me for one summer."

"Oh, Jonas Jones isn't in the least like Miller Jenkins." She shook her head in an emphatic negative. "Not in the least. I've known him ever since I was a tiny little girl and he's one of my closest friends."

"Is it possible," I asked with a frown, "that I scent a rival?"

"Well, he may be a bit old for that, and he seems to be perfectly contented to remain a widower, but he's a very nice man just the same. He has a little shop about a mile from here where he paints furniture and does beautiful cabinet work. He has delightful red hair and a marvelous sense of humor, and his favorite hobby is arithmetic. It is, really! He declares the arithmetic is the only book that proves what it says. You'll like him. See if you don't."

I sighed. "Well, I'll take a chance as long as you'll guarantee that he won't jump out of some dark corner and bite me on the leg as I'm passing by. My nerves are just a trifle frayed, after Brother Jenkins."

When supper was over that night, Marian redeemed her promise to have Iantha tell us her pet story, the story of the supposed "curse."

We were all four in the small library which opens from the dining room and the front hall. There is no electricity in the house and the only light in the room was supplied by a small lamp on the table where Gregg was pretending to study his chess problem. He had heard the tale before but was still interested in it apparently, for I glanced in his direction once or twice during the narration and could see that he was listening intently.

Marian and I sat side by side in the deep shadows, and Iantha rocked rhythmically in a chair by the window.

Iantha related for us the events of 1883—the events which are now so clearly fixed in my mind that it seems as if I had always known them. I will not repeat her words for she has already written the account in detail. Plainly it was, as Marian had said, her pet story and she told it well. So well, and with such awe-stricken earnestness, that I was actually startled when she suddenly ceased rocking and leaned forward in her chair to point a thin finger at the far side of the room.

"There'll be trouble come from that—and the rest you've set up around," she declared, with conviction. "If you'll take my advice—which, being young and know-it-all, I suppose you won't—you'll cart every single one of them wicked things up attic again. That's what you better do, mark my words."

I glanced in the direction she indicated and made out the little wooden figure of Buddha which I had placed on the top of the bookcase that very afternoon. Most of it was merely a vague outline in the murk, but a stray ray of light from the lamp gave the grotesque face a ghostly illumination.

"What did I tell you?" Marian broke the tension with a rather uncertain laugh. "Didn't I say that if Iantha once got started, you'd jump every time you saw your shadow for a week or two? She's entirely too good a story-teller to suit me."

Gregg nodded his big head thoughtfully and toyed with one of the chessmen on the board before him. "It is not only an excellent story but a very interesting one. What did it all mean? How do the parts fit together?" He glanced up at us. "The parts *would* fit together, you know, if we knew how to sort them."

Marian shook her head. "It was all very strange, and it didn't stop being strange even after Captain Freeland died. There was some kind of a weird message, you know, that came for him a week after the funeral. I wonder Iantha did not tell us that."

"A message!" Gregg sat up straight in his chair. "I never heard anything about a message."

Iantha smiled grimly. "Well, there was one, and if you can fit *that* together, Samuel Gregg, you're a better fitter than anybody else who knew about it, then nor since."

"What was it?" he demanded. "Who sent it?

"The 'who sent it' part," replied Iantha, "is easy enough to tell. It was sent by a man named Burke that was mate of the *Pride of the Fleet* when she come aground in our front yard, as you might say."

She went on to tell of the mate's injury, his death in the Boston hospital and of the letter the nurse had written to Freeland Blair, the letter containing Crossley's message and which came a week after Captain Blair's death.

It was all familiar to Marian, of course, but I found it very intriguing and interesting. So, too, did Samuel Gregg. It seemed to excite him greatly.

"Bless my soul!" He bounded to his feet and paced up and down the little room. "Bless my soul! Why wasn't I told of this? It might be the key to the whole problem." He turned upon Iantha. "What was that message? Can you remember the message?"

"I don't exactly know as I can." Iantha frowned. "Jethro Gould, he thought it might mean something, but Aunt Rebecca vowed it was just nonsense. 'Whether it is or not,' says she, 'I mean to forget it and I want you to.' Aunt Becky was the boss, so me and Jethro tried to do what she said."

"But don't you remember the message?" the fat little man pleaded. "Can't you remember anything about it?"

Iantha continued to frown. "Well, as far as I can recollect at this late day it said somethin' about everything bein' all right. Then it went on with the craziest rigmarole. It said, 'Look out of one eye at one leg,' or some such nonsense."

Marian and I burst out laughing. Gregg, however, did not even smile.

"What!" he demanded. "Surely those were not the exact words."

Iantha pondered. "It don't seem as though that was exactly it, but it was all about lookin' at or for some parts of the human frame. I am sure of that much."

Samuel Gregg clicked his tongue, shrugged his shoulders sadly, and sat down once more at the chess table. "Bless my soul," he murmured. "What a shame! That message may have been important; it may have meant something. If we had the exact wording we might be able to solve the puzzle; for apparently there is a puzzle. . . . Hum. . . . Oh, well, the whole thing is doubtless of small importance, but I have a distinct aversion to unsolved puzzles." He sighed. "Yes—I would be greatly interested in the exact wording of that mysterious message."

Marian patted him consolingly on the shoulder. "Don't be too downhearted, Mr. Gregg. There's a great box full of Aunt Rebecca's letters on the top shelf of mother's closet, the one from the nurse might be among them. I don't think she ever threw away a great deal of her correspondence."

Iantha sniffed. "Miss Rebecca never threw *anything* away," she declared. "She saved up enough string in her lifetime to fetch from here to Hong Kong and back, and never used more than six foot of it. She was a saver, if ever there was one."

Samuel Gregg did not seem greatly comforted. "That letter was written more than forty years ago," he pointed out, "and it hardly seems possible that it is still in existence."

Marian beckoned to me and turned to the door. "It is little more than a bare chance," she admitted, "but if you're still interested, we'll have a look for it one of these days. Just now Bill and I are going to wreck our nervous systems by a trip to the movies in Orham."

We left Mr. Gregg hunched over the table, his bald head gleaming brightly in the lamp light. He seemed rather forlorn to me—as though he would like to engage in a heated game of chess but saw the futility of suggesting it.

III

The next morning was a busy one at the old Blair house. We had no more than finished breakfast when a tall, powerful negro appeared at the back door and announced that he was Mr. Blodgett's man and had come to take away the boss's purchases of the previous day. Iantha, with appropriate comments, showed him the way to the attic, and he soon rattled down the drive with the clock, chairs, and settee in the back of his station wagon.

Then we had another visitor. This individual, long, lean, loose-jointed and extremely lugubrious, presented himself sorrowfully as one Abel Peak, assistant to Mr. Miller Jenkins, antique dealer of East Orham. He brought with him hammers, saws, and certain lengths of wood with which he intended to crate the three Sheraton chairs for immediate shipment to Boston. His raspings and thumpings resounded through the house for the greater part of the morning. His employer made a brief visit later on to inspect the work.

I was not altogether idle. To the contrary, I think I may say that I was thoroughly active.

There was a stove in the living-room which, I was told, served to heat it during the winter months. It was a huge, black, ungainly thing which stood squarely in front of what had once been the fireplace. A length of stovepipe sprouted from its top and disappeared into the chimney through a hole cut just above the mantel.

Marian viewed this stove with a coldly unfriendly eye. It was an eyesore, she maintained, and as such it must be exiled to the barn. "We can take it out through the French doors to the porch," she asserted cheerfully, "and we can cover up the hole left by the stovepipe with that ship picture up in the attic. It ought to be perfectly simple."

Iantha remonstrated with her. "I don't see any sense," she declared stoutly, "in luggin' away something that'll have to be toted right back again in two or three months. Maybe it don't look so pretty right now, but it looks a sight prettier, I can tell you, along about December when it's cold enough to freeze the handle off a hot teakettle."

Marian was firm. The stove could be brought back before it was needed, but until then its resting place was to be the barn. I was appointed to see that it got there. "You can start in," she told me, "by taking the pipe down. Jonas Jones will be here in a little while and he'll help you with the stove itself. I don't want to ask Mr. Gregg because I'm sure it would be too much of a strain on his weak heart."

It all sounded very simple, but when I set to work I found that it was not so simple as it sounded. The pipe was in two sections and it stubbornly resisted my efforts to loosen it. I pushed and pulled until my face was a fiery red and my temper near the breaking point. Then, all at once, when I swung my whole weight on it in desperation, the piece nearest the stove gave way and I descended heavily to the floor. The fall was painful and I was nearly choked by soot. I am afraid I uttered words which should never pass a gentleman's lips.

When I struggled to my feet I saw Marian and a man I did not know, regarding me from the doorway "You look," said Marian sweetly, "like the hero of a two-reel movie comedy. I hope you're having a good time."

I wiped the soot out of my eyes and laughed without mirth. "Angels," I assured her, "could ask no more!"

She advanced into the room and turned to the man who followed her. "Mr. Jones," she said with a smile, "this is Bill Thornton. He sometimes looks even better than he does at present, but perhaps you may have noticed that he has been working on the stove."

Mr. Jones, a stocky man of medium height whose bright red hair was beginning to turn gray at the temples, smiled pleasantly and insisted upon shaking my hand. "Pleased to meet you, Mr. Thornton," he said heartily. "I'm always glad to meet any friend of Marian's, especially—" his bright blue eyes twinkled—"especially when he's the kind of a young man that loves exercise. That's what you and the stove was having—exercise—wasn't it?"

Marian laughed. "You'd better not hand out too many wise remarks about that stove, Jonas Jones, because I'm going to ask you to help Bill get it out to the barn."

"Oh! Hum! Sho! You don't say! Dear me, this is a world of disappointments, that's a fact." His right eyebrow rose to a point almost an inch higher than its brother, and he shoved one hand deep into his trousers pocket. "I came over here to look at antiques and to bring a little present to Iantha—she's my best girl, Mr. Thornton; you ask her sometime if she ain't. That's what I thought I came for and now it turns out I came to move a stove. Well, well! live and learn. Here's Iantha's little remembrance."

He waved a brown paper parcel with his free hand and placed it tenderly upon a neighboring table. Marian regarded him with suspicion. "Do you think it's decent at your age," she inquired severely, "to bring presents to a respectable maiden lady?"

Jones looked at her reprovingly. "This present is different," he said, solemnly. "This is food for the mind. I was comin' over to pay my respects to Iantha when all at once, thinks I, 'What Iantha needs is to have her mind fed.'" He pointed to the parcel. "So I wrapped the mind fodder up and there it is."

Marian's severity did not abate. "So it's a book, is it? I'll bet *The Murders in the Rue Morgue* or something like that."

Jonas Jones was sorrowful. "You ought to know better than to think I'd bring Iantha any light, frivolous readin' like that. No, sir! This book is something that'll stick to the ribs, as you might say. I wish I could be around while she is readin' it."

During all this conversation I had been giving my attention to the second piece of stovepipe which protruded from the wall like a sore thumb. I tugged at it violently but soon saw that it would present the same difficulties that the first piece had. At length I appealed to Jones. "If you'll give me a hand with this thing," I suggested, "perhaps we can get it loose."

"Well, well!" he exclaimed, turning, "if I hadn't almost forgot that stove. You'd be surprised, Mr. Thornton, how easy I forget some things—hard work for instance."

He walked up and down before the pipe, humming tunelessly between his teeth, and inspected it carefully from all angles. "Well," he remarked gently at last, "I judge by the looks you've been tryin' to do this thing so far by division, Mr. Thornton. Let's try subtraction a second."

He reached up tentatively, gave the pipe the slightest possible twitch, and it came away clear in his hands. Marian laughed. "Do you see, Bill, how easily it can be done when you know how!"

Jones shrugged. "Mr. Thornton deserves all the credit," he said. "He had it so it was ready to fall down. All I had to do was blow hard and out she come."

I knew that that was not an accurate statement, but I did not resent it. I decided at that moment that Jones and I were going to get along splendidly.

The stove was moved out to the barn. It was not half the job that I had anticipated, for Jonas seemed to have a faculty for getting things done with a minimum of effort. He was as calm and unruffled as ever when the ponderous thing finally came to rest in a corner of an unused stall. "And now," he said with a smile to Marian, who had accompanied us, "if there's no more stoves to tote, I guess I'll hop up to the attic and take a look at those antiques. By the way Sam Gregg blesses his soul over 'em they ought to be worth lookin' at."

"Bill and I will go back to the house and wait in the living room," said Marian after she thanked him. "I want to get that ship picture up before somebody comes in and sees that great hole in the wall. You'll have time to stop in there won't you, before you go home?"

Jones nodded and turned away. "Sartin sure!' he promised. "I left Iantha's mind-food on the table in there, for I wanted to give it to her with my own fair hands. It seems to me, lately, she's been lookin' kind of hungry. Well, if that yarn don't satisfy her appetite, nothin' will."

He strode off across the back yard, humming industriously between his teeth.

Marian and I went in and hung the ship picture in the living-room; at least, I hung it and she bossed the job. It was an unusually big canvas in a heavy ebony frame, and it depicted the *Pride of the Fleet,* a square-rigged vessel under full sail. As Marian had predicted, it looked very well above the mantel and it completely covered the sin of the missing stovepipe. We placed a bronze elephant, caught by the sculptor in the act of trumpeting, in the center of the mantel beneath it and stood away to observe the full effect.

"If you dare tell me," said Marian, "that this room doesn't look better than it did before, I'll run away from home and go into the movies. It *does* look well, doesn't it!"

"Yes." I put my arm shamelessly about her. "It looks marvelous."

We were still, unaccountably, regarding the ship picture when Jones came into the living-room some time later. Marian turned to him in anticipation. "Did you have a good time in the attic? Haven't we some fine things up there?"

"Yes." He nodded. "I had a good time, and I must say that Sam Gregg's advertisin' isn't as touched up as most advertisin' is. There's some mighty interestin' stuff in that attic."

She tried not to appear anxious. "Did you see anything you liked? Anything you liked particularly, I mean?"

His hands disappeared into his trousers pockets and he hummed absently for a moment before he replied. "Most likely," he said slowly, "you'll think I'm kind of queer in the head when I tell you what it was in that attic I specially hanker for. Of course, there were lots of things I'd like to have if I was made of money, but not bein' built that way— worse luck—I had to content my cravin' with one item."

"What was it?"

He grinned at us. "Well, it was that cabinet thing, the Chinese one, with the carvin's on it. Yes, I sort of fell in love with that. . . . Don't tell Iantha; I wouldn't want her jealous."

Marian stared at him in amazement. "Do you actually mean to say, Jonas Jones, that you want to buy that horrible box with all the ghastly faces and things carved on it."

He scratched his head. "I guess that's what I mean. Maybe it does sound sort of foolish when you stop to think of it. But it does explain, don't it, why Iantha and I are soul mates. We both have a fancy for horrors. She likes hers in books and I like mine on boxes."

"Well, if you aren't a queer one!" Marian laughed and shook her head. "But if you want that Chinese cabinet,

you certainly can have it. I'll guarantee that. What did
Mr. Gregg say?"

"He didn't say anything; he wasn't there."

"Wasn't there?" I was surprised. "Why, thought he had
been in that attic all morning. Abel Peak was there pack-
ing up chairs and so was Miller Jenkins, for a little while.
I thought Gregg was with them."

"There wasn't anybody there." Jones shook head. "My
only company was a heap of shavin's which from what you
say must have been the leavin's of Abel Peak. I didn't see
anything of Sam Gregg—and he'd be a hard one not to see,
if he was anywheres within a half a mile."

"Well, he must be somewhere about the house." Marian
turned to me. "Will you please find him, Bill? Tell him
that Mr. Jones wants the Chinese cabinet, and that I say
he is to have it. Ask him the price, and tell him not to
make it too high."

I went upstairs, and on my way out to the back part of
the house I tried Samuel Gregg's door. It was locked, to
my surprise, so I knocked with my knuckles on the panel.
"Mr. Gregg!" I called. "Mr. Gregg."

There was a long pause and then I heard his voice.
"Well?" it answered irritably. "Well? What do you want?"

"I want to speak to you for a moment, if I may."

There was another pause and I heard rustling inside the
room. Then the door was jerked open. "Yes, Mr. Thornton?"
Gregg inquired sharply. He seemed excited and nervous.
"What can I do for you? It just happens that I am very busy."

"I won't keep you long," I assured him. "Marian just
asked me to tell you that Jonas Jones wants to buy the
small Chinese cabinet and that she has decided to sell it
to him."

"The Chinese cabinet? Bless my soul!" My news appeared to perturb, rather than please him. "Are you positive that she wants to dispose of that cabinet?"

"Quite." I nodded firmly. "She has told Jones that he can have it and she wants to know what the price is to be."

"Bless my soul, how inconvenient!" He seemed more irritated than ever, but at last he shrugged his shoulders. "Will you please tell Mr. Jones that I have not been able to decide upon the price as yet, but that I shall have done so by tomorrow morning. The piece shall be put aside for him until then."

"You're sure," I asked doubtfully, "that you can't give me the price now."

"I am." He nodded his head with great emphasis and, muttering more apologies about being very busy, shut the door in my face.

Marian received the message with annoyance and would have hastened upstairs to consult with Gregg personally had not Jones prevented her. "There's no hurry," he assured her. "I can wait till tomorrow just as well as not, and by then Sam will have made up his mind. Right now I'm goin' out to the galley and have a little talk with my best girl." He picked up the brown paper parcel from the table. "Just wait till she sets her teeth in this yarn," he chuckled. "She'll scare herself into a conniption fit. She's happiest when she's that way, so all hands will be satisfied."

Marian turned to me with a frown when he had gone. "What on earth is the matter with Mr. Gregg? I never knew him to act this way before."

"I don't know," I shrugged. "It certainly looks, at any rate, as though he had something very special on his mind."

When dinner was ready Iantha confirmed my diagnosis. She came into the dining-room with an expression of solemn wonder on her face. "Somethin' awful," she informed us, "is the matter with Samuel Gregg."

"What is it?" I pushed back my chair.

Iantha shook her head. "He says," she announced impressively, "that he don't want any dinner!"

"Oh, is that all!" I laughed in relief. "I thought that at least he had cracked a couple of ribs."

Iantha did not laugh. "You wouldn't say, 'is that all,' Mr. Thornton, if you knew him as well as I do. He's been in this house now for years and never until this very minute has he ever as much as hinted he didn't want to eat. And eat enough for three strong men and a boy at that. No, sir-ee." She shook her head. "He says he isn't sick, but I'm thinkin' of sendin' for the doctor, just the same."

We refused to take the matter seriously, even in the face of Iantha's most conclusive evidence. We got along quite cheerfully by ourselves and had almost forgotten Gregg's existence when, in the middle of the afternoon, he poked his head in the door of the small library and spoke to Marian.

"I wonder," he began with hesitance, "if you would have the kindness to do me a great favor."

"Of course." Marian looked up from her work and smiled at him. "Would you like to have me get you something to eat from the ice box? You must be awfully hungry."

"Hungry?" The idea seemed to confuse him. "Oh, no, I have no craving for food, I assure you." He looked about him vaguely. "The favor I am about to ask has to do with our conversation of last night. You understand, of course, what I mean."

Marian looked bewildered. "I'm afraid I don't."

"You said something about some letters. You thought that there might be a possibility—a bare chance, that is—"

"Oh. You're talking about that letter from Mr. Burke—Captain Crossley's mate. I said that there was a chance that it might be among some old stuff belonging to Aunt Rebecca."

"Exactly." He rubbed his bald head in relief. "I wondered if it would be possible for us to examine those letters of your aunt's."

"Oh." Marian frowned. "You want to hunt through them this afternoon? I'm really awfully busy."

Gregg flushed and stammered, but he stuck stubbornly to his guns. "I'd like—I'd consider it a great favor—"

"I tell you what I'll do." Marian's face cleared. "I'll give you the box of letters and you can go through them yourself. Will that be all right, Mr. Gregg?"

It appeared that it would be a great deal better than all right. Gregg followed Marian up the steep front stairs with numerous "Bless my soul's" and profuse expressions of gratitude. He seemed more unexplainably excited than ever.

Marian returned to the library after a short interval with a smile and a shake of the head. "He grabbed those old letters," she told me, "as though they were a million dollars in gold coin, and disappeared with them into his room like a rabbit into its hole. I'm beginning to think he must be just a trifle nutty."

"At least," I laughed, "we have the solution to the mystery of the omitted dinner. He evidently thinks he's hot on the trail of Iantha's pet curse."

"I don't see why he should think so any more than he thought so last night. There's only a slim chance that he'll find that letter from the mate, and a slimmer chance that he'll be able to make anything out of it if he does find it." She shrugged and turned to the wot at hand. "Well, more power to him, anyhow."

The unaccountable Mr. Gregg appeared for supper, and it was quite evident that his temporarily mislaid appetite had been found. He ate with a tremendous verve that must have reassured Iantha as to the state of his health, but his customary flow of conversation was notably absent. He seemed lost in a world of dreams, and it was only by speaking his name with great distinctness that Marian was able to rouse him from them.

"Mr. Gregg!" she said loudly. "Did you have any luck with the letter? Did you find the one from the mate?"

"Letter?" He stared at her for some time without any apparent understanding. "Mate?"

"Yes. Did you find the letter containing the mysterious message we were talking about last night?"

"Oh—I see what you mean." He shook his head. "No—no, I could find no trace of it. Most disappointing, I assure you."

He shook his head again and would have sunk back into his lethargy if Marian had permitted. "Then Iantha's curse is to remain unexplained for always?"

"I greatly fear so." He sighed. "A most regrettable state of affairs, but unavoidable—absolutely unavoidable."

We questioned him further but could learn nothing more. He seemed unwilling to discuss the matter, and went to his room directly after supper without so much as glancing in the direction of the chessboard.

The next morning was dull and gray. The cold wind swept in from the ocean and howled mournfully about the old house. Iantha shook her head when a particularly violent gust made the windows rattle in their frames. "We're in for a no'theaster," she announced, "though it beats me why we should have one at this season of the year. It'll be rainin' like all possessed before dinner time, you mark my words."

Samuel Gregg kept to his room and emerged only when Jonas Jones came to inquire about the Chinese cabinet. They went out to the storeroom together, and after a time Jonas came downstairs with his purchase in his arms. "Well, she's mine," he announced with a grin, "and cheap enough at the price. I don't think Sam was exactly anxious to get rid of her, but he don't seem anxious to get rid of anything up in the attic, for that matter. I made him an offer on a little table that took my eye, but he said no. Accordin' to Sam, it ain't for sale."

"Did he say that?" Marian got to her feet grimly. "Then I think it is just about time that Mr. Gregg and I had a little conversation. He's been acting very strangely for the last twenty-four hours, and as long as he confines his strangeness to refusing his meals I don't care. But when he begins to say that things I am dying to sell aren't for sale, then it's time to ask questions."

She returned from Gregg's room after a short interval, with a sigh and a shake of the head. "He says that he's got some marvelous idea for making me a mint of money, and he begged me to trust him for just a little while longer. He wouldn't tell me what the plan was, but he seemed tremendously serious about it. Well, I'll give him just about one day more and then I'll take things into my own hands. I'm beginning to think that either Mr. Gregg is goofy, or *I* am."

Iantha was right about the rain. It began about noon, and by the time we sat down to dinner it was beating a fierce tattoo against the window panes on the ocean side of the house. The wind, if anything, had increased in velocity. Marian shook her head at me sadly. "There's one thing certain, Bill, and that is that there'll be no golf today. You had better resign yourself to a domestic afternoon."

I grinned. "You may not believe it," I told her earnestly, "but if there's one thing I crave more than any other, it's a really domestic afternoon!"

We spent it in the little library with the wooden Buddha beaming down on us from the top of the bookcase in the role of chaperone. Gregg, happily, sulked in his stronghold, and there was no sign of Iantha until late in the day when she came in with a book in her hand and settled herself in the rocking-chair by the window.

"I do hope you'll excuse me," she begged with a sigh, "if I set here with you for a little spell. I been up in my room readin' this book Jonas Jones brought me until I declare I couldn't stand it any longer. It got so that every time a board creaked I pretty nigh jumped my soul out of my body."

Marian laughed. "Is the book as bad as all that, Iantha?"

"Bad!" She shuddered. "It's the most awful thing I ever set eyes on—all about some frightful critter that comes creepin' out of his grave in the dead of night and sucks the heart's blood out of innocent folks while they're layin' peaceful in their beds."

Dracula!" I whistled. "Did Jonas Jones lend you that thing?"

"Yes. He said he thought I'd find it real snappy readin'."

"I should think you might!" Marian shook her head. "If you keep on with it, Iantha, we'll find you out in the woodshed, one of these days, barking like a dog. You'd better give it to me."

"No!" Iantha clutched the volume tightly as though she feared someone might wrest it from her. "I got to keep on readin' till I find out whether they catch the thing and drive a stick through its insides, or whatever they have to do to kill it dead. I wouldn't rest peaceful till I knew about that."

Iantha continued to read the book, uttering periodic moans of delighted horror. She was able to put it down barely long enough to get our supper, and retired with it to her room immediately thereafter.

"She won't be able to sleep a wink all night," Marian predicted, "and she'll be as nervous as a cat in the morning, but there's no stopping her."

As Gregg seemed to prefer his own company to ours, we were alone in the library all evening with the wind whistling a dreary tune outside the windows. Marian went off to bed about eleven-thirty, and left me with a magazine which I read until just after midnight, when I also took my lamp and went upstairs.

I had taken a bath in the tiny room at the head of the stairs, and was just ready to return to my own room when I noticed, all at once, how quiet it had become; apparently the storm was over, the wind seemed to have stopped blowing, momentarily at least.

I pulled my bathrobe tightly about me and stood still for an instant, listening. There was not a sound except the gentle drip of the rain, and the rhythmic thump of a loose blind somewhere in the distance. I shivered, picked up my lamp, and turned to the door.

My hand was already on the knob when, suddenly, from somewhere far in the back of the house, came the reverberation of a heavy crash. It was followed, after a breath of absolute silence, by a long, quavering scream.

IV

For what seemed an age I remained perfectly motionless, conscious only of the heavy pounding of my heart and of an odd prickle of fear which began somewhere near the base of my spine and traveled upward. Then with an instinct, I suppose, for taking the shortest way, I recrossed the bathroom and knocked sharply with my knuckles on the door which connected with Mr. Gregg's room.

"Mr. Gregg!" I called in a sort of hoarse whisper. "Mr. Gregg!"

There was no reply. I twisted the knob and entered, calling his name once more. A lamp, with the wick burned low, flickered palely on the small table at the side of the bed, but the bed itself was empty and had not been slept in. A glance told me that he was nowhere in the room, so I crossed swiftly to the door on the far side.

I had stepped out into the dark corridor beyond with the lamp held high above my head, when Marian's door opened and she came running toward me down the hall. "Bill!" she whispered in a small, frightened voice, and caught my arm. Her face seemed pale and unnatural in the uncertain light. "I—I thought I heard something." She shuddered. "Something terrible."

"So did I." I tried to keep my voice calm. It was probably just something knocked over by the wind.

"I thought I heard someone—scream." Her grip tightened on my arm. "Listen!"

We were silent for a time and perfectly still, presenting, I have no doubt, a strange tableau. My straining ears could catch no sound beyond the gentle whining of the wind and the dismal, pulse-like thump of that confounded blind.

"I'm perfectly sure," I began with entirely false cheerfulness, "that—"

There was another piercing scream from somewhere in the back part of the house. It was louder this time, and more hysterical.

"Oh!" Marian gasped and slumped heavily against me. I supported her with my free arm and tried to mutter something about not being afraid. "What is it, Bill?" she was murmuring desperately against my bathrobe. "Please, please, tell me what it is!"

"I don't know." I got myself together with an effort. "I don't know, but I intend to find out. You stay here."

"No!" She clung to me. "I—I can't."

"All right," I ordered, "come along, then, but see that you keep behind me."

We proceeded, silently and cautiously, until we came to the door which led to the ell and to the top of the back stairs. This I opened very, very slowly, and took one step to the landing beyond.

All at once someone moaned.

"Who is it?" I lost all sense of caution and shouted foolishly into the darkness. "What do you want?"

There was another groan, and this time it was quite evident that it came from below. I raised the lamp high above my head and peered down into the murk of the stair well. There was a vague, indistinct heap on the landing at the bottom, and at last I was able to see a face staring mutely up at me. The face was drawn and terrified, and from one corner of the mouth a thin trickle of blood zig-zagged down to the point of the chin.

"Iantha!" I was conscious of being pushed rudely to one side and that Marian was flying down the steps in front of me. "Iantha, dear," she was saying over and over, "what is it? Tell me! What has happened to you?"

Somehow I managed to get down those stairs myself, and somehow Marian and I half dragged and half carried Iantha's limp form to a chair in the kitchen. She was trembling violently, and her sobs as she rocked back and forth with her hands over her face had a hysterical quality. I should have merely stood and stared at her indefinitely, I think, had not Marian taken charge of the situation.

"Get me a clean dish towel," she ordered sharply, all trace of fear gone, "and wet it. Hand me that bottle of ammonia on the shelf there, too. Hurry!"

I hurried, and then stood helplessly by while Marian worked. The wet dish towel was passed over Iantha's face and I was tremendously relieved to see that the blood had come from only a very slight cut at the corner of her mouth. The fumes from the ammonia bottle seemed to revive her somewhat and she stopped that endless rocking. She continued to sob, however, quietly.

"Iantha, dear," Marian was urging gently at last, "you must try to tell us what happened. Did you fall? Please try to tell us."

Iantha did her best, and finally we were able to piece together some sort of an account of what had occurred.

It appeared that Iantha had been reading *Dracula* in her room, and that just when she had reached a most irresistibly horrible point in the story, her lamp had gone out from lack of oil. Iantha then found herself, of course, half way between the devil and the deep blue sea. She had an overpowering desire to continue her reading, but in order to be able to do so she must find her way downstairs in the pitch blackness and refill her lamp from the can in the woodshed.

The prospect was not alluring, but neither was the prospect of going to bed in a room full of vampires still unslain.

She finally decided on the bolder course, and with her empty lamp in one fearful hand she began her descent in a blackness which, she assured us, was "filled up with bat wings a-flappin'." Everything went well as she stole through the corridor and started down the back stairs. She had reached the landing on the ground floor and was steadying herself with her left hand by leaning rather heavily against the door into the library, when all at once that door swung silently open.

At this point in her narration Iantha began to sob and tremble once more, and Marian patted her soothingly on the shoulder. "I see what happened, Iantha, she said gently, "and it's a darn shame. The door into the library wasn't shut quite tight and it opened when you leaned against it. It gave you a nasty fall."

"What?" Iantha straightened. She pointed toward the library. "Don't talk foolish, Marian Fisher! That door didn't open by itself. I tell you somethin'—somethin' awful in there opened it! I felt it! It stepped right onto me as I was lyin' there on the landin'!"

"There, there." Marian smiled at me and made gestures with her hands to imitate the motion of wings. "I don't think anything really stepped on you, Iantha. You must have imagined that part of it."

Iantha's indignation got the better of her fear. She struggled to her feet. "Somethin' stepped on me, I tell you! Don't you suppose I know whether I'm stepped on or not? It stepped right on top of me and come on out here into the kitchen." She swung about and pointed past my shoulder. "If nothin' didn't step on me," she demanded, "how do you account for that? Eh? Talk to me about imagination! How about *that?*"

We turned in the direction she indicated, and once more I was conscious of that little, uncomfortable prickle in the small of my back. The kitchen door stood wide open.

There was an interval of complete silence while we tried to reconcile ourselves to this new development. Then I laughed with no degree of conviction. "You must be getting careless in your old age, Iantha. You evidently forgot to lock up when you went to bed."

"Rubbish!" Iantha's voice was fast regaining its strength. "Never you mind how old I be, Mr. Thornton," tartly. "I ain't so old that I ever forgot to lock that door in all my years of livin' in this house. I didn't forget it tonight, neither. It was shut up tight as a drum when I went upstairs. I suppose you'll be sayin' next that I'm just imaginin' that it's open this minute."

"No, it's open, all right." I went over and examined the lock which showed no signs of having been forced. "And it couldn't have opened itself; unless, of course, the wind may have done the trick."

Iantha sniffed. "The wind," she pointed out with impatient contempt, "is blowin' from the east'ard, and besides, I've never heard of a wind that would blow open a door when it was locked tight. *Don't* talk such trash!"

Her logic was unanswerable, so I merely shut the door and locked it carefully. Marian glanced about her anxiously. "Perhaps—perhaps, Bill, you'd better take a look around."

I nodded. "I'll do that, but I'm almost sure I won't find anything. If Iantha's reasoning is correct, whoever opened that library door stepped across her as she lay on the landing, came out here into the kitchen, and made his getaway through the back door."

I walked across the room and examined the place where Iantha had fallen. Bits of the broken lamp chimney lay scattered about the floor and on the bottom step of the back stair. It was evident that one of those pieces had caused the small cut on her chin. The base of the lamp itself had rolled into a shadowy corner, and as I stooped to pick it up I noticed another object lying close beside it. I whistled.

"What is it, Bill?" Marian asked sharply. "Have you found something?"

"Yes." I straightened slowly and turned back into the kitchen. "I've found something—something I don't understand."

In my right hand I held out a small piece of wooden statuary. Its head had been broken off cleanly, and there was a long deep crack which ran straight down through the body, but it was easily recognizable jus the same. Marian gasped.

"Why," she murmured in complete bewilderment, "it's that little figure that we just brought down from the storeroom. It's the wooden image of Buddha that came from the *Pride of the Fleet!*"

Iantha rose from her chair with a choking cry, and then sank back again. Her moanings recommenced and she rocked back and forth with her hands over her face. She seemed to be repeating something over and over, but the words were indistinguishable.

For some time Marian administered the ammonia bottle without apparent effect, but suddenly Iantha stopped rocking and pointed an accusing finger at me. "I told you so!" she cried almost triumphantly. "I knew it would happen! I knew it! Didn't I say so, right up in that attic? Didn't I?"

"Hush, Iantha," begged Marian, "hush! What did you say? What did you know would happen?"

"The curse! That everlastin' old curse and the bad luck and all! I told you if you put them heathen idols up around the house, somethin' awful would happen. And now—" She began to weep again, "and now it's landed right on the top of us! Oh, why did you stir up them things?"

Well, of course, it was all perfectly idiotic, wildly ridiculous and absurd. But, as I stood there with the broken wooden statuette in my hand, I found myself gazing almost with apprehension into the black shadows of the library. And then, all at once, there was a heavy step at the top of the back stairs.

It was only Samuel Gregg, and if our nerves had not been badly frayed I am sure we should have smiled as he came bouncing down to join us in the kitchen. He was wearing silk pajamas of a violent purple hue, the voluminous legs of which protruded grotesquely from beneath the huge shaggy overcoat he had donned in the interests of decency. He held a lamp in one plump hand and with the other he was industriously rubbing his eyes.

"Bless my soul!" he exclaimed as he peered at us from the landing. "Bless my soul! What's all this? I was awakened by some sort of frightful commotion. Is someone ill?"

"No." I shook my head. "Iantha was coming down here in the dark to fill her lamp and—she had an accident. She fell on the landing there."

"Bless my soul!" He hopped off the landing as though it were red hot and gazed anxiously at Iantha. "She was not injured, I trust. No serious ill effects?"

"She was badly frightened. No wonder!"

I told him Iantha's story and the fact that the back door had been found wide open. I showed him the broken statue of Buddha. "It was found," I explained, "on the landing there, beside the base of her lamp. What do you make of it, Mr. Gregg?"

Gregg was greatly excited. He examined the back door with care and he clucked in wonder over the image. Then he turned to me with the air of a man who has made a startling discovery. "A burglar, Mr. Thornton!" he announced impressively. "There is not a doubt in the world but that some miscreant forcibly entered this house with intent to pilfer. Not a doubt in the world!"

"It looks that way," I admitted, "but at the same time, there are things that I don't understand. Why should anyone want to steal a small wooden Buddha? It wouldn't be worth five cents to a thief."

Samuel Gregg did not seem dismayed. "The workings of the criminal mind," he informed me with a solemn shake of the head, "are beyond comprehension. I have made some little study of the criminal mind, and I know whereof I speak."

He trotted across the room and peered cautiously into the empty woodshed. "I suggest, Mr. Thornton," he said as he turned away, "that you and I conduct a search of the house. It is possible that the scoundrel may yet be lurking somewhere about the premises."

"I wish you'd do that, Bill." Marian looked up at me. "There probably isn't anybody within a mile of here by this time, but I think we'd all sleep better if we were sure about it. You and Mr. Gregg look around the house and I'll take Iantha up to my room. She can spend the rest of the night with me. I'm sure neither of us wants to be alone after this."

Gregg and I examined the house thoroughly, but as I had expected we found nothing new. Nothing was missing or out of place, and the only reminder of our unwelcome visitor was the broken wooden image that I held in my hand and the unoccupied space on the top of the bookcase in the library.

My companion maintained an unbroken flow of conversation. He regaled me, as we inspected doors and windows and poked into dark closets, with stories about the
workings of the criminal mind. I didn't listen to him for
just then I wanted to think. I finally steered him into his
room and shut the door on a windy explanation of the
relation between crime and the immigration laws.

Then I retired to my own chamber to trouble my brain
with the annoying mystery of the busted Buddha.

I had placed the headless statue upon my bureau, and
had stared at it for no more than a minute when I had
a sudden thought. It was not a brilliant thought and it
should have come to me long before. I thumped myself on
the top of the head, took four or five turns up and down
the cold floor, and then went out in search of Marian.
There was a thread of light under her door, and she re-
sponded immediately to my knock.

"If you can leave Iantha for a minute," I whispered quietly, "I'd like to talk to you."

She nodded, slipped silently out in the hall, and followed me back to my room. It is fortunate Iantha did not
see us, for I closed the door carefully without giving a
thought to the proprieties.

"Marian," I demanded earnestly, "is there anything
about this business tonight which strikes you as being
peculiar?"

She smiled, rather wanly. "If there is anything about
this business tonight," she retorted, "which does not strike
me as peculiar then I wish you'd tell me what it is." Her
lips trembled. "To tell you the truth, Bill, I'm scared stiff.
I don't think I'm any more cowardly than anyone else, but
just the same—"

"I know." I patted her hand. "It isn't pleasant to be
awakened out of a sound sleep the way you were wakened

tonight. I turn sort of green myself when I stop to think of it. The point is, nevertheless, that we've darn well got to find out what it all means." I looked at her closely. "Then you didn't notice any one thing tonight which seemed stranger than all the other strange things?"

"No." She shook her head slowly. "Did you?"

"You didn't think it was funny that in spite of all the screams and crashes and running around that went on— that in spite of all the noise, Gregg didn't come downstairs until it was all over?"

"Why, no, I didn't think of that." She looked at me in some surprise. "It does seem funny, now that you mention it, but—" she shrugged her shoulders—"he may be a very heavy sleeper. That would explain it."

"It would," I nodded, "except that I happen to know he wasn't asleep at the time!"

"You do!" Her head came up. "How do you know that?

"I know because I was in the bathroom when I heard the first scream, and because when I heard it, I knocked on Gregg's door and went in. He wasn't asleep then, and his bed hadn't been slept in. Not only that, but he wasn't in the room at all!"

"Then—then, where was he?"

I shrugged. "I have my own suspicions as to where he was."

She stared at me with growing excitement. "You mean— you mean you think Gregg may have been the one who bumped into Iantha on the landing?"

"I wouldn't place any bets to the contrary."

Marian seemed bewildered. "But what was he doing? Why was the back door open? How did he get back to his room?"

I really was immensely satisfied with myself. "If you'll listen for a minute," I said, "I'll tell you how the thing shapes up to me. Suppose, for some reason we don't know,

Gregg wants to get hold of the wooden image in the library without our knowing anything about it. He waits until everyone has gone to bed and then sneaks down and gets it. He is coming back with it to his room when he has the hard luck to run into Iantha on the landing of the back stairs. The image as well as the lamp smashes to the floor. His first instinct is, naturally, to beat it, so he steps across Iantha, runs into the kitchen, and barges out of the back door."

"But, but—"

"Wait! What happens next? You and I come rushing down to the kitchen at the sound of the scream, and the coast is clear. With his latchkey he lets himself in the front door, goes up to his room, and gets into his pajamas. Then all he has to do is to come down to the kitchen and act dumb." I smiled triumphantly. "How does that strike you?"

"It—it sounds all right." To Marian the whole idea was too sudden for immediate comprehension. "But—but doesn't it sound almost too good to be true?"

"I know, but the more you think of it the more logical it seems. You must remember the important fact that Gregg wasn't in his room when I entered it. If he hadn't had anything to do with the business downstairs, why did he tell that lie about having been asleep the whole time? Why didn't he tell a straight story?"

"I believe you are perfectly right!" Marian was convinced at last and she was in favor of immediate action. "The thing for us to do now is to give Mr. Gregg the third degree. There are several questions I'd like to ask Mr. Gregg."

"I'm not so sure." I frowned and shook my head. "I'm darn well interested in why he was so keen on the Buddha as to go hunting it in the middle of the night, and why he was so keen on not being caught that he'd go running around out in the front yard."

"Well," she replied impatiently, "we'll find all that out, won't we, by asking him."

"I don't believe it. I think he'll either wriggle out of it some way, or else he'll just get mad and pull out in the morning, bag and baggage. We couldn't stop him, you know. We haven't anything definite against him."

"Then, what *are* we to do?"

"I suggest we lie low and watch. You must remember, Marian, that we are one up on Gregg. We are perfectly aware that he is up to something, and he doesn't know that we are aware of it. He thinks that his little trick worked perfectly—as it would have worked except for the accident of my going into his room. He thinks that he is entirely unsuspected, and for that reason will feel free to try again. Let him feel that way, I say. I'll catch him red-handed the next time."

That was the way the matter was left, although Marian had her misgivings. She did not altogether approve of allowing a crazy person, perhaps even a dangerous person, to roam unhampered about the house, and it was only after I had assured her most earnestly that I would permit neither her nor Iantha to come to any harm that she consented to go back to her room and to try to get some sleep.

I doubt if any of us, with the exception of Gregg, slept very much that night. I know that I remained in the bathroom with my ear to Gregg's door until the dawn. As far as I could tell from his heavy breathing, he slept, without interruption, the celebrated sleep of the just.

Life in our establishment for the next two or three days was not exactly one gay, carefree carouse. It resembled more closely, I think, the conventional picture of the condemned man making every effort to dispose of a hearty breakfast.

Gregg was the only one to put on any kind of front, and he rather overdid it. His conversation at the table became

more continuous and erratic than ever and he suddenly
acquired the vicious and unnatural habit of telling jokes.
If the jokes had been amusing or well told they might
have provided comic relief, but they were neither. He had
culled them, I gathered, from the *Chess Lover's Weekly*, and
on each occasion he either forgot the point altogether or
put it in at the wrong place.

His efforts to be the life of the party were not convincing and I was interested to note that in unguarded
moments he was apt to fall into deep, frowning reveries.

Iantha went about her work with a grim, set face, and
she jumped at the slightest unexpected noise. Marian was
little better. She took to glancing furtively over her shoulder and when I laughed at her about it she became defiant.

"I can't stand this much longer, Bill, and what's more
I won't. If you don't find out something, and find it out
soon, I'm going to Gregg and get the truth, if I have to
shake it out of him!"

"Hold your horses," I begged her, "a little while longer.
He's just waiting for the last storm to blow over before he
starts another. Something is bound to break, and break in
a hurry."

Something broke the very next morning, but it broke
in a quarter I had never expected.

I was called to the telephone shortly after breakfast to
receive a peculiar message. It caused me to hang up the receiver with a perplexed frown, and it caused me to tell Marian a more or less feeble lie. "Do you mind," I asked her, "if
I use your car? There seems to be a night letter for me at the
telegraph office and can't get it straight over the 'phone."

I drove the little flivver out of the front yard and turned
right on the road leading to East Orham. I did not, however,
proceed as advertised to the telegraph office. I followed
the road skirting the sea for perhaps half a mile and then
turned right again on a private drive. There was a signboard

at the entrance of that drive, and on it in assertive black letters were printed the words "Harvey Blodgett."

Mr. Blodgett, I discovered, was a tall, well-built, red-faced man, who reminded me for some unexplainable reason of a retired fireman. He was seated in his shirtsleeves in the midst of the bachelor confusion of his living room and he greeted me with a deep, booming voice when I was announced by his negro servant.

"Good morning, Mr. Thornton," he began, after shaking my hand with great vigor. "It was decent of you to show up in answer to a fool message from a perfect stranger." He laughed heartily. "You're probably thinking right now that I'm some kind of a nut."

I murmured some politeness to the contrary but he did not listen. "You're probably wondering why the blank Harvey Blodgett asked you to come see him without saying anything to anybody. Well, I'll tell you why." He pointed a big red finger at me impressively. "There's some funny business going on around here, Mr. Thornton—some damn' funny business!"

I blinked. "Really?"

"Yes." He pounded his fist on the table. "It's funny enough, all right, and it's my motto to leave women out of such stuff. They get excited and squeal, but they don't do any good. That's why I asked you to keep mum and come over here. See?"

"Yes." I nodded with growing apprehension. "What is this—this funny business, Mr. Blodgett?"

He pondered for a moment and then came to a decision. "I'll tell you the whole thing so you'll get it straight." He nodded. "You seem like a sensible young fellow so I'll put all the cards on the table."

He began by informing me that he collected antiques. He wasn't sure why he collected them, but he did. He collected nothing but the best antiques and he never let anything interfere with getting a piece that he wanted. That was why he had put aside his dislike for Gregg, whom he described as "a fat, conceited numbskull who thinks he knows a lot more than he does," and consented to view the antiques in the attic of the Blair house. In that attic he found, among other things, a mahogany clock which pleased him greatly. He bought the clock then and there and had it brought to his house.

"All fair enough," declared Mr. Blodgett, "but then what happened?"

I assured him that I could not guess, so he enlightened me. A few days later, he said, Gregg had come to him and had tried to buy the clock back. He had offered an absurd price for the thing and in the end had been greatly excited and even indignant when Blodgett flatly refused to sell.

"What do you make of that?" I was asked with great vigor. "Does that make any sense? If a man wants to keep something does he go and sell it? And when he has sold it does he go out the next day and try to buy it back? No, not if his brains are O.K."

It was perfectly obvious what Mr. Blodgett meant, and I was beginning to think that perhaps I agreed with him, but I made no comment.

"That isn't all!" He pointed a finger at me again. "Don't think I dragged you over here to talk about whether Sam Gregg is crazy or not. I don't give a darn whether he's crazy or whether he isn't." He got to his feet and continued impressively. "What I want to tell you about is what happened last night. Last night Tom, my man, and I were both out, and when I got home about eleven o'clock I found that somebody had broken into this house!"

"Honestly?" I was really startled by this time. "Was—was anything gone?"

"Yes, and that's the funny part of it. There's a lot of valuable stuff in this room, and yet there was only one thing taken." He paused briefly in the interest of dramatic emphasis. "That was the clock I've been telling you about. Now how does *that* strike you, Thornton?"

It struck me a lot harder than liked to admit but I could see that I must say something. "Do you mean," I asked with reluctance, "that you think Mr. Gregg has your clock?

"No." He laughed grimly. "I'll bet my shirt that that he *took* the thing, but I happen to know he hasn't got it now."

It was all too much for me. "I—I don't understand."

"I'll say you don't!" He laughed again. "Nobody with any sense would understand, and I'll tell you why. This morning, just before breakfast, we found the clock down by the foot of the drive. Come and take a look at it!"

He led me across the room to a small table and showed me his clock. Perhaps it would be more accurate to say that he showed me what had once been his clock, for in its present state it resembled more closely than anything else the jumbled pieces of a jigsaw puzzle. Twisted bits of metal and tiny fragments of splintered mahogany were all that was left of what had once been a valuable antique. It looked to me as though someone had inserted the clock in the jaws of a large and particularly efficient meat-grinder.

I shook my head in complete bewilderment. "It—it might have been run over by a ten-ton truck."

"It looks that way," he admitted, "but that isn't the answer. The answer is that the thief took the thing to the edge of my yard and then chopped it into hash with a hatchet. If you look at the junk closely you can see the marks."

The more I looked and the more I thought, the more firmly I became convinced that Samuel Gregg had completely lost his mind. I shrugged my shoulders, at last, hopelessly. "What do you want me to do?"

He lit a long black cigar and gazed thoughtfully at the smoke before he answered. "I'll tell you, Thornton, the way I see the thing. When all is said and. done, the big fact remains that I'm out a damn' expensive clock. And it stands too that I've got better than a shrewd suspicion who swiped it from me. Am I right?"

"Well, I—I imagine you may be."

"Sure I am! And I can do one of two things. I can go to the cops, hand them the dope, and see what happens. That would be the natural move and I'll take it if necessary. At the same time—" he looked at me closely—"I don't like to make trouble, and I hope I won't have to."

I saw then, of course, what he was driving at. If the money he had paid for the clock was refunded to him, he was willing to forget the whole affair; if not, there would be trouble. The town police would be called in and there would be all sorts of unpleasant notoriety. After a moment's thought I anticipated what I was sure would be Marian's wish, and told him that I would bring him a check the following morning. We parted with many expressions of good will on his part.

The rest of that day was more or less of a nightmare. I knew that I should go directly to Marian and tell her the whole story, but I hesitated to do so. She would undoubtedly be greatly alarmed and, more than that, she would put an immediate end to any possibility of my finding out what Gregg was trying to do. I finally decided to keep my own counsel until the following morning and in the meantime to be more watchful than ever.

I tried a little experiment that afternoon when Gregg and I chanced to be alone in the living room. In the most casual of manners I related as a bit of diverting gossip the fact that Blodgett's clock had been stolen from his house the night before. The reaction was about what I had expected. Gregg appeared greatly interested. He seemed excited and even agitated. He asked about a million questions, declared that these invasions of private property were becoming an outrage, and even went so far as to suggest informing the Orham constable. I remember thinking, as I calmed him, that his acting would be much more convincing if it were more restrained.

I did not let him out of my sight for more than a minute all that evening, and even after he had gone to his room I sat in the bathroom near by until a succession of lusty snores informed me that it was safe to go to bed.

I do not know how long I had been asleep. I had been involved, I remember, in a series of mad adventures in which the leading figures were Samuel Gregg, the wooden Buddha, and the mahogany clock. I had just come upon the Buddha, which had grown to startlingly lifelike proportions, in the act of stuffing the clock down the fat little man's throat, bit by bit, when all at once I sat bolt upright in bed.

Marian, a dim figure in the dark, was shaking me by the shoulder. "Bill!" she was whispering over and over. "Wake up! You must wake up!"

"What is it?" I was thoroughly conscious at last. "What's up?"

"Oh, Bill!" She made a little sound, almost like a sob. "I think—I'm sure I heard a noise down in the living room."

"Good!" I grabbed my bathrobe, slipped it over my shoulders, and rolled out of bed. "I've been waiting for something like this. Now we'll find out what's what."

"What are you going to do?" She was clinging to my sleeve. "I—I'm terribly afraid."

"There's nothing to be afraid of," I whispered reassuringly. "It's nobody but Gregg. First I'm going to peek into his room to make sure he isn't there, and then I'm going to take a jaunt downstairs."

Gregg wasn't in his room. A lamp burned low on the table beside his tumbled and empty bed. I stole back into the corridor where Marian was waiting for me, placed a finger on her lips as a warning to be quiet, and crept slowly to the head of the front stairs. She followed with a hand on my shoulder.

Halfway down in the inky blackness I paused, held my breath, and listened. There was not a sound. I put a cautious foot on the step below, and all at once the board cracked like a pistol shot under my weight.

For an instant nothing happened, and then, from the living room came a soft thump, a shout, and the sound of running feet.

V

The rest of those steps down into the front hall I took at one bound, my ankle twisting painfully as I landed. I staggered, and only my outstretched hand against the far wall saved me from falling. Then I was in the living room.

"Gregg!" I cried sharply into the gloom. "Mr. Gregg! Where are you?"

There was no answer, and from the other end of the room came a puff of cold, damp, night air.

We found a lamp upon one of the tables and, between us, managed to get it lighted. As the flame strengthened and grew steadier I could see that we were quite alone. There was no sign of Gregg, and the only evidence that the room had been disturbed at all was a heavy armchair which lay on its side in the middle of the carpet—that and the door leading out to the porch. The porch door was open, swinging gently in the breeze.

"Damn! He's worked it again!" I had sworn disgustedly and had started for the porch when Marian caught me by the arm.

"Please, Bill," she begged almost tearfully, "don't go out there. Don't leave me alone. I can't stand it!"

Just then there was a cry from the top of the stairs and Iantha made a tempestuous descent to join us. Her hair, in curl papers, stood out in weird little pointing fingers from the top of her head and her eyes were staring. I could see all the signs of an approaching emotional cyclone, so I did my best to head it off.

"There's nothing to get excited about, Iantha," I said sharply. "Absolutely nothing. Mr. Gregg has just gone out into the yard for some reason, and I'm going to find him. You stay here with Marian."

"Why—why—"

"It's nobody but Gregg," I interrupted rudely. "You aren't afraid of him, are you? He went outside for a minute but he'll be right back. He—"

Once more I swore aloud, for I had a sudden complete realization what Gregg's movements would probably be. I grabbed the electric flashlight which always lay on a chair by the front door, muttered something or other, and dashed off through the library toward the kitchen. Even as I ran I kicked myself mentally for being stupid beyond belief. Gregg, of course, had run out to the porch when he heard the stair tread creak under my weight, and at that moment would be trying to get back to his room by entering one of the doors at the back of the house—always granting, I reflected irritably, that he had not already succeeded in doing so.

My flashlight showed me that the kitchen door was shut tight and I soon discovered that it was locked from the inside. The woodshed door was the same way. I hastily placed chairs, bearing a number of pots and pans, against both of them and then ran up the back stairs to Gregg's room. It was empty.

Hurrying back to the living room I found Marian and Iantha huddled close together upon the haircloth sofa. The porch door, I noticed, had been closed in my absence. "Well, well!" I remarked brightly with some vague idea of relieving the tension. "What would life be without those jolly little midnight parties? I'm getting so that I thoroughly enjoy them."

Iantha tried to speak, but contented herself at last with a snort of indignation at my flippancy and a groan which ended in a shudder. Marian's lips trembled. "Did you find anything?" she asked. "Did you find Mr. Gregg?"

"No, but I'm not worried about him. He'll be back as soon as he has finished his game of hopscotch, or whatever he's playing out there in the shrubbery. I expect his cheery knock any moment now."

We waited, in uneasy silence, for ten minutes or more, but no knock came. Then Marian looked up at me with apprehension in her eyes. "You don't suppose that anything could have happened to him, Bill, do you? Anything serious, I mean?"

I was beginning to wonder that very thing but I tried not to show it. "Oh, no," I replied carelessly, "nothing has happened to him. I imagine he has found out that the place is locked up tighter than a drum and is cooking up a good story to tell before he bangs on the front door."

Marian shivered. "It must be awfully cold out there in the dark. Do you think he's dressed?"

That was an idea which had not occurred to me, and I ran upstairs once more to investigate. His clothes, lying in a neat pile upon a chair, seemed to indicate that Gregg was wandering about the lawn clad in nothing at the most more substantial than bathrobe and slippers. It was time, I decided, that something drastic was done, so I crossed to my own room and put on shoes, trousers, and a heavy sweater. Marian and Iantha regarded me anxiously when I returned to them.

"I'm going out," I told them as casually as I could, "to take a look around. It may not do any good but it certainly won't do any harm."

"What did you find upstairs?" Marian demanded. "Is he dressed, or isn't he?"

"Oh, yes," I lied cheerfully, "he's dressed all right. Don't worry about that, and don't worry if you hear someone yodeling about the premises. It'll just be your little friend calling to his mate."

I made them a bow, trying not to look at their white, fearful faces, and skipped out to the porch with a joyousness that I most certainly did not feel.

That next half hour I cannot place among the more happy intervals of my brief career. I kept the flashlight in my pocket at first and made a complete stealthy circuit of the house and barn. The darkness was complete, and while I am not an overimaginative person, it seemed to me that every shadowy clump of bushes was packed full of menace. Of Samuel Gregg I found no trace.

At last, and with a cowardly feeling of relief, I switched on the electric torch and abandoned caution altogether. I made another complete tour of the grounds, lustily shouting Gregg's name at short intervals and throwing the beam of light into every conceivable hiding place. I even searched the dusty stables and the lofts of the old barn, but my only discoveries were a number of healthy rats which scuttled hastily to cover as I advanced, and the ponderous body of the old stove sitting in sullen majesty in a far corner. I finally admitted defeat and went back to the house.

Time, I discovered, had been of very little assistance to matters in the living room. Iantha, on the sofa, was still shuddering and moaning forlornly in the circle of Marian's arm, and Marian herself seemed on the verge of tears. She gazed at me hopelessly as I came in out of the dark.

"What are you going to do, Bill?" she pleaded in response to the negative shake of my head. "We—we simply must do something."

I decided it was time to assume the role of the stern male. "Look here," I declared in a tone which I hoped was facetiously reproachful, "I can't see any reason for all this weeping and wailing and gnashing of molars. Sam Gregg is a fully developed specimen, and just because he decides to take a walk in the middle of the night is no excuse for calling out the fire department. It's beautiful weather, cool and refreshing, and I suppose he answered the call of the open. What would be more natural?"

"Natural!" Iantha choked and extended both arms to a disinterested heaven. "A full-grown man comes tiptoein' down stairs at twelve o'clock in the night time, upsets a chair, yells like a loon, and goes tearin' out into the yard in his shirt, and—and you say it's natural! Oh, my soul and body!"

I saw that it was no use, and made a pleading motion to Marian. "Well, there's nothing to be scared about even if it does seem queer. Not only that, but there's no sense in all of us sitting up all night waiting for something else to happen. You two go on up to bed and I'll do the waiting. I promise you you'll be safe enough!"

Iantha, of course, made vehement protest. She not only should not sleep that night but she had no expectation of being able to do so in the future. The curse, she declared, had descended upon us, and the evil day had come.

It was only after earnest persuasion and upon Marian's solemn promise to keep her company that she finally permitted herself to be led upstairs to her room.

"But I shan't go to bed," she declared, with unalterable determination. "Nobody can make me go to bed. I'll be sittin' up there in a chair, with my clothes on, waitin' for the call. And the Lord only knows what that call may be!"

I was smoking my second cigarette in the living room when Marian came running down to me again. "I mustn't stay but a moment," she said. "Iantha will be flying after me if I do. But, oh, Bill," she whispered desperately, "you must tell me what you know, and what you think. You must tell me because—I'm almost crazy."

There was no possible way to comfort her although I would have given anything to cause that look to leave her eyes. "I know very little," I admitted reluctantly, "and I'm thinking even less. It's all a fog to me."

"Is he dressed? Are you really sure that he's dressed?"

Nothing was to be gained by deceiving her further, so I shook my head. "No, Marian, I'm afraid he's not. As far as I can make out his clothes are lying just where he put them when he got ready for bed."

She gasped. "Then—then he's been out there somewhere all this time in just his nightclothes. Why, something terrible might happen to him! If it hasn't already!"

"I know, but what can I do. I've looked everywhere and I can't find him. There isn't any sense in getting the police, is there?"

"No. There aren't any police, or practically none. I suppose there isn't anything we can do, but it just seems so awful."

"I know, it seems terrible." I patted her hand "But isn't there just a chance, old dear, that we may be getting ourselves all steamed up about nothing? What do we know, after all? Gregg's clothes are undoubtedly on the chair, but he may very well have put on something different for his little excursion. I think he's perfectly capable of taking care of himself, and I wouldn't worry at all if he'd only poke his ugly nose through that door in about one minute."

Marian sighed. "If he only would."

Iantha shrieked her name from the top of the stairs and she went up and left me to my vigil. It wasn't a pleasant vigil, for I was more anxious than I liked to admit. The memory of Harvey Blodgett's shattered clock was all too vivid in my mind and I found myself wondering as the

long hours dragged by whether Gregg was entirely sane. If
he was mentally normal why had he run out into the night
in his pajamas, and more than that, why had he failed to
come back?

My question remained unanswered when the first
streaks of light appeared in the east. I had spent endless
hours in searching the living room for a clew to the mystery
and in periodic excursions through the lower floor of the
house. The living room told me nothing. It had remained
untouched, as far as I could see, except for the chair which
Gregg must have knocked over in his flight. My careful
examinations of every door and window on the ground
floor were fruitless. They had not been tampered with.

As soon as it was light enough for my purpose I let myself out of the house and once more searched the grounds.
This time I omitted nothing. From the road, to the bluff
on the ocean side, I inspected every yard of turf. I prowled
through the barn again. I poked inquiringly into each
clump of shrubbery. I had given up hope and was trudging
wearily back to the house when my eye was attracted by an
object lying half hidden in the long grass just beneath the
living room window. I bent over and picked it up.

In my hand I held an old, shapeless bedroom slipper. It
belonged, unless I was greatly mistaken, to Samuel Gregg,
and unless I was equally mistaken he had lost it in his
flight of the evening before.

I stood there for some time turning the thing over and
over and digesting its significance. It settled beyond any
reasonable doubt the question of Gregg's costume. When
he heard my clumsy step upon the front stair he had run
out into the dark in his night clothes. Where had he gone,
and why had he failed to come back? It was the same old
query and I could find no answer to it. I shook my head,
stuffed the slipper into my hip pocket, and returned to
the house.

People were moving about in the bedroom upstairs, and in a few moments Marian and Iantha, both fully dressed, came down to join me. There were dark circles under their eyes, mute evidence to a sleepless night, but they seemed more cheerful in the reassuring light of day.

Marian smiled at me. "Poor boy, I'll bet you've spent one of the better evenings. I'm sorry."

"Don't be sorry. Solitude and reflection are good for the soul and I've had a little of both."

"Nothing happened, of course?"

"Not a darn thing. The lack of happenings was a most monotonous. Why did you and Iantha burst forth at this ungodly hour?"

"Well, we have neither of us slept a wink, of course, so we decided it would be just as well to get up and have breakfast. There'll probably be plenty to do later on."

I agreed with her, and by way of being prepared for those doings I went upstairs, bathed, shaved, and put on fresh clothes. Then I went down to Marian in the library. "Well," she inquired bravely, "what do you think we'd better do now?"

"You've got me. What on earth do people do when one of their number goes out for a walk in his nightshirt and doesn't come back? Bloodhounds are the only things that occur to me, and they sound more like *Uncle Tom's Cabin* than anything else."

"I don't like the looks of it, Bill, do you?"

"No, I don't. I like the looks of it so little that I suppose we'll have to call in the police—much as I hate the idea."

She shrugged impatiently. "There's only one constable in East Orham and he wouldn't know what to do any better than we do. We might get the state police, I suppose."

I thought that over, but in spite of the obvious common sense of the suggestion I did not like it. "There is something about cops," I admitted finally, "that doesn't appeal to me. They nose around, they ask a lot of questions, they get people into the papers. I wish we could carry on on our own hook, for a little while at least."

"So do I," Marian nodded. "But, Bill, what are we going to do? We can't just sit around and do nothing, you know."

I rubbed my forehead wearily. "The old brain seems to have curled up and quit. I can't squeeze a decent idea out of it. I'd give my hat if there was only some other man to talk to somebody with sense, and somebody we could trust."

Marian had an idea. "How about Jonas Jones?" she demanded. "He has sense and you certainly can trust him. Why don't you telephone him right this minute?'

The thought of Jonas Jones was so pleasing that I could have kissed Marian from pure joy and relief. As a matter of fact, I did. "There are moments," I assured her solemnly, "when you have flashes of positive intelligence! Jonas Jones is right. He's not only right but he's perfect! What's his phone number?"

Jonas was apparently a heavy sleeper. His bell rang and rang until I had almost decided that I should be forced to get out the flivver and descend upon him in person. His voice, however, when it finally came to me across the buzzing wire, was cheerful.

"Mr. Jones?" I announced myself impatiently. "This is Bill Thornton. I'm sorry to have waked you up, but—"

"Well, well, Bill, good mornin'! Don't you worry about wakin' me up. I'd ought to have been up a long time ago; would have been if I hadn't been born lazy. What can I do for you—sell you an antique?"

"No, but you can do something else for me if you will. Something darn funny—or it may not be so funny—happened over here last night and I'd like your advice about it. Do you suppose you could come right over? It's rather important."

He did not ask any questions. "Sure pop! I'll be there just as quick as I can climb into my duds."

"Shall I come for you in the car?"

"No, no, don't you do that. I'll take the short cut over there before you can get your car under way."

I hung up the receiver and went to my breakfast in a much more happy frame of mind. Why the prospect of Jones' help should have pleased me so greatly I do not know, except that I had come to have a great respect for his intelligence and capabilities. I felt that a great load had been lifted from my shoulders and I was able to listen to Iantha's lamentations with more patience.

Marian had told her, apparently, of our suspicions that Gregg was responsible for her adventure at the foot of the back stairs, and she had already decided upon the reason for his strange actions.

"He's crazy," she informed us solemnly. "Just as loony as—as a loon. You can't tell me he ain't, and you don't have to tell me the reasons why he is. It's that chess and those puzzle things that begun it, and handlin' them things in that back attic finished the job. He's gone clean out of his head. Well, I've been expectin' one of us would go that way pretty soon." She shook her own head emphatically. "You mark my words, they'll be callin' us on the telephone now any minute to say they've found him ravin' distracted. Sarah Mary Hall's grandfather went crazy one night all of a sudden, that way, and they found *him* out in the henhouse, cacklin', thinkin' he'd laid an egg. Oh, you can laugh! But you won't laugh long. You mark my words!"

We were marking her words—there were plenty of them—and making a pretense of breakfasting, when Jonas Jones arrived. He walked into the dining room with his hat in his hand, and I noticed as he greeted us that he did not seem to be his usually cheerful self. He did not smile, and what was more odd, he had no jovial remark for Iantha.

"Oh, Mr. Jones," cried Marian, "you have no idea how glad we are to see you. We've had a perfectly ghastly night."

He nodded briefly. "Bill was just tellin' me there was something stirrin'. If he'll come outside with me now I'd like to hear the whole yarn."

"Oh, you needn't go outside," objected Marian. "He can tell you here just as well. And you haven't had your own breakfast, have you? Sit down and eat with us. Please do."

I should have echoed her invitation if I had not been watching Jonas, who frowned at me and made a quick backward motion with his head. I pushed back my chair and got to my feet with a little quiver of apprehension. "All right, Jones," I said carelessly, "breakfast can wait a minute or two. I'm sure Iantha can keep something hot until we get back."

Jonas led me out through the back door and around the corner of the house, where he halted. "Now, Bill," he said abruptly, "let's have it."

I told him as briefly as possible what had happened the night before. He listened silently and shook his head when I finished. "Well, now!" he said in slow wonder. "Well, what do you think of that!"

"I don't know what to think of it, and I don't know what to do. Have you any suggestions?"

He stirred a twig with the tip of his shoe. "You say that you searched the place, searched it careful, and didn't find anything?"

"Not a thing but that slipper, and that didn't tell me much. Why?"

I looked at him closely and noticed for the first time a strange tightness about the corners of his mouth. I caught him by the arm. "Why? Have you found—something? Tell me!"

He nodded, gravely. "Yes, Bill, I've found something. I've found something, and I guess you'd might as well see it."

I followed him once more, without a word. I suppose I knew then what we were going to see, but there was a strange confusion in my brain and I could not summon words to ask the question. We walked swiftly along the path to the front gate, passed through it, and crossed the main road.

On the other side of that road a well-beaten path led through a thick grove of pines and twisted away across the fields to the west. Jonas stopped me as we entered it. "I don't have to tell you, do I," he asked gently, "what we're going to find? You know, don't you?"

My voice seemed to me as though it came from a great distance. "Yes. I—I suppose I do."

I knew, and yet as we bent over that still figure in the brilliant purple pajamas as it lay half in the path and half in the low bushes beside it, my mind refused to believe.

"Gregg!" I cried involuntarily. "Mr. Gregg!"

"There's no use, Bill," said Jonas sadly. "Not the slightest bit of use."

Even as I straightened, I knew that he was right. I knew that, incredible as it seemed, Samuel Gregg had played his last game of chess.

VI

A man, they say, shows his real worth in a moment of crisis. I sincerely hope that that axiom does not always hold water, for I am anything but proud of my behavior during the minutes that immediately followed the discovery of all that was left to us of Samuel Gregg. Death was a new thing to me. I had never encountered it before and it was beyond my grasp. At the time I was not conscious of sorrow, or of anything but a selfish and very terrible feeling of guilt.

"It's my fault," I murmured hopelessly, "all my fault. If I'd found him last night this wouldn't have happened."

"Nonsense, Bill!" Jonas shook me roughly by the arm. "How in the nation could you have found him way out here in the dark?"

"I ought to have known. I ought to have stopped him from coming." I shook my head. "If he died of exposure it's my fault and nobody else's."

Jonas took hold of the situation with a firm hand. "We don't know what he died of," he said shortly, "and it isn't our business to find out. That's up to the doctor. In the meantime, there are plenty of things that we *can* do. Are you ready to help?"

"Of course." His coolness had its effect upon me. "What do you want me to do?"

"I want you to go back and tell Iantha. Tell her straight out and then come back to me. I'll be waiting here."

"Tell Iantha? Why—"

"You do what I say. Iantha may fly off the roost about little things but she's right on the perch when it comes to big ones. You'll see quick enough."

He was perfectly right. I saw a different Iantha Hallett that morning, an Iantha that made me ashamed of myself and gave me new courage. She was washing dishes when I came into the kitchen, and when she glanced at my face her own turned pale. She put down the wet cloth and turned to me. I know, she said, with a little gasp. "I know! I—I had a feelin'. Somethin' has happened to Mr. Gregg."

"Yes," I nodded. "I'm afraid it has."

"Oh!" She choked and her eyes filled with tears but she did not break down. "I was almost sure of it," she said gently at last. "I was scared it would turn out so. If it wasn't craziness it was bound to be somethin' worse. Where is he, poor soul?"

"Out there." I made a vague motion with my head. "Jonas is with him. We—"

"Is it—is he—?"

"Yes, Iantha."

"You go right on back." She was taking off her apron. "I'll fetch the doctor and fix up the room best I can."

"Marian—" I began.

"Leave Marian to me. I'll tell her, and I'll keep her out of the way. Don't worry about things in the house. You go back to Jonas."

Poor Samuel Gregg was in his own room at last, and Jonas and I were in the library waiting for the doctor— Iantha's phone summons had brought him over—to come down stairs. Jones paced up and down before the window, grimly chewing an unlighted cigar.

"Did you find out anything?" I asked him. "Have you any idea what caused it?"

"No." He shook his head. "There wasn't a mark on him that I could see, and no signs of a scuffle anywhere."

"He had a bad heart, you know. That was why he came down here in the beginning."

"I've thought about that, and I guess we'll find out that's the answer. His heart gave out on him when he run so hard and so far. But what beats me is why did he run at all, and what was he doin' way out there in the pines in the middle of the night. That's the part I can't figure."

"The poor fellow was out of his mind," I said wearily. "There isn't a doubt of it."

"Well, I can see plain enough why you think so; but, Bill, a man don't generally turn crazy as sudden as that. There's usually signs of it comin' on, ain't there?"

"There were plenty of signs, Jonas. I've been watching them for a week or more. I was only waiting to be sure, but like an idiot I waited too long. I ought to be shot."

He looked at me keenly. "What are you talking about, Bill Thornton?" he demanded, coming over to me. "What are you hintin' at? What do you mean?"

I had to confide in someone, so I told him. I told him all about Iantha's adventure on the back stair landing and about the fact that Gregg had not been in his room at the time. I described Gregg's strangely secret manner of late and his suddenly developed habit of sulking in his room. I even related the unexplainable incident of Harvey Blodgett's clock.

"With all those things added together," I admitted in the end, "any person with a grain of sense would have known he was off his head and would have done something about it, but I, of course, was too smart. I refused to believe what was staring me in the face until it was too late."

Jonas, who had been listening to my recital with intense interest, shook his head. "Humph!" he grunted. "Well, I declare! But you mustn't blame yourself, Bill. I don't blame you at all. I can hardly believe it myself even now. It don't seem—well, to square up, somehow."

"It's been proven, hasn't it? I thought at first that maybe he was just running away from me, but if he was doing that he wouldn't have run way across the road and into the pines. No, nobody but a crazy person would do that."

Jonas pondered for a time and then offered a new idea. "Isn't it just possible, Bill," he suggested, "that Sam might have heard somebody in the parlor and have gone downstairs to find out what was goin' on? If he'd found—well, say a thief—he might have chased him way out to the pines."

"You mean, it might have been—murder?" I shrugged my shoulders. "I can't believe that, Jonas, and I can't believe there was even a thief. Nothing was touched in the living room, and you, yourself, say there were no signs of violence on Gregg and no trace of a scuffle. More than that, you've got to remember all the things Gregg had been doing this past week. Remember that business about the Buddha, and remember Harvey Blodgett's clock."

"Yes." Jonas nodded. "You make out a strong case, Bill, and you may be right, but I just can't seem to swallow the notion that poor old Sam Gregg was crazy. I can't hardly believe it, even if it does add up that way. Seems as if there must be somethin' wrong with the figurin'. It—no, it don't sound like good arithmetic—not yet—to me."

We were silent for a time and then something else occurred to me. "What are you going to tell this doctor?" I demanded. "He's going to want to know a lot of things and he's going to ask a lot of questions. Must I tell him all about Blodgett's clock and all the rest of the mess? I'm sure Marian wouldn't like to have it spread all around the town."

"No, she wouldn't." He frowned. "And I don't know as it'll have to be spread. If that doctor comes down and says Gregg died a natural death you can just tell him the old chap has been actin' funny lately. Tell him you found him out in the yard in his night clothes once before. That'll be plenty, so long as the verdict is heart disease, or somethin' like it. If that verdict is different—well, then the thing is out of our hands. You'll have to tell all you know."

The doctor—he was a young man whose name was Bartlett—saved me the necessity. He came down to us after a long wait and shook his head in the manner of one whose expectations have been fulfilled. "Heart disease," he announced briefly and with finality. "Not a doubt in the world of it. Mr. Gregg has had a bad heart ever since I have known him, and I warned him time and time again that the slightest overexertion might be fatal. He was not a man, however, to pay much attention to advice."

He asked me for details of the night before and I gave them to him as accurately as I could. I told him also that Gregg had been acting very strangely for the past week and that I believed his mind was not altogether sound. He listened with interest and some surprise.

"That's odd," he said when I had finished. "I had no inkling of anything like that.

"It strikes me funny too," Jonas agreed strongly. "Mighty funny! Tell me, Doctor, does it very often happen that a fellow who had been runnin' smooth in the upper story for years slips a cog all of a sudden?"

Dr. Bartlett pondered. "Well," he offered judicially at last, "I couldn't say that it was a common occurrence, but on the other hand it might very well happen. From what Mr. Thornton says it seems to have happened in this case."

The question of Gregg's insanity did not particularly interest me. I had the answer to that, I was certain. Just then I was worried about more important matters. "You are sure, of course," I said hesitantly, "that death resulted from natural causes. There couldn't be any possibility of violence, or anything like that?"

"Not the slightest." His dignity, I am afraid, had been offended. "I made a most careful examination and can assure you that Mr. Gregg died of heart failure and nothing else. I have made out the death certificate to that effect and will stake my professional reputation upon it."

Jonas winked at me when the doctor left the room. "Kind of ruffled him the wrong way, didn't you, Bill? These young fellows just out of the doctor factory don't like to be asked if there's any chance they might be wrong."

"I just wanted to be sure," I shrugged. "You put the idea that it might be something else into my head, so I asked him about it. I hope you're satisfied."

"Why, yes, I suppose I'll have to give in that I am. Bartlett isn't yet exactly what I'd call a bright and shining light at his job but he isn't so green but that he'd know murder when he saw it. I'll swallow the heart disease part, all right, but it'll take a sight of provin' before I'm satisfied that poor old Sam Gregg was crazy. It don't figure, Bill. It don't add up right at all."

I left him wandering about downstairs and went up to Marian. The shock to her, of course, had been as great or greater than to any of the rest of us but, like Iantha, she showed her courage in the face of real trouble. "It's all very awful, Bill," she said wearily, "and I can't realize it even yet, but I suppose it has to be faced. If only there were some one here—some one older, I mean—who has faced it before."

"There's Jonas," I reminded her gently. "He is one of the coolest and most sensible people I have ever met and I'm sure he'd be glad to help."

"Oh, Bill, if only he would! Of course, he has helped so much already, but will you ask him, for me, if he won't keep on a little longer? Ask him if he'll tell us, and help us to do—all the things that must be done. Please go down and ask him now."

I found Jonas in the living-room and he assented readily when I relayed Marian's request. "Sure!" he said heartily. "Sure thing. You tell Marian not to worry her head. Just leave everything to me and I'll take care of it."

I had thanked him and had turned away to report to Marian when he stopped me. "Say, Bill," he said casually, "when did you folks sell the box? The sandalwood one, I mean. The one with all the little ivory figures and things on it."

"Sell the box?" I looked at him in bewilderment. "What are you talking about? We haven't sold anything for the last week, ever since things began to happen."

"Sho! My mistake, then." He whistled softly between his teeth. "I kind of thought you must of sold it, but I suppose it's just been moved. I've been sort of used to seein' it on that table over yonder."

I stared in the direction he pointed and noticed, for the first time, that the sandalwood box was not in its place. There was an empty space in the corner of the table where it usually sat. "Why," I stuttered foolishly, "it isn't there!"

Jonas nodded. "Not unless my eyes have gone back on me, it ain't."

"Then," I demanded in complete confusion, "where is it? It was there last night. I know because Marian and I were talking about the inlay on it."

"You don't tell me!" His eyebrow lifted and he whistled softly once more between his teeth. "Well, perhaps Iantha lugged it off somewheres. The further away any of this old stuff is the better she loves it, you know."

"Why on earth would she lug it off? It wouldn't make any sense, but I'll go ask her, just to be sure."

"Hold on!" Jonas was decisive. "Come now, Bill, you don't honestly think Iantha or Marian moved that box, do you?"

"No."

"Then what do you think?"

"I—I don't know."

He leaned toward me. "Well then, suppose I tell you what you think—or what you're beginnin' to guess. You're beginnin' to suspect, same as I do, that that box went out of this room durin' the hurrah last night. Am I right or not?"

"I—I don't know. You mean you think Gregg took it out with him?"

"Well, either Sam took it—or somebody else."

"Somebody else? Are you actually still fooling with the idea that there was a thief in the house last night? Didn't the doctor say that Gregg died of heart failure and nothing else?"

"What in blue blazes of it?" Jonas was impatient. "If Sam caught somebody makin' off with the box he would have chased him, wouldn't he? Seems to me anybody would. And Gregg might have kept on chasin' until he dropped down dead of heart failure in the pines. That makes sense, don't it?"

"No." My brain was in a whirl but I refused to accept the idea. "In the first place what would a thief want with a sandalwood box, and in the second place, why should you think it wasn't Gregg who took it? He was the one who had the Buddha the other time, wasn't he?"

"There, there, Bill, don't waste your steam. I'm not sayin' for sure it wasn't Sam. But if Sam took it, I wish you'd tell me where he took it *to*. Where is it now?"

"It might be almost anywhere. He may have dropped it in the yard or even over in the pines. We didn't make any search, you know."

"That's so, we didn't," he agreed; "and I'd say the next thing to do is to make one now. Ten to one we won't find anything, but we may as well have a try."

"Look here, Jonas," I said impatiently, "will you tell me why you're so set on this thief idea?"

"Why, yes, Bill," scratching his head in some embarrassment, "I'll tell you. If Sam Gregg took that box last night and ran with it way over to those pines, then he must have been crazy. Yes, sir, crazy as a coot, and I can't believe that. I don't believe—I *can't* believe that he was any crazier than I am or you are."

"Well, I don't agree with you," I told him flatly; "and what's more I'll make you a little bet. I'll bet you we find the box somewhere around. If we do find it you'll have to admit that Gregg took it and that I'm right."

He turned to the door. "If we do find it," he said with a sniff, "I'll own up that my head is in worse shape than you figure Sam's was."

We made a careful search, beginning at the front porch and working our way slowly to the front gate. Jonas hunted with the air of a man who expects no success but he hunted carefully, just the same. When we had crossed the road and had progressed quite a way into the pines I was beginning to wonder if perhaps I had not been wrong, after all.

Jonas pointed to a spot just ahead and shook his head. "There's where we found him, Bill, and if that box ain't between here and there, then it looks as if you've lost your bet."

I nodded and continued to edge along the left-hand side of the path, with Jonas kicking in the bushes to the right. All at once I heard an exclamation and turned to see my companion rising from a stooping position with something in his hand. That something was the sandal-wood box.

"Well, I do swear!" muttered Jonas with an expression on his face of combined amazement and chagrin. "Well, I'll be everlastin'ly blistered! You're right, Bill—and yet, by the Old Harry, everything else is dead wrong! It is—I vow it is!"

My triumph gave me little satisfaction. Obviously my theory that Gregg was insane and, in his mad midnight rush out of doors, had taken the sandalwood box with him, seemed proven now. Why he had taken that particular thing, or anything, was hazard speculation—for me, at that minute. I was beginning to be conscious of an overwhelming weariness.

Jonas would have liked to talk. As we walked back to the house he kept muttering to himself.

"I don't know when I've been so off in my arithmetic," he observed as we entered the front hall. "I was just as certain it wasn't Sam who took that box and that you and I wouldn't find it as I am that the tide'll come in this afternoon. And yet he must have taken it—because here it is. Tut, tut, tut! I better go back to primary school, I guess."

I broke in on his self-depreciation. "Jonas," I said, desperately, "I just can't guess,—or even think, another minute. I haven't slept since God knows when and I'm completely played out. The only thing I am sure of is that I want to locate a nice, broad, downy couch and curl up on it. If you'll excuse me, I think I'll go and find one."

I left him and went upstairs to bed.

The next few days were a nightmare which still remain a blur to me. I do not know what we should have done without Jones. It was he who found Gregg's will in the Orham bank. It was he who made all the arrangements for the funeral and saw that they were carried out. It was he who shouldered all the responsibility and left us with nothing to do but to sit by with folded hands. I had appreciated

Jonas before then I think, but afterwards I regarded him almost with reverence.

Samuel Gregg's will was a simple document, but it was surprising in a way. He had no relatives, it seemed, or none that he wished to remember in a substantial manner. He expressed the desire to be buried in the East Orham cemetery and had set aside enough money to cover the expenses of the ceremony. He left a small amount to a Boston museum, and one thousand dollars to Iantha Hallett. The remainder of his property, which was not extensive, was to go in toto to Mrs. Mary Fisher, Marian's mother.

"She has given a home to a lonely man," he had written in explanation, "and I leave her this small remembrance as a wholly inadequate expression of my very deep gratitude."

Jonas Jones had a great deal of quiet fun with Iantha concerning her unexpected bequest. "I don't understand it," he said with a mournful shake of the head, "I don't like even to think about it. I haven't got what you'd call a jealous disposition, but, honest, Iantha, the thought that a bachelor man should leave a whole pile of money to you, the only steady girl I ever had, is—well, it hurts my feelin's. Of course, I realize there may have been more between you two than I knew about or suspected—"

"Stuff and nonsense!" Iantha broke in, impatiently. "How *can* you talk so unlikely, Jonas Jones! I guess there wasn't anything between me and poor Mr. Gregg, unless it might be a good many plates of hot biscuits. He was a man that liked his food and he had sense enough to be grateful to them that cooked it for him. The milk of human kindness ain't beyond *my* understandin', Jonas Jones, even if it's beyond yours. Somethin' between him and me! The idea!"

Jonas shrugged his shoulders and muttered darkly that he wasn't completely satisfied. "At the same time, Iantha," he added, in conclusion, "I'm man enough to say that I won't let your bein' a thousand dollars richer come between us. No, sir, I'll put up with it as best I can. I've always wondered how I was goin' to be provided for in my old age."

Things swung gradually back to normal. It seemed almost callous the way we accustomed ourselves to the absence of Gregg's genial chatter and to the fact that his chess problem no longer stood upon the table in the library, but I suppose it was only natural. People adjust themselves rapidly to new conditions. Then, too, the strain was gone. It was a relief to be able to go to bed without the uneasy suspicion that sleep might be shattered at any moment by an unearthly scream, or by the sound of a crash somewhere in the lower part of the house.

Marian, in writing to her mother of Gregg's death had not mentioned those strange occurrences. "I couldn't see any sense," she told me, in spoiling her vacation. She'd worry her head off if she knew everything that has been going on here, and she might even feel that she ought to come tearing right home. I just told her the truth, that Mr. Gregg had died suddenly of heart disease, and let it go at that. Now she can have the rest of her visit in peace."

Yes, life was becoming almost pleasant once more, and I had just reached the conclusion that my niblick might serve in a more dignified manner than as a weapon, or as a tool with which to open boxes in the back storerooms, when all at once something happened which sent us off on another hectic, and even more confusing trail.

I was reading a book in the library late one afternoon while Marian was doing an errand in the village, when I heard Iantha calling my name from somewhere upstairs. "Mr. Thornton!" she cried, and there was a noticeable ring of excitement in her voice. "Mr. Thornton, would you mind comin' up here a minute? I want to show you something!"

She was in the room which had belonged to Samuel Gregg. She had a dust cloth in one hand and in the other a small book which she waved as I came in the door. "What do you think I've found?" she demanded eagerly. "What do you think I've just come across right here in this room?"

"It isn't another thousand dollars is it, Iantha?" I asked with a smile. "These seem to be your lucky days."

"How ridiculous you do talk! What would a thousand dollars be doin' kickin' around loose in a table drawer?"

"I don't know, but nothing would surprise me any more. If you turned into a cat at this moment, Iantha, and began to mew, I wouldn't be surprised. I'd just yawn politely and say, 'Well, well, here's some more good clean fun.' I'm past the point where I can be surprised."

"Oh, is that so!" Her chin came up. "Well, I'm not figurin' on turnin' into a cat, or any other critter, but I shouldn't wonder if I could surprise you. just the same. What do you think this is, Mr. Thornton? Look at it."

She handed me what at first glance seemed to be a small commonplace book. It was bound in imitation red pebbled leather which was blotched and spotted as though with mildew. A small slip of paper, now yellow from age, had been pasted in the middle of the front cover, and on it in faded ink were the figures 1883.

"Eighteen-eighty-three," I murmured. "Hum! there's something about that date that seems familiar."

"You don't say!" Iantha snorted, in huge disgust. "Well, if you'll stop starin' at the cover and look on the inside you'll find something that'll be even a mite more familiar, maybe."

I took her advice and opened the volume. On the inside of the front cover were written, obviously by the same hand which had inscribed the date on the yellow slip, the name and address:

"Freeland A. Blair
East Orham, Mass."

A hasty examination of the first few pages showed that they were filled with a series of entries all written in the same small, regular script. Some of them were long and some of them occupied but a line or two. Each entry was prefixed, in the left margin, by a date. The book, obviously, was Freeland Blair's diary for the year 1883.

"Well," I whistled, "this is interesting, sure enough. Wasn't 1883 the year that—"

"It was the year of all our troubles," she interrupted triumphantly, "and that book there is Captain Freeland's diary about it. I knew that he kept one, everybody in the house did, but Aunt Becky and I couldn't find it anywhere after he died. We hunted hard for it, too, because we figured it might tell us somethin' we didn't know about all the awful goin's on. No siree, it had vanished right off the face of the earth, and yet here it is back again, after forty years and more. Now, Mr. Thornton, I guess likely you're ready to say I've surprised you some,—even if I haven't started caterwaulin'."

"You've surprised me, all right," I admitted. "Where on earth did you turn it up?"

"Right in that drawer there." She pointed to the little table beside the bed. "I come across it just now when I was dustin' and cleanin' up."

I frowned. "Do you really suppose that it's been in that table drawer for the last forty years?"

"I know it hasn't." She shook her head emphatically. "I know because that table ain't any more than a year old. Mr. Gregg bought it so's he could read comfortable in bed."

"Then—then—" I was struggling with a new idea—
"you think Gregg must have found it somewhere?"

"That's what I think. Mr. Gregg must have come across
it when he was pawin' around in those things in the attic,
though *where* he come across it beats me. Aunt Becky and
I went through everything with a fine-tooth comb—or we
thought we did. Sam Gregg must have found it and he
must have brought it in here to his room where he could
read it over by himself."

"Why didn't he say anything about it to the rest of
you?"

"Don't ask me, Mr. Thornton." Iantha made an expres-
sive gesture with her hands. "Crazy—crazy! that's the
answer, I guess. All I know is that he must have found it."
She hesitated. "I know something else, too, or I *almost*
know it. I know that Mr. Gregg had been readin' it the
very night when he was struck stark loony and run out
into the front yard."

"What on earth makes you think that?"

"I'll tell you what makes me think so. That mornin'
when you come into the kitchen and told me that—that
something had happened to the poor man, I come right up
here to get the room ready. Things was in a awful mess,
and I wasn't, naturally, payin' attention close to what I was
doin', but I think—yes, I'll almost take my Bible oath—
that that very leather book—Captain Freeland Blair's
diary—was lyin' open on top of this table here. Unless I'm
way off in my rememberin', I slapped it shut and shoved it
into that drawer to get it out of the way. That's what I'm
sure now that I did, although I clean forgot all about it
until I opened the drawer again this afternoon."

I sighed and regarded the diary in perplexity. "Well,"
I confessed, "I'm darn sure it's all beyond me; but I'll tell
you what I'll do. I'll take this thing to my room right now
and read it from cover to cover. It may help to clear up

what was going on before Captain Blair died, and better than that, it may tell us something about what was biting Sam Gregg. We'll give it a try, anyhow."

I crossed the hall to my room, shut the door, and pulled up a chair by the window. I had seated myself and was fumbling for a cigarette before I began to read, when something slipped from between the pages of the small red book and fluttered to the floor. I stooped to retrieve it and saw that it was a letter, a very old letter, addressed to Captain Freeland Blair. The edges of the envelope were yellow with age, and the writing was even more faded than the writing in the diary. The postmark was badly blurred, but at last I was able to make out that the letter had been sent from Boston.

It seemed to me that the letter provided as good a starting point as anything else, so I pulled it from the envelope and spread the crackling sheets of paper open upon my knee. It had been written, as the postmark indicated, in Boston, and the date in the upper corner was January 10, 1884. I began to read, and before I had finished the first paragraph I leaned back in my chair and whistled aloud.

I had tumbled, unaware, upon an old friend.

That letter was the one Iantha had told us about; the one which had come some time after Blair's death; the one containing the mysterious cryptic message. It had been written by the nurse who took care of Burke, mate of the bark *Pride of the Fleet,* during his last illness in a Boston hospital, and its contents were almost exactly as Iantha had remembered. Only the wording of the thrice-relayed, and never-delivered message from George Crossley to Freeland Blair, was different.

According to the nurse's letter, that message was as follows: "Tell him that everything has been done just as we agreed. Tell him that I've hid it safe. Tell him to look for one foot, one hand."

One foot, one hand! I shook my head and marveled. No wonder Aunt Becky and the rest had been unable to make anything out of it. No wonder they had given it up as a bad job and had put the letter away. No wonder—

Once more I whistled, for I had had a sudden startling thought.

What was that letter doing in Freeland Blair's diary? It had arrived after Blair's death, when the diary, according to Iantha, had vanished off the face of the earth. The letter, however, had fallen into Aunt Becky's hands and she had taken care of it. How could the two things have come together after all those years?

I had pondered only a very little while when the whole matter became clearer. Gregg, of course, had found the diary somewhere in the attic. He had discovered the letter in the mass of Aunt Becky's correspondence which Marian had handed over to him later. He had placed the letter in the diary.

It was all very simple—except for one thing.

In answer to Marian's question Gregg had stated flatly that the letter from the nurse was nowhere to be found. He had searched diligently, he assured us, with no success. What was the solution to that? He had lied, obviously, but why had he lied?

"What was the sense in it?" I demanded aloud of four unsympathetic walls. "What in heaven's name was he trying to do?"

I got no response, so I gave it up and turned my attention to the diary itself.

VII

The first few entries, beginning with the one under the date of January 1, 1883, were of no particular interest. They consisted largely of reference to obscure business deals, of notes concerning persons whose names meant nothing to me, and of reiterated expressions of hope that the new year might prove more successful to the writer than the old one had been.

I read hurriedly until I came to the top of the second page, where I found a heavy cross in blue pencil in the margin beside the first item. The pencil marks seemed fresh, I noticed, and I wondered if Gregg had been responsible for them. If so, what did they imply?

"January 10th," the entry opposite began. "Was very much surprised to receive note from George C. today. And more surprised to learn that he is in Boston, for his bark, the Pride of the Fleet, is in San Francisco, loading there for Calcutta. Bliss told me so last month when I was up to Boston and called at their office. Bliss said then that it was their intention to pick up return cargo either at Calcutta or Singapore or Hong Kong and have Crossley bring back bark to Boston because she was in need of overhauling. So I did not expect to see George for months. He must have crossed from Frisco by train, a mighty expensive trip, and one he would not be liable to take without good reason. It hardly seems as if it could be private business that fetched him over, and yet from the little he says in his letter I judge it is partly that, anyhow. He must have money these days. Made a lucky strike somewhere maybe. I wish to God *I* could see any luck ahead. Things are worse and worse. If I do not—" (A line or two scratched out here.) "George writes he is coming down on the morning train to see me on a very important matter for both of us. What that means is too deep for my guess. He knows I am pretty hard up, for I told him a little last time we were together. Of course he nor nobody else knows how hard. Pray the Lord they never will know. Shall meet him at the depot."

That was that, and I was glad to realize that I could make a little sense out of it, at any rate. His "George C.," of course, was the Captain Crossley I had heard so much about, and his remarks about hard luck were understandable enough in the light of what had come out after his death. It was evident, poor bird, that he was seeing the beginning of the end, even then.

The next entry had been made three days later, and was also distinguished by a penciled cross in the margin. I was certain by that time that the crosses were Gregg's work, and I was conscious of growing excitement.

"George C. has gone," Captain Blair informed me in his small neat script. "I have made a plunge that may save me. It is a gambler's chance, but I have got to take chances. It is neck or nothing, and I have agreed to risk $15,000 on it. If I lose I might as well blow my brains out. If I win, and if the gamble is as good as George says it is, it ought to put my head above water and keep it there. He says he is sure the thing is worth at least one hundred thousand, and more likely, half again as much more. Under our agreement he is to have $10,000 himself for putting the deal through. I shall go to Boston tomorrow with the securities and raise the $15,000 cash on them. It takes the last of M's government bonds. Well, if I win she will lose nothing by it, that I take my sworn oath to. The whole yarn as George tells it sounds like a fairy tale, but he vows it is true to the last word."

I wasted no more time with any entries except those marked with the cross, and I found the next one, so marked, under the date of January sixteenth.

"Back home again. Gave G. C. the $15,000 and saw him off for Frisco. He expects to sail from there in about three weeks from now. I shall not hear from him for months, and the waiting is going to be the very devil. He has promised to cable me the word, 'Done' as soon as he has the thing safe in his hands. He will write, too, but it will take Lord knows how long for his letter to get here. That is why I made him promise to cable. He told me more about the thing itself. He is a shrewd fellow and was always a keen hand at a trade, so I do not believe he could be fooled easy. And, besides, he made P. take it to—" (Several lines were scratched here.) "If that man knows his business it must be worth all or more than C. calculates. Well, if it was twice that, I could use every cent."

The plot was thickening too rapidly for me to be able to follow it intelligently, so I read all of the remaining marked items in the little red book without pausing for thought.

"January 17—I couldn't sleep last night but an hour or so. All I could do was think and think about this gamble of ours. It sounds crazier and crazier the more I do think. About the craziest of all is the idea that he should have met up with Ike P. I have not heard of him since my own seafaring days. He was a rascal then, and from what G. C. says, he is a worse one now. Keeping a kind of sailors' boarding-house and thieves' nest on the water front over there. But—how did he ever get hold of such a thing as this? The less questions asked about that the better, I should not wonder. But I am in no shape to be fussy about another man's honesty. If it comes to me and fetches me the money I have got to have, where it came from in the beginning, and whether or not throats were cut in getting it, is the least of my worries. That shows how low I have sunk. Wonder what my father would say if he could know about the boy he used to be so proud of."

The next marked entry was dated more than three months later.

"April 3—No cable from G. C. yet. Things in the market are worse than ever. I am about down to hard pan. Running this place keeps me sailing close to the wind and I barely manage to get by even at that. I am beginning to wish I had not risked the fifteen thousand. If that goes I shall have to go with it. I will not face the disgrace, to say nothing of the punishment."

"May 7—Cable came today. It said 'Done. Have written.' Thank God for that much mercy, at any rate. It means that he has it in his hands at last, and that he will bring it to Boston as fast as the Pride of the Fleet can sail. I am praying for fair-winds."

"July 19—Had another horrible dream last night. I have them in plenty nowadays. Sometimes I think my brain is beginning to go. No letter yet. Should not reasonably expect one for another month or so, but I do just the same. I wonder where the Pride of the Fleet is now. I wish I was aboard her. It came across my mind, after I woke up from that cussed dream, that maybe I ought to write down a little more about the deal with G. C. If anything happens to me before he gets here I should like Rebecca and M. to know that I was trying to square myself. So I am going to set it all down, just as G. C. and I talked it over. G. C.'s yarn was this: When he was in port at —" (Apparently the name of the city had been written here and scratched out very carefully later on)—"a tough looking customer came up to him on the dock one day and called him by name. C. did not know him at first, he was so much older, but then he did. He was a man who had gone cook with me way back when George was second mate. He was a rum-swilling rapscallion even then, a fighter and a regular hellion with women, in spite of his being worse than a cripple. He run away from the ship at Manila and neither of us had seen nor heard from him since. He told G. C. he was keeping boarding-house there at —" (More erasure)—"and that he had been hanging around hoping to meet an American skipper, somebody he knew preferred, because he had something to tell the right kind of

man, something that was well worth hearing and
that meant money. G. paid no attention to him or
his talk at first, but as he was so persistent, at last
he took him aboard the ship and listened to what he
had to say. And, after he had heard it, he went with
him to this boarding hole of his, a regular dive it
was, so G. says, and there Ike showed him—"

It was here that two pages had been torn out of the
book. The entry at the top of the third page began in the
middle of a sentence.

"and was afraid of his life, so G. C. was sure. That
was why he was so anxious to get rid of it right off
and for so little. And he could not, for the same reason, dispose of it there in —" (The name was again
scratched.)—"where they were after him. Finally, C.
and he made a bargain. C. gave him $1,000 in cash.
Partly owners' money it was, but C. was sure he
would not need it till he got home and he knew he
could borrow it personal in Frisco and replace it if
needful. The balance, $14,000, was to be paid over
to Ike when C. came back to that port again, which
he knew he would do within eight months or a year.
Knowing Ike as he did he would not trust him, of
course, so the thing was put in the bank where C.
did business. Neither him nor Ike was to touch it or
reclaim it, without the other, inside of a two year
limit. G. C. had had me in his mind all the time.
Being so sure it was worth upwards of seven times
the $15,000, he was certain I would finance the
rest of the deal and we would both get rich on it.
According to G. C. it is—"

And here a third page had been torn out. In the next, nor in fact in any entry for the next two months was the deal with Crossley mentioned. Then the mentions were but casual and gave no further details. The writing in the diary became steadily more irregular, and the entries briefer and more disjointed. There were frequent prayers for forgiveness from heaven, and over and over again:

"No letter yet. Not one word. Where is the Pride of the Fleet? What *shall* I do! God pity me!"

The final dated entry was November twenty-third. It was only a few lines and so shaky and blotted that I could hardly read it. As nearly as I could make out it was a prayer that the writer's health and sanity might be preserved.

"I am beginning to see faces and hear voices . . . cannot sleep nights . . . must keep going somehow . . . die not yet . . ."

This was the end of the diary proper, and to my mind it was plenty, but at the top of the next page I found something else. In blue pencil, the freshness of which was in sharp contrast to the rust-colored entries preceding it, were a number of notations in a precise, neat handwriting, which I immediately assumed had been made by Samuel Gregg. These were as follows:

"1. Why did not Blair destroy this diary altogether, as he did Crossley's letter, provided the letter Iantha says he received just before his death, was from Crossley? Of course, there is a possibility that that letter might have been from someone else. He said it was from a man named Bangs, but the chances are he lied. Evidently he wrote all particulars concerning his transactions with Crossley in this diary and then lost his courage. He probably erased and tore out pages as a preliminary measure of protection before burning the whole thing. I have no doubt that sudden death alone saved this volume from the fire.

"2. *Probabilities:* That Crossley must have had this 'thing' with him on board Pride of Fleet. That, realizing he was going to die before the voyage was over, Crossley hid it somewhere and hid it well. That he hid it among his personal belongings for he had willed them to Blair and knew they would come to Blair after he died. Hiding it there would be his safest method of transporting it to its destination without confiding in a third person. That his personal belongings were all brought ashore from the wreck and stored first in the barn and then in the attic. That, consequently, they have never been disturbed. That, finally, the 'thing' has never been disturbed either. It is still there.

"*Unless*—1. Valuable item was not hidden in Crossley's personal effects. (I'm almost willing to swear it was. Blair evidently thought so, too, for he was searching among them before his death.) 2. Personal effects were not all brought ashore from the wreck. (I think they were, for the wreck did not break up, according to Iantha, for several days.) 3. Blair found the thing before he died. (For obvious reasons not to be considered seriously.) 4. Valuable item was taken when barn was robbed shortly after salvage from wreck had been stored there. (I doubt this, for it would have been pure luck on the part of the thief. Is, however, a bare possibility.) 5. Valuable item left house with things we have sold to Jenkins, Blodgett, and Jones. (This is very possible, and I must my best to reclaim them. Jones has Chinese cabinet. Sorry for that. Shall offer him a high price for it. A rare piece, in any event.)

"3. I would give almost anything for a list of Crossley's personal belongings. It will be almost impossible, without it, to sort those belongings from the great mass of odds and ends in the attic. There are certain things, of course, which I am sure belonged to Crossley, such as the Buddha, the sea chest, and the sandalwood box. Must examine them at once. The lack of the list above mentioned is what makes this puzzle most difficult. It will be like hunting for a needle in a haystack.

"4. *Very Important*. I must fix my attention on the letter from the mate's nurse to Captain Blair. I must concentrate on the message—'Look for one foot one hand.' This is not as foolish as it sounds, in my opinion. Probably the key to the puzzle, and if it had reached Blair before his death would have enabled him to find what he was looking for. I must learn to use it."

That was the end. The remainder of the pages in the diary were blank.

For a long time after I had finished my reading I sat there with the little red book on my knee and stared aimlessly out of the window. I am not sure what I was thinking. There was a great confusion of facts, probabilities, and possibilities in my mind, all so new and so startling that I could not classify them. I was conscious, too, of a constantly growing excitement; of an urge to be up and doing, if only I could determine what was the sensible thing to do.

I pawed hastily through the pages of the diary once more, reading small snatches here and smaller snatches there, and learning absolutely nothing. I felt like some castaway upon a desert island who had stumbled upon half a map leading to a hidden treasure; a map which told him a little but nowhere near enough.

At the height of this disturbing mental condition I spied Marian coming in the drive in the flivver and I had a sudden idea. I shoved the diary and the letter into my coat pocket, dashed down the front stairs and out the door. The little car had no more than come to a stop when I reached it, and I jumped into the front seat before Marian could cut off the motor.

"Keep moving," I ordered breathlessly. "Give her the gas and take me down to Jonas Jones's shop as fast as you can get there!"

"Why, Bill!" She instinctively slipped the lever into first speed and we began to move. "What is the matter with you? What on earth has happened?"

"Nothing!" I laughed. "Nothing unpleasant, I mean. Tell you about it when we get there. Step on it, will you please?"

We made an undignified descent upon Jonas, who was working on a table in his back room. As I came bustling in the door with Marian at my heels he glanced up and whistled in surprise. "Well, well!" he observed, putting down his sandpaper. "What's up? You look, Bill, as if you'd stepped on a crab, or somethin'."

"He looks worse than that," replied Marian with some annoyance. "If you ask me, I'd say he'd gone completely off his trolley."

"Is that so!" I reached into my pocket and pulled out the diary in the manner of a magician producing a rabbit from a tall hat. "Well, what would you think if I told you that I'd found Freeland Blair's diary for the year 1883—or at least that Iantha had found it?"

"Oh, is that all." Marian shrugged her shoulders disgustedly. "I thought at least you'd found a million dollars or so. Why all the excitement about an old diary?"

"Wait a minute, Marian." Jonas Jones, as usual, had his wits about him. "Wasn't 1883 the year Captain Freeland died? Wasn't that the year when this mystery of ours first stuck its head out of the hole?"

"Why, so it was!" Marian was interested at last. "Does the diary explain anything, Bill? Where did Iantha find it?"

I sighed with exaggerated patience and placed the volume on the table. "If," I suggested sarcastically, "you will lay off on the insults and quit asking a hundred foolish questions a second I'll be glad to tell you all I know about everything."

They subsided then and gave me the floor, so I told them of Iantha's discovery. I explained that it was evident Gregg had made the original find. I produced the letter from Burke's nurse and read it to them as a sort of appetizer.

"Well, now!" exclaimed Jonas. "What do you know about that! So old Sam found that letter, after all, and kept mum about it. Kept mum about the diary, too, didn't he. . . . Humph! Surprisin'!"

"Surprising enough," I admitted with relish, "but not so surprising as some other things. Wait until I read you some of the more interesting entries from this old diary. Just prick up your little white ears and listen to them!"

They listened.

I read nothing but the entries marked with the blue crosses, and I read them slowly and distinctly. When I had finished my audience was silent, observing me with fascinated eyes. "And now," I observed gently, "we will close with a brief but careful consideration of a few notes and observations written in neat blue pencil by the late Mr. Samuel Gregg. Your attention, please."

The request was unnecessary. They hung breathlessly upon my every word, and when the last one had been spoken they gazed at each other and at me in increasing wonder.

"Well, well, well!" Jonas whistled softly between his teeth. "What do you know about that! By the Old Harry! That certainly does beat the Dutch—and you know what they say the Dutch beat. Well, I'll be blistered!"

Marian seemed to be struggling with some strong emotion. "Why—why—" she stammered. "Why, Bill!"

I smiled. I was enjoying the sensation I had created. "Can it be possible," I inquired sweetly, "that the mere prospect of finding a hundred thousand dollars or so lying about the house somewhere has aroused your interest? You amaze me!"

Marian paid no attention to my persiflage. She crossed over to me, her eyes shining, and shook my arm. "Bill, do you think it's possible? Do you really think there's a chance of anything like that?"

"It looks very much that way, doesn't it?"

"Come on, then!" She almost dragged me toward the door. "You come along too, Mr. Jones!"

"Here, here! Heave to a minute, Marian!" Jonas had taken the diary from my hand and was studying it earnestly. "Where are we headin' for? What are you aimin' to do?"

"What am I aiming to do?" She laughed excitedly. "Why, I'm aiming to go home and find that thing, whatever it is. I'll take everything in the house to pieces if I have to, but I'll find it somewhere."

"Yes, yes! . . . Well, I know how you feel." Jonas nodded. "I know just how you feel and I don't blame you. I'm pretty much the same way myself; only, you see, I've lived a couple of hundred years longer than you young folks and I've found out that it generally pays, afore you jump, to calculate where the jump will land you. Where was you plannin' to hunt, Marian, when you got home?"

"Why"—the question seemed to confuse her—"why, I hadn't exactly thought. I'll look through all the old stuff, I suppose. All the old stuff we've put around the house and everything that's left in the attic."

"That'll take quite a spell of lookin', won't it? There is an awful pile of that stuff if I recollect right."

"What of it? I'd tear the whole of East Orham to pieces for a hundred thousand dollars."

"So would I." He nodded again. "I would, that is, if I thought there was any chance of my findin' it that way— or if I couldn't find it any easier way."

"Easier way? What do you mean?"

Jonas scratched his head. "Well, I'll tell you how this business strikes me. There's a lot of things in this diary of Captain Freeland's, a lot of things—some of 'em loomin' up clear and some pretty much in the fog. I haven't had any time to figure 'em out yet, of course, but, even now, it looks to me as if there were reefs in the channel, it ain't goin' to be all plain sailin'. Now, honest, don't you think we might save time in the end if we set down and reckoned up what we do know, and what we don't know, before we run for the ax and started to smash up all the furniture in me old Blair house? What do you say, Bill?"

Like Marian, I craved action, but I could see that Jonas was right. "I suppose we ought to have some plan," I agreed; "but let's make it snappy."

"Good enough." Jonas went to his desk, took out paper and pencil, and sat down. Marian sighed impatiently and sat down also.

"Let's start this job arithmetic fashion," he began. "Let me tell you, first off, what *I* get out of this diary of

Captain Freeland's, and you two listen and see if you get the same things." He began to turn the pages of the little red book slowly. "The first thing I get out of it is something that I knew before, and that is that poor old Blair had used up most of the money that rightfully belonged to Mary Fisher, her that was Mary Blair then. He had only about fifteen thousand left, he says, and he decided to risk all of that on a gamble that George Crossley put up to him. He says that, himself, don't he? Yes. All right then, what was the gamble? As far as we can tell it had to do with some 'thing' that Crossley said he could pick up cheap in a foreign port. He would have to pay fifteen thousand for it over there, but he was sure it would be worth seven times that much in the States. What would such a thing be, do you suppose?"

"Diamonds!" cried Marian. "Buckets of diamonds!"

Jonas grinned. "Maybe you're right. Anyhow it was something that this man, Ike, who must have been a tough customer, had got hold of and was willing to sell. Not much doubt but what he stole it in the beginning, but that's neither here nor there for us, now. The important part is that Crossley raised the fifteen thousand from Captain Freeland, handed it over to friend Ike, who handed him the 'thing.' We can be sure of that much because we know Crossley cabled the word 'Done' to Blair. And I judge we can bet our spare change that Crossley took the 'thing' aboard ship with him and set sail for Boston.

"So far, so good, but what else do we know?" Jonas leaned back in his chair and stared at the ceiling. "We know that Captain Freeland got pretty nigh crazy with worry as time went on and he didn't hear nary a word from Crossley. The *Pride of the Fleet* bein' so long overdue didn't help his peace of mind, neither. Then, accordin' to Iantha's tell, the old man finally got a letter that cheered

him up considerable. We can guess that it was from Crossley, but we can't be sure, and anyhow it's gone for good
now."

"Do you think that letter is important, Jonas?" I interrupted. "Do you think it would be worth our while to
hunt for it?"

He shook his head. "It would be interestin' to see, of
course, but when Crossley wrote that letter, remember, he
didn't know he was goin' to die. He thought he was going to bring the 'thing' home and hand it over, personal,
to Captain Freeland; so he probably didn't say anything
about hiding it anywhere. And, anyhow, it was most likely
burnt up. Let's stick to our knittin', and see what happened next."

"What happened next was the wreck of the ship," Marian put in, impatiently. "We know all about that."

"Yes, she come aground here in East Orham and she
stayed in one piece for a considerable number of days before she broke up in another storm. The stuff from the
cabins was brought up to your house and stored there.
Captain Freeland, who was a mighty sick man, finally
learned about the wreck and that George Crossley was
dead. That news finished him. The thing he had counted
on to save him from ruination was gone, and he couldn't
find it. He pawed around in Crossley's goods some, but I
think it's safe to say that he died without ever finding it.
Then what?"

"Then came that message from the mate," I said. "Can
you make anything out of that at all, Jonas? Gregg said in
his notes, you know, that he thought it was the key to the
puzzle."

"Well, I tell you, Bill." He scowled in concentration.
"Of course that message ought to have a lot of time spent
on it, but right now, not havin' given it any time at all,

it looks to me like this: When the voyage was about half
over, Crossley began to think that he wasn't goin' to live
to reach port, so he did what almost any man would do.
He hid that thing somewhere, and he hid it good. He had
to tell Captain Freeland somehow where he had hid it, and
not darin' to write a letter or to take anybody else into the
know, he gave the mate a message to carry. He knew that
Burke couldn't make head nor tail out of it and he didn't
want him to. He must have been pretty darn sure, on the
other hand, that Blair could."

"Then you agree with Gregg," I asked, "that if Captain Freeland had received that message before he died he
would have been able to find the 'thing'?"

"I don't know, Bill." He shook his head doubtfully.
"That's just the point I can't be sure about at all. He might
have found it if he'd had the message, and on the other
hand, he might not."

"I don't see that at all," Marian objected vigorously. "It
seems to me that the message wouldn't have been sent if
it hadn't been clear enough to be of use to Captain Blair.
What would have been the sense in it?"

"It was probably sense all right, Marian, but you're forgetting one important thing. When Crossley worked up
and sent that message, he thought the *Pride of the Fleet*
was going to come safe to port in Boston. He didn't know
she was going to be wrecked, remember."

"What of it?"

"Just this. He might have hid that hundred thousand
dollar 'thing' of theirs under the floor boards of his cabin. In that case, even if the message had come to Captain
Freeland, clear as crystal, it wouldn't have done him any
good with the ship scattered in two-foot lengths from here
to Race Point."

"Then why did he hunt through all that stuff in the
attic?"

Jonas was patient. "He never got the message before he died, so he didn't have anything to go on."

"But," I pointed out eagerly, "Gregg says in his notes that the thing was hidden in Crossley's personal goods."

"I know he does, but he didn't have proof of it. He was just guessin'. I'm not sayin' it wasn't good guessin', mind you, but I'm sayin' there isn't anything to back it up. No, sir, that precious 'thing'—a barrel of diamonds, or whatever it was, may still be hid in the stuff from the *Pride of the Fleet,* but on the other hand it may be soakin' in twenty fathom of wet salt water."

We looked at him in dismay. We realized, of course, that his reasoning was perfectly sound but we resented it, at the same time. Marian voiced something of our feeling. "What of it?" she inquired with asperity. "Just because this thing may be lost at the bottom of the sea isn't going to make us fold our hands and do nothing, is it? It surely isn't going to stop us from doing what we can."

"No." Jonas shook his head. "Of course it isn't. I just told you all this because I don't want you to think you can run home and find your keg of diamonds in about one minute. I want you to realize that you may find it only after a long, hard, pretty blind hunt—and maybe never."

"Don't worry!" Marian laughed good-naturedly. "You've succeeding in ruining a perfectly good day, and now I want to know what we *are* going to do about it. What's the next move?"

"The next move, as far as I can see, is to get on the band wagon along with Samuel Gregg. We'll agree, because it's the only thing we can do, that he was right in guessin' that the thing was hid, and still is hid, in George Crossley's belongin's. Let's have another look at Gregg's notes." He turned to those pages of the diary which were covered with neat, blue-penciled writing. "You'll notice," he continued, "that underneath Sam's 'pretty sures' are a whole lot of 'unlesses.'"

"They're just like your bottom of the sea proposition," Marian pointed out. "We'd might as well forget them."

"We'd might as well forget most of them, I'll grant you, but there's one 'unless' that hits my eye. Sam says, 'unless valuable item left house with things we have just sold to Jenkins, Blodgett, and Jones.' What about that?"

"We must buy those things back," I said. "I think we ought to do it even if they cost a lot more than we sold them for. We can't afford not to."

"Right." He nodded approvingly. "We'll set out to do that right away, but first let's look at one more of these notes of Sam's. He says here that he'd give almost anything for a list of Crossley's goods, because it'll be so hard to sort 'em out from all the rest of that stuff in the attic. He says that that's the worst part of the whole puzzle, and I don't know but what I agree with him. There isn't a list of that stuff anywhere around, is there?"

"Not that I know of," said Marian doubtfully. "I never heard of it if there is one." She had a sudden idea. "What about Iantha?" she demanded. "Iantha was here when the wreck happened and she helped put the things in the attic. She should remember some of them. Let's go back right this minute and ask her."

"I'd thought of Iantha," Jonas admitted, "and I guess she's the ticket. Anyhow, she's the only ticket we have. She may be able to remember a little somethin', even after forty years and more. She'll remember all her heathen idols, that's sure. She groans about 'em enough. She's tied her 'curse' tag on every one of *them.*"

Marian demanded immediate action, so we decided to go back to the house, taking Jonas with us. He was struggling into his coat and vest when all at once he looked at me and grinned. "Tell me, Bill," he inquired, "what do you think of Sam Gregg now?"

"What do I think of Sam Gregg?" I had no notion what he was talking about. "What do you mean?"

"I mean, what do you think of the state of his mind. Do you still think he was off his nut all that time before he died?"

I had not thought about the matter at all, as a matter of fact, but now that he put me the question I considered it swiftly and was forced to smile. "Well, Jonas," I admitted, "I'm beginning to have my doubts. Reading this diary and his notes at the end of it, does put a new light on some of the things that he did."

He chuckled. "Sort of clears up what he was doin' down in the library that night with the Buddha, don't it?"

"Yes, and it clears up why he stayed in his room the way he did. It also explains why he stole Harvey Blodgett's clock and smashed it up at the foot of the drive. He was hunting for the 'thing.'"

"Well, I swear!" Jonas whistled. "I declare I'd forgot about that business of Blodgett's clock." He frowned. "I suppose it does explain that; though I'll be blessed if I can picture meek little Sam Gregg breakin' into somebody's house and stealin' things. It don't seem like him, but I suppose you can't tell what a man will do for a heap of money. Yes. Yes, that's so; it all hangs together."

"All," I agreed, "except one thing. I don't yet understand why Gregg ran away out into those pines with that sandalwood box the night he died."

"No more do I, but there's a lot of landmarks lost in the fog yet. Perhaps they'll all blow clear in the course of time. Who knows?"

We all went back to the house together and questioned Iantha. We told her something about what had been found in the diary, admitted that there was just a faint possibility that there might be something valuable hidden among

Captain Crossley's things, and asked her to tell us what she remembered of them.

She was tremendously excited, of course, and very eager to help us, but it was soon evident that her memory had dimmed with the years. There must have been a list once, she believed, because Judge Saunders and Mr. Bliss had checked over what they left in the Blair barn, but she had never seen it—nor, she was sure, had Aunt Becky or Jethro Gould. There were certain things such as the sea chest, the wooden Buddha, the bronze elephant, the Chinese cabinet, and the sandalwood box, which she remembered perfectly and identified without hesitation as having belonged to Captain Crossley. There were a great number of pieces, however, both scattered about the house and remaining in the storerooms, that she could not be sure about.

"There's so *much* stuff," she confessed at last, "that it gets all hashed up in my head like—like mincemeat, kind of. First off, I thought I could recollect everything, but now it seems I can't. It does beat all how a body can forget."

Jonas consented to stay for supper, and we spent the evening in examining the things of which we could be sure. The sea chest was given a thorough inspection but it revealed nothing. "I didn't have much hopes that we'd find anything here," said Jonas. "In the back of my head that consarned message keeps jumpin' up and down. 'Look for one foot, one hand,' it says, and there's no hands nor feet on this box, that's sure."

"If hands and feet are all you're looking for," I snorted, "there are enough of them to drive you crazy. There are hands on the Buddha, there were hands on Blodgett's clock; and there are hands *and* feet on all those inlaid ivory figures on the sandalwood box; and feet on the bronze elephant, feet on all the chairs, tables—"

"Hush, Bill," he begged me. "Hush. Don't tell me about all of 'em or I'll go crazier than old Freeland ever was. Let's take 'em one at a time and do the best we can."

It was after midnight when we finally admitted defeat. We had found nothing, although we had done everything to the things which we knew, or suspected had come from the *Pride of the Fleet,* except attack them with a hatchet. Jonas would not hear of that.

"There's time enough," he declared, picking up his hat, "without choppin' up a lot of good antiques. If this 'thing' is still here, it has been here forty-four years and I guess it can wait while we move slow and do some real thinkin'." He turned to the door. "We're licked tonight, all right, but we're not through yet, by a long shot. I'll figure over that message some more when I get home, and I'll have another go at the diary. In the meantime, you folks go to bed and sleep easy and peaceful without botherin' your heads about such trifles as a couple of hogsheads of diamonds. I'll be back first thing in the mornin'."

We took his advice and went to bed. I for one did not rest peacefully, for my sleep was troubled with dreams. It would have been troubled a great deal more, however, had I had any inkling what I was to find when I next came downstairs.

VIII

Like a small boy on the morning of the Fourth of July I awoke very early, conscious that there was something about which to be excited but not able for the moment to remember what it was. I lay on my back for a time, blinking dazedly at the ceiling and wondering at the complete stillness of the house. Then all at once the happenings of the day before returned to me and I leaped out of bed.

Disregarding the fact that there would be no breakfast for more than an hour, I dressed hurriedly and crept to the head of the front stairs. There was a vague idea in my head of examining the sandalwood box and other things at my leisure. Perhaps—who knew?—I might be able to fill Marian's glass with diamonds in place of her customary orange juice. That would be a thoughtful little touch, I reflected, and one that should please her.

I trotted cheerfully down the stairs and through the door into the living-room. Then I came to a complete and flabbergasted stop. If such gymnastics are physically possible, I am sure that my eyes bulged from their sockets.

That living-room was in a state of considerable disorder. My sandalwood box lay on the floor in a far corner with its trays and drawers piled in a heap beside it. A lamp and some other small articles which had been on the top of a small stand near the fireplace were now resting on the bricks of the hearth. The top of the stand itself, I noticed in my first bewildered survey, had been removed and placed on the seat of a near-by chair. An overturned box lay beside another table, with its contents—a number of Japanese pictures painted and embroidered on silk—scattered about the carpet.

I rubbed my eyes and stared. I wandered aimlessly from one pile of debris to another, swearing softly under my breath. Then I turned and flew, like a homing pigeon, to the telephone. I suppose it must, by this time, have become an instinct with me, in moments of emergency, to summon Jonas Jones.

"Jonas," I said quickly when his voice came to me over the wire, "I wish you'd hop over here in a hurry, I'm in over my head again."

"In over your head?" His voice sounded anxious. "What do you mean, Bill? Has somethin' more happened? Don't tell me there's somebody else missin', or hurt!"

"No, it isn't as bad as that, but it's bad enough. Some one evidently busted in here last night and took the place to pieces to see what makes it go. You never saw such a mess!"

"Good Lord!" He seemed almost as amazed as I felt. "Well, I'll be blistered! More thievin', eh? Anything gone?"

"I don't know. I just came downstairs this minute and haven't had a chance to look. All I know is that my head is buzzing."

"I should think it might. Tut, tut! Sho! Now who on earth—? . . . Well, I'll be over in half a shake. Meantime don't touch anything. Let every thing lay right where it is. Tut, tut; . . . Well, now, don't this beat all!"

The more I looked about me after I had hung up the receiver the more I agreed with him. It certainly did beat all! I was standing helplessly in the midst of the clutter in the living room when Marian, fully dressed, appeared in the doorway. She stared about her and shook her head sadly.

"What in *heaven's* name, Bill," she demanded, "have you been doing? Have you gone crazy?"

"I think so," I replied. "I'm almost positive of it, in fact."

"I should think you might be. Do you honestly think you can find my treasure by spilling everything all over the floor?"

"Oh, I see what's troubling you." I smiled grimly. "You think I'm responsible for this. Well, I'm not."

"You're *not!* Why—why—" She ran over to me. "You didn't? Then, who—"

"Don't ask me who. Don't ask me anything, because I don't know anything, except that I found this room just as you see it."

"But—but somebody must have broken in!"

"It looks that way."

"But why?"

I sank wearily into a chair. "You win again, because I give up. Jones is on his way over here now, thank the Lord, and perhaps he'll be able to make some sense out of it all. I can't."

We were still sitting there asking each other foolish questions, when Jonas appeared at the porch door. I let him in, and after he had said good morning he glanced about the room and shook his head. "Well, I swear!" he observed reflectively. "Humph! . . . I *do* swear and that's a fact! . . . Say, this is a nice new kettle of fish, now isn't it?"

"It's all of that," I agreed, "and what's more, I'll tell you what I'm going to do. I'm going to put an ad in the paper saying, 'Plain and fancy mysteries for sale at the old Blair house, East Orham. Prices low, as owner is leaving town. Can you make anything of this particular mystery, Mr. Sherlock H. Jones?"

He looked up from a window he was examining and nodded. "I can make out that, whoever your sociable friend was last night, he got in this way. If you look close you can see the marks of his special patent latchkey on the outside of the sash right here!"

"Interesting," I admitted, "but not new nor particularly illuminating. What we want to know is, who was he, and why did he call?"

"Do we? Yes, I shouldn't wonder if we did, now you mention it." Jonas nodded again, calmly, and bent over the sandalwood box. "That's some of what we all want to know, I give in. . . . Well, Bill, maybe if we take things slow, and one at a time, perhaps we might find out here and there an item." He picked up the little trays and drawers, one after another, from the floor, turned them over in his hands, and slipped them back in their places. "Was there anything in this box, Marian?" he asked. "Anything you'd figure anybody might be particular anxious to steal?"

"No. It was absolutely empty, as far as I know."

"Yes? . . . Well, it looks to me as if your callin' friend had a notion there might be somethin'. Ye-es, it does. Now what—?"

He shoved his hands deep into his pockets and went over to the small stand by the fireplace. "He had a squint at the insides of this nice little piece, too," he observed reflectively. "Pretty little table, afore he got after it."

The stand was one of the articles I had brought down from the attic. It was of shiny black lacquer, and the front of its single drawer was inlaid with mother of pearl. The top, which Jonas picked up from the chair, was also decorated with mother of pearl. Black and white squares of the material alternated on its surface to form the design of a chessboard.

"Humph!" he grunted. "This looks as though it had been made to order for Sam Gregg to play with. Didn't belong to Sam, did it?"

Marian answered. "No," she said, "we found it up in the attic."

Jonas moved the drawer in and out absently. "Your new friend took the top off," he pointed out. "Yes, and you'll notice he did a real neat job of it. . . . Humph! I wouldn't say 'twas hard to guess why he did it, either. See here!"

We looked over his shoulder and saw what he meant. The drawer of that stand did not extend to the full depth of the box, but ended at a partition about three inches from the back. The remaining space would not have been accessible unless the top of the table had been removed.

"That hole might be a nice place to hide somethin', mightn't it?" Jonas asked, exploring the compartment with his hand. "There's nothin' hid there now, though, that's sure."

"Look here!" I demanded excitedly, "do you think—"

He stopped me with a wave of that same hand. "I'm not thinkin' anything yet, Bill, and I don't want to. No use to begin addin' up till we've put down whatever figures are in sight. Let's finish our lookin' first."

We looked at the Japanese pictures next, which were interesting enough from an artistic point of view. There were perhaps a half dozen of them, done on stiffened pieces of silk. The scenes were painted in formal Japanese manner, and each was embellished with bits of beautiful silk embroidery, portions of which having been heavily stuffed, stood out in bold relief.

"I suppose," said Jonas when he had gathered the pictures up and laid them on a neat pile on the sofa, "that these were dug out of the attic, too. Kind of look as though they had been."

Marian nodded. "I'd almost forgotten it, but we did bring them down from upstairs. We thought they were rather pretty, as well as being curiosities."

"Look here—" I began again hurriedly, but once more Jonas stopped me.

"Steady as she is, Bill," he advised. "Let's stick to the main channel for a while yet. These things may tell us somethin' else we want to know."

He was turning the pictures over slowly, one at a time. Suddenly he paused and uttered an exclamation. The scene which he held in his hand had for its background a large embroidered representation of Fujiyama. In its original state the mountain must have stood out more than half an inch from the silk, but now it had been ripped from base to peak with some sharp instrument, and most of the stuffing had been taken out.

"Aha!" muttered Jonas. "See that? Yes, yes; just about what I expected to find."

He riffled hastily through the rest of the pictures, and gathered them together. "And now," he said decisively, "I wonder if we couldn't have a short session with Iantha? She's downstairs by this time, isn't she?"

"I think I heard her out in the kitchen," said Marian. "But, Jonas, what do you want of her? You don't want her to come in here now—and see all this mess—and ask questions? Oh, I hope you don't! Her nerves are only just beginning to settle down; they have been, as you know, positively standing on end since Mr. Gregg's death. Now they are subsiding a little bit; I haven't heard her mention the family 'curse' for almost a week. But if she should learn that there has been *another* robber, or whatever he was, in this house—well, I should just have to go *out* of the house, that's all. I simply couldn't stand it."

"Marian's right, Jonas; she mustn't know," I put in, emphatically. "She wouldn't sleep, she wouldn't eat, and, worse than all, she wouldn't stop talking. Iantha's all right in her way—nobody is stronger for her than I am—but this is one of the times when her ignorance is bound to be our bliss. We've got to keep her out of it, if we possibly can, for a while anyway. Don't you see?"

Obviously Jonas saw. He nodded.

"Sure, sure!" he agreed, heartily. "She mustn't be told, not yet, that's a fact. . . . Well, maybe she won't have to be. Bill, we've seen about all there is to see this minute, so far as these things are concerned. Let's you and I set 'em straight again, 'twon't take but a jiffy."

With Marian's help he and I put the pictures back in their case, picked up the lamp, and generally brought a semblance of order to the room. As a finishing touch Jonas set the top of the lacquer stand in place, although of course he made no attempt to fasten it.

"There!" said he. "Now everything's ready for the Uncle Tom show, isn't it? Looks so to me. Good enough! H'ist the curtain and you two set around and look careless while I go fetch little Eva."

He hurried out of the room and, a few minutes later, he reappeared, ushering in Iantha, who was talking steadily.

"And if you can tell me, Jonas Jones," she was saying, "what in the wide, wide world you're doin' over here at this hour in the mornin', and why you drag me away from my breakfast cookin', and— Oh, good mornin', Marian! Good mornin', Mr. Thornton. Well, maybe you can tell me: Is this man struck silly as he sounds or what is it all about, anyhow?"

It was Jones who answered. He put his arm about her shoulder, or would have done so had she not pushed it impatiently away. "Iantha," he said, tenderly, "don't you understand yet, after all my explainin'? Haven't I told you the dream I had about you, about you havin' given me the go-by and taken up with another fellow? I woke up from that dream with the tears runnin' down my face, and thinks I, 'I must see Iantha right off and find out it isn't so.' So over I came, runnin' every step of the way, and—"

"Oh!" Iantha gave him another push. "Can't you ever talk sense, Jonas Jones?" she demanded. "Marian, for

mercy sakes, you tell me. What is he doin' here and what
do you and him want of me?"

Marian rose to the occasion. She even laughed. "Why,
Jonas had some more questions he wanted to ask about
those things from the wreck," she said. "He came over to
ask you, for of course he knew you would be up early. When
he found we were up, too, he stopped to talk with us."

"Oh! . . . Well, there's some sense to that, even if there
ain't much. I should have thought them questions might
have waited until we'd all had a mouthful to eat. They
must be dreadful important. What are they? Come, you
Jonas, hurry up and ask 'em! I've got things to do."

Without further persiflage Jonas pointed to the lacquer
stand and asked her directly whether or not it had come
from the *Pride of the Fleet*. She did not think so at first,
but after an extended probing into the shadowy places
of her memory she was inclined to reverse her opinion.
"Seems as if it must have," she admitted. "All shiny black
like it is, and with that pearl stuff set in all over it, it must
have come from foreign parts somewhere, that's sure. I
wouldn't wonder a mite if it came in that wreck stuff. But
there! I just can't say for certain."

She was much more positive concerning the Japanese
pictures. "I remember them now," she affirmed, with an
emphatic nod of the head, "just as clear as day. I snum, I
don't understand why I forgot 'em when you asked me all
those questions last night! I remember Jethro Gould and
me lookin' at 'em when we brought 'em in from the barn
to the attic, and I remember my sayin' that they weren't
my idea of Christian pictures. Yes, I know they come from
the *Pride of the Fleet*. I don't have to think twice about it."

Jonas thanked her for her help, and would have again
dilated upon his "dream," but she bustled off to the kitch-
en declaring that in all probability her toast was "all
dried up to splinters by this time." Marian and I stood

and looked at one another perplexedly when she had gone. Jones, however, seemed moderately satisfied.

"And a part of that's that," he announced, with a nod. "We don't know much, but we know what we know." He pointed first to the sandalwood box, then to the pictures, and last to the lacquer stand. "We know that that came from the wreck of George Crossley's bark; we know that that did, too; and we've got pretty fair reasons for guessin' the same thing about the stand. Now what does the whole thing tell us?"

"It tells us," said I, "just what I've been trying to say for the last half hour. It tells us that someone else is in on the party. It tells us that there's somebody besides ourselves hunting for the 'thing' that Freeland Blair—yes, and Sam Gregg, were hunting for. But how—"

Jonas lifted his hand. "Let the 'hows' wait a second, Bill," he broke in. "What you've just said is the answer to one 'why,' as I reckon it. The fellow who broke in here last night didn't come to steal whatever stood handiest. He came to look for somethin' 'special; that's *why* he came."

Marian gasped and struggled for expression. "But, but—"

"Yes," I began. "What—"

"I know, I know." He waved us to silence. "Of course there's a 'what'; just the same as there's more 'whys' and a 'who,' and 'when,' and 'where,' and a million other questions. We're afloat without a compass, and maybe driftin' onto a lee shore—I know it, same as you do. Seems almost as if we ought to do somethin' about it, don't it?"

"You bet it does!" cried Marian. "I'm not going to let somebody else get my diamonds. Not if I can help it!"

"Granting that we've got to do something," I put in, "will you please tell me what it's going to be?"

Jones's right eyebrow lifted. He scratched his head. "Well," he drawled, "first off, why wouldn't it be a good start if you two went and had your breakfast?"

"Breakfast!" we protested almost in chorus. "We don't want any breakfast."

"I know," he said, "but it's all ready, and if you don't eat it Iantha will ask questions. I've had my breakfast, so I'll have a chance while you're eatin' yours, to take the pieces of this new puzzle and try to put 'em together a little closer. Then, when you've done, we can set down together and have another committee meetin' same as we had yesterday afternoon. How does that strike you?"

It did not strike us at all, but we finally agreed, just to please him, and went off to the dining-room. Neither of us was able to eat. We stirred our food about and talked trivialities for Iantha's benefit, and were more than glad when we were permitted to leave the table.

We found Jonas seated at the desk in the library with his inevitable piece of paper and pencil. He motioned to us to come in and to shut the door. Then he rubbed his chin thoughtfully and proceeded to business.

"Well," he began, "I've done a lot of figurin' and more scratchin' out and I don't know as any of it has got me anywhere. This whole business is so mixed up in my head that I can't seem to straighten it—yet. Perhaps you young folks can help me."

"Shoot!" said I, drawing up a chair for Marian and one for myself. "What do you want to know?"

"I want to know what the first question you asked yourself was, after you came to realize that somebody besides us was huntin' for George Crossley's hundred-thousand-dollar 'thing.'"

"That's easy," I replied. "I wanted to know, and I still want to know, how anybody else got hold of the dope. I want to know where he got his information."

"Fair enough. That was the first thing that hit me, too. Now, have either of you got any half-way satisfyin' answer to that question?"

"I don't think there's much mystery about it," said Marian. "Somebody must have overheard us yesterday when we read the letter and the diary in your shop. He must have heard all our talk, and he must have decided to beat us to it."

"I see. . . . Yes, there's a bare chance of that," Jonas admitted with a doubtful shake of his head; "but some way or other I can't make myself believe it really happened."

"Why not?"

"Well, in the first place, whoever did the listenin' must have slid himself into the front room of my shop awful quiet, and he must have eased himself out the same way. It don't seem likely that we wouldn't have heard him just as quick and as plain as he heard us. Not only that, but there's other objections to the whole notion." He tapped his pencil thoughtfully on the top of the desk. "Just stop a minute, Marian, and think what this fellow you had here last night did after he had got into the house. He looked at the sandalwood box, the Jap pictures, and the lacquer stand. That's what he looked at, and that's *all* he looked at."

"What of it? If he was hunting for the treasure, he'd be bound to look at things from the wreck, wouldn't he?

"He would—and he did." Jonas nodded emphatically. "But the thing that stumps me is—how did he know that the Jap pictures and the lacquer stand came from the *Pride of the Fleet?* He didn't find out from us, that's sure and certain, because we didn't even know it ourselves until this mornin'."

I whistled. "That's an idea! It makes it look as though our caller got his dope from somebody besides us, all right."

"Then where did he get it?" Marian demanded rebelliously. "Nobody else knew but Mr. Gregg, and he's dead."

"Wait a minute!" I cried excitedly. "Isn't it possible that Gregg might have told somebody else about the whole thing before he died? He could have had a partner, couldn't he?"

"Of course!" Marian agreed eagerly. "That's exactly what must have happened. Why on earth didn't we think of it before?"

Jonas smiled. "Easy! Let's not go too fast. I'll give in that Sam Gregg's havin' had a partner looks mighty likely when you first think of it, but the more you think the less likely it looks. For instance now—what reason would Sam have had for tellin' anybody?"

I had an answer for that. "Just this. You remember his note at the end of the diary, don't you, where he said that he must get back the stuff he had sold to Blodgett, Jenkins, and you, because of the chance that the 'thing' might be hidden in some of it?"

"Sure I do! What about it?"

"Wait. Suppose he tried to buy something back from you, for instance, and you wouldn't sell at any price. What could he do then? He could either steal the thing from you, as he stole Blodgett's clock, or he could take you into the secret. See what I mean? Gregg may have been forced to spill the whole works, and as a matter of fact I think that's exactly what did happen."

Jonas's eyebrow went up. He looked interested and scribbled for a time upon his piece of paper. "That's pretty smart figurin'," he admitted at last. "Let's suppose for a minute that it's true. Who were the folks Sam Gregg sold things to out of that attic?"

"Jenkins, Blodgett, and yourself."

"Right," Jonas nodded. "Now let's take those folks one at a time. My name can be scratched off right at the start because Sam never told me his story, believe it or not."

I laughed. "I think we're willing to admit that."

"All right, then we're left with Harvey Blodgett and Miller Jenkins. Blodgett's clock was stolen and smashed up, remember, so it looks as though we'd have to count him out, too."

"How about Jenkins?" I got to my feet in triumph. "We can't count him out, and I'll bet a cooky he's the one! He's just the kind of a bird who would do something like this. Am I right or not?"

"Maybe you are." Jonas ran the pencil through his red hair. "Perhaps you are, Bill, but I—well, I can't hardly think it, not yet. I can't just figure Miller havin' the nerve to break into other folks' houses. It would take him so long to make up his mind which window to tackle first that the night would be over afore he got in at all. Not only that, but I can't figure Sam Gregg tellin' his secrets to anybody. Sam wasn't the tellin' kind, to my way of thinkin'."

"What's the alternative?" I demanded impatiently. "If Gregg didn't have a partner, how did the thing leak out? You can't really believe that Gregg and this other person were working from two completely different sources of information, can you?"

"That's just it, Bill, I can't. It don't seem possible."

"Then if it isn't possible they both must have been working from the diary. How could they have done that if they weren't partners?"

"I don't know," said Jonas with a shake of the head, "but I'm almost willin' to swear there was no partnership, just the same. I'll tell you why. If they had been partners, one would have known as much as the other, wouldn't he?"

"Of course."

"Well, he didn't."

"How do you know that?"

"I'll tell you how. I know because of those Jap pictures and that lacquer stand. Don't you forget them for a minute, Bill, because they're the most important numbers we've got so far in our example. They're important because they show, plain as can be, that whoever broke into this house last night has some kind of a list of George Crossley's personal goods."

He got up from his chair and paced up and down with his hands deep in his pockets. "Gregg didn't have any such list—he says so in his notes—so it looks as though any partner of his must have known more than he did. Which, to my mind, pretty much wipes out the partner idea."

I threw up my hands in defeat. "Well, then, if they weren't working from different starting points, and they weren't partners, what have we left? Have we got to swallow the wild idea that the second person read the diary without Gregg's knowledge?"

Jonas grinned ruefully. "It's a large mouthful, I'm free to admit, but it isn't all. Accordin' to our figurin', this other fellow, besides readin' that diary on the sly, must have got hold of an extra string to the puzzle—one that Gregg didn't have at all. I'm talkin' about the list. Can you gulp that down with the rest?"

"I can't." I shook my head in bewilderment. "It seems worse than absolutely impossible."

Marian had been listening to our guesses with increasing impatience and now she interrupted firmly. "As far as I can make out," she declared, "you people have been talking and talking, and all you've decided is that everything is impossible. I hope you won't be annoyed if I break in on your reflections to ask practical questions."

Jonas laughed and went back to his chair at the desk. "I don't blame you for gettin' mad, Marian. Bill and I have been tackin' back and forth and it hasn't got us anywhere in particular. It's your turn now. What do you want to know?"

"I want to know, if it isn't an impertinent question, what we are going to do next."

"I shouldn't call it impudent," said Jonas with a nod. "It's a question that's got to be answered, somehow. I've thought a little about it myself and it seems to me that the next thing to do is to get hold of the fellow who was so busy in here last night."

"Why, Jonas! What possible good would that do?"

"It might do a lot of good. Have you stopped to think that maybe he found what he was so darned anxious to find?

"I'll say I have! I can't think of anything else. Oh, Jonas, do you really suppose he did?"

"Don't know. He may, and then again he may not. It seems to me, anyhow, that the bare chance is enough to make it worth our time to hunt for him."

"Suppose we catch him and then find that he hasn't got it?"

"That would be almost as good. He knows somethin' that we don't, that's sure, and we might scare that somethin' out of him."

Marian was not altogether satisfied. "In the meantime," she demanded, "what's to prevent his coming back again?"

"Nothin' much, but I'm afraid he won't. If he did, it would give us the chance we want to get our hands on him."

"We didn't get our hands on him last night," Marian pointed out, "and we might not the next time."

"You'd be watchin' for him the next time, and that might make all the difference. Tell me, Marian, isn't there a little bedroom on the ground floor here—over on the ocean side of the house, I mean?"

"Why, yes, there is. Why?"

"I was just thinkin' that maybe Bill might sleep down in that room from now on. If he did that he might have a better chance of catchin' any middle of the night visitors that happened along."

That seemed like a good idea to me and I assented to it at once. "With both of my doors open," I said, "I don't think anybody would have a ghost of a chance getting away with anything."

Marian had another suggestion. "How about locking up all the stuff from the *Pride of the Fleet,* just to be on the safe side?"

"You can lock up everything you're sure of," Jonas agreed, "but you've got to remember that there's a lot of things you ain't sure of. You can't lock up all the furniture in the house, you know."

"No, I suppose we can't." Marian shook her head and then went off on another tack. "Speaking of the things from the *Pride of the Fleet* that we *are* sure of," she insisted stubbornly, "I still think we ought to examine them closely. I think we ought to chop them into bits if necessary."

"Suppose we do that," he said patiently; "and then suppose we found nothin' at the end—which would be more than likely. Then you and your mother would be hundreds out of pocket instead of, perhaps, thousands in. Seems to me smashin' up that rare old stuff would be what the Orham doctor called cuttin' off Eben Gallup's leg. Eben had been hittin' up the jug pretty regular, which was a habit of his, and he was makin' heavy weather of it when he rolled into the doctor's office. 'Doc,' says he, 'I want you to saw off my starboard leg. The durn thing's no good; it's weak, seems so; I can't keep it on the course. Saw it off, you hear? I'll wait around while you do it.'

"The doctor looked at him. 'Gallup,' says he, 'don't you think cuttin' off your leg would be too drastic an operation? Let me cut off your head. That's the weakest part of you.'"

We laughed. "Well, Jonas, what less drastic thing do you want us to do?" I inquired.

"Nothin', so far as you two are concerned. Just wait a spell."

Marian wrinkled her nose in disgust, but I was watching Jonas closely. "Marian," I said, "this man has some idea of his own and he doesn't intend to tell us what it is. Jonas, you'd like us to leave things in your hands for a while, wouldn't you?"

"Why, yes—if you'd just as soon. I'd be obliged if you'd let me take the wheel alone for a few days. I *have* got one or two notions, such as they are. Of course, they may come to nothin'; a lot of my notions come to less than that."

It was finally settled that way and Jonas took himself off to begin his investigations. We did not hear from him again until after dinner that night, when he telephoned.

"Just thought I'd report to headquarters," he observed cheerfully, and I thought I could detect a note of satisfaction in his tone.

"What have you found out?" I demanded. "Is it anything important?"

"Well, now, I can't say as it's so everlastin' important, but on the other hand it's kind of interestin'. I've found out that Sam Gregg didn't steal Harvey Blodgett's clock."

I refused to believe him at first, but he finally convinced me. It appeared that Jonas had been asking some questions about town and had found out that on the night of the theft of Blodgett's clock Gregg had been at a meeting of the Ostable County Historical Society in Harniss. The meeting had lasted until after eleven o'clock and a friend of Jonas's had driven Gregg home afterward. He had set him down at the front door of the old Blair house at about five minutes past midnight. As Blodgett's clock had been stolen some time between the hours of eight and eleven, this new evidence provided Gregg with an absolute alibi.

"Look here, Jonas," I stammered at last, in bewilderment, "do you realize what all this new development does to us? We can't be sure now that Gregg was responsible for Iantha's adventure; we don't know who took Blodgett's clock; we don't know what really happened the night Gregg died!"

"Never mind, Bill," he chuckled. "We're pickin' up chips here and there and one of these days we may be able to build a real fire. Just you leave things to me for a spell. I'm beginnin' to think that as a furniture painter I'm a pretty darn good detective."

I left things to him, just as, now, I am going to leave this story to him. If he does as well with the story as he did with his detective work, it will be worth reading. At any rate, ladies and gentlemen, I am now signing off until further notice.

Please stand by for Mr. Jonas Cahoon Jones!

PART THREE

Some Figuring and Much Guessing
and What Came of Them.

Recorded by the Guesser and Figurer,
Jonas Cahoon Jones

I

Bill Thornton is a good fellow. I liked him the first time I met him and better the second. By now I am almost ready to say that he is good enough to marry Marian Fisher, which is saying considerable more than a whole lot. And he seems to like me—does a good job of making believe at it, anyhow.

And yet, here and now, as I see it, he has played me about the same kind of trick that, according to what Iantha Hallett says Jethro Gould told her, George Crossley's mother played on that Liverpool foundling asylum. Crossley's ma left her baby in a washboiler on the asylum front steps, kissed it good-by, rang the bell and went for a walk. This was along in the eighteen-forties and, up to the last bulletin posted, she was still walking.

See what I mean, don't you? Bill Thornton lifted this story out of Iantha's lap, took care of it for a spell, and now he has hung it on my doorknob. I realize, I guess, how those asylum folks must have felt when they answered the bell. They were better off than I am though, for they had the washboiler, which might be worth something, and, besides they probably knew—having had considerable experience—what to do with somebody else's baby. I am blistered if I know just how to start in playing dry nurse to somebody else's yarn.

225

However, I must get under way somehow, I suppose, but, before I do, let's get this much straight and understood: In spite of Thornton's calling me "Sherlock H." Jones, I am no story-book detective. No, sir, I am not! I have wished, more times than a few, that some day I might run across one of those book detective fellows, the kind who can find footprints in the middle of winter when the ground is froze, and look at an old shirt collar and tell from it what complexion the person was that wore it and what church he belonged to. As I say, I should like to meet one of that kind, but the only detective ever happened my way was one that the insurance company sent down after Alpheus Creel's billiard saloon burnt. The first thing *he* did was ask Al if he thought likely the fire was set on purpose. Surprising as it may seem, Alpheus said "No," and the detective gave out his opinion that it was mighty cold weather down here—which, it being February, was true enough—and took the next train back to Boston.

No, in spite of Bill's jokes, I was no detective. And I am no puzzle hound, the way poor old Sam Gregg used to be. If I have got any trick of my own at all, outside of painting up and fixing over old furniture and, maybe, picking out a 'specially good piece from a room full of half-ways—if I have any knack of my own, it is in sticking close to arithmetic, or trying to.

To my mind the arithmetic is the best book ever put together. There is nothing but plain, straight truth in it— facts, that you can't beat. Add two to two and you have got four. Multiply two by two and it is four again. Divide four by two and there is the two you started with. There is no way around it—it is truth. And truth in this world is scarcer than genuine Duncan Phyfe tables at a tent auction in summer time.

So then, that forenoon following the meeting of what you might call the Blair house Ways and Means committee—

the get-together that Bill Thornton has written about, the one where he and Marian agreed to leave matters in my hands a spell—after that meeting I went back to my shop and sat down at my desk. Walking home by way of the short cut across the fields I had done a little thinking and even that much made me realize that I had let myself in for a ticklish job. Just why I had done it is kind of hard to explain. The fact is, I guess, that all the mysteriousness which had been going on up there had stirred up my curiosity, had kind of got me riled, as you might say. You remember how, when you was a youngster, some other fellow would dare you, "stump" you, to do some fool thing or other and you made up your mind you just wouldn't be stumped. Well, that is the way this business at the Blair place had got hold of me. It had stumped me to find the answer and I had taken up the dare. Already, before I got home that morning the size of the job I had tackled so cocky was beginning to scare me. Those two young folks had given me my way—the way I had asked them to give me; now, naturally, they would expect results. Yes, sir, I had bit off a man's size chunk; the question was, after all, whether or not I could chew it.

I had some ideas, some notions of my own—yes. But they were not very clear ones, and the more I went over them the less worth while they looked. I took a sheet of paper out of my desk drawer and a pencil out of my pocket and squared my elbows. I can always seem to think easier if I can scribble and figure at the same time. There is no better way, as I see it, to go at a thing than by tackling it arithmetic fashion.

I wrote the word "Diary" at the top of my sheet of paper just to give me one number to start from. If I was certain of anything it was that all the new trouble—that later than 1883, I mean—centered right around that diary. It was Sam Gregg's getting hold of Freeland Blair's diary

that had started him on the ransacking cruises that ended
by his being found dead there in the pines across the road.
Gregg had found that diary somewhere amongst the *Pride
of the Fleet* stuff in the attic. Where he found it was not
so much matter just now; found it he had, and it had set
him going.

Was he alone when he found it? I did not know, of
course. In the beginning I had taken it for granted he
was, but now, since this new breaking and entering, I
began to wonder again. And that very afternoon, after I
had spent hours staring at my paper and getting nowhere,
I learned for sure that it could not have been Sam who got
into Blodgett's bungalow and stole and smashed the clock.
That evening, sitting down alone to figure once more,
although I left the word "Diary" standing, I wrote down
"Attic" underneath it.

The diary came from that attic—it must have—Gregg
got it there—he must have. He was working from the diary and, I was almost sure, from the diary alone. He had
no list of the Crossley property, he said so in his notes—
wrote down that he wished he had some such list. This
other fellow—whoever he was—might have read the diary
and be partly working from it, but he was working from a
list *too,* or it seemed so. The way he manhandled one item
and left the next untouched—and the untouched one, you
would say, the more likely of the two to have something
hid in it—made me almost certain that he knew just which
of the furniture and things in the Blair house had come,
not only from the attic and back storeroom, but from the
Pride of the Fleet. The clock, the sandalwood box, the Japanese pictures, they had all been Crossley's—Iantha remembered them. The only piece of the lot this fellow had
touched that she was not certain of was the lacquer stand
and even of that she was almost sure.

Of course, you might say that Sam Gregg had tackled the Buddha image and the sandalwood box. Well, it was pretty safe to figure he was the one who had smashed the image. But the box—well, there was a lot of doubt about that. I believed now that it was this other fellow who had carried the sandalwood box out of the house the first time and had come back again last night and taken it to pieces.

Well, there is no use going into all this again because Thornton has written how he and Marian and I reached about the same conclusions during our committee meeting. *I* went into it, of course—went over every bit of it again and again—but that one word "Attic" still stared at me, important as ever. There had been no outbreaks and inbreaks until the things in that attic was disturbed. The diary came from that attic. The list—if there was a list—or, at any rate, whatever second string there might be leading to the hundred-thousand-dollar "thing" George Crossley and Freeland Blair had gone partners to buy and fetch home, *must* have come from that attic. There seemed no other likely place it could have come from.

And so, the big question was: Who had been in the Blair house attic since the things there were disturbed? If we could get hold of the right one who had been there— the one who had not only read the diary, but had found the list, or the second string I just mentioned, we could probably scare him, or her, into letting us in on whatever extra information he or she had. And, providing—and this was by no manner of means impossible—he or she had already found the "thing," we could hold jail or state's prison over their head until they handed that back to its rightful owner, who was of course Marian's mother, Mary Fisher.

All this, or the biggest part of it, had been in my mind when Marian and Bill and I had our talk. Names had been mentioned and I had brushed them all to one side, pretending I did not take much stock in any one of them as a possibility. That was mostly make-believe and my reason for doing it was that, when you set a mouse trap, you don't go stamping and hollering around the place where you set it. No, sir; you go on tiptoe, so as not to frighten away the mice. I believed a trap ought to be set, but that only one person ought to set it—or even know it was there. Well, I had unanimously elected myself to be that person and—now what?

Underneath my words "Diary" and "Attic" on my paper I wrote down next nine names. I will set them own here, just as I did then. They were: Marian Fisher, William Thornton, Iantha Hallett, Samuel Gregg, Harvey Blodgett, Abel Peak, Jonas Jones, Miller Jenkins, Tom Davis.

Nine of them altogether, you see. They were my real starting numbers. Some of them could be rubbed out afore the start was made. Sam Gregg, of course, was out for good. And Marian and Bill and Iantha could be rubbed out, too. So could I, for I did not have any good reasons for suspecting myself. There were five numbers gone. Five from nine leaves four. These four were: Harvey Blodgett, Abel Peak, Miller Jenkins, Tom Davis. They were my remainder. Take them altogether or separate, how did they figure out according to arithmetic?

I knew them all first-rate, Blodgett and I had had a lot of business dealings and sometimes one of us came out ahead in the trade and sometimes the other. You had to keep your eye peeled when you dickered with Harvey Blodgett. He loved to buy and sell antiques, not so much, I always thought, because of the antiques themselves—although he was a good judge of them—as for the fun he got in beating the other fellow. He was well-off, sharp, and honest up to a certain point. After that it always seemed to me that his honesty had considerable elastic in it. It generally managed to stretch until he got what he was after.

Harvey Blodgett had been in that attic and back store-room three or four times looking at the things Marian and Gregg was sorting over. Sometimes Gregg was with him, but at least once he was left there alone. If he found the diary, or the list, or it might even be some other thing putting him on the scent—something of which we knew nothing at all, which seemed too far-fetched to consider, hardly—I would not put it past him to slip what he found in his pocket. Only I could hardly see him sharing his find with Samuel Gregg, letting Gregg have the diary to keep. He and Gregg, after their row over chess or whatever it was, were scarcely on speaking terms. And yet that might have been bluff, mostly. Bluff and bluster were Harvey's strongholds.

But Harvey Blodgett's own house had been entered and the clock he bought from Gregg taken outdoors and smashed. One answer to that was that it might have been part of the bluff. A fellow as smart as Blodgett, if he calculated to do a little burglaring, or have it done for him, might be keen enough to burglar his own house first; there could not be a much better way to throw people off the track.

Totting up under Harvey Blodgett's name then, what did I get? That he was in the attic and might have found the diary—or something else, or both. That he was smart enough to realize what his finds might mean and not so honest as to feel it necessary to tell. I could hardly see him breaking in through Marian Fisher's porch window, but I could easy see him hiring somebody else to do it—that Tom Davis, his colored man, for instance.

Harvey Blodgett was worth taking serious account of as a possibility. There was no doubt of that in my mind.

Abel Peak was the next number on my list. Generally speaking I should have rated him as about a cipher—minus. Long-necked, long-faced, long-legged and gangling, that was Abel. He was Miller Jenkins's hired man in the Jenkins' antique shop at East Orham village. He was what you might call one of the "fairly goods" of this world, the kind who are so likely to get the fairly poor wages. A fairly good carpenter and furniture repairer and polisher; a fairly good bookkeeper—he did what bookkeeping his boss had to be done: a fairly good salesman—sometimes: when selling was easy. He was one of the Trumet Neck Peaks, and none of them was ever bright lights. He was single and had a room up over the antique shop, where he slept nights. He took his meals down at Sarah Ellis's boarding-house. About thirty-five years old, would be my guess.

I should not have given Abel Peak a serious thought—I never knew anybody else who did—if it was not for the sure fact that he had been in that Blair attic for hours, crating the chairs that Miller Jenkins bought of Sam Gregg. He was there and so he had to be one of the numbers in my example. But as for him playing housebreaker—well, hardly! You might as well expect a tame rabbit to get vicious and bite people. Such actions, both for him and the rabbit, was possible, but I'll be blessed if they were probable! As I sized up Abel Peak, he was weak in the knees and weaker yet in the head. He was on my list because he had to be, but I didn't waste much time figuring him out.

That took two away from my four. Miller Jenkins was next. He was different. He *was* worth a lot of figuring. And when you figured Miller you needed a sharp pencil. He was a slick boy. No plane nor sandpaper could have made him any smoother than he was. And sly—and 'round the corner—whew! Put *him* on the track of an extra dollar and he would never leave it unless somebody else got to the end of the trail first. You would never guess he was in

the hunt at all—that is, you would not unless you knew
him as well as I did. The thing he was after was the thing
he never mentioned. He would talk about the weather, and
pat you on the back, and beg your pardon, and look out of
the window and talk weather some more. Then he would
beg your pardon again and go home. It was not until he
had shut the door that you woke up to realize the dollar
you, yourself, had come there to get had gone with him.

A mighty good antique dealer Miller was—if you didn't
put too much emphasis on the "good."

Of the four, Blodgett, Peak, Jenkins and Davis, Jenkins looked to me the most likely of the lot, in spite of
what I said to Bill and Marian. And yet some of the same
objections hung to him that hung to the others. If he
found the diary—providing that diary was a part of what
he was working from—he would never let go of it unless
somebody gave him ether and pulled it from him by main
strength, like a tooth. And poor Sam Gregg was no dentist.

There was only one number left in the sum I was laying out and he was Tom Davis, the negro who did Harvey
Blodgett's cooking and housekeeping. I did not know so
very much about him, for he, being the only colored person in East Orham, flocked pretty much by himself. He
was a big, strapping chap, most generally good natured
and on a broad grin, but with once in a while a sour streak
when he would say scarcely yes or no to a civil question.
These streaks, so folks seemed to think, followed on after
Blodgett had been giving him a blowing up for something
of other. Blodgett was a hard driver, I guess likely, a regular old time Bucko mate when he set out to be, but he
paid liberal wages and so Tom hung on to his job. He was
scared half to death of his boss, so much was plain for all
hands to see. As for his honesty—well, I don't know as I
would have trusted him in my henhouse the night afore
Thanksgiving, but I take my oath he would not know a

diary, or anything like it, from a dictionary. If he was mixed up in the thieving and all around mysteriousness it was because he was acting under orders from some one else. I did not rate him any higher than ordinary seaman, and mighty ordinary at that.

So, you see, all my adding and subtracting and multiplying and dividing so far left me not much further ahead than when I started. It still seemed sure and certain that somebody besides Sam Gregg must, someway and somehow, either before or after Sam got hold of it, have seen and read that diary of Captain Freeland's. If not the diary, then some other piece of information just as definite, and tempting enough to make him do such desperate things as had been done. That this second person had a list of the Crossley things I was pretty well convinced of, but a list alone did not figure to me quite enough. The diary *and* such a list together might be—but, confound it; it was nobody but Gregg who had that diary at the finish—his finish, I mean.

What this second fellow *might* have done I could guess; but I was a long, long ways yet from knowing who he was—or why—or how.

The channel ahead looked pretty foggy, that was a fact. I put my sheet of paper back in the drawer for that session. The only result I had got from all my calculations was that I must make a beginning somewhere and it might as well be somewhere amongst the owners of those four names. It would not do any harm and it might do some good. One of the four—or, perhaps, two of them together—*might* know at least a part of the answer to my example. If I could only get hold of what he or they knew and add it to what Bill and Marian and I knew already, then—why, then we ought to be a whole lot nearer to knowing what George Crossley knew and meant to tell Freeland Blair when he sent that message by Burke.

Oh, well! The first thing before knowing what anybody knew was to get hold of the one, or ones, who knew it. How could that mousetrap of mine be set? The course to be steered for the present seemed to me to lay close aboard those four—Blodgett, Peak, Jenkins and Davis—Blodgett and Jenkins in particular. Keep in close touch with them and wait and watch. Bill Thornton, I know, would be standing watch up in the old Blair house and if one of my four took another crack at the things in that living room and library Bill would be up and doing. Meanwhile I must hang around with my eyes and ears open.

Of course there was always the bare chance that the person concerned with George Crossley's left-overs might be some one away outside my calculating. If that was so, then—well, then I should have to tear up my paper and start all over on a fresh sheet.

II

Harvey Blodgett's name was Number 1 on my list of worth-watching folks, you remember. I decided to drop in at Blodgett's home the next morning and have a talk with him. The reason I meant to give for calling and talking was to be his smashed clock. Bill had given him Marian's check to pay for the damage, I knew, but my idea was to ask him if he had kept the pieces of the clock and, providing he had, to suggest that he let me take them and see if I couldn't put them together again. Considering what I had heard about how badly the clock was busted the chances were that he hadn't kept the remains, or that, if he had, nobody short of Ezekiel—the Bible fellow who stirred up and sorted out a whole valley full of dry bones—could do anything with them. That part did not bother me. All I wanted of that clock was to use it as an excuse for getting in touch with Harvey Blodgett.

As it happened, I didn't need any excuse. Just as I was getting ready to start for his house he walked into my shop. I declare it gave me a start to see him open the door. It was like something in one of the books Iantha reads herself awake with nights, where, just as the heroine is about to give up all hopes and heave herself down the well, the hero's ghost sticks its head out over the well curb and says, "Don't be in a rush" or "Nothing doing" or something

similar. Last she heard of him he was in Africa or on top of
the North Pole, so naturally she is considerable surprised
to see his appearance hoisting itself up in the bucket. She
had been thinking of him, but she wasn't hardly expecting
him. See what I mean?

Well, I had been thinking of nobody but Harvey
Blodgett ever since I woke up, so when he walked in on
me I was astonished. If I hadn't had it drilled into me ever
since I was a boy in Sunday School that the prayers of the
wicked gather no moss I swear I should have thought one
of mine was answered.

Anyhow, there he was, rigged regardless of expense, hat
listed a little mite to port, cigar in the starboard corner of
his mouth—cool and patronizing and satisfied with himself as ever.

"Hello, Jones!" says he. "Well, how's tricks?"

Unless I was clear off in my reckoning he knew a lot
more tricks than I did, but I said they were doing as well
as could be expected and he laughed and handed me over
a cigar.

"Just thought I'd drop in a minute," he said. "Haven't
seen you for a long time. Been busy, have you?"

I gave in that I had been fairly busy and asked him if
he wouldn't sit down. He did and I did and we sat there
smoking and talking scandal about the weather and other
things that neither of us was particularly interested in. It
was my guess that we both had something up our sleeves;
I did sure, and I thought he did, by the way he acted. He
kept looking past me and around the shop. By and by one
of the things in his sleeve began to slip down into sight, a
little at a time.

"How is Marian Fisher these days?" he asked, careless. "Don't suppose you see as much of her since her boy
friend—what's his name? Thornton—got here, eh?"

"I see her every once in a while. She's first-rate."

"That's good. Getting over the shock of old Gregg's death, is she?"

"Seems to be."

"That was a queer business. Old Sam had gone nutty, that's my answer. He was next door to it for years. His coming up to try and buy back that clock after selling it to me himself proved he had bats in his loft. And climbing in my window and stealing what he couldn't buy settled all doubts. Poor damn' fool! Well, now he is dead I'm glad I didn't jail him for it."

That gave me my chance to say one of the things I intended to say if I had gone to his house same as I planned.

"Mr. Blodgett," said I, "it wasn't Sam Gregg who got into your house and took that clock. I've got proof that it wasn't."

I put it just as blunt as that, for I wanted to see how he would take it. And the way he took it disappointed me a little. Either he was genuine surprised or he was as good an actor as ever came to the Orham Center town hall.

"What!" he sang out. "You've got proof of *what?* What the devil do you mean by that?"

"Mean what I say. Gregg never stole your clock."

He glowered at me for much as half a minute.

"Are you drunk?" he wanted to know, finally. "Of course he stole it; stole it first and then smashed it. A crazy man's spite, that's what it was. He has had it in for me ever since I caught him playing a crooked game of chess. You're talking through your hat, Jones."

So far as their chess row went I remembered mighty well Sam Gregg's hinting to me that it was Blodgett who played crooked. However, that didn't interest me then nor now. I went on to tell him what I had found out about Gregg's whereabouts the night his clock was taken. His playacting—if it was acting—kept on being as good as ever. He even let his cigar go out.

"Well, I'll be blanked to dash!" says he, or something like it. "You mean to say—? Why, it couldn't have been him, then. . . . Who in blue blazes was it?"

"Don't know. The clock was a nice enough antique and worth stealing, perhaps. Only why, if the thief wanted it *for* an antique, did he hammer it to pieces?"

He didn't know. He made me doubt that he had the least notion. He kept asking more questions and scowling and swearing under his breath. The way he looked and behaved went a long way towards proving to me that my surmising he might have broken into his own house to bluff the rest of us was away off.

"Humph!" he said, after a spell. "Humph! Well, all right. Let it go for now. Eh? Suspicions? No, I haven't' got any suspicions. I may have later, when I have time to think. *If* I do, I'll— Well, forget it. . . . See here, Jones; have you sold that Chinese cabinet yet? The one you got from Marian?"

I caught my breath. This was what he had up his sleeve. I knew there was something.

"Chinese cabinet?" I says, innocent. "Oh, yes, yes! that one. I haven't hardly looked at it since I brought it down here, but I haven't sold it. Don't know as I will. It's a pretty rare piece, that cabinet is."

"Where is it? Mind if I look at it?"

It was in the back shop just where I had dumped it down when I brought it from the Blair house. We went out there together. He walked around and around it, stooping down to finger the carving on the sides.

"Ugly as the very devil, isn't it," he said. That didn't fool me much; I have been trading antiques more or less for twenty years and I can tell when a person's fingers are itching. He was crazy about that Chinese cabinet.

"Homelier than a turkey's neck," I agreed. "Queer that anybody would have such an outrage in the house."

He straightened up. "That's the way you feel about it, eh? Well, I don't blame you. . . . What will you take for it, cash, this minute?"

I shook my head. "It is so everlasting ugly that I guess I won't sell it, Mr. Blodgett. Being no beauty myself I get considerable comfort in knowing there's something handy by that's even worse looking. No, it is not for sale."

"Give you so and so much," says he. And he went on raising bids for quite a while. At last, seeing I meant it, I presume likely, he gave up.

"All right," he said. "Matter of fact, Jones, I wouldn't take it as a gift."

"I know. And I shan't give it to you, so we're both satisfied. If I ever do think of parting with it I will let you know. Nothing else I've got you'd be interested in, I suppose?"

We was back again in the front shop by this time. His hand was on the doorknob, but now he turned to look at me.

"Nothing you've got—no," says he. "There is one thing some other folks have got that I'd like, but they don't realize the value of money any more than you do. I stopped in at the Blair house the other day and made an offer for one piece that came from the same attic your cabinet came from. Marian and her little Willie were there and they gave me to understand the thing wasn't for sale. That made me want it more than ever, naturally. . . . Say, you and they eat out of each other's hands; I wonder, providing I made it worth your while, you'd try to buy it for me. They might sell it to *you*."

"What is it?"

"It is that square sandalwood box with the ivory inlays on the sides. Next to that cabinet of yours it is the finest thing in their whole collection. I fell for it the first time I saw it but I wouldn't give Gregg the satisfaction of seeming too eager. Next time I called he wouldn't sell that or

anything else, the crazy bug. . . . I want that box. See if
you can't get it for me, will you?"

I don't think I answered right off—fact, I know I didn't.
He had surprised me this time, for sure. Surprised I was,
and interested.

"Well?" he barked out. "What's struck you now? You
heard what I said, didn't you?"

I nodded. "Why, yes, Mr. Blodgett. I heard you. So you
would like that sandalwood box?"

"I would. So would anybody that knows a fine thing.
Jones, you try to buy it, that's a good fellow. I'll pay a good
liberal commission. Pretend you're getting it for yourself
and then slip it to me. Come! What do you say?"

I said about the only thing I could say, which was that
I would think it over and see what I could do. He ordered
me not to waste time thinking, but to go ahead and get
busy. Then he walked out of the shop. I went to the window and looked after him. Here was a brand-new figure to
add into my calculations.

That sandalwood box had been in those calculations
pretty strong for a spell, but lately it had been shoved one
side. Bill has told how he and I found it out in the bushes
nigh where Sam Gregg dropped down dead. A few days
after that I had lugged it to my shop and gone through
it thorough, I thought, finding nothing whatsoever. So
Bill and I had about come to the conclusion that it had
been picked out haphazard, either by Sam, or—as I was
beginning to think now—by the person he might have
been chasing, and that it didn't cut any special figure in
our arithmetic example—any more than any other item in
George Crossley's property, that is.

But Blodgett's talk had set me to wondering if it might
not be important after all. Anyhow Harvey was mighty
anxious to get hold of it. Of course he wanted the Chinese
cabinet, too—or pretended he did—and that cabinet and

the sandalwood box really were about the two rarest bits in that attic collection. Blodgett was a fellow who collected with judgment, and it might reasonably be that his interest in the cabinet and the box was only because they were fine specimens. But it was curious, just the same, that one of the two things he wanted most should have been the very one that Sam Gregg—or somebody—had taken out of the Blair house the night Sam died.

I set this down here because it shows a little of the muddle my brain had got into already over this Freeland Blair-George Crossley puzzle. Any straw that blew my way just then loomed up big as a ship's mainmast. A little realization of the state I was in came over me as I stood there thinking and I decided to go out doors and take a walk and see if the fresh air would not breeze a little common sense into my skull.

It was a fine forenoon and I tramped along by the road and across the fields until I got to the village. My walk hadn't done me much good so far, for I was wondering and speculating every step of the way. When I woke up, so to speak, I was close abreast Miller Jenkins's place and, as Miller and Peak were two of the numbers in my watching list, I stopped in to pass the time of day.

Abel Peak was the only one in there at that minute. He was half asleep in a chair in front of his boss's desk. It was just like Jenkins, and gave you his measure, that, although there was at least a dozen desks in his stock out in the shop, he would spare only one for him and his clerk to use in common. This one was a banged-up old walnut roll top and when Miller wasn't writing letters or figuring out his bills at it, Abel used it to post up his ledger and cash book on. When he heard me open the front door he came to life and gangled out into the front room, hair tousled and hands in his pants beckets, same as usual.

Miller, he told me, had gone out on the trail of some antique he was trying to make a deal for. What it was this time Abe didn't know—and cared less, I judged. The only point he seemed anxious about special was whether or not I had any chewing tobacco. I hadn't, but I did have a cigar and he took that as a substitute. It seemed to brighten him up a little mite for he talked considerable, for him.

By and by, he mentioned that he shouldn't be surprised if Jenkins was up to the Fisher girl's place. Miller was still pretty keen about some of that stuff that had been in her attic. Hadn't give up all hopes of buying more of it, provided he could get it cheap enough.

"One thing he would like more than another," drawled Abel, "is that Chinese chest of drawers you got yourself, Jonas. You kind of beat him out on that trade, and it hurt. Calculate you could make a good profit on that chest, if you would sell it to him."

"Um-hm," said I. "Well, it isn't for sale, not for the present. It can't be my cabinet that sent him up to see Marian. What else does he want up there?"

"Don't know. It's something. I ain't real sure whether he wants it for himself, or to buy it for somebody else on commission. Harvey Blodgett and him are pretty sociable these days. Harvey was in here a little while ago, just afore Miller went out."

"Humph! You don't say! Was he so?"

"Yes, he was and he and Miller had their heads together about something."

I had a feeling that maybe I could guess what that something was, but I didn't say so. If Miller Jenkins was up to the Blair place I knew I could find out from Bill Thornton what he was there for. I changed the subject.

"Well," I said, "poor old Sam Gregg isn't calling on you folks any more. You must miss him, he used to come so regular."

Either it was imagination or Peak didn't seem to want to talk about Gregg. He shut up like a clam and pretty soon mumbled something about having to go ahead with his bookkeeping and went back to the desk. The last I saw him doing was spearing the stub of the cigar I had given him on the little blade of his jackknife, so as not to lose the comfort of the last half inch.

That evening when I called at the old Blair house, Marian and Bill told me that Jenkins had been there that day, sure enough. What was he after? Well, that was a question of course—what Miller Jenkins was ever really after was always a question. He had backed and filled and hemmed and hawed over a number of things, even though Marian told him she had decided to keep every one of them.

"Did he hem and haw over any one thing more than another?" I asked.

Bill laughed. "It is hard to say," he told me. "You know him. He did seem to us more interested in that box with the ivory inlays than anything else. I really think he would have offered a good price for that, if we had given him the least encouragement."

It was what I had expected to hear, but, having heard it, I was still floundering. The chances were Blodgett had asked Miller to buy the sandalwood box for him, as he had asked me to do the same thing; but it was possible that Miller wanted it himself. And why did either or both of them want it? I made up my mind to give that sandalwood box another overhauling, although I was practically sure I had not missed anything the first time.

Another week went by without anything happening out of the regular run, except that I was struck all of a sudden with a rush of business. Old Mrs. Slater, who has the big summer place over to Orham Center, sent me down a curly maple dining-room set that she had bought, a piece at a time, of every antique dealer betwixt here and New

Bedford—or so she said. She wanted every piece scraped and repaired and refinished and nobody on earth must do it but just me. And she was in a tearing hurry, same as she always is. So I

had both hands full every minute and hardly as much as found time to run in on Marian and Bill, to say nothing of my "best girl," Iantha.

Bill came to see me sometimes, though, and he did not have much to report. No, there had been no more breaking in and taking to pieces up his way. . . . Unless—

"What is the 'unless'?" I asked him, for he had stopped short. He laughed, sort of uneasy, seemed to me.

"Oh, nothing, I guess," he said. "I have the jumps nowadays, I suppose, like the rest of our household. I am sleeping downstairs now, in the little sewing room—you know that, of course—and night before last I woke up, as sure as could be that some one was on the front porch."

"And was there?"

He laughed again. "When I got there—which you can bet didn't take me long—there was nobody, and the porch door was locked. So—"

"Yes? And so? What's the rest of it?"

"Well, next morning it did seem to me as if I could make out muddy marks on the porch floor. It had rained that night, you remember. All fancy, no doubt. At any rate, if we had a visitor, he was scared away and has not come back. I only wish he would."

That was all he had to tell. You notice he didn't ask me how I was getting along with my end of the riddle, the end I had taken over so chipper. And Marian never asked either. I judged they had agreed not to mention it to me until I mentioned it first. They was keeping to their part of the bargain and were giving me free hand.

It was fine of them and I appreciated it, but it was making me feel ashamed, just the same. So far I had not

gained one single inch. I had as many, maybe more, suspicions than I started with; but for proof of those suspicions—nothing.

I changed the subject. "How is Iantha making it?" I
asked him. He grinned.

"She goes around looking like the prophet Jeremiah;
that is to say, the way he must have looked if his face
matched his lamentations. It is all settled in her mind
that the curse connected with the Blair-Crossley corporation has been resurrected and is doing business at the old
stand. It killed poor old Gregg—she knows it—and the
only important question is which of us is next on the list
of sacrifices."

I grinned, too. "You tell her her beau will be in some
of these evenings to cheer her up. I only wish I could find
another *Dracula* to distract her mind. Seems to me there
is an old copy of Fox's *Book of Martyrs* in amongst the
books in that secretary over yonder. I took that secretary
in trade of Obed Coles's widow last March, and the books
were chucked in for good measure. Some of the pictures
in that *Book of Martyrs* ought to help Iantha out. Did you
ever see them, Bill?"

He had not, but I told him about them. I had seen
them when I was a kid and I hadn't been able to forget
them since.

"I read once in the paper," I said to him, "that the way
to stop a person from being poisoned was to keep giving
him little doses of arsenic and Rough-on-Rats and such.
After a course of that treatment he is shape so that nothing as mild as everyday poison will take. You leave Iantha
to me and that martyr book."

It was a couple of days after this when we commenced
to have the stretch of unseasonable hot weather. It was
not time for August dogdays by a long ways, but the heat
that struck down on us was strong enough to satisfy any

dog—or cat either. I was slaving away over the Slater dining-room set and after I got back from supper the second night of the hot spell the very sight and smell of paint and shavings was too much for me. I had intended to work for a couple of hours longer, but I just couldn't. I made up my mind to walk over and see Bill and Marian instead.

There was nobody home but Iantha when I got to the Blair place. Bill and Marian had gone out for a little ride in the auto, she said.

"They will be back pretty soon," says she. "They know I don't like to stay alone in this house after dark. Won't you come in?"

"You bet I will!" I told her. "Well now, Iantha, this is fine, isn't it? You and I can be alone together and have a real sociable chat, same as steady company like us ought to have. My, my! you get better-looking every day, seems so. How do you manage it? You haven't taken to painting and powdering-up, have you, like the rest of the girls these times?"

That started the fireworks, same as I knew it would. Iantha is always a great comfort to me. She is one of the dependable kind; you can always count on her to get mad in the right place.

"Sometimes I do declare I think you are crazy as poor Mr. Gregg was in his last days, Jonas Jones," she snapped at me. "Paint and powder—the idea! Just for that I've got a good mind not to let you inside this house at all. It would serve you right if I let you stand and cool your heels on that doorstep."

"Well, anywhere that would keep any part of me cool just now wouldn't be so dreadful bad, that is a fact. Tell you what we'll do: You come out and set alongside of me on the step, Iantha. Then we'll look just like regular sweethearts. Eh?"

That settled it. She shooed me into the house like a policeman taking up a tramp. She had been sitting in the library and she marched me in there, pulled up a chair and plumped herself into another one.

"Now," she says, "if you are through foolishness, and *can* talk sense, for mercy sakes talk it. It is bad enough being left alone in this lunatic place, even for a little while, without having another loon come to air his ravings. Tell me all the news you've heard, talk about how hot it is— talk about anything *outside* of this house. Don't you dare whisper about the dreadfulness inside it. I want to forget that for a few minutes, if I can."

She did not mean it. The very things she wanted to talk about were all inside that house. I hadn't more than commenced on the town news before she was asking me if I thought Sam Gregg had really died of heart disease.

"Why, sure," I told her. "There is no doubt of that. The doctor's examination proves it."

"Yes, I know he says it does."

"Well, it does, doesn't it? What do *you* think he died of?"

She looked at me as if she was half ashamed and half stubborn. "I think he died of exactly the same thing that killed Captain Freeland. That's what I think, and I don't care if I do—so!"

"Well, that was heart disease too, at the finish."

"Umph! I suppose *you* will be the next one to say I am superstitious. Don't you dare say it, because I ain't."

I told her I wouldn't say it for the world. That didn't calm her as you might expect.

"You know what I was just doing when you come?" she wanted to know. "I'll tell you, but don't you tell Marian or Mr. Thornton. I went up to Mr. Thornton's room and I got that old diary of Captain Freeland's. They keep it hid

away, because Marian says looking at it makes me nervous.
My heavens to Betsy! As if I could be any more nervous
than I am already! Well, I got it and I was setting here
reading it when you rang the bell. I was intending to put
it back before they got home. Don't you say one word to
them about it, now will you?"

I swore to keep mum. "I have got a book up to the
shop I meant to fetch over to you, Iantha," I said. "I must
try and remember to bring it next time I come. It is an
old-timer, but it's got some nice cheerful pictures in it.
You will enjoy looking at those pictures."

"Humph! I do hope I haven't read it already. What's its
name?"

"Fox's *Book of Martyrs*. I don't know who this fellow
Fox was, but he must have been lively company in his day."

Here was one time when Iantha was not dependable,
instead of acting happy and eager, same as I had expected,
she just sat back in her chair and sniffed.

"Oh, *that* old thing!" says she. "Mercy on us! we had
that book in our house when I was a child. My grandmother left it to us; she left that and a wax wreath with
some of grandfather's hair on it and a picture of the death
of President Andrew Jackson and—oh, quite a lot more."

"You don't say! Well, well! Her name wasn't Fox, was it?"

"Fox? No! It was Beasly. What on earth made you think
it was Fox?"

"Well, I didn't know but she might have been the wife
of the man who wrote that book. Sounds as if they had
tastes in common. . . . All right, Iantha; I won't bring
over the *Book of Martyrs*. I will see if I can't find you some
other joke collection instead."

She rambled along about her grandmother who, I
judged, must have been about as sunshiny around the
house as a yard of crape. The Freeland Blair diary was
lying on the table and I picked it up and began to turn the

pages. I knew every word by heart already, but there was a
fascination about the confounded thing.

Iantha was watching me. Pretty soon she said: "You
know where I think Mr. Gregg found that diary? In that
old sea chest or somewheres where Captain Crossley's
clothes used to be. I am almost sure that's where it was
hid, though how Aunt Becky and I missed it when we went
through everything I can't see."

Neither could I, nor could Bill nor Marian, though we
had tried to enough times, goodness knows.

"It must have been in with them clothes," Iantha went
along, "because people's clothes are very often laid away
in camphor and you can smell camphor on that diary this
minute. Now where else could there be camphor—up in
that storeroom and attic? Of course that Chinese cabinet thing you bought was partly camphor wood—or seems
to me I remember 'twas—but Aunt Becky and I went all
through that afore it was put away. Now— For the land
sakes, Jonas Jones, what is the matter? What ails you? . . .
Don't look like that! Man alive! do you want to scare me
to *death?*"

I guess likely I must have looked strange. I certainly
was feeling strange enough. I leaned back in my chair.

"Iantha," says I, after a second or so, "did you ever see
a complete darn fool?"

"Eh? My Lord! What are you—"

"Because, if you never did afore, you are looking at one
now."

She screamed. I calculate by this time she was sure that
the "curse" she was forever laying the family troubles to
had got hold of me, along with the rest. I didn't stop to
explain. I grabbed up my hat from the chair and started for
the door. She yelled after me to know where I was going.

"I'm going home," I called over my shoulder. "Maybe I
will be back later. Good night."

I all but ran the whole way across the fields to my shop. Once inside, I locked the door behind me, took down one of the bracket lamps I had left burning, and with it in my hand, went out into the back room. That Chinese cabinet was there on the corner of my bench just where it had been since I brought it from the Blair house attic. I put the lamp down alongside it, pulled up a chair, sat down myself and went to work.

I couldn't have worked more than twenty minutes when I found what I was hunting for—what, if I had had the sense the Almighty gives a jackass, I would have known right off must be there.

Underneath the lowest drawer of that cabinet was another, a secret drawer. It opened when you took out the main drawer altogether and pressed a false screw head. This secret drawer was empty—did not disappoint me, for I expected it would be—but it was made of camphor wood, just as was all the inside of the cabinet and when I pulled it out and held it to my nose it smelled strong enough of camphor to pretty nigh make me sneeze.

I had found something at last. Of course, if I had not been what I called myself to Iantha—a complete darn fool—I would have guessed and found it long ago. Bill and Marian, and I have talked this over fifty times since and we cannot understand yet why we didn't, any one of us, connect the camphor smell of that diary with the camphor wood inside of that cabinet. Marian says she did, in a way, but she herself had looked through the drawers and cubby-holes the very first time she and Sam Gregg took the thing out of the storeroom, and they were all empty, so, although the thought came to her, she didn't mention it. And Bill had not had experience with old things, so he should not be blamed.

But me—a man who had taken to pieces as many old desks and chests and boxes, and had found the land knows

how many secret drawers! Why *I* should not have guessed
right off! Well, it is beyond explaining. I had not really
examined the cabinet careful since I brought it home
and—to grab at every excuse possible—I will say that I
had paid hardly any attention to the inside of it; it was the
hard wood carved outside that took my fancy. But there—
what's the use? Absolute darn fool, that is the answer. Let
it go at that.

However, as I say, I had—thanks to Iantha's hint—found
something at last. I knew I had found the place where old
Freeland Blair, in those last days of his, just afore he died,
hid his diary to keep anybody else from reading what he
had written in it. In that secret drawer he had put it and
there it had stayed for forty-four years, until Gregg—or
somebody—took it out.

I was sitting there, with the empty drawer in my hand,
when there was a pounding on the front door of the shop.
I tiptoed in and peeked out of the window. Bill Thornton
was the one who had knocked, so I let him in, of course.
He was out of breath. When he and Marian got back from
their auto ride Iantha had met them with a wild yarn about
my having, as she said, gone raving distracted and torn out
of the house, foaming at the mouth.

So Bill, naturally, had galloped over to see whether to
get a doctor first and a keeper next, or the other way
around. When I showed him what I had found and told
him about it, he was excited as I was—more just then, for
I was calming down. We talked it over and he agreed with
me that there was no doubt this was where Freeland's diary
had come from.

But pretty soon he said what I had been expecting he
would say.

"Good enough, Jonas!" said he. "Smart work and score
up one for you. . . . But—well, I—I don't exactly see—"

I finished for him. "You don't see that it gets us much if anywhere, after all. . . . Well, I'm with you there. It doesn't, confound it! We had the diary anyway, so settling where Gregg found it don't help much."

"Jonas, have you— No, that isn't my business. Sorry, old man."

"Oh, that's all right. . . . Bill, I—I wish I could honestly say I was making progress. I can't not yet. This pesky muddle is outside of my arithmetic, I'm commencing to think. If I had studied algebra—but I never have. The end of the grammar school was the end of my education."

He clapped me on the back. "You have done more so far than the rest of us put together. You will get the answer for us some day."

"Humph! Wish I could think so. Bill, you are a college man. Isn't it in algebra that they figure in what they call the 'unknown quantity'? What we need on this job is more of that unknown quantity—call it luck, if you want to. It was nothing but plain luck—my being on hand when Iantha coupled the smell on the diary with that cabinet— that got me even as far as this drawer. If we could have another streak of luck we might get further. Without it— well, I don't know."

I was pretty down at the heel when I said that. And yet, right off, the next day, that streak happened along. Seems sometimes as if luck did run that way—in streaks, good or bad. The weather stayed just as hot, or even hotter, and, in the middle of the afternoon, I slung my varnish brush into the corner, vowing I would not turn myself into a grease spot for anybody's maple dining-room set. I had a couple of letters to write, so I sat down and wrote them. Then I walked down to the village to mail them at the post-office.

I had walked pretty nigh as far as Miller Jenkins' antique shop when I remembered I had promised to telephone Mrs. Slater and tell her how her work was getting on. So, for fear I might forget it if I it off, I decided to drop in at Miller's place and use his phone.

His shop was on the corner and, when I crossed the road and came abreast the window of his back office, that window was open and, looking in, I could see Harvey Blodgett sitting at the roll-top desk, writing. His coat was off, he was in his shirt sleeves and smoking his usual big cigar. Seeing him there, making himself so much at home with Jenkins' belongings, started my suspicion mill working again. He and Miller surely were mighty chummy nowadays. Of course they always had been friendly on account of Blodgett's interest in antiques, but, just the same—

I went on around the building, came up the front steps and in the front door of the main shop. Jenkins was there— he had shed his coat too—and out in the workroom next to the office I could see Abe Peak, peeled down to trousers and a calico shirt, fitting a piece of veneer into the back of a mahogany chair.

Miller was awful glad to see me, so he declared, and I said I was terrible glad to see him. Having swapped even so far—and, I guess, both of us realizing the worth of what we'd got in the trade—I asked him how business was. He said it was about the worst he ever see and I said mine was worse than that. Then I told him what I'd come for.

Why, yes, yes—certain! I could use his phone just as well as not. Where was I figuring to phone to? Well now, nigh as he could recollect, the toll charge to Orham was fifteen cents. Of course he wouldn't think of letting me pay it, you understand, but—

I cut in. "That's all right, Miller," said I, "I hadn't any idea of paying you fifteen cents, so don't say another word."

He didn't, but he looked as if he wanted to say a lot. I took a dime out of my pocket and handed it to him.

"The Orham charge is ten cents," I said, "and there it is. Now we are all square, except that I'm much obliged. I will wait until Mr. Blodgett finishes his letter, or whatever it is, and then I'll try to get my money's worth out of the telephone company."

I did not have to wait, for that minute Harvey himself came out of the office.

"Go ahead, go ahead, Jones," says he, condescending as always. "I have finished what I was writing and the rest can hang over until you are through."

I thanked him and went in and sat down in the chair he had just left. It did not take me long to get Mrs. Slater on the wire and report progress on her work. Blodgett had left his coat hanging on one corner of the chair back and, when I went to get up, I hit it with my elbow. Being top-heavy, the whole business, chair, coat and all, went over backwards. The coat opened and spread-eagled and something from the inside pocket flew out and slid along the floor.

Harvey and Miller were talking together by the front door and they did not pay any attention. I picked up the chair and the coat first and then stooped to get what had slid out of the pocket. It was a pocketbook, one of the long, old-fashioned kind, faded red leather with a strap around it, and Blodgett's initial, a big B, stamped in rusty gilt on the flap. There were a pair of snaky-looking whirligigs in gilt—fact is, they *were* snakes, or dragons, or similar—one above and one below the B. It struck me that it was a shabby old-fashioned sort of wallet for a man of Harvey Blodgett's class to be using. However, that was none of my affairs—if he stretched his love for antiques as far as pocketbooks, *I* should worry—so I started to put it back into the coat pocket it had come from. And then, as I lifted it as high as my nose, something else struck me— yes, and struck me hard.

I took one good sniff to make sure. There was no doubt about it. That pocketbook reeked of camphor as strong as Captain Freeland's diary did.

For a second I sat there holding the thing against my face and wondering if I was going camphor crazy. Then I heard Blodgett's voice, it sounded as if he was crossing the outer shop towards the office. I jammed the wallet back in the pocket of the coat and walked out to meet him.

I didn't hang around there many seconds. I wanted to get outside where I could think. The only words I remember hearing said—and I did not really remember them until afterwards—was Blodgett's telling Miller Jenkins that he would not be in to see him again until day after to-morrow.

"I am going to Ostable to-morrow, Jenkins," he said. "But the next day I shall be here about two o'clock. You think over that proposition of mine. I made you a good offer and, unless you are a fool, you'll take it."

That speech must have sunk into my head without my knowing it. I am glad it did, for, as it happened, it helped out my plans later on. I went wandering off up the road, the letters I had come down town especially to mail forgotten altogether—they stayed forgotten in my pocket for a fortnight—my head down and my mind steaming off, like a switch engine, on this new track.

That pocketbook was an old-fashioned one and it reeked of camphor. Why should Harvey Blodgett be using a dingy, camphor-soaked pocketbook? It did not seem like him; everything I had ever seen him carry—like his watch and gold pencil and cigar case—was new and expensive, and right up to date. Of course the pocketbook might be a rare antique he had picked up somewhere, but, if so, it was funny he should have spoiled its antiqueness by having his initial stamped on it.

And then I stopped short in the middle of the step I was taking. There was only one letter on that pocketbook. The gilt stamping was not H. B., but just B. And B stood for other names besides Blodgett.

For instance, one of the names it stood for was Blair.

III

I was, maybe, half of the way home by this time, but I didn't go any further. I whirled off to the left and, tramping right through bushes and weeds instead of going around them, I made a bee line across lots for the Blair place. I went in the back way and around to the woodshed door. It was Iantha Hallet I wanted to see just then and I was hoping neither Bill Thornton nor Marian would see me until I had my talk with her.

The good luck which had hit me the day before, and had kept right with me ever since, hung on now. Iantha was alone in the kitchen when I walked into it. She had not heard me coming and so, of course, she hopped clear of the deck when I hailed her.

"Good goodness alive, Jonas Jones!" she squealed at me. "Don't you know better than to creep in on anybody like that? My nerves are all ravelings nowadays and first thing you know I shall jump right out of my skin. I will, sure as you live!"

"If you're going to jump out of your skin," says I, "this is good weather to do it in. All a person needs for comfort just now is a suit of bones. Sorry I scared you, Iantha. I just ran in to beg pardon for the way I ran out last night. Mr. Thornton told you why I did, I suppose? It came over me that I had left a lamp burning in the shop. With all the shavings and stuff around, why—well, it don't pay to take chances."

It was the excuse I had given Bill to give her and there was just truth enough in it to get by. I *had* left a lamp burning, but I did it on purpose.

"So he said," says she. "Though why that should make you call yourself a fool I don't know. I will say, though, that you acted like one that minute; I was about set to telephone the Taunton asylum."

She and I talked while she bustled around the cook-stove. Little by little I was steering the talk towards what I really came for.

"Did you put Captain Freeland's diary back where you took it from?" I asked her.

Yes, indeed she had and she reminded me that I was not to tell Marian or Mr. Thornton that she ever fished it out.

"Queer old thing that diary is," I went on. "Funny that it should turn up after this long, long time. You hadn't missed it, I suppose, way back there when you and Miss Rebecca looked over her brother's things?"

"Sartin sure we missed it. Two or three little things of his were missing, as I recollect, but we were too much upset to hunt for them long. That was an upset time! Poor Mr. Gregg's being took the way he was brings the other awful spell back to me so plain! Well, you know how *I* feel about it all. Call me superstitious much as you mind to, I still say—"

She was getting up steam and, as I knew from experience, if she really got under way on that bad luck and curse cruise of hers, there would be no land in sight for an hour.

"Yes, yes—sure! I agree with you," I cut in, quick. "Oh, well, such is life and we are here to-day and tomorrow the rent is due, as the fellow said. . . . Speaking of that diary, Iantha, it seems queer to me that a well-to-do man like

Captain Freeland Blair should have used such a shabby old book to keep his log in. But there! I remember well the pocketbook my dad carried during his last years. That was shabby enough, mercy knows, but he would never have swapped it for one right off the store counter. He was used to it and he liked it, you understand. I presume Captain Freeland liked that diary. It was kind of homey and—er—rusty, like the rest of his things. . . . Well, well, we are all notional, more or less, that's a fact."

That scraped a tender spot, same as I hoped it might. Iantha might, and did, feel herself free to criticize anybody and anything connected with the Blair family, but she never kept still when an outsider did it. She bristled right up.

"I don't know what you mean by the 'rest of his things,'" she said, sharp. "He had as good things as anybody in this town—yes, and better than most. That gold watch and chain of his—the one Mary has in her bedroom now and tells time by nights—that was bought in London and cost I don't know how much money. You wouldn't call that watch and chain rusty, I shouldn't say. Well, scarcely!"

"I wasn't thinking about gold watches. They don't get shabby like—well, like diaries and pocketbooks."

"Who said Captain Freeland's pocketbook was shabby. He had two or three, far as that goes. Some he used a lot and some he didn't."

"Sure! But I'll bet the one he fancied and used most was about like my dad's. That was a chunky old black leather wallet, tied 'round with a piece of string."

"No such thing! I'd have you understand that a man like Freeland Blair didn't tie up *his* pocketbooks with no string. The idea! The one he carried most of the time had been bought abroad, same as his watch and chain. He bought it in—in China or the East Indies, where he used to go voyages in his younger days. It wasn't fat and chunky either. I ought to know, I saw it times enough. Why, now that you remind me, I can see him this minute, taking it out to pay Jethro Gould his wages. It had a strap around it and there was a big gold B—his initial, you know—on the front. Yes, and some kind of wiggly gold ornaments—like worms I used to think—at top and bottom. That pocketbook was a real nice one."

"Must have been. Sounds like a genuine antique. It might be worth more these times, as a curiosity, than it was at the beginning. Mary Fisher has got it now, I suppose. Humph! I should like to see it. Such things always interest me."

She turned and looked at me. "Jonas Jones," she said, "what in the world made you set me remembering that pocketbook?"

"I don't know. I was recollecting the one my father carried."

"Well, it is funny you should mention it, for that very pocketbook was one of the things belonging to Captain Freeland that neither Miss Rebecca nor me could find after he died. She remembered it, same as I did, although of course it wasn't as familiar to her as it was to me. We figured he must have lost it along in his last days when he was half crazy and careless."

"That so? Then I guess you won't be showing it to me. Too bad!"

I had stirred her up, that was plain, for she began to sputter.

"Dear, dear!" she snapped. "Why on earth did you have to set me thinking about Captain Freeland, Jonas Jones? Now I shall dream about his dying and

all, and I have dreams enough without raking *him* out of his grave. . . . I declare you have pestered me till I have forgot how long that johnny cake of mine has been in the oven. Oh, you *are* a nuisance sometimes!"

I wasn't one much longer for I went away right after that. I had got what I wanted. I spent the longest half of that night in my bedroom up over the shop, trying to think what this new find amounted to and what more I could make out of it. I got out my sheet of paper with the names on it. That pocketbook, as I saw it, must be put in just one column and the name at the top of that column was Harvey Blodgett.

Blodgett had been in that attic, with Gregg and without him. The diary had been—I was dead sure—in the secret drawer of the Chinese cabinet. I was just as sure now that Freeland Blair's wallet had been in the same drawer. How did it get out of that drawer and into Blodgett's pocket?

I didn't know, of course; but it was there, and, what was a whole lot more important, I believed there was, or had been, something in it that was responsible for the breaking in at the old Blair place—the break that had happened after Sam Gregg's death.

My first idea was that I would see Bill Thornton and Marian right off after breakfast and tell them what I had found and what I suspicioned. I had not told Iantha because, although I knew she would promise to keep still, and mean to, she would be so excited that the first person she met would guess something was up. And, after I had thought a while longer, I decided not to tell anybody just yet. I had no plan and I must make a plan. I must dig out some way to force Blodgett—or Blodgett and Jenkins, provided they were working together—to tell how he or they came by that pocketbook and what was in it.

All that day I did not much of anything but plan and plan. Every idea that struck me seemed worse than those I thought of sooner. My notions concerning the sandalwood box I hove overboard, for the present. If Blodgett or Jenkins had any reason for wanting that box other than because it was a rare antique, I must not waste time guessing what they were.

The Chinese cabinet, though, I knew now, had been mixed up in our mystery from the very start. The diary and the pocketbook had been hid in it. And Blodgett—yes, and Miller Jenkins too—still wanted to get hold of that cabinet; they were willing to pay high for it.

Well, it was that Chinese cabinet that gave me the start on the plan I finally worked out and decided to try. It was not much of a plan. If I had tested it by arithmetic I should have had to own up that the chances against its coming to anything were at least fifty to one. But, as I saw it, it was a possible bait for the mousetrap and I made up my mind to try that fifty to one chance.

About half past one of the next afternoon I locked my shop door and started down to the village again by the road. On the way I met Bill Thornton; he had been coming over to see me. I told him I had an errand down town and would be glad of his company. We were almost at Miller Jenkins' corner when, as luck would have it, I saw that Tom Davis, Blodgett's hired man, coming down the post-office steps. I had not expected him, nor I hadn't counted him in on my precious "plan," but, as long as Providence was handing him to me, I gave him a hail.

He came across the road to meet us, his teeth shining in his black face like a steamer's cabin portholes at night.

"Yes, *suh!*" says he, bearing down hard on the "suh," which was a habit of his. "Yes, *suh,* Mr. Jones. How is you to-day?"

I told him I was fair to middling and asked if his boss had got back from Ostable yet.

"Yes, suh, Mr. Jones, Mr. Blodgett he got back home last night. He's down town here now somewheres, I reckon!"

"All right. Maybe I will run across him myself, but, in case I shouldn't, you give him this message from me. Tell him I have found out something new about that Chinese cabinet he is interested in. Be sure and say that I am going up to Boston on this afternoon's train, but I will be back the day following. Got that?"

"Yes, suh, I got it."

"Good enough! Tell him what I found out is going to surprise him."

"Surprise him? Yes, suh!"

"Yes; and be sure and say that it will be no use going to my shop to see me this evening, because there won't be anybody there all night."

"Yes, suh, I'll tell him. . . . Now what was that last, Mr. Jones? That you nor nobody wouldn't be to yo' shop all night to-night?"

"That is just what I said. Don't you forget it, Tom."

"No, *suh!*"

We walked on and left him. Bill turned to me.

"So you are going to Boston this afternoon, Jonas?" he said. "Sudden trip, isn't it?"

"Um-hm. Sudden enough."

I guess likely he expected me to tell him why I was going, but I didn't and he isn't the kind to pry. We walked a few steps further and then he said, "Why did you tell him there would be nobody in your shop all night?"

"Eh? Why not?"

"Why—well, he is probably honest enough himself, but he may tell other people and— Humph! Sounds to me like issuing a general invitation to whatever thieves may be about, if any."

I laughed, "I declare it does sound so, that is a fact. Bill, I am going in here to Miller's place a minute. Come along with me, if you have got nothing else to do."

When we first stepped across Jenkins' doorsill I was considerable disappointed. It looked as if there was nobody there but Abel Peak, who was sandpapering for dear life at a chair back. However, that of itself ought to have proved to me that he was not alone; Abe never worked as hard as all that when there was nobody to watch him. And, next minute, Miller came out of the back office, with Harvey Blodgett at his heels.

I don't know whether or not they were glad to see us, but I do know I was glad to see them. During the attacks of thinking I had been suffering from most of the day and night just past, it had run across my mind what Blodgett said to Jenkins about calling in on him at two o'clock that afternoon. So I had timed my own call to fit.

"How do you do, Mr. Blodgett?" said I. "How are you, Miller? Don't get your hopes up; I didn't come to buy any antiques you have got."

Jenkins smiled kind of feeble, but Blodgett, as usual, had a prompt comeback.

"Well then, did you come to sell any of your own?" he asked. "I am still in the market for bargains. I told you that the other day."

"Yes, I recollect you did. And Mr. Thornton here says Miller was up to the Fisher house hunting along the same line. Well, there is no harm in trying, I suppose, only I might as well warn you both that prices are rising with me every minute. Fact is, I was happening by and I couldn't help stopping in to make you fellows more jealous than ever. That Chinese cabinet of mine *was* a bargain. I thought so when I bought it and now I know."

They looked at each other and then at me.

"What is all this, Jones?" blurted out Blodgett. "What are you giving us?"

"I'll tell you one thing I *ain't* giving you, or anybody else, and that is that cabinet. I may sell it, sometime or other, if anybody is interested. . . . Are you interested, Miller?"

Jenkins shifted his feet and looked foolish. "I don't know as I'm exactly what you'd call much interested," he said. "Of course, if I could get the thing cheap enough to make it worth while I might be. . . . What do you mean, anyhow; talking about making us jealous?"

I laughed. "I just said that because I have got a mean disposition. I gave that cabinet an overhauling yesterday and I found something. What do you suppose it was? Give you three guesses."

For a man who wasn't much interested Miller Jenkins gave a poor imitation. Far as that goes, I had all hands interested by this time. Even Abe Peak stopped his work to listen and, out of the corner of my eye, I could see Bill Thornton staring at me as if he thought I had gone crazy. Harvey Blodgett spoke first.

"Come, come! can the hot air, Jones," he ordered. "You know darn well I want that cabinet. How much?"

I waved my hand. "All I said was that I might sell it sometime. That time isn't now. I am only beginning to take a fancy to that cabinet. I always had an idea there was more to it than meets the eye. There is, too. I haven't had a chance to go at it the way I mean to, but I have found one secret drawer and—well, that is a start, isn't it?"

Nobody said a word for a second, though I have a strong notion that Bill was on the point of speaking. I judge his suspicion that I was crazy was close to a certainty by this time. As usual, though, it was Harvey Blodgett who had his say. "A secret drawer," he snorted. "Well, what of it? There are likely to be—"

But Miller couldn't wait any longer.

"What was in that drawer?" he wanted to know.

I grinned. "Why, nothing—maybe. Perhaps there was nothing at all in that particular one. Or perhaps—but never mind. That isn't the whole thing. There are two or three spaces in that cabinet that I can't account for and—humph—well, I shouldn't wonder if they might be worth looking into when I get the time. Where there is one drawer there may be others. . . . Oh, well, I won't stir up your jealousy any more, just now. I am going to Boston on this afternoon's train, but I shall be back to-morrow night and then I mean to have a regular hunt. I just wanted you fellows to know that that cabinet is worth money and it is going to take money to buy it. . . . Think it over. I will see you again in a couple of days."

I started for the door. Jenkins hurried after me and caught hold of my arm.

"Now, now, don't hurry, Jonas," he begged. "What's your rush? I tell you what let's do: Let's you and me go right back to your shop now, and—"

Blodgett was right at his heels. "No, you don't!" he sung out. "Look here, Jones—"

I did not let him finish. "No, no," I said, laughing again. "You will have to wait, both of you, till I have made this Boston trip. Yes, and after that, until I have given that cabinet the looking through I mean to give it. After that I will talk to the highest bidder—maybe."

Miller was just going to speak again, I think, but once more Blodgett wouldn't let him.

"Shut up, Jenkins!" he ordered. "When are you going to Boston, Jones?"

"Now, on the next train."

"And you will be back—when?"

"To-morrow evening, early."

"Umph! . . . All right. I will see you then, or the next day sure. Don't you sell that thing until I do see you; understand?"

Bill and I walked along the sidewalk. He had not taken his eyes off me since we came out of that antique shop.

Finally, judging that nothing would be said unless I said it first, I spoke.

"It is a dreadful thing to have softening of the brain, ain't it," I said.

He grunted. "You ought to know, I'd say!" he answered, emphatic. "See here, Jonas, what the devil—?"

"That is the question, sure enough. It is the only one I want you to ask just now, and even that I can't stop to answer till later on."

He grunted again. "I'll be hanged if I can see—" he began. Then he shook his head. "Why on earth you took pains to advertise that secret drawer is beyond me. However, you have some reason, of course. . . . But about those others you said you expected to find in that cabinet? You never mentioned them to me, nor to Marian."

"I never mentioned them to anybody till five minutes ago. . . . Now, Bill, will you go home and get Marian's car and call for me at my shop just as soon as you can? I'd like to have you take me to the depot."

"Of course. . . . But, Jonas, do you think it is safe to leave that shop of yours, with nobody in it, all night? Especially now, after you told that negro and the rest you were going to?"

"No, I don't think so. At least I am hoping it isn't safe. . . . Bill, you and Marian and me had a sort of bargain, didn't we? About leaving things in my hands for a spell?"

He nodded. "We did," he agreed. . . . "All right. I will get the car and call for you in time for the train."

He and the car were on hand inside of half an hour. We shook hands on the depot platform and I took pains that everybody up there saw us doing it.

"I will be back to-morrow night," I said, and said it good and loud. Then, under my breath, I added, "Bill, I want you to stay home this evening. Will you?"

"Certainly. But why?"

"I will tell you that, and a lot more, pretty soon. . . . So long!"

I waved to him from the car platform as long as he was in sight. Then I went inside and sat down. I stayed seated but for nine miles, though. When the train pulled up at North Harniss I got out on the side away from the depot platform and hurried down the road. I ate supper at the Anchor Inn in the town and then I rang up the Fisher house on the hotel telephone.

As good luck would have it Bill himself answered.

"For heaven's sake!" says he. "You are not in Boston so soon, are you?"

I told him where I was. "Now," I went on, "I wish you would ask Marian, on the quiet, if she will be willing to let you out for—well, for a good part of the night, maybe. Tell her I don't believe there will be any breaks up at her house while you are out and that I need your company. Yes, and you might say that what I want you for is in connection with our puzzle. Ask her that, but don't let Iantha know you are planning to stay off watch so long. She would hang onto your coat tails and you would have to drag her with you."

He went to ask Marian and he was gone not more than two minutes.

"She says, 'Of course,'" he told me.

"Good! She is a brick and you tell her I always knew it. Now take the auto and come over here to the Anchor Inn and get me."

He came flying; I don't believe the Fisher flivver had ever moved as fast afore. I climbed in on the seat beside him.

"Drive to my shop," was my next order; "and take the back roads, I don't want anybody to see me. Now listen, while I tell you what it's all about."

I did tell him, beginning with my finding the pocket-book when it fell out of Harvey Blodgett's coat pocket and

what Iantha had told me about the wallet Captain Freeland Blair used to own. He listened, hardly saying a word
until I had finished.

"I see," he said, quiet enough, although I could tell
by his voice that he was excited. "I get now why you told
Davis you were going to be away from the shop to-night.
Yes, and why you told Blodgett and Jenkins the same thing
and about suspecting there were more secrets in the Chinese cabinet. Yes, I get that. But, honestly, Jonas, you
don't really suspect a man like Harvey Blodgett of being
the one who broke in at our house. It does not seem as if—
and yet, of course, if he *did* have any inside information
that we have not got—"

"*Somebody's* got some such information," I interrupted.
"They must have. And, whatever it is, we want it. Of course
this grand plan of mine is only a fifty to one chance, but it
might work, mightn't it? And I do declare I have not been
able yet to think of any other."

He drove quiet and slow along the road to my place
and we parked the auto in the pines a hundred yards or so
off to the left. Then we sneaked up to the shop and I let
him in by the side door. It was all black dark in there, but
I had an electric flash lamp in pocket and, by its light, I
piloted him in behind a stack of empty boxes I had built
up in one corner of my front room. Right abreast of a
peephole I had left between the boxes was the Chinese
cabinet on a maple table I had taken from stock.

I had put a couple of chairs behind the boxes and I sat
down on one and made him sit on the other.

"Now," I said, "there is one thing more. Here! You hang
on to that."

It was my old revolver I gave him and, when I turned
the flash light on it, he whistled.

"Good Lord!" he said. "You don't expect me to shoot
anyone, do you?"

"You would have a sweet time doing it with that thing. It has not been loaded for all of five years. No, there won't be any shooting—on our part anyhow—but even an empty revolver is a dose of soothing syrup sometimes. . . . There! now I am going to put out the light and all you and I will have to do for a spell is think about what pesky foolishness all this is most likely going to turn out to be."

IV

Summer nights are supposed to be the shortest we have, but there was nothing short about that one. Seems to me I have already said, as much as once or twice, that if there was any book I pinned my faith to, it was the arithmetic. That stretch of waiting there in the pitch dark—waiting for something that might turn up at any time, or no time—came nearer to unpinning that faith than any other experience ever I had. The table says there are sixty seconds in a minute and sixty minutes in a hour, but if there was not sixty years in those three or four hours then I was losing my knack at figures.

At the beginning we whispered to each other a little, but by and by we stopped even that and just sat still. Every once in a while, when I had decided that it must be close to the edge of morning, I'd push the flash-lamp button and look at my watch and find it was only twenty minutes later than when I looked at it last. It got to be eleven o'clock, then twelve, and then half past—and still nothing but the smell of varnish in the shop and the faint whistle of the breeze outside in the pine trees and the far-off growling of surf along the outer beach.

And, of course, with every minute my hopes were dropping lower and lower and my opinion of my wonderful "plan" and of myself, the idiot who was responsible for it, shrinking like a new flannel undershirt on wash day. When it got to be quarter past one and the nothing which had happened so far was still happening as slow as ever, I was ready to haul down the flag. I laid my hand on Thornton's knee.

"Bill," said I, still whispering, but only from force of habit—I was long past the point of believing that a howl would have done any harm—"Bill, I am sorry that revolver of mine isn't loaded."

He started; I should not wonder if he had been asleep, or on the edge of it.

"Eh?" he said. "What is that? Why are you sorry?"

"Because this lunatic scheme of mine is nothing but a wild-goose chase and the wildest goose in the county is roosting on the chair right next to you getting wilder every second. It ought to be shot and it is a shame you haven't anything to shoot it with. Bill, I am sorry I kept you out of bed for nothing, like this."

He chuckled. "Why, you are not surrendering so soon, are you, Jonas? It is early yet for callers. I scarcely expected. . . . *Sshh!*"

He didn't need to do any hushing. I had heard the same thing he had. We did not so much as breathe for a jiffy and then we both heard it again—a kind of scraping noise out back somewheres, a fumbling and scratching like.

He reached over and gave my leg a squeeze. I felt in my pocket to make sure the flash lamp was where I could get it out in a hurry. There was an instant of quiet and then more fumbling and scratching; then a long rasping squeal. Somebody was prying up one of the windows opening into the back shop.

We heard the sash moving up in its grooves and then everything was still again, but not for long. There came a sound of scuffling and scrambling, followed by a soft thump. The fellow, whoever he was had climbed into the back room.

Pretty soon he began to move again. A streak of brightness shone in through the door from that other room; it moved up and down and around; I was not the only one with an electric flash in that building. The spot of white light at the end of the streak slid along the walls and floor, over our pile of boxes and Mrs. Slater's maple set, until it hit the little table with the Chinese cabinet on it. There it stopped and stayed.

Another spell of quiet. Bill and I had our heads together at the peekhole, but of course we could see nothing but the streak of light. The person who was holding the flash lamp was just a blacker blotch against the rest of the dark. Then he came forward and moved toward the table. The light centered on the Chinese cabinet and lit up the carved heads and faces on it. It stayed right there until, all at once, a shadow blocked it out. Our visitor had scrooched down and was taking a close look at the cabinet.

I nudged Bill with my elbow and we both got to our feet. I took my own flash from my pocket and tiptoed out from behind the heap of boxes.

"Well, well!" said I. "This is a pleasure for sure! Glad to see you, neighbor. Nice of you to drop m this way."

The fellow before the cabinet jumped up with a sort of yowl, like a cat with its tail trod on. The flash lamp he was holding fell to the floor with a bang and a jingle. He swung around toward us and the beam from the light I was pointing at him struck him right in the face.

Then I wanted to yowl, too. It was Harvey Blodgett I was expecting to see; if not him, then Miller Jenkins sure. And this fellow was neither Jenkins nor Blodgett, but that Shanghai-legged, ostrich-necked Abel Peak!

I certainly had not expected to see *him!* If you can imagine a man who had baited a shark hook finding that he had caught a gudgeon, you can imagine a little of how I felt.

However, I did not have much time to think of anything. Peak stared at us, for a jiffy, with his big mouth sagging open like a schooner's hatch. Then he let out another scream and made a bolt for the back room. Bill Thornton was after him like a bluefish after a sand eel and grabbed him around the waist and both arms.

"I have got him, Jonas," he sang out.

"Good boy!" said I. "Hang on to him tight."

He was hanging on, judging by the thrashing and banging where he and Abe were having their wrestling match. I flew across the shop and lit two of the bracket lamps on the walls.

"There!" I said. "Now we look more sociable and ready for company. Give him to me now, Bill. . . . Stand still, you crazy jumping-jack, or I'll break you in two."

He did not seem to have any idea of standing still, but all at once I felt him go slack all over. I looked up and saw that Thornton had taken that old revolver of mine out of his pocket. It was the revolver Peak was looking at and it would not be any exaggeration to say he looked interested.

"Shall I shoot him, Jonas?" asked Bill, solemn as a church.

"Oh, not quite yet," says I. "Let's have a little fun with him first."

Peak was quiet enough now in one way, but in another he was not. He had stopped kicking and squirming, but now he began to beg.

"Don't shoot! Oh, please don't shoot! Don't kill me— please! I—I haven't done nothing! I didn't mean nothing! *Please* don't shoot me!"

I shifted my hold from his waist to his shirt collar. I really did not need to hang on to him at all; the sight of that pistol had taken all the starch out of *his* back-bone. I think he was just going to cry, he sounded as if he was.

"All right, all right," I told him. "We will give you time to say your prayers. Be still! Stop your noise!

I reached out with my foot and kicked one of Mrs. Slater's chairs towards him. "Sit down on that," I ordered. "Sit down and behave yourself. Mr. Thornton and I want to look at you. You don't realize what a welcome sight you are."

He sat down on the chair without waiting for another invitation. He did not take his eyes off the revolver though, not once. Bill and I looked him over.

"Well," said I, after a breathing space, "here you are, Abe, ain't you! I can't say we exactly expected you, but we are glad you came, just the same. . . . Now then, tell us all about it. What did you come here for—and why? Who put you up to this? . . . Come! Out with it!"

He didn't answer; just stared at the revolver and shook and shivered. He surely was a pitiful show for anything that called itself a man. I could not make it out at all. It didn't seem possible that *he* was the one responsible for all the burglaring and disturbances up at the Blair place. I would about as soon have expected an ague chill to turn into an earthquake.

"Out with it—all of it!" I ordered again. "No? You won't? All right, Bill; put him out of his misery."

That turned on the spigot—a little. Peak began to beg and pray some more. Finally he started to tell a few things, but they didn't amount to much. He had come to hunt through that Chinese cabinet.

"I—I wasn't going to steal nothing, Mr. Jones," said he. "Honest truth I wasn't. I—I— Well, you said—I heard you say up at our place—that you had found one secret drawer in that Chinese box and—and that you was sure there was more of them, so—so—"

"Yes, yes! And so?"

"And—and you said you was going up to Boston and there wouldn't be nobody in your shop all night. And so—so I—well, I thought I would come down and hunt through that box afore you had another chance. That is all 'twas. Honest, it was! *Please* let me go! Oh, *won't* you?"

I could not help winking at Bill Thornton. I was feeling a little better than I had been during the last half of our watching and waiting session. My great plan wasn't altogether a wild-goose chase; my trap had caught something, even if what it caught was a mighty small mouse.

"We will see about letting you go later on," I said. "We haven't decided whether or not to shoot you yet. What we do with you depends on how much you tell. Understand that?"

"But I *am* telling you! It was just nothing but that Chinese box thing I came here about. I wanted to find them other secret drawers afore you or anybody else did. That is all. I just—"

"Hush! What on earth did you want of secret drawers, provided there were any?"

He looked up at me, then at Bill and the revolver, and then around the room.

"I don't know as I wanted nothing," he mumbled. "I just—well, I know about secret drawers in—in desks and boxes and places. I have seen a lot of them; yes, and I have found two or three on my own hook. There is—sometimes there is things hid in them drawers, money and rings and such."

It was a fact—so there were, and every fellow who has anything to do with the antique business knows it. My confidence that we were close to at least a part of the answer to my arithmetic example began to slip its cable. Abel Peak had worked on antiques about as long as he had ever worked at anything. He did know about secret drawers and that, sometimes, cash, or things that could be sold for cash, were hid in them. His explanation sounded reasonable, too confounded reasonable and believable to please me. It was about down to his measure; it was about what he would think and do.

But I could not give up yet.

"Bosh!" I said. "That isn't all that set you to breaking and stealing. I don't believe it. Tell the rest! Tell the whole yarn!"

He stuck to it that there was no more yarn. That was why he came and for nothing more. Bill asked him who had sent him, who had put him up to the job. Nobody had put him up to it. He didn't know anything about Blodgett's clock or the sandalwood box. He wanted to find those drawers I had said I was sure were in that cabinet and, being as I was going to leave my shop all alone all night, he had taken a chance. That was all; we could believe it or not, just as we had a mind to.

He was getting over a little of his first scare. He was realizing, I guess, that we had not the least idea of shooting him and he was getting more sullen and stubborn every second. We cross-questioned and bullied and badgered him, but he just shook his head and declared he had told all there was to tell.

I was coming to be sure he had, too, and the thought made me so disappointed that I was about sick. I could see that Bill believed him, for he had dropped out of the cross-examination after a while and just stood there, twirling the revolver around his finger, and smiling at me, kind of mischievous and amused. That smile made me stick to my guns longer than I otherwise might have. I was mad clear through.

"Rings!" I scowled. "Suppose you had found a ring in one of those drawers, what on earth would you do with it?"

He shifted a little on the chair. "Well," he said, ugly but kind of ashamed too, "I—well, you see, I have got a girl over to South Harniss."

That was too much for Bill Thornton. The idea of any girl taking a fancy to Abe Peak struck him funny. He burst out into a roar of "Ha, ha's."

"Oh, for heaven's sake, Jonas!" he said, between his laughs. "Don't waste any more time on him. He is a dud, if ever there was one. Kick him out and let him go."

Abel Peak did not seem to mind the kicking part. It was the notion that he might be let go that struck him hard. He jumped up off the chair.

"Yes—yes!" says he. "That's it, that's it. Oh, God bless you, Mr. Thornton! I'll never forget you as long as you live."

"You bet you won't!" I growled, between my teeth. "And you will remember me, too—every time you go to sit down for the next fortnight. You leave the kicking to me, Bill."

I made a move towards Peak and he squealed and jumped away from me. His jump took him over nearer the wall, where the light from one of the bracket lamps struck full on him from head to foot.

And all at once I noticed something I had not noticed before.

"Wait!" I shouted. "Stand still! . . . Grab him, Bill! Don't let him go."

Bill grabbed him. I stepped over and took another long look. Yes, it was so. I couldn't be mistaken—and yet—

"Where did you get those clothes you are wearing?" I asked, sharp and sudden.

Thornton has never told me what he thought when he heard me ask that question. The expression on his face was funny enough, if I had been feeling funny just then. But Peak's was funnier still. He stared at me, his mouth opening and shutting.

"Wh-wh-what?" he stuttered. "Clothes? . . . Wh-what clothes?"

"That suit of clothes you have got on. Where did it come from? Does it belong to you?"

"Eh? . . . Why, of course it belongs to me! What you talking about, Mr. Jones? I—I don't know what you mean."

"Where did you get it?"

I presume likely he had come to the conclusion that I thought he had stolen the suit. At any rate, he stiffened up. For a fellow who had been caught climbing in through another person's window he gave the best imitation of injured innocence I ever saw.

"I don't know as I am called on to tell you or nobody else where I get my clothes," he snarled, his voice jumping. "I got them and I paid my own money for them, and that's enough."

"No, it isn't. Where did you get them? Quick! Have that revolver of yours handy, Bill."

The mention of the revolver did the trick; even yet I guess Abe was not quite sure we might not murder him. His answer this time was mild enough—and prompt, too.

"I bought this suit over to the New York Store at Wapatomac. You ask them over there and they'll tell you I did. . . . What—what difference does my clothes make, anyhow? I—"

"Be still! Has anybody else except you ever worn them?"

"*What?* Why, course they ain't!"

"I see. . . . Wait a second now. Let me get this straight. You remember when I came into Jenkins' shop the other day—not the last time, but the time before? . . . Yes. Well, Mr. Blodgett was sitting at your boss's desk writing a letter. After he came out I went in and used the telephone. You remember that?"

"Yes . . . Yes, sir."

"Blodgett was in his shirt sleeves and there was a coat hanging on the back of his chair. That coat wasn't his, it was yours? It was this very coat you have got on now?"

"Eh? Why—why, yes, it was. I had been in there doing some bookkeeping, and it was terrible hot weather, so—"

I didn't wait for the end. Where I had made my mistake was plain to see now. I had taken too much for granted, something that no good figurer should do.

"Hold him tight, Bill," I ordered.

Bill held him. I guess he, too, was beginning to sniff a scent of the truth. I caught hold of Peak and rammed my hand into the inside pocket of his jacket. The pocket was empty and, for a second, my breath caught. Then the feel of something hard under my hand set it going again.

I let go of the coat and, taking hold of the top button of the vest, I jerked it open, then, from the inside pocket of that vest, I pulled out a long, leather pocketbook smelling strong of camphor and with a gilt B on the flap.

I could have danced a jig, but I didn't. Ordering Bill again to hold him tight, I stepped back right under the lamp and opened that wallet. In it were two sets of papers and I took them out. One, the thinnest of the two, was a long sheet of foolscap, yellowed from time and worn at the folds. I spread it out.

It was headed: "List of Personal Property Belonging to me, George Crossley, in Cabin and Stateroom of Bark *Pride of the Fleet*. To be Delivered, in Case of My Death, and With Enclosed Will to Captain Freeland Blair, East Orham, Mass., U. S. A."

The other set of papers was thicker, a dozen sheets or so at least, and covered, both sides of each sheet, with close-together lines of handwriting. It was a letter. I looked at the top of the first page. It began:

> Hong Kong, June 2, 1883.
>
> "Dear Captain Blair:"

I turned to the foot of the last page. It was signed:

"Yours truly,
George Crossley."

Then I *did* take a jig step or two. My fifty to one chance had won, after all. My wild-goose chase had bagged a bird, even if it was not the one I thought I was aiming at.

Yes, and I could write "Proved so far" under one column of figures in my arithmetic example.

PART FOUR

Captain Crossley's Message

The Story Continued by
William Todd Thornton

The picture of Jonas Jones, as he stood there under the bracket lamp in the back room of his shop that night, will always remain vivid in my memory. In one hand he held a shabby leather pocketbook, in the other a wad of time-yellowed papers, and he gazed at both with an expression of mingled wonder, relief, and intense satisfaction. He looked like a child who had just awakened from a nightmare to discover it was Christmas morning.

"Well, I'll be blistered!" he was murmuring softly. "I'll be everlastin'ly blistered!

I still maintained a firm grip on the lanky body of Abel Peak, but the precaution was wholly unnecessary. He had gone limp in my arms and was whining a pitiful and abject plea for mercy. I shook him savagely and ordered him to be quiet.

"What have you found?" I demanded eagerly of Jonas. "Is it as much as you'd hoped?"

He nodded, placed the pocketbook and the papers in his pocket, and turned to us. "Yes and, maybe more," he said briskly; "and now, Bill, if you'll just plunk that thing you're hangin' onto into a chair, I'll ask it a few straight questions. . . . Thank you."

He walked over to the cowering Mr. Peak and shook a stern finger under his nose. "Now look here, Abe, you

long-legged mess of nothin'," he began, "this has been your
night so far. You've had all the fun—now it's our turn. Mr.
Thornton and I don't want to hear any more about rings,
and best girls in South Harniss, do you understand? We
want the whole yarn, and we want it straight and in a
hurry. If you keep anything back, and if you tell any more
lies, we'll—"

I picked up the empty revolver and fingered it lovingly.
"How about a little dose of lead, Jonas?" I asked, with
intense solemnity. "Don't you think that might help?"

Jonas appeared to reflect. Then he shook his head in
the negative. "No, Bill, no," he said. "It's the right pre-
scription, but I guess we can't give it just yet. Business
afore pleasure, you know. Besides, I'm sure the Ostable
County jail folks will save us the trouble. They're apt to
be kind of rough with robbers—and murderers."

"No!" Abel emitted a half-strangled scream and tried to
struggle to his feet. "Oh, God, Mr. Jones, don't say that!
I ain't a murderer. Honest, Mr. Jones, I ain't! I never even
laid hands on him. I'll swear it wa'n't no fault of mine.
He—"

"Shut up!" Jonas looked at him and then at me.
"Humph," he grunted, with a nod. "I thought as much.
There it is, Bill—see? So you *was* in the Blair house, Abe,
the night Sam Gregg died, and he caught you there, into
the bargain. Chased you, too, didn't he, 'way out across
the road into the pines? I thought so."

"Yes, yes, I was—but—but I didn't do no murder!"
Peak's face was considerably whiter than his dingy shirt
and his teeth were chattering so violently that he could
scarcely speak. "I just ran away from him as fast as I could
run, and I never laid hand nor finger on him. I didn't have
nothin' to do with his dyin'. Oh, my Lord, Mr. Jones,
don't tell 'em I killed him! *Please*—! Oh, *don't* you believe
me! Don't you hear what I say?"

Once more Jonas silenced him. "I hear you all right, but believin' a fellow who has told so many lies already is different. Whether you killed him or not remains to be seen, and whether Mr. Thornton and I take you to Ostable depends considerable on how straight you talk now. If you want to save your skin you'll come across with the whole yarn. You'll begin at the beginnin', you won't leave out anything, and you won't add on any trimmin's. We're listenin' to you. Now go ahead."

Abel went ahead. He told the whole story, with many irrelevancies to be sure, and with numerous pleas for mercy, but it was evident that he was, at last, sticking closely to the truth. The fear that he might be implicated in the death of Samuel Gregg—a fear that must have been his bedfellow ever since that death occurred—was so real that he had no thought of further evasion.

The whole thing had begun, he assured us, on the morning when he had come to the Blair house to crate those of Miller Jenkins' purchases of the day before which were to be shipped to Boston. He had found himself alone in the attic storeroom and had taken the opportunity to do a little private investigating. The Chinese cabinet interested him because he knew from experience that such cabinets usually contained secret drawers. He also knew from experience that valuables, and money even, were sometimes to be found in hidden compartments.

He set to work, in his honest, straightforward way, and in less than five minutes had found what he was seeking, the inevitable secret drawer. He pulled it out and carried it over to the window, where the first thing that met his delighted eye was the sight of a long leather pocketbook. Mr. Peak's acumen was not great but he knew a pocketbook when he saw it, and he realized that this one might very well contain a just reward for his diligence.

He had taken the pocketbook from the drawer and was about to examine it when he heard a step in the outer storeroom. He had time only to slip the wallet into his coat pocket when Samuel Gregg appeared in the doorway.

"Wait a minute," Jonas interrupted sharply. "Not too fast now, Abe. There was somethin' else in that drawer wasn't there, besides the wallet? Even though the wallet was all you had time to hide before Sam Gregg showed up? Don't hold anything back. Wasn't there somethin' else?"

"Yes—yes, sir."

"I thought so. Well? What was it?"

"I—I don't exactly know, Mr. Jones. Honest I don't. As nigh as I could make out it was a little red book. Mr. Gregg, he grabbed it—as soon as I'd told him I'd found the secret drawer for him."

"Oh, you told him you'd found it so's to save him the trouble. He must have thought that was kind of you. I see. You forgot to mention the pocketbook, I suppose—eh?"

Abel hung his head. "Well, I—I didn't say nothin' about that."

"I'll bet! That's about what I'd expect you to do. Did Sam show you the red book? Did he tell you what it was? Out with the truth, all of it! Keep that revolver handy, Bill."

"No—no, he didn't. I swear he didn't! He just grabbed it and pawed it over. He seemed kind of excited like, but he never showed it to me or told me what it was. Honest—"

"Be still!" Jonas winked at me and I could see that he was hugely pleased. "I'll believe you, Abe, for once. Go on with the rest of the yarn. If it's as interestin' as what you've told already, it'll be worth hearin'!"

Peak continued. He had been very much frightened when Gregg walked into the attic because he knew that he had no right to be meddling with anything there. He begged Gregg not to say anything about the matter to Jenkins as it undoubtedly would cause him to lose his job. Gregg seemed to pay little heed to his plea at first, but finally—and to Peak's great surprise—agreed to keep silent. The secret drawer was replaced in the cabinet and Abel was allowed to go his way. He did not understand why, nor did he stop to inquire.

Later, in the privacy of his room over Jenkins' shop, he examined the pocketbook. To his great disgust, it contained nothing but a lot of old papers. His disappointment was keen, and he was on the point of throwing them away, unread, when his curiosity got the better of him. He scrutinized his find carelessly at first, and then with growing interest. In the end it dawned upon him that he had unearthed something worthy of attention, after all.

Abel Peak was far from being a man of great intelligence, but he had a certain mean shrewdness coupled with an insatiable lust for easy, even if dishonest, money. He asked guarded questions of people in the town, among them Iantha Hallett. He added the answers to those questions to the information he had gleaned from the papers in the pocketbook, and in the end he found himself convinced of three things. One was that a man named George Crossley had hidden something of immense value in his personal goods. Another was that he—Peak—was the only living person with the knowledge that such a thing existed. The third was that Crossley's effects had, in all probability, remained intact and undisturbed in the attic of the Blair house until very recently.

From then on, Abel assured us, he had acted only as any sensible man would have acted in his place.

"Sure!" Jonas nodded grimly. "Any sensible man with a chance of findin' some money that didn't belong to him would be sure to go around thievin' and breakin' into other folks' houses; and doin' a little murder now and then just to liven things up. That would be only natural. Yes, indeed!"

Once more Peak hit the roof. He begged us, tearfully, to believe that he was not a murderer. He was an honest, God-fearing man, he protested vehemently, and the very thought of doing violence to a fellow creature was almost more than he could stand.

"There, there," Jonas soothed him, "don't get so excited. Realizin' as I do what a sensible, honest, God-fearin' critter you are, Peak, I ought to have known your feelin's would be tender. I do hope you'll excuse me for hurtin' 'em. Now stop cryin' all over the place like a sprinklin' cart and answer me this: You'll swear, will you, that all the information you had came from those papers in the wallet? You're sure you never saw that little red book you turned over to Sam Gregg—never read it, I mean?"

Abel raised a solemn hand. "As I hope for salvation, Mr. Jones, I'll swear to mercy I never so much as laid an eye on the inside of it."

"Humph! Well, for once more I'll believe you. Gettin' so I'll believe 'most anything these days, that's a fact." Jonas turned to me: "You hear, Bill? He never read the little book! Don't that show you how far from the truth the calculations of mortal mind can slip? Well, be that as it may, let's hear some more of this honest man's sensible actions—about his stealin' Harvey Blodgett's clock, for instance."

"Cl-clock?"

"Yes, yes—clock. We know all about that. You'd be surprised, Abel, how much we do know. We can always jog your memory if you forget anything—which I wouldn't do, if I was you. Now heave ahead with the yarn."

One of the most useful things that Peak had found in the old wallet was a detailed list of Crossley's personal effects. It had given him what Jonas and Marian and I had never had—a definite field in which work. Some of that field he discovered to be close at hand. In addition to the Sheraton chairs which had been sent to Boston, Miller Jenkins had purchased a mahogany writing desk and a maple chest drawers. Both of the latter items were stored temporarily in the shop, and Abel knew from his list that they had come from the *Pride of the Fleet*. He examined them at his leisure and with great care, but he found nothing.

His stubborn determination to find the hidden "thing" increased, rather than diminished, and the thought of being able to offer riches to the girl in South Harniss gave him the courage to break into Harvey Blodgett's house and to steal the mahogany clock. Not daring to carry it home with him, he had smashed it at the foot of the drive, and once more had failed to find anything.

"Wait a minute, Peak," I interrupted. "Jonas, how about that business of the Buddha? Do you think—"

"No, Bill, I don't. We'll ask him about it later, but let's hear what else he has to say first."

The next step, our prisoner told us, was his attempt to rob the Blair house on the night Samuel Gregg died. He knew that there were a number of things from the *Pride of the Fleet* in the living room, and he hoped, by breaking in in the dead of night, to be able to look at some of them. Hard luck, however, trotted close behind him. He had crept in through the porch door, which had carelessly been left unlocked, and had no more than laid his hands upon the sandalwood box, when he was interrupted.

Abel was not very clear about the details of that interruption. He knew only that something had fallen with a thud close behind him and that someone had shouted. He fled in terror, still clutching the box, and with his pursuer close behind. He had run swiftly across the yard and had gained the group of pines on the other side of the road, when he stumbled and fell heavily. The box flew from his hands as he crashed to earth, but he did not attempt to reclaim it. He scrambled desperately to his feet and did not stop running until he was safely at home.

"Honest, Mr. Jones," he burst out, feverishly, once more, "I didn't have nothin' to do with Sam Gregg's dyin'. I never even touched him. I didn't know he was dead till next day. I—"

"All right, Abe," cut in Jonas, brusquely; "we'll let that go for now. We haven't forgotten it, remember, and we are not satisfied about it by a long shot, but right now we want to hear the balance of the story. What was the next sensible and honest thing you did?"

The sensation created by Gregg's death had quieted Mr. Peak for a number of days. Then, when he was satisfactorily assured that no suspicion had been directed toward him, he went to work once more. He was able, on his second midnight foray, to inspect, at his leisure, the sandalwood box, the lacquer stand, and the Japanese pictures. He had had every intention of leaving them in such a condition that the occupants of the Blair house would never suspect they had been touched. An unexpected noise, however, had prevented that and had caused him to make a hasty exit through the open window.

"Did you have any luck that trip?" I demanded. "Did you find what you were looking for?"

"No, I didn't, Mr. Thornton. Honest truth, I didn't find nothin'."

"For the third time," Jonas nodded, "I believe you, Abe. Belief has got to be a regular habit with me. I believe you because if you *had* found anything you wouldn't be here to-night. You thought there might be a little present for you in my Chinese cabinet, of course—eh? I'm surprised you haven't called sooner."

Abel admitted that he had long been anxious to search the Chinese cabinet, as his list told him that it had belonged to George Crossley in the beginning. He thought his opportunity had come at last when he had heard Jonas say that he was to be absent from the shop over night.

"But," Peak faltered, "but—"

"But the cat came back, eh?" Jonas laughed grimly. "Well, that's a habit cats have, Abe, and you want to remember it afore you start on your next house-breakin' picnic. Now is there any more to this yarn of yours? If there is, you'd better get it off your chest. Confessin', they say, is good medicine for the soul. I should judge yours needed all the doctorin' it could get."

Abel vowed and protested he had nothing further to confess. He had told us everything, and if Mr. Jones and I would only think it over, he was sure we would admit that he had acted only "just natural, same as anybody would." He intimated that he would be glad to bring his present visit to an end.

"Wait a minute," I protested. "About that Buddha business? Did he have anything to do with that?"

Jonas questioned him closely, but his bewilderment and declarations of innocence seemed convincing. "I didn't have nothin' to do with it," he repeated doggedly. "I didn't have nothin' to do with anything I ain't told you about. . . . Now will you let me go home? Please, Mr. Jones, let me go home! I didn't mean to do any harm."

"Not so fast, honest man, not so fast!" Jonas was emphatic. "You won't go home for a spell yet, if we let you go at all." He turned to me. "Any more questions to ask, Bill?"

"Not that I can think of."

"Well, there's one that's just come to me. I want to say somethin' to you, Abe, and I want you to listen close and tell me if you know what it means. Think hard now, and don't try any of your tricks." He paused, stared at his captive intently, and then said, "Look for one arm, one nose."

Abel Peak's face was a study in absolute bewilderment. "Wh-what?" he stuttered. "One nose! Whose nose? Why—why, Mr. Jones, what on earth—?"

"Nothin'." Jonas laughed. "I just wanted to know if you belonged to the lodge, but I see you don't." He shrugged. "Well, it looks as though we'd squeezed everything out of you that there is to squeeze, Abe. Now it's up to us to decide what to do with you. What do you say, Bill?"

I could see no use in playing with the pitiful creature any longer. "I'm sick of the sight of his face," I said. "Let's let him go, if he promises to keep his mouth shut and to give up stealing other people's property."

Abel was about to swamp me in a deluge of gratitude but Jonas stopped him. "You hear what Mr. Thornton says, Peak? He says to let you go, in spite of the fact that you're a thief, and a housebreaker—and a murderer, maybe, for all we know. He is for lettin' you go scot free instead of puttin' you into state's prison for ten or fifteen years, which is where you belong, you know. Well, it proves he's a kind-hearted chap, and I like him for it, but I don't know that he is right. I don't know as it is safe to let you go."

Peak burst into a torrent of prayers and assurances. If we would only forgive him he would never again stray from the path. He would become a paragon of virtue and a credit to the nation. He would never think about Crossley's property again, much less meddle with or mention it to a living soul.

Jonas heard him through, stolidly. "That sounds good, Abe," he admitted in the end, "but sound is only noise, after all. I might be willin' to take a chance if I was sure you'd do what you say, but how can I tell? What do you think, Bill?"

"Oh, tell him to beat it. We know enough about him now so if he tries anything again, we can get him and get him right. He can remember that—and I strongly advise him not to forget."

"Dear, dear!" Jonas sighed. "It must be nice to be young and soft-hearted. I suppose I'll have to give in, much as I hate to." He glanced longingly at Peak and then at the revolver in my hand. "Hadn't you better drill him in the leg just once, so's he'll have somethin' else to remember?"

I grinned. "I hardly think that will be necessary. He'll remember, I think. He'd better, anyhow."

Jonas sighed again. "Then can't I give him one good healthy kick to sort of help him on his way?"

"You might," I agreed, heartily, "that is, if you can catch him. Mr. Peak seems to be in a hurry."

Abel had sprung to his feet and was rushing to the door. He flung it open and leaped frantically into the darkness in an attempt to escape Jonas' punitive boot. He was not altogether successful.

Jones shut the door, locked it, and returned to me with a smile of satisfaction. "I don't think, Bill, that we'll need to do much worryin' about that particular skunk. Unless I miss my guess, he'll lie low and play dead for the next ten year or more. Well, that's as it ought to be."

"Yes," I agreed impatiently, "let's not bother about him any more. I've lost all interest in him, personally."

"So have I, but I was mighty interested in him a little while ago, I'll tell you that." He shook his head in wonder. "Abel Peak! Who would have thought it! Honest, when I first saw what it was my mousetrap had snapped shut on, I could have swore out loud from disappointment. I thought I'd set up all night, and made you set up too, waitin' for a—a grizzly bear, at least—and then hadn't caught any-thing but a weasel."

"He did look a dud at first, all right."

"He did, Bill, he certainly did. But what makes the shivers run up and down my spine is how close he came to *keepin' on* lookin' like one. I had my mind nailed so fast to the idea that that coat of his belonged to Harvey Blodgett I couldn't pry it loose for a spell. That's what a fellow gets for takin' things for granted, instead of workin' 'em out arithmetic fashion."

"Yes, Jonas, yes," I agreed hastily; "but the point is that everything worked out all right in the end. Now what have you found in that pocketbook? I've been on pins and needles for the last half hour. Is it something that's going to help us find what we're lookin' for?"

"I don't know but it is! I declare I don't!" Jonas forgot for the time his wonder at the capture of Peak. He took the shabby leather pocketbook from his coat pocket and slapped it down on the table with an air of triumph. "Of course, I haven't had a good chance to look at it yet, but I've seen enough to know that *all* my calculations weren't away off the mark. No siree, some of 'em were pretty fair figurin', if I do say so."

"*Is* there a list? Is there really a list of all that stuff from the *Pride of the Fleet?* I can't believe it!"

"Neither can I, but it looks as if we'd both have to." He pulled the wad of papers from the wallet and separated two from their number. "It's written in George Crossley's own hand and appears as if he had set down every last thing that belonged to him. . . . Bill, what do you know about that!"

"Hot towel!" I executed a small war dance in my excitement. "If this isn't the ball game then I'm a Hindoo snail hound. All we've got to do is take that list and trot home with it. Jonas, you're a genius!"

"Easy, Bill, easy!" Jonas smiled with pleasure at my childishness. "Thanks for the flowers, but don't waste all the bouquets at once. If you followed friend Peak's chatty remarks close, you ought to guess there's somethin' else in this pocketbook; somethin' that—if it is what I think it is—may turn out to be even more of a help than the list."

"Go on!" I protested. "'There ain't no such animal!' What could be better than a list?"

"I'll show you." Jonas sat down at the desk and spread the remaining yellow sheets out before him under the light. "Do you remember that George Crossley wrote Freeland Blair a letter after he had cleaned up the deal in China, or wherever it was? He cabled 'Done. Have written.' Remember?"

"Sure I do."

"Well, my boy, I honestly believe this is that letter. It is *a* letter, anyhow—and it is from Crossley to Freeland Blair. We knew, from what Iantha said, that Blair had probably received a letter from George, but we took it for granted that he had burned it up along with the rest of his papers. All of which goes to show once again that you shouldn't take things for granted."

Even then I did not grasp the importance of this second find. "Suppose it is the letter," I said, stupidly enough. "What can it tell us?"

Jonas was patient. "I don't know, Bill, because I haven't read it yet, but I shouldn't wonder if it could tell us a lot. It was written after Crossley had bought that 'thing' of theirs, and it might give us a hint where he hid it. Perhaps it'll save us from smashin' up all his stuff, you can't tell. Anyhow, the surest way to find out what's in it is to read it, and I, for one, can't wait another minute. Want to hear it? Or aren't you interested? . . . Oh, all right—all right! Set down and cool off. I'll read it out loud."

The letter was dated from Hong Kong on the first of June, eighteen hundred and eighty-three, and was as follows:

Dear Captain Blair,

I cabled you from S. as according to our arrange
ment and I guess you were glad enough to know that
the deal had been put through and that I had the
goods. I said Done in the cable, same as we agreed,
but I said Have Written, too, and that wasn't quite
so straight, for I had not written then although I
meant to right off that very afternoon. I really commenced a letter but I never finished it and you will
understand why when tell you everything that has
happened. I have had a mean time since then in a lot
of ways and now I am about half sick and just crawling around. I shall be thankful to be at sea again
and homeward bound. Maybe I will commence to
gain strength when I get out on salt water. I shall
feel a whole lot safer anyway, that I do know.

Well, as soon as we docked at S. and I could get
clear of the ship's business for a few hours I went
right off to see I. P. I had quite a job getting in to see
him. He had a blackguard of a Lascar servant at that
boarding-house of his, who seemed to be in charge
when Ike wasn't on deck. This Lascar swore up and
down that he was not on deck then, was out of town
and he did not know when he would be back. It was
not till I gave my name that the scamp as much as
shifted an inch in his lies. Then he looked more
interested and owned up that there might be a chance
that Ike had come home unbeknownst to him. There
was a lot more backing and filling but, to make the
yarn short as I can, I may as well say that finally he
piloted me off up a lot of the filthiest, darkest back
entries and stairways I ever expect to cruise through
and shut me into a room with only one window in
it. And there was Old Ike, after all.

He was glad to see me too, there was no doubt of that. He swore steady for three or four minutes which, as you remember, was always his way of showing joy. He vowed he had about given up hope of ever clapping eyes on me again although he had no reason for talking that way as the bark had made a quick voyage and I was really ahead of the time I had said I should probably arrive. And besides he had the $1,000 deposit, although he had spent that long before, I imagine. It seemed to me he had aged since I saw him last. The same fat, dirty, rum-soaked scalawag he always was, but the fat on his chin was hanging in folds now, and his mean little eyes kept shifting hither and yon as if he expected somebody or something to jump out at him from every corner.

Of course he wanted to know right off if I had got the rest of the $15,000. When I said I had he had another swearing streak. Was I ready to pay it over and take charge of what it paid for? I told him I had not come for any other reason. "Get on your hat," I said, "and we'll go after it this minute."

I expected he would jump at that, as high as a man with a timber toe could jump, but he didn't, not exactly. He acted scared and shifty. Finally he rung a bell for his Lascar supercargo and they jab-bered together in what I suppose was Lascar lingo for a while. The Lascar kept shaking his head and, unless I was a whole lot mistaken, he was fright-ened. At last though, Ike gave him an order and he went away, coming back pretty soon to jabber something that must have meant "All ready," for Ike stumped down the stairs and passageways on his wooden hoof, and I after him, to another door on another alley, where there was one of those man-hauled little carts they use over here waiting for us.

We got in and rode up to the banker's place, the one I told you about when we had our talk together, the place where I had insisted on having the thing put for safe-keeping. I. P. pulled his hat way down over his eyes before we came out of his boarding-house and kept it down that way the whole trip.

We didn't have any trouble at the banker's. He had the thing in his safe and—after looking at it alone by myself, of course, to make sure—I paid over the $14,000 and took it out of there in my pocket. I said good-by to I. P. before we came out into the daylight. I wasn't exactly proud of being seen in his company (the banker man thought our being so chummy mighty queer, I could see that) and I wanted to be rid of the rascal as soon as possible.

The last word Ike said to me I could not understand the meaning of. He said, as nigh as I can remember, "You've made a damnation fine bargain, Crossley, and if things was not as they are with me you never would have got it for three times fifteen thousand. All I have got to say to you is keep your weather eye skinned till you and it are back home in the States. I hope you both get there safe."

He was stumping off when I caught hold of him. "What do you mean by that?" says I. He pulled clear and gave me a funny look from those bloodshot little eyes of his. "Maybe I don't mean nothing," he said. "Only remember this, Captain George. You and me ain't the only folks interested in that thing you've got." That was all he would say and the last I saw him do was climb aboard that ricksha and haul his timber toe in after him.

And the last I heard of him was when I read two days later in the English paper they get out in S.

that the keeper of a sailor's boarding-house in the native quarter had been stabbed to death in a row at his place, and the name he went by was—well, you know what it was and can guess how I felt when I read it.

The letter broke off here and began again at a date a week later. The writing now was less regular and somewhat shaky.

I intended writing more particulars, but I was interrupted then and I have had another attack of this cussed sickness of mine and it has knocked me out for five whole days. What ails me I do not know. I am better again just now and we set sail tomorrow, thank the Lord. I am beginning to worry a little about myself, for, if anything should happen to me on the voyage home I would want you to get this property of yours somehow and I declare I can't think of anybody I could trust with the truth about it. Burke, my mate, is an honest man so far as I know, but honesty that will stand the strain of a hundred thousand dollars is scarce, according to my experience. I have made up my mind not to carry the thing around with me but to hide it carefully somewhere in some of the stuff belonging to me on the bark—the stuff in the cabin and in my stateroom, I mean. I have drawn up a sort of will leaving everything I own to you, Captain Blair, and I shall make a list of my property on board the Pride of the Fleet. If I do not make Boston alive and should not be able to deliver what we bought to you personally, be sure and claim every article on that list. What you are looking for will be hid in it somewhere, although I have not made up my mind just where

yet. I do not dare write more plain even in this letter. I am trusting Burke to mail it, for the doctor
will not let me step foot on shore on account of
my having been so sick. Besides, I am pretty nigh
certain that the ship and myself are watched nowadays. I went on deck for the first time this morning
and, unless I am more mistaken than I think I am, I
caught sight of that Lascar stevedore of I. P.'s, hanging around the wharf. Probably you will think this
is just a sick man's notion, but I do not believe it is.
What was he doing away over here?

As for the bargain we have made, I must tell you
it surely *is* one. I have not hardly dared look at the
thing since I brought it aboard, but I have two or
three times, and why Ike ever let it go for the price,
I cannot see. Except, and I guess it is the right answer, he had come by it by theft, and, just as likely
murder, and was scared of his own life either to
keep it or even sell it to anybody on this side of the
world.

Well, that is all until I see you. Of course I mean
to see you and I hope and trust I will be permitted to. If I should not, do not forget to hang on to
and hunt through every piece of property I own on
board the bark.

Yours truly,
George Crossley.

When Jonas had finished reading he sat back in his
chair, absently tapping the little stack of dingy paper that
lay before him on the desk. "Well, Bill," he said quietly,
"there's the thing we've been huntin' for so hard. There's
our extra string to the puzzle. What do you think of it?"

II

A sense of disappointment, of anti-climax, was foremost in my mind. "Since you ask me," I said disgustedly, "I think it's a flop—an absolute flop."

"Do you, now? Do you really? You know it seems kind of interestin' to me."

"Oh, yes, it's undoubtedly interesting enough read-ing—good local color, an excellent picture of the times, and all that rot. But what does it tell us? It doesn't say what the 'thing' is or where it was hidden. I can't see that it gives us a word that's going to be any help."

"I don't know, Bill." He shook his head doubtfully and shuffled the pages of the letter. "I don't know as I agree with you. It seems to me that it tells us at least one mighty important thing."

"And what is that?"

"Well, it lets us know for sure that Crossley didn't hide the 'thing' in the floor of his cabin or any place like that. We can be sure now that our diamonds aren't lyin' under twenty fathom of salt water. This letter makes it certain, if anything can be certain, that he hid 'em somewhere in his personal stuff."

"What of it? I never had much doubt of anything else."

"Didn't you?" Jonas smiled. "Well, I did. I had so many doubts, to tell you the truth, that it almost made me sick thinkin' about 'em. I'm thankful for this letter, even if it don't do anything but ease my mind. Now I know we're huntin' for somethin' we've got a chance of findin'. I say a chance, mind you, only a chance. It's a much better chance than it was before, but there's a lot of doubt still."

"Oh, Jonas, for heaven's sake stop your croaking. If we don't find that 'thing' after all this, I think I'll go jump in the creek. We simply *must* find it!"

He nodded quietly. "We must if we can, or if anybody can. We will, too, if tryin' will do the trick. I just don't want you to think it's goin' to be all fair wind and plain sailin'. You say yourself that this letter don't help much. Well, that bein' so, all we have to go on is this list—the list, and the 'One foot, one hand' message. If *only* I could make some sense out of that rubbish!"

I was becoming more and more impatient. "Rats with the message! I think it's just what you've called it, rubbish, and I don't think it will ever do us the slightest bit of good. The big thing is the list! We've been howling about that list for the last couple of weeks and now we've got it in our hands. Let's have a look at it."

"Help yourself." Jonas handed the thing over to me and sank back in his chair. He seemed to be thinking deeply.

The list, in faded ink, had been written by Captain Crossley himself. At the top was the heading, "List of Personal Property Belonging to Me, George Crossley, in Cabin and Stateroom of Bark, *Pride of the Fleet*. To be Delivered, in Case of My Death, and, with Enclosed Will, to Captain Freeland Blair, East Orham, Mass., U. S. A."

The catalogue itself ran as follows:

1. Folding writing desk
2. Barometer
3. Table, walnut

4. Chinese cabinet
5. Painting, Pride of the Fleet—ebony frame
6. Clock
7. Table desk with drawers under—maple
8. Idol, wood
9. Chart case with charts
10. Sea chest
11. Elephant image, metal
12. Black lacquer stand—chessboard top
13. Teakwood stool
14. Set Japanese pictures in case
15. 3 chairs
16. Sandalwood box, carved
17. Armchair, stuffed seat
18. Case liquor bottles and glasses
19. Picture Ship Dreadnaught, mahogany frame
20. Large chest of drawers, maple
21. Model Chinese junk
22. Revolver
23. Silk umbrella, ivory handle
24. Metal tobacco box
25. Silver inkstand
26. Marine glasses
27. Sextant
28. Quadrant

That was the end. I read it through twice and then glanced up to find Jonas smiling at me. "Quite a large order, isn't it?" he observed. "Be quite a job to sort out all that stuff and hunt through it, don't you think?"

"Terrible," I admitted. "But it can be done."

"I guess it can, if we can lay hands on everything. Yes, I guess likely it can be done in time."

"Come on then." I shoved the papers in my pocket and got to my feet briskly. "Let's go home and get busy."

Jonas looked at me and then pulled an old-fashioned gold watch from his vest pocket. "Half past four," he remarked doubtfully. "Don't you think that's a pretty late hour of the night—or an early one in the mornin'—to begin a big job?"

"What do we care?" I demanded hotly. "What's the loss of the fag end of a night's sleep compared to finding a hundred thousand dollars or so?"

"Not much, Bill, I'll own up, and I know just how you feel." He ran his fingers through his hair. "But just listen to me for a minute. If we go back to your house now, we'll have to wake Marian up and tell her all about it. That'll take time. Iantha will probably wake up too and then there'll be a rumpus for fair. Then we'll spend the little left of the night gettin' together the stuff on this list. By the time we've done that and are ready for the hardest job of all, it'll be pretty nigh to-morrow's—or to-day's—dinner time. We'll be so tuckered out by then that we'll have to give up and go to bed anyhow." He sighed. "I declare I hate to be always the one that says 'No, no,' and 'Wait, wait,' but I don't see how I can say anything else."

"Never mind, Jonas." I admitted defeat and patted him reassuringly on the back. "You're right. You have the disgusting habit of being always right. What do you want me to do?"

"Well, Bill, I won't give in to the always bein' right part, much as I'd like to, but I'll tell you what I want you to do. I want you to go home now and get some sleep. I'll get some too, after I've done a little more figurin', and I'll be over first thing after breakfast. Don't you worry, Bill, I'm just as het up over this as you are. All I'm tryin' to do is save time, and it strikes me that the best way to save it is to start fresh."

I left him, sitting there at his desk, and went home. I put the little car away and let myself in the front door of the dark house as quietly as possible. There was no sound, and I had come to the conclusion that everyone was safely asleep, when Marian's door opened and she came running to the top of the stairs.

"Bill," she called softly, "is that you? Where on earth have you been? Do you know what time it is? Did you find out anything?"

I knew very well that I should obey instructions and tell nothing then, but excitement got the better of me. "Yes," I said, "we found out something, all right. We found out something darn important."

She had run down those stairs and was shaking me by the arm before I could move. "What was it, Bill? Will it help us find the treasure? Tell me!"

"Don't you think," I protested half-heartedly, "that it would be better if we waited until by and by—ten o'clock or so? It's almost daylight already, you know, and we haven't much time left for sleep."

"Sleep!" She was utterly disdainful. "I haven't been able to sleep a wink all night, and I won't be able to, either, until I know everything. Please tell me, Bill, just as fast as you can."

"Come on then." I shrugged my shoulders as though telling her were not the one thing I was most anxious to do, and turned toward the library. "Let's go in here where we can sit down. It will take some time."

My last statement was more than accurate. We were still talking, and with constantly increasing animation, when Iantha came downstairs to get breakfast.

She, of course, had to be taken into the secret. There was no help for it now and, in any event, we decided it was time she knew a little more of what was going on. She listened to my story in wide-eyed silence, and her reaction to it was peculiar. She freely admitted that the puzzle of the hidden "thing" was remarkable, even wonderful, but it was evident that she found that aspect of the matter less intriguing than our discoveries concerning Mr. Abel Peak.

"Abe Peak!" She shook her head in complete astonishment. "To think that that long, lazy, dead-and-alive actin' object has been goin' around thievin' at night, and scarin' honest folks almost into their graves! If that don't beat the Old Scratch then I give up! I'll be gettin' so, soon, that I won't even trust old Mr. Milliken, the Orham Baptist minister. I do hope you've got him locked up safe."

"Who?" I inquired. "The minister?"

"The minister!" She regarded me in amazement. "What on earth would I want poor old Mr. Milliken locked up for? He's the feeblest, dreamin'est, goodest old soul that ever trod this earth. No, I want to know if you've shut up that scalawag, Abe Peak. I shan't breathe easy until I know he's out of harm's way.

I finally was able to convince her that Peak's claws had been drawn effectively and that he no longer was an important part of our problem. "What we must do now, Iantha," I told her, "is find that 'thing' Captain Crossley hid. It must be around here somewhere. Just think, you may be sitting on it this very minute."

She jumped out of her chair as though it had suddenly become red hot. "Don't you go talkin' like that to me, Mr. Thornton," she warned me solemnly, "Or I'll scream right out loud. I've got a thousand dollars of my own to take care of, and that's trouble enough gracious knows. It gets on my nerves so I can't hardly sleep nights—havin' so much money does. If I should find, all of a sudden, that I was settin' on a hundred times as much, like a—like a hen on an egg, I don't know what I mightn't do. No, sir, the quicker you dig it out and take it away from here, the better I'll be pleased."

Jonas appeared shortly after our late breakfast, and I noticed at once that there were dark circles under his eyes.

"I trust," I remarked suspiciously, "that you rested well, Mr. Jones. You realize, of course, how necessary it is to be thoroughly rested before tackling a big job!"

He grinned sheepishly. "Don't hit a man when he's down, Bill. I'll admit I didn't do much of any sleepin' after you left. Couldn't seem to turn my mind off, if you know what I mean."

"I know your game," I retorted. "You just wanted to get rid of me so you could do some more of your precious figuring. Well, I hope it got you somewhere. Marian and I have been wide awake too, and we aren't any wiser than we were before."

We went, once more, into executive session, with Iantha serving as a newly elected member. The letter was read again and discussed thoroughly. The list was given careful attention. The diary itself, even, was produced for the hundredth time and combed from end to end. Jonas finally laid the three parts of our puzzle side by side on the desk.

"Well, fellow members," he said quietly, "it looks as though we had about all the get-at-able evidence in the case. It strikes me that we've got more, probably, than anybody has ever had. We've got the diary, the list, the letter, and the message. Captain Freeland, he had everything but the message. Abe Peak didn't have the message or the diary either. Sam Gregg was short the list and the letter. It kind of seems as though the four of us was elected, and ought to do some business."

"Fair enough!" said Marian eagerly. "How shall we begin?"

The obvious thing to do first was to check the things in the house which had belonged to Crossley, with the list which had come to us the night before. We began light-heartedly enough, and soon discovered that the ointment was not to be entirely free from troublesome insects. When we counted noses, after hours of hard work, we found that we could positively identify only sixteen items that had come from the *Pride of the Fleet.*

"That ain't so bad," Jonas nodded, swiftly scanning the list in his hand. "If you count the three chairs Crossley mentions, as one, there's only twenty-eight things written down here. No, that isn't bad at all."

"Not bad!" Marian groaned. "Do you realize that it means there are twelve things that we haven't got. Why, it's perfectly terrible! I don't think we have a chance in the world."

"Wait a minute. Let's not give up just yet. One of the things we haven't counted in is that wooden idol—Buddha, or whatever 'tis—that Sam Gregg dropped. You've got that somewhere, Bill, haven't you?"

"Yes, it's up in my room, but it's split right down the middle. I'll guarantee there's nothing hidden in it."

"Never mind. It brings the number of things we can account for up to seventeen. Now there's another one we've all hands forgot, and that's the Chinese cabinet down in my shop. How about that?"

"True enough," I agreed. "That cuts the number of missing items down to ten."

"Only ten?" Marian inquired with some sarcasm. "It seems to me that ten out of twenty-eight is plenty. Oh, dear, I wish I'd never laid eyes on that darn diary! I'm getting more discouraged every minute."

Jonas was studying the list attentively. "Let's look close," he remarked, "and see if there isn't some more light in the darkness, sailor, as the hymn says. Now take this item marked '3 chairs.' Unless I'm more mistaken than I think I am, those chairs are still in this house. You haven't sold 'em or given 'em away or anything, have you?"

Marian shrugged. "No, they're still here, but how are we going to identify them? How are we going to pick them out from a million other chairs?"

"Well—I don't know, but never mind. They're around here somewhere, so they can't be counted as missin'."

"Nineteen down, and nine to go!" I was becoming more cheerful every minute. "Is there any more good news you can spread, Jonas? Can you think of anything else that may be lying around the house?"

"No, I'm afraid I can't. On the other hand it comes to me that there's a thing or two lyin' around, not so very *far* from the house. There's the walnut table you sold to Harvey Blodgett, for instance; and the folding writing desk and maple chest of drawers that are down at Miller Jenkins' shop. We might be able to lay hold of all of them in a pinch."

"So we might!" Even Marian was beginning to come to life. "We'll go see if we can't buy them all back the first thing to-morrow. How do we stand now, Jonas?"

"We stand twenty-two accounted for, and six not. One of those six, into the bargain, is the mahogany clock Abe Peak stole from Blodgett and smashed up. If anything had been hid there, the chances are Abe would have found it."

I executed a few impromptu steps of the Highland Fling. "Better and better! That brings our red figures down to five. What are the chances on any of them, Jonas?"

"Not very good." He sighed and scratched his head. "So far as I can see, they've gone up in smoke, so to speak. I wonder where they did go to."

"You don't suppose," Marian frowned, "that they could have been stolen when the barn was broken into, shortly after the wreck?"

"I've thought of that. That's probably what did happen. They're the sort of things a thief might take if he was in a hurry." Jonas nodded. "Yes, I guess that's the answer to them."

Oh, dear!" Marian was greatly perturbed. "You don't think it's possible that the 'thing' might have been in one of them, do you? If that happened I'll just curl up and die."

"It would be mighty tough luck for us if it did," he agreed; "but, on the other hand, we can't say for certain that it didn't. The 'thing' had to be hid somewhere and it *might* have been there."

"What were the things that were stolen?" I demanded. "Do they sound like good hiding places?"

"Here's what they were. Anyhow, here are the five missin'." He read aloud from the list. "One umbrella, one revolver, one pair marine glasses, one silver inkstand, one case of liquor bottles with glasses. All light enough and fairly easy for a sneak-thief to carry, do you see?"

"Yes," I pointed out, sticking to my idea, "but they don't seem like very good places to hide something. You can't tell me Crossley hid a hundred thousand dollars' worth of something or other in an umbrella—no, nor in a revolver either."

"How about the case of liquor bottles?" Jonas inquired. "And how about that silver inkstand? It seems to me he might have hid something in either one of them—the bottle case 'specially."

"For heaven's sake stop!" Marian interrupted us impatiently. "What on earth good is all this doing? If the 'thing' has been stolen, that's all there is to it. Let's stop being glooms and take a look at whatever hasn't been stolen. What'll we take to pieces first?"

That question occasioned considerable argument. We had sixteen items at hand from which to choose. Some of them, such as the sextant, quadrant, chart case, bronze elephant, barometer, and tobacco box, seemed to hold only faint possibilities, so we passed them by for the time. Others, including the sea chest, lacquer stand, Japanese pictures, and sandalwood box, had been examined more or less closely in the past. Jonas said that he was by no means through with any one of them, but he consented to forget them for the present. The only other things from the *Pride of the Fleet* left in the house, therefore, were two ship pictures, a teakwood stool, a table desk with drawers, a stuffed armchair, and a model of a Chinese junk.

"There are two ways," Jonas pointed out, "of startin' in to hunt. We can take the most likely stuff first and work down, or we can go the other way."

Marian and I were united in our desire to begin with the best. We felt that there was no use in wasting time with improbabilities.

"All right," Jonas consented; "but I warn you right here and now that we'll have to spend considerable time with every one of 'em. Now what do you want me to begin on? This little desk looks like a good prospect. It has drawers, you'll notice, so there may be more in it than meets the eye, as the carpenter said when he noticed the jug in the deacon's pantry."

We agreed that the table desk was exactly the thing, and we watched anxiously as Jonas went to work upon it. He proceeded with maddening deliberation, measuring and tapping every inch of the way. He removed the drawers and studied them thoroughly. He unscrewed the top and explored the regions beneath. He unscrewed the four legs one after the other.

It was nearly midnight when at last he rose to his feet with a little groan. "If there's anything hid in there," he confessed, "it's hid too smart for me. I give up, so far as this little pet is concerned, although I'd be the first to say that that 'thing' of George Crossley's *may* have been starin' me in the face for the last two hours."

"Nonsense," said Marian. "It just plain isn't there or you would have found it. What'll we try next—to-morrow morning, I mean?"

"There's lots of things to try." Jonas rubbed his chin thoughtfully. "I can have a go at the teakwood stool or that stuffed armchair in the library. Both of 'em will be big jobs."

I sighed. "Gosh! This is going to be a long haul, isn't it. You were perfectly right about that."

"Yes, Bill, I'm kind of afraid I was. It's going to take a long time and a mighty sight of patience. Not only that, but nobody's got any gilt-edged guarantee that we'll have found anything when we get through. . . . Well, that don't stop us from tryin'."

"No," said Marian impatiently, "it doesn't. Will you come over early in the morning, Jonas?"

He looked thoughtful. "I'd like to, Marian, you know I'd like to, only—"

"Only what? You aren't going to leave us in the lurch at this late date are you, Jonas?"

"No, no! Nothin' of the kind. It's only that I'm bothered about that dinin' room set of Mrs. Slater's. I promised her it would be ready to-morrow night, and I kind of hate to go back on a promise. The poor woman's so set on havin' it that it seems a shame to disappoint her."

"Oh, dear!" Marian was greatly troubled. "This is terrible! Can't you put her off again, Jonas? Can't you make her let it go for just another day or two?"

I could see that Jones hated to refuse, but I could also see the position in which he found himself. "Look here, Marian," I put in, "I don't see how we can expect Jonas to give us all of his time. He's already given us most of it for the last two or three weeks. Why not let him finish Mrs. Slater's work during the day to-morrow, and then we can start in on this again right after supper. You and I can probably find plenty to do in the meantime."

"That's the ticket, Bill!" His face cleared. "You just give me time enough to dose my conscience with a little of

Mrs. What's-her-name's celebrated soothin' syrup—children cry for it—and everything will be fine. I won't walk out on the job again, I promise you that."

"Of course, Jonas," said Marian contritely. "You take just as long as you want to. I didn't mean to be as selfish as I sounded. This business has put me in such a state that I can't think of anything else."

"Tut, tut," he interrupted, "don't you say another word! I know just how you feel and, to tell you the honest truth, I feel the exact same way. I'd heave Mrs. Slater's maple set into Herrin' Creek if I didn't think she'd be kind of put out if I did."

"Oh, to-morrow will go fast enough," I lied cheerfully, "and perhaps it won't be entirely wasted."

"You bet it won't!" Jonas nodded vigorously. "There's two or three outside things that have got to be done, and there isn't any reason why you and Marian shouldn't be doin' 'em. For one, you can try and buy back that walnut table from Harvey Blodgett; and for another you can see if Miller Jenkins will part with his mahogany desk and chest of drawers. You'll have your hands full with either job, unless I miss my guess, but you ought to try. Any one of those pieces is a prospect and we mustn't let 'em slip through our fingers if we can help it."

"We'll get them if we have to use main strength," I boasted, "and they'll be all lined up for you when you come to-morrow night. Just leave it to us and don't worry about it."

"I won't." He nodded and turned to the door. "I'll have plenty of worryin' of my own to do, and it won't be about Mrs. Slater or her job, either. Well see you at prayer-meetin'."

Marian and I were sitting in the living room the next night when he arrived. He threw his hat on a chair, rubbed his hands, and surveyed us with a grin. "Well, brethren, sisters, and children in arms," he said, "the entertainment is about to commence. Mrs. Slater's set has been finished off and delivered, my conscience is clear, and my head is achin' from goin' 'round and 'round in circles. How about you?"

Marian and I glanced at each other. "We," I observed bitterly, "are sunk—absolutely and completely sunk. We don't care whether school keeps or not."

"You don't say!" He regarded us keenly. "Come to think of it, you *don't* look exactly like a parson's family after a donation party. What's the matter? Did old Big Heart Jenkins make trouble?"

"Trouble," I retorted, "is our middle name. We find it hanging from almost every bush and we're getting so we're disappointed when it isn't there. You'll be overjoyed to hear, Jonas, that Harvey Blodgett has gone to Boston and won't be back for a week."

"Honest? Well now, isn't that too bad! I don't blame you for bein' set back. Looks as though we wouldn't be able to shake hands with that walnut table for some time, eh?"

"Not only that," Marian informed him wearily, "but Miller Jenkins has sold both the chest of drawers and the writing desk. He sold them a week ago to some dealer from New Bedford and he hasn't the remotest idea where they are now."

Jonas shook his head and murmured little phrases of regret. He walked up and down the room whistling softly between his teeth. Marian watched him grimly.

"If you find yourself in too high spirits," she continued, "it may help you to learn that Bill and I spent the whole afternoon trying to pick out those three chairs that belonged to Captain Crossley. We found about fifty chairs, more or less, but they all look exactly alike to us. Any time you happen to be in the mood you can take all fifty to pieces. It won't keep you busy more than a year or two."

Jonas threw back his head and laughed aloud. "It never rains but it pours. That sayin' isn't exactly new, but like an old shoe, it fits all right. Humph! No wonder you both look as though you'd lost your last friend."

"We feel worse than we look," I assured him. "We've just about decided to take the diary and the letter and everything else and throw them in the fire. How do you feel? Have you, by some miracle, something cheerful to report? If you have, break it gently, or the shock may be too great."

His eyebrow lifted. "I have something to report," he said, dryly, "but I don't know as you'd exactly call it cheerful. I finished my other work about four o'clock this afternoon and I have been overhaulin' that Chinese cabinet once more and ever since."

"I see." Marian nodded calmly. "The answer is, of course, that you didn't find anything."

"Not a thing." He shrugged his shoulders expressively. "Not a darned thing."

The silence after that was long and painful. I stood it as long as I could and then I got to my feet. "Well," I demanded irritably, "what are we going to do next? What's the next move?"

"If you ask me," Marian replied, "I suggest that we get out the car and go to the movies. They say there's a good show over in Harniss."

I nodded. "You mean quit, of course—quit for good."

"Why not? We aren't doing anything here except run around in ever widening circles, getting nowhere. Why drive ourselves crazy over something we'll never find? It doesn't seem to make sense."

"Heave to a minute," said Jonas quietly; "let's not go too fast. We've had a lot of discouragin' things happen to-day, but I don't know as they're so bad that we'll have to abandon ship just yet. Harvey Blodgett has gone to

Boston, but he'll be back. Miller Jenkins has sold the desk and the chest of drawers, but that don't say we can't ever find 'em. They haven't been burnt up or thrown in the ash heap. Most folks pay enough for anything bought of Miller to keep it under glass ever after. And, besides, Abe Peak told Bill and me that he overhauled those things and found nothin'. You two haven't been able to pick out Crossley's three chairs, but they're still here and we can find 'em if we have to. I didn't have any luck with my cabinet, but, to be honest, I didn't expect to." He shook his head thoughtfully. "No, I wouldn't say it was time for us to haul down the colors. Not yet, anyhow."

Marian was unimpressed. "All right, Jonas, if you want to keep on hunting we'll stick with you till the last gun fires, but we honestly don't think you'll find anything. What do you want to start to work on now—the teakwood stool or the armchair in the library?"

Jonas scratched his head. "To tell you the truth," he admitted, "I don't know that I want to start work on either one of them. I swear I don't!"

"Then what do you want to do?"

"That's just it. I'm not sure *what* I want to do." He grinned ruefully. "As I told you before, I've been thinkin' about this whole thing all day until my head is goin' around in circles. I've thought and I've thought, and the only thing that keeps comin' back to me is that fool message, 'One foot, one hand.' What does it mean? What's the sense to it? If we could only answer that one question I think we'd save ourselves a pile of trouble and I think we *might* find what we're lookin' for."

"No doubt," I agreed without any particular interest, "but what chance have we of answering it? It might possibly have meant something to Captain Blair if he'd lived to receive it, but I don't, see how it can ever mean anything to us. The only thing I can get out of it is that perhaps the 'thing' is hidden in something that has hands or feet, or both. Suppose it is. What good will that do us?"

"Not much," Jonas agreed. "Almost every item on Crossley's list has the one or the other. There's hands on the barometer, the clock, the wooden idol, and on all those carved figures on the different boxes. There's hands enough, Lord knows, but there aren't half as many hands as there are feet. Why, there's feet on every table, every chair, every—"

Marian, who had been wandering about the room during all our talk, stopped in front of the fireplace and waved an impatient hand. "Oh, feet, feet!" she exclaimed disgustedly. "What's the use of talking about them?" She picked up the small bronze elephant from the mantel shelf and held it out. "Why, even this creature has four feet. What of it? We couldn't take it to pieces even if it had fourteen!"

Jonas reached out his hand and took the elephant from her. He looked at it absently for a moment and then shook it once or twice, apparently to see if it was hollow. "No," he agreed, "I don't think we could get this apart. Seems to be one solid chunk. For that matter, I don't think Crossley could have got it to pieces either."

He had moved over to the mantel in order to replace the elephant when his attention was attracted to the picture which hung above it. He studied it silently for a moment and then grunted.

"Humph!" he said slowly, "I thought this was a picture of George Crossley's bark."

Marian turned in surprise. "Why, it is. There's the name, *Pride of the Fleet*, in gilt letters at the bottom."

"Yes, yes, I see that. But Crossley wasn't in command of her when this was painted. It says, "Bark *Pride of the Fleet*, Isaac Peters, Commander. Hong Kong, July 19, 1879."

"Really? I hadn't noticed that. I just read the name of the ship and took the rest for granted. It never occurred to me that somebody else might have commanded that ship before Captain Crossley, but I suppose it is perfectly possible."

Jonas was still looking at the picture when Iantha entered the room. He turned when he heard her and immediately asked a question. "Iantha," he inquired, "did you ever hear Captain Blair mention a Captain Isaac Peters? He was skipper of the *Pride of the Fleet,* before Crossley took charge."

"Isaac Peters?" Iantha frowned. "No, I never heard the name before. What did you say he was?"

"He was the captain who had the *Pride of the Fleet* before Crossley."

"You don't say." Once more Iantha frowned. "Now that's kind of funny. Seems as though I recollect Jethro Gould tellin' me that the *Pride of the Fleet* was bran-new, just off the stocks, when Captain Crossley took command of her. I thought he skippered her right from the first, makin' regular trips to India, China, and the East Indies."

"You must have thought wrong, unless the letterin' under this picture lies. It says 'Isaac Peters, Commander,' as plain as the nose on your face. No, Iantha, your recollector must have broke a main-spring. And yet," he added, with a frown, "it does seem kind of odd Crossley should have a picture of this particular ship with another skipper's name on it. You'd naturally expect he'd have had one painted for himself, with his own name. He sailed the *Pride of the Fleet* a long time. Yes, sir, it seems kind of funny."

"What of it?" I inquired indifferently. "To quote a favorite song, 'What does it matter?'"

Jonas did not answer. He was still staring at the picture of the bark. Then, all at once, he whistled.

Iantha jumped nervously. "What on earth is the matter with you, Jonas Jones? Won't you please stop that? Are you tryin' to scare a body to death?"

Jonas shook his head and stepped across the hearth so that his eyes were not more than six inches from the canvas. He stared at it intently for another long moment and then he whistled again.

"What is it, Jonas?" Marian demanded sharply. "What do you see?"

"Nothin,' Marian, nothin' . . . That is, I presume likely it's nothin'." He turned back to the room, and could see that his eyes were shining. "I've just got another crazy notion in my head, that's all."

Iantha was still ruffled. "I should think there was enough of that kind in there already," she observed,

Jones did not retort. He walked swiftly across the room and picked up his hat. "If you'll excuse me for a jiffy," he was saying as he backed toward the door "I think I'll run down to my shop. Got an errand there. Be back in less than ten minutes."

"Wait a minute, Jonas," I cried. "What's the idea? What—"

I was wasting my breath, for he had gone. We could hear him running rapidly down the walk to the front gate.

Marian and I looked at each other in bewilderment, and Iantha sank onto the haircloth sofa with a little groan. "Oh, dear, oh, dear!" she exclaimed fearfully. "The awful things are goin' to begin all over again. I know they are! I know it!"

"Don't be silly, Iantha," Marian ordered. "Nothing is going to happen. Jonas has just had an idea, that's all."

"Don't say a word! Don't try to tell me!" Iantha refused to be comforted. She began rocking back and forth on the sofa. "Oh, dear, oh, dear! I know it! I've got what they call a presentation. I feel it in my bones. Somethin' *awful* is goin' to happen!"

III

It seemed as though we waited for hours, but my watch told me that only nine minutes had passed before we heard the sound of Jones' footsteps returning. He came panting into the living room and I noticed that he was carrying a small black bag almost like a doctor's satchel.

"And now," he announced briskly, "we shall see whether there's any sense in my notion, or whether it's as crazy as they usually are. Give me a hand, will you, Bill?"

"Look here, Jonas," Marian interrupted rebelliously, "do you think you're being very nice? One minute you act perfectly rational and the next you tear out of the house muttering nothing in particular. You've put Iantha into a terrible fever, to say nothing of Bill and me. Do you mind telling us what everything's all about?"

"I wish I could." Jonas laughed and walked over to the fireplace. "The trouble is, Marian, that I'm not sure everything is about anything. It was just that, when I was lookin' at this picture a few minutes ago, an idea—or what might possibly be an idea—flew up and hit me. You see—Oh, well, we'll all either see, or not see, in a jiffy. Meanwhile I do hope you'll excuse me for runnin' first, and explainin' afterwards."

"We'll excuse you, all right," Marian assured him, "if you'll just put us out of our misery. What is your idea, and why are you so excited about that old picture?"

325

He drew two chairs to the hearth and hopped up on one of them. "If Bill will just help me get this picture down," he replied, "I'll try to show you what strikes me funny about it. It don't hardly seem as though it could be so, but I won't rest easy until I've made sure."

Between us we removed the canvas from its place on the wall and lowered it to the floor. Jonas then jumped down from his chair and looked about him with a frown. "Let's go into the dinin' room," he suggested. "The table there will be a good place to work, and the light will be better. If you'll carry the picture, Bill, I'll fetch my tool kit."

We proceeded hurriedly to the dining room, where I laid the canvas in the center of the big table and lighted the hanging lamp overhead. "That's the ticket," Jonas nodded approvingly. "Now we can see where we're headin'."

He opened his little satchel and from the clutter of things it contained, drew out a bottle, a number of brushes, and a soft white cloth. Marian was standing close at his right hand, and Iantha and I arranged ourselves on the other side. We watched in silent fascination as he extracted the cork from the bottle and dipped one of the brushes into it.

"I tell you," he began, almost apologetically; "the thing that hit me in the eye about this picture was the printin' underneath it. Do any of you see what I mean?"

Marian shrugged. "I suppose you mean the name, 'Isaac Peters.' That may be peculiar, but I can't see that it's anything to get excited about."

Jonas nodded and wiped his brush carefully on the mouth of the bottle. Then he began to apply it gently to a portion of the gilt lettering in the inscription. "Yes," he admitted, working deftly and cautiously, "I was surprised to find this 'Isaac Peters' name on here. What you'd naturally expect, of course, would be 'George Crossley.' It made me stop and look close, and that made me notice somethin' else."

"What?" I demanded with growing excitement. "For heaven's sake, tell us!"

"Well, Bill, I noticed that the letterin' in that Peters name isn't done as careful and neat as the printin' on both sides of it. If you look sharp you can see for yourself that it isn't."

"You're right!" The thing was obvious, even at a casual glance. "What do you make of it?"

He continued to manipulate the brush, which was beginning to remove the top layer of paint. "Well, it looks to me as if the name had been painted over top of somethin' else, and by somebody who wasn't a regular letterer by trade. . . . See? . . . Look there! There's a tiny speck of gilt showin' through the black underneath. And that special bit of black is a little different, too. Now, why? . . . Unless—eh? . . . Well, let's see what luck we have."

He went on, working with utmost care and deliberation. We watched breathlessly as the "Isaac Peters" name was removed and as the blotch of black upon which it had been painted disappeared little by little. Suddenly Marian cried out.

"Look! There's something painted in gilt underneath. It's a name! I can see some of the letters. There's an "r" and two "s's," and—why, it's 'Crossley.' 'George Crossley'!"

She was right. The lettering became more and more distinct until, at last, Jonas threw down his brush with an air of finality. "It's 'George Crossley,' all right," he said, with decision, "and you'll notice that the letterin' of it is just the same as the rest of the regular printin'. The other name was painted over it by somebody else."

We looked at each other in growing wonder and bewilderment. "But—but," Marian stumbled, "who did it? Who would have gone to all the trouble to paint another name over the right one?"

"It seems to me," Jonas replied slowly, "that there's only one likely answer to that. The picture belonged to Crossley. He had it right up to the time he died."

"You mean Crossley did it himself?"

"Sort of looks that way. Don't you think so?"

"Yes—yes, but why? Why did he do it?" I had a sudden startling idea. "You don't think—is there a chance that it might have something to do with his hiding the 'thing'? By gosh! if—"

"Why, Bill!" Marian was on the verge of jumping up and down. "It must be that! It can't be anything else!"

Jonas was more conservative, but he could not keep a tremor of excitement from his voice. "We mustn't get our hopes up, I suppose," he said, "but, honest, I don't know but it *might* have somethin' to do with it. Humph! Now I wonder if it could. What was that name that was painted on top? 'Isaac Peters,' wasn't it?"

"Yes," I agreed, "that was the name. But who on earth is Isaac Peters? I've never heard of him, have you?"

"No." He shook his head slowly. "I can't say I have, and yet—"

"Wait!" Marian grabbed his arm. Her face was flushed and she tried to speak so rapidly that the words tumbled over each other. "What about all that in the diary—yes, and in the letter—about—about I. P.? Wasn't he the old crook Crossley bought the 'thing' from? Weren't that man's initials 'I. P.'?"

"Yes!" Even my feeble brain was beginning to swing into action. "Not only that, but Crossley in that letter called him 'Ike,' don't you remember. By gosh! I wonder—"

Jonas slapped his leg resoundingly. "Go get that letter and diary," he commanded, his excitement now as great as ours. "Go get 'em quick!"

I ran upstairs and came down with the letter and the diary. We then sat down at the dining-room table and proceeded to make a thorough if hasty examination. We found a number of references to "I. P." in the old diary, and Marian found him designated as Ike" in Crossley's letter.

"It's as plain as A, B, C," I exclaimed confidently at last. "Ike, or I. P., or whatever you want to call him, is nobody else but Mr. Isaac Peters. If you try and tell me he isn't, I'll break down and cry."

"I guess you won't have to do that, Bill," commented Jonas quietly. "It looks as though so much of the case was proved."

"But why?" Marian demanded. "Why on earth was it done? What does it mean?"

"That's what we've got to find out." He nodded and began to study the picture again, closely. Then suddenly he stiffened and leaned forward. "Here! Hold on!" he ordered, his voice shrill and eager. "Doesn't it say something in the diary about I. P. being a cripple?"

"Yes." I could remember the wording of the diary almost literally. "If I'm not mistaken, Blair called him 'worse than a cripple.' Why?"

"Not only that," Marian put in, "but in the letter Crossley says something about I. P.'s 'timber toe' . . . But, why do you look like that, Jonas? What is it?"

Jonas had bent down close to the painting and was pointing with his forefinger. We crowded over his shoulder and saw that he was indicating the small figure of a man represented as standing on the deck of the bark, just forward of the wheel.

"Do you see that?" he demanded.

"Yes," said Marian. "I see a man there, but what of it? There are half a dozen others painted about the deck."

"Sure there are! But that fellow is supposed to be the skipper. The folks who painted these ship pictures always put in the old man standing aft like that, givin' orders. It was the captain who contracted to have the picture done and so the painter put him in it to tickle him and to make him easier satisfied with the job. That chap standing there was meant, you can bet, to be George Crossley himself."

"Well?" I asked. "Suppose he was Crossley? What of it?"

"That's just what I asked myself. And now—listen! If he was George Crossley to start with, why did George label him 'Isaac Peters' down below? . . . Eh? . . . Unless—"

"Yes, yes!" Marian urged. "Unless what?"

"Why, unless he knew Captain Freeland—who, he's sure, would go through everything mighty careful—would wonder why the 'Isaac Peters' name was painted in, and look at the ship from stem to stern. Yes—and at the folks painted aboard her."

"Well?"

Jonas' finger moved down the tiny figure of the of the *Pride of the Fleet's* captain. "Look there—look close," he commanded, "See anything funny about that fellow?"

We looked, and all at once Marian clapped her hands.

"He—he has only one leg!"

I felt a shiver run up my back as I leaned forward to look more closely. "By gosh!" I muttered, "so he has. You're right!"

Jonas' eyes were sparkling, "Not exactly," he cried. "He has got one whole leg—and there it is. And part of another. But, if you look sharp, you'll notice the lower end of that second leg has been blotted out with a little daub of paint. That daub don't match the rest. It was put on afterward. He had two whole legs to start with—yes, and two feet. Now what he has got is—"

"One foot!" Marian almost screamed the words. She began to dance up and down like a child. "One foot! One foot!"

"You've hit it, Jonas!" I felt like a person walking in a dream. "You've smacked it right on the nose!"

Jonas was staring at the picture in a sort of dazed wonder. "I—I swear, I don't know but I have! There's a one-footed man anyhow. Now as for the hand—"

"*He* has only one!" Marian almost pushed Jonas to one side in her eagerness. "See? There's only one hand showing in the picture."

"Yes, that's so. . . . Eh? And that hand is painted pointin'—see? Well, of course about every captain in these old pictures was painted pointin' for'ard, givin' orders to the crew. . . . And yet, I don't know—"

"Where is he pointing?" I interrupted.

"Why, for'ard, where the sailors are. You see—"

"Wait, wait!" Marian cried. "Oh, Jonas! don't you think—don't you think he might be pointing at, at—I mean don't you think Captain Crossley may have meant for my uncle to—to look where his one hand pointed? At—at the frame, perhaps—or something like that?"

Jonas whistled. "I'm blistered if that isn't a notion!" he exclaimed.

He seized the picture and turned it over, face downward upon the table. The back was covered with a large sheet of brown paper glued to the edges of the frame, which he quickly removed with his jackknife. There was nothing visible underneath except the back of the canvas itself.

"Nothin' doin' so far," he nodded. "Oh, well, that isn't surprisin'. Let's have a little closer squint."

"Yes," cried Marian, "the frame! Oh, it might be in the frame! Take the picture out, Jonas—hurry!"

He delved once more into the black satchel and produced a small chisel and a hammer. With these he proceeded to loosen, one after another, the small wooden wedges holding the picture. At last he lifted the canvas on its stretcher carefully from the frame and laid it to one side on the table.

"Now!" Marian whispered. "Now!"

With Iantha, Marian and myself crowded close together peering over his shoulder, Jonas began to examine the edges of the frame. The side toward which the hand of the little figure had pointed was one solid piece of wood from top to bottom. Under the light it was obvious that there was no scratch, mark, or irregularity anywhere on its surface. Jonas studied it intently for a long moment, ran an inquiring finger up and down its length, and then looked up at our stricken faces.

"Humph!" he remarked with quiet sarcasm, but it was plain that he, too, was greatly disappointed, "it don't look as though we were skunked or anything, does it?"

Marian was on the verge of tears. "We can't be," she protested vehemently. "We simply can't be! If we are, I—I don't know what I'll do."

Jonas shook his head. "We may not be licked for good, Marian, but I swear it does begin to look as though we were on the wrong trail so far as this frame goes. The inside edge of it is solid, all the way round. You can see it is."

He picked up the heavy frame, and held it closer to the light. "Yes," he murmured, "it's solid. . . . *No!* Eh, what? Why, by the everlastin'! I—"

He stopped short in the middle of his sentence and drew a deep breath. Then he set the frame down on the table again and struck his forehead wonderingly with his knuckles. "Well, I'll be blistered! Of all the hopeless blind fools I ever—"

"What is it, Jonas?" Marian caught his arm. "Tell us what it is. Please!"

He chuckled and picked up his chisel. "It's just this, Marian: This frame is made of ebony, see? It's dark and heavy the way ebony ought to be and is."

"Yes, but—"

"But the inside edge of it *isn't* ebony—that's the thing! No, it ain't! It's some horse of a different color, and why I didn't notice it from the word go is beyond me."

"Then—"

"There must be a thin strip of this other wood all around the inside edge of the frame. I *thought* the picture didn't fit in very good when I first looked at it. . . . *Now* let's see!"

He bent down and made tentative gestures with the chisel, while once more the rest of us crowded about in absolute silence. After an instant there was a small, tearing sound, and a long, thin piece of wood fell upon the table. Jonas did not even look at it. He was staring intently at the darker wood underneath, which was obviously part of the frame itself. All at once he uttered an exclamation.

"Aha! Look there!" he shouted. He was pointing with his chisel. "What do you make of that?"

It was easy enough to see what had caught his attention. On the inside edge of the frame there were faint lines forming a rectangle about two inches wide and eight inches long. Little streaks of glue made them stand out very clearly.

"*Now* boys and girls!" crowed Jonas in triumph. "It looks as though we might be strikin' ile at last!"

Once more he set to work with his little chisel, this time upon one of the longer lines.

"A nice neat job, whoever did it," he muttered to himself. "Crossley must have been a handy man with tools. Set in just to fit and glued fast. Forty odd and yet— Ah! *There* we are!"

There was a sharp snap and an oblong slip of wood flew up from the edge of the prying chisel. It was a lid covering a cotton-filled cavity beneath. As we watched in tense excitement, the silence broken only by Iantha's heavy breathing, Jonas lifted out the top layer of cotton. Beneath was a small oblong parcel wrapped in coarse paper.

With fingers which shook a little Jonas gently pried it from its place until it lay in the palm of his open hand. Then he looked up at us. "Well," he said with a long, slow breath, "and—now for it! Eh?"

He pushed the frame to one side and placed the paper-covered parcel on the dining-room table under the strong light. Then he motioned to Marian. "You open it, girl," he directed. "It's yours, you know."

None of us spoke. We merely stood and watched as Marian moved forward, and began, with trembling fingers, to unwrap the package. The paper rustled dryly as it was laid back, and then all at once something gleamed dully under the light.

We had come, unbelievably, to the end of the road!

There was a long, long moment of complete silence as we gazed at the confusing little heap that lay before us. I, for one, could make nothing out of it. It was a tangle of many dim colors—dull gold, blue, deep green. It seemed to have no order, and no form.

Marian reached out and picked it up with uncertain thumb and forefinger. There was a heavy jingle as it untangled and, like a many-hued cascade, poured its length before our eyes.

Iantha was the first to speak. "Humph!" she said "My soul! Nothing but a string of old beads!"

The rest of us continued to stare, wordlessly and stupidly, until Marian pointed with her free hand. "Bill!" she cried, in soft, incredulous wonder. "Why, Bill! Do you—do you suppose it's possible that those are real pearls?"

"I—I don't know." I shook my head and came forward. "But if they *are,* and if those four are emeralds—*if* they are—why, this thing is worth— Good Lord! I don't know what it's worth!"

Jonas was the only one of us who seemed to have complete control of his faculties. He scarcely looked at our find, but sat down in a dining-room chair and wagged his head in complete wonder.

"And it was nothin' but dumb luck that set us onto it!" he exclaimed unbelievingly. "Just dumb luck, and not arithmetic at all! Why—why, even Abe Peak could have found it! Well, I'll be everlastin'ly blistered!"

IV

We sat up, as was rapidly becoming our habit, most of the rest of that night. For half an hour or more we merely gurgled idiocies and shook each other's hands like a group of delegates at a convention of the feeble-minded. I even have a faint and shameful impression that we indulged in song, but perhaps I am wrong.

Finally, at any rate, we simmered down to the point where we could view with some degree of calm the thing which Jonas had extracted from the depths of the ebony picture frame.

It was a sort of necklace, or collar, of gold; about fifteen inches long and crudely made. The ancient, clumsy clasps were at each end of a cord braided from a number of strands of gold wire. From this cord hung eleven small gold panels, heavily chased and ornamented, but with bits of the chasing worn down by time. Each of the two panels at the extreme ends was in the shape of a triangle with the upper point cut off. Each, also, was decorated with a more or less conventionalized tiger's head, the mouth open and snarling. The eyes were small rubies.

The nine panels forming the main portion of the necklace were also semi-triangular in shape, but each one of these had for its center a precious stone set in a chased gold mounting. All of the stones were large; not huge, but of good size. The four, two at each end of the panel portion of the necklace, were emeralds. The four, two on each side of the center panel, were rubies.

In the center was a beautiful gem, which from its very definite shade of blue, Marian and I concluded must be either a very pale sapphire or some variety of semi-precious stone. We discovered later, however, that it was a diamond, of such purity and rare color that it was by far the most valuable item in the necklace.

Suspended from the center panel and from the two on each side were five large and beautiful pearls. Other pearls, forty-five in number, but much smaller in size, were set between the tops of the panels and the gold cord upon which they hung.

The emeralds, rubies, and the diamond were cut in ancient Oriental fashion. According to the standards of our place and time, therefore, they were poorly cut. One of the emeralds was not particularly good in color, and one of the rubies contained a small and not particularly noticeable flaw. Other than these, all the stones were clear and of fine depth and color. The blue diamond was something about which to shout from the housetops, as were the five larger pearls.

That first night, of course, Marian and I could not be sure of all these details concerning the necklace, but we were sure that we had found something so marvelous that we could talk about nothing else. Iantha, on the other hand, was frankly skeptical, and offered her opinion that the stones were nothing but glass and might be counted on to bring in the grand total of five dollars. Jonas Jones was more optimistic, but now that he had unearthed what he called "Marian's bucket of diamonds," he seemed to have little interest in it.

What interested him then and what continued to interest him later, were the details of the puzzle. He wanted to

know how such a piece of jewelry ever came into the hands
of the rascally keeper of a sailor's boarding-house in some
Far Eastern port. Where had it come from?

The experts who have examined it recently have not
been very helpful. One high authority is certain that it
came from Thibet and was intended to hang about the neck
of an idol in some temple there. Two others are equally
certain that it was a Hindoo creation and that it was made
in India—probably Burma. They all agree that it is at least
a thousand years old.

Jonas says he doesn't give a snap of his fingers about its
age. He wants to know where Isaac Peters laid hands on
it and how. That question, in my opinion, will never be
answered. It was stolen, of course, and there is little doubt
that blood and murder are component parts of its history.
Peters, obviously, was afraid of his life as long as it was in
his possession, and it is highly probable that his death was
connected with it in some way.

Another thing that seems remarkable to all of us is that
a Yankee sea captain like George Crossley should have rec-
ognized its value, and should have been willing to gamble
a thousand dollars on the chance of obtaining it. Crossley
knew that Peters was a crook if not worse, and it seems
surprising that he should have dared to buy anything of
value from him. Peters must have convinced him of the
genuineness of the stones, and the judgment of the person
to whom, later, the necklace was submitted for examination, must have confirmed that conviction. Crossley was
sure that he "had a bargain," and told Blair so in their
interview at East Orham—see Blair's entry in the diary.
Crossley also repeats the assurance in his letter. It is quite
probable too that Peters told him something about the
history of the theft of the "thing," for from what we know,
it seems evident that the scruples of both Blair and Crossley were easily satisfied.

We have been able to learn very little about Isaac Peters. Forty-four years seem to have obliterated his memory almost entirely. Jones made a number of inquiries among the old salts left alive in Orham and the surrounding towns. One of them—who lives in Wellmouth and is more than ninety years old—had, as a youth, sailed one voyage with Freeland Blair. He remembered that the cook on that ship was called "Ike Peters," and that his nickname among the crew was "One Foot Ike," or just plain "One Foot." Both Crossley and Blair must have known him as such.

Jonas was not altogether satisfied with the message, "Look for one foot, one hand." He thinks now that originally it was "Look at One Foot's hand," or something similar. It was transmitted by word of mouth from Crossley to the mate, and from the mate to his nurse. It seems likely that it may have been so garbled that it would have been of doubtful use even to Captain Blair, had he lived to receive it.

"Even if it *was* 'Look at One Foot's hand' when it started," said Jonas with a shake of the head, "it would have been a pretty tough puzzle for Captain Freeland to figure out. Yes, sir, he'd have scratched his topknot over it considerable, accordin' to my way of thinkin'. Crossley took a long chance when he hid it as good as he did, but you've got to remember that, even then, he was a sick man and *had* to take chances. He probably knew Blair would think of the 'One Foot' right away when he saw 'Isaac Peters' at the bottom of the picture, and that, havin' got so far, he'd find the necklace before he got through. That must have been somewhere nigh the way of it."

We all realized, of course, as soon as we were able to realize anything, that the necklace we had found belonged to none of us, but to Mrs. Fisher, Marian's mother. We telegraphed her the next day to come home, saying "Good news," so as not to alarm her. She came at once and was mildly surprised and pleased, to say the least. She was more than willing to listen to suggestions as to our next step, so it was finally decided that I should take the necklace to a very good friend of my father's, who is a member of a large jewelry house in Boston.

If it were not for the fact that minor disturbances mean nothing to me after the events of this summer, I should have been pleased with the sensation created when I exhibited our little trinket for the jeweler's inspection. He did everything but burst into tears of pure joy. He summoned his partners and they held an admiration meeting which lasted about two hours. The upshot of the matter was that they offered to relieve me of my burden for a trifling sum in the neighborhood of one hundred and fifty thousand dollars.

I must have paled visibly, for they hastened to assure me that that amount did not represent anything like the full value of the necklace, which was in truth a museum piece and almost beyond appraisal. If I cared to leave it with them they would try to sell it elsewhere at a more satisfactory price.

At this writing the necklace has not been sold. My jeweler friend writes me, however, that negotiations are under way, with several would-be purchasers bidding. One, a well-known steel manufacturer, is particularly insistent. His latest bid was a careless $200,000, but my agents are holding out for an additional fifty thousand. The joke is that they seem to think they will get it.

Oh, well! Big numbers are just big numbers, after all.

We had to engage a lawyer, of course. What would life be without a lawyer? He has been employing his odd moments of late in attempting to decide whether we should all become rich, or go to jail as receivers of stolen goods. Then, too, there was the small question of duty which was not paid when the necklace was brought into the country.

He assured us, all but smacking his lips, that the matter involved a number of interesting legal problems.

Nevertheless, in spite of these evidences of professional appetite, he did not turn and bite the hand that was feeding him. After a great deal of learned beating about the bush he informed us, almost with tears of manly regret in his eyes, that we were perfectly safe. There was no positive proof, and could never be any, that the necklace had been stolen. It would be manifestly impossible, after a lapse of nearly fifty years and the death of everyone concerned, to make any sort of investigation. We did not even know more than the initial—"S"—of the port where Crossley had bought it from Peters. And he—Crossley—*had* bought and paid for it.

Not only that, but the awful bugbear of the United States Customs turned out, in the bright light of day, to be but a playful kitten. No one now living had been guilty of an attempt to smuggle. The only persons against whom such an accusation might ever have been brought were Crossley and Blair, and there was no actual proof that they intended evading duty. With the passing of the executor of Captain Blair's estate, moreover, it seems that the government lost its last potential victim.

What could a poor lawyer do? Nothing, I assure you, but fold up his fee like a particularly downhearted Arab, and silently steal away.

Mrs. Fisher has recently brought forth a most startling proposition. She wishes to divide the profits from the necklace with those concerned in the finding of it. Who ever heard of such an idea? We merely laughed heartily when she first suggested it, but she seems determined. As the direct heir of Freeland Blair, she is willing to keep one half of the proceeds, but the remainder is to be distributed among Marian, Jones, Iantha, and myself.

Poor Iantha is by far the most upset. She flies to arms whenever the subject is mentioned, declaring that she has no desire for further riches. "My sufferin' soul, Mary Fisher!" she demands, frantically. "What in time would I ever do with *more* money? Haven't I got the thousand dollars poor Mr. Gregg left me, and isn't that more than enough to put me into my grave comf'table when my time comes? Worryin' about that thousand is drivin' me to the cemetery fast enough, as 'tis. I've got a home here with you long's I live, ain't I? You keep tellin' me I have. Well, then!"

Jonas Jones, of course, is the one who really should receive the lion's share. He did all the heavy work and it was his thinking that brought results. We keep pointing this out to him as firmly as possible, but he merely laughs.

"Thinkin'!" he protests, with his right eyebrow elevated. "Say, now, a joke's a joke, but you folks needn't rub it in. I did plenty of thinkin', that's a fact, but where did it get me? Nowhere. Arithmetic didn't have a thing in the world to do with finding that necklace—not a thing in the world. It was plain luck that turned the trick—just plain, dumb, backyard luck! No, Mrs. Fisher, don't give me any money. If you did, I'd feel as though I'd been robbin' the Sunday School collection plate, and Iantha would quit havin' me for steady company."

It is possible that Jonas and Iantha may escape their just rewards—but I have my doubts.

Marian and I are in a somewhat different situation. I make loud and repeated declarations that I will not consider the matter—declarations which are perfectly sincere. I can not, and shall not consider it. Something, however, tells me that there is a weak spot in a vital part of my armor, because Mrs. Fisher says that if I do not accept my share she will add it to Marian's and thus achieve the same purpose.

That idea has a certain cunning, but it could be easily beaten if it were not for Marian. Marian, I am ashamed to say, is utterly brazen. "Well, mother,' she says, "if you insist on showering me with gold, what can a poor girl do? Nothing, I assure you, especially if she has hopes of getting married. You have supplied a twig, if not three, for a new nest!"

What can be done with a girl like that? I shall fight fiercely, of course, to a glorious finish, but I have a strong suspicion what that finish will be.

With all of these things settled, or nearly settled, everything should be peaceful in the vicinity of the old Blair house in East Orham, but everything is not. The story of the necklace has somehow leaked out.

I do not know whether or not my jeweler friend is guilty of having spread the tidings, but I do know that they have been spread. We have burst forth in all our glory, in company with the latest murder, divorce, and South American revolution, on the front pages of America's newspapers. The entire story of the necklace, highly seasoned and piping hot, has been served to the public.

Reporters lurk behind every bush, and the joyous clicking of cameras is heard in the land. Marian, Jonas, Iantha, and myself have been interviewed until we are worn out and surfeited with questions. The necklace, the house, the inmates, the grounds, and the surrounding terrain, have been photographed, and photographed again. Jonas stoutly proclaims—in her hearing of course—that Iantha has been offered a vaudeville contract, and only yesterday he showed me her picture in a Boston paper. It had been taken, when she was a girl of seventeen, by a "tintype" artist at the Ostable County Fair, and, if not awarded a blue ribbon at that exhibition, deserved one.

"Mad!" Jonas chuckled wickedly. "Why, Iantha pretends she's mad enough to sue that newspaper, but, between you and me, she isn't—she loves it. It's all like one of those book stories of hers come to life, excitin' and grand, you know. Speakin' of excitement, wouldn't old Sam Gregg have gloried in all this! Why, he'd be flappin' around here like a chicken with its head cut off, blessin' his soul about forty times a minute!" He sighed. "Too bad, his havin' to go the way he did. I always liked Sam, and, do you know, Bill, I can't help believin' that he wasn't doin' what he did just for his own selfish sake. I'll bet if he'd lived to find that necklace he'd have turned it over to Marian. She says he hinted he was goin' to make her a mint of money, remember."

I nodded. "I shouldn't be surprised if you were right. He didn't seem like the kind to do anything crooked."

"So I say. He was crazy over puzzles, Sam was, and he liked the fun and excitement of working 'em out on his own hook. We've all got a crack in our heads, of one kind or another, that's a fact. Yes, and we're all like Iantha too, underneath—we make believe we hate excitement, but we don't."

Once more I think he was right. I know that I was finding the excitement agreeable, and one day when Marian and I had escaped from the house and had gone for a walk on the beach she showed me that she, too, was enjoying it.

"It'll seem pretty tame, won't it," she remarked quietly, "when this is all over, and you have gone to work in Chicago."

"Why bring that up?" I frowned. "It'll seem a lot worse than tame. I hate to think about it, it'll be so awful."

"I wonder," she pursued softly, making a small mark in the sand with the tip of her shoe, "if there isn't something we might do to help the situation."

"Help it? What on earth are you talking about?"

"I just thought that perhaps—" She looked up at me with a peculiar little light of laughter in her eyes—"we might fix it by—by getting married, right away."

"Get married!" I stared at her in complete bewilderment, and then grasped her by the shoulders. "Get married right away! What are you talking about?" I shook her gently. "You know there's nothing in the world I'd like better, but perhaps you'll tell me what we'd use for money."

She would not meet my eye. "You'll have a job, won't you?"

"Of course, but I won't get enough salary to keep a humming bird from starving!"

She shrugged. "Well, you'll get something, and in a little while you'll be getting more. In the meantime, we might scrape along if we used a little—a very little of the money mother is going to give me when she sells the necklace. Half of it really belongs to you, you know."

The carnage was truly frightful. I waved my arms and became red in the face. I cried aloud in horror and asserted myself generally. In the end I fell back upon my manly dignity.

"Impossible," I said coldly. "Absolutely impossible! We not only won't discuss the matter any further but we won't even think of it. The subject is closed. Positively nothing doing!"

And so we are to be married.

The wedding is to take place sometime in the fall and will be small but gaudy. All the really worthwhile people will be there. The groom, who, as he recently announced to Iantha's horror, is about to be supported in the style to which he is accustomed, will be attired in navy blue with a neat pin stripe. The other costumes are of small importance, but it may be worthwhile to note that the bride will wear a gold collar, of Oriental design and set with precious stones, which is to be borrowed for the occasion. After the first of the year the young people will make their home in or near Chicago, Illinois. They will be disgustingly happy.

All papers please copy.

PART FIVE

The Necessary Touch

Added by
Iantha

When I signed my name at the end of the beginning of this chronicle—"chronicle" is what the book-writing folks call their stories and I must say I think myself it is a kind of high-sounding word—when I signed my name there at the end of the commencing of this chronicle and laid down my pen, I supposed, of course, that I had laid it down for good. Now it appears that I did not do any such thing; I must take it up again and write the end of the ending, if you know what I mean.

When Mr. Thornton and Jonas Jones had finished their part, the writing they had allotted themselves to do, Mr. Thornton and Marian handed it over to me to read.

"Your opinion is what we want, Iantha," says Mr. Thornton. "Jonas and I are greenhorns at this sort of job, you are an expert. Now give us your candid opinion. Have we left out anything?"

I took all the writing—and the land knows there was enough of it—up to my room and I went over it careful. It took me quite a spell, three long evenings, to get through with it, for even Mr. Thornton's hand of write is hard to make out when he gets going fast, and as for Jonas Jones's—well, hens' tracks are print alongside of *his* scrabble.

I read it, though, finally—every last word of it. On the whole I do not know as I would state that I have much fault to find. They both of them have considerable to say about me and some of it is just stuff and nonsense—like my having hysterics that night when poor dead and gone Mr. Gregg trod on me at the foot of the back stairs. Yes, and Jonas's making out he was so cute when he got me to tell about Captain Freeland's lost pocketbook without as much as hinting what he was driving at. As for hysterics, I never had such a thing in my life, and, even if I had them then—which I take my Bible oath I did not—I should like to know how anybody would feel to be knocked down in the pitch black of the middle of the night and have an unseen foot tramp right on your stomach. As for Jonas Jones's cuteness—well, *those* sort of smarty-cat actions are beneath notice and all I wish to say is that I have my own opinion of them.

So much for that much; but I do ask them just this: Where would *they* have been if I had not remembered so clear all that happened away back there in 1883? Who was it called to mind the message in the nurse's letter? Yes, and also and moreover, who was it found Freeland Blair's diary in Mr. Gregg's table drawer? I ask those questions—and there are plenty more I might ask—and I am sitting right here this minute waiting for the answers.

I will give in, though, that neither Mr. Thornton nor Jonas have called me any more names in this writing than they have called themselves. And I presume probable they have tried to tell the whole truth as they saw it. It is only that—well, I was reading my Testament the other night and I came across a place (Deuteronomy xxxiii: Verse xv) where it said that a person name of Jeshurun—whoever he was; it is not very plain right there—"waxed fat and kicked." Well I can not help kicking when they try to make out I am subject to hysterics.

But to get back to what makes me take up my pen again. As I say, I read all they had written, and when Mr. Thornton asked if I had any criticizings to make I was ready for him.

Says I, "I have got one. When it was decided amongst us that this story of ours was to be set down, I told you then that, if it was going to amount to anything, it ought to have romance in it. You agreed with me, and, at the very beginning, you *have* put a little mite in. But, afterwards, when you get going about the mystery and all, where is your romance? *I* do not see any. You and Marian might have been a couple of twin brothers and sisters, so far as what the books call 'love interest' is concerned. That is my criticism, Mr. Thornton, and I make it open and free—take it or leave it."

He and Marian looked at each other. It was Mr. Thornton who saw fit to answer me first.

"By George, Iantha," he says, "I guess you are right! It is a shame I left out the love interest, but it is too late to do anything about it now, I am afraid."

Jonas Jones was there, same as he is more than half the time these days, and he had to put in his oar.

"Oh, no, it is not, Bill," says he. "Leave it to Iantha. Let her do it for you. She began this yarn of ours, let her finish it. She will take care of the romance shipshape fashion. She can handle yours and Marian's and, when that is done, she can sling in a little about hers and mine. *That* love match has been going on years and years longer than yours, Bill. That is so, ain't it, Iantha?"

I snubbed him up, of course, same as he deserved to be, but the talk ended in my promising to add on a little more at the end of this chronicle.

"Just give the necessary touch, Iantha, do," says Marian. "I am sure you know what that may be far better than we do."

"That is the idea. Go to it, Iantha," agreed Mr. Thornton.

So I am going to it, such as it is, and do not blame me if that such is mighty little.

The wedding is going to be sometime in the late fall— the exact date is not set even yet—and it will be right here in this house where, of course, it ought to be. What I can get ready to wear troubles me most, but Marian and Mary have promised to help, so I trust I shall look fit to be seen. If I am to make an appearance afore all them Chicago and Out West folks I do want it to be a respectable and genteel one. I am planning now to have my green taffeta turned and made over, but that I shall have to buy a new transformation seems certain, for the one I use Sundays is kind of scant in places and shows my own hair through.

Mr. Thornton's vacation is all but over and pretty soon he will be traveling off to Chicago where, so the plan is, he is to go into business along with his father. It is also part of the plan for Mary and Marian to go out there, too, for a little visit with his folks. They will stay only a short while and then come back to get ready for the wedding. The Thorntons, all three of them—there is a daughter name of Dorothy—have been on here already visiting us. I presume likely they wished—which was only natural—to kind of look over the family their son was marrying into.

I hope and trust they was satisfied with us. They seemed to be and, on the whole, we was very well pleased with them. Mr. Thornton—the father, I mean—is a real jolly, pleasant kind of man and his wife is a nice woman. Dorothy—that is our Mr. Thornton's sister—is a pretty girl and, except that she wears her skirts up to her knees, is well behaved and ladylike. However, so far as skirts go nowadays, hers are not much if any shorter than anybody else's, even her own mother's. What this world is coming to I do *not* know.

The Thorntons were, all of them, terribly excited about the finding of Captain Freeland's necklace thing. I do not know how many times I had to tell my story, that about the wreck of the *Pride of the Fleet* and all, and Dorothy spent about half her time up in the attic and the back storeroom gloating, as you might say, over the places where all the doings had started from. So far as that goes, the whole town has been all wrought up over it and Jonas Jones declares that every garret from here to Ostable has been overhauled and rummaged. He goes on to say—but you never can tell how much truth there is in what *he* says—that at least four secret drawers have been found in old desks and tables, but that so far all that has been found in them drawers was a set of lower teeth that had belonged to Captain 'Zekiel Kelly. His daughter—her that was Sophronia Kelly—had bought them for him, but he hated them, would *not* wear them, and finally, they calculate, must have hid them away in that secret rawer, pretending they was lost.

All I can think of as the days go by is about next winter, when Marian is gone to Chicago with her husband and Mary and I will be alone in this big house once more. I can just hear the wind howling and screaming, and the blinds rattling, and the snow and sleet whizzing against the window panes. You might think I ought to be used to it by this time, and in a way I suppose I am, but there has been so much going on here ever since spring that how I can ever settle down to just doing housework with Mary and reading the books Jonas vows he is going to bring me is more than I know.

"I should like to have you tell me, Jonas Jones," I said to him only yesterday, "what sort of story you can ever fetch in now that will be as nerve-racking and horrible as what I have had to undergo, myself. Why, that Poe man's nightmares—yes, even that *Dracula* outrage—would be nothing but an *Elsie* book out of the Sunday School library compared to what I have lived through this summer. I only wish I could forget it, but I can not."

He shook his head. "Iantha," says he, "you would not sell out your recollections of those thrills for a million dollars a shiver. Don't talk to me about forgetting! Why, you have had the time of your young life."

Be that as it may—anyhow they keep saying, Marian and Mr. Thornton do, that sometime early in the winter Mary is to go out to their new house in Chicago to make a long visit and that I am going with her. I do not look forward to it. Chicago, I am afraid, is going to seem dull enough after the excitements I have got used to here in East Orham.

I had written as far as this—yesterday evening it was—when Jonas called. He came in the kitchen door and found me sitting by the table and asked me how I was getting along with touching in the romance. I shook my head.

"I am not getting along at all," I told him. "If you will show me any romance connected with the love affair in this house I will be obliged to you. I am sick and disgusted."

He got up out of his chair. "Is that so!" says he. "Well, I happened to look in at the parlor window as I came by. You follow me."

He tiptoed through the dining room and along the entry-way leading to the living room. I followed him. The door from that entry to the living room was partly open and he made signs for me to look in through the crack.

I did, and there on the sofa in front of the fireplace mantelpiece over which the painting of the *Pride of the Fleet* had been hung up again, sat Marian and Mr. Thornton. Her head was on his shoulder and, judging from what I could see of his arm, it was where it ought to be. They was not saying a word, they were just sitting there together. We looked in at them for a second and then tiptoed away.

When we was back in the kitchen Jonas turned to me.

"There, Iantha," he says, "there is your love interest and your romance. Take your pen and ink, old girl, and touch them in."

So I have, and here they are. Not a great deal, I grant you, but even so much gives me more hope for what the book folks call the "rising generation."

I almost forgot to say a word about Captain Freeland's necklace thing. It has been sold. That iron man has bought it for his wife and is going to pay $250,000 for it, too. Such crazy extravagance about a mess of heathen gewgaws is away beyond my understanding. Both Marian and Mr. Thornton are set and determined that it must not be turned over to them iron folks until after the wedding, because Marian must wear it while she is being married—"just for luck."

Luck! My heavens on earth! What kind of luck is *that* thing liable to fetch anybody? Oh, well, I have said all *I* can. Live and learn, I suppose, has got to be their lot in life, same as everybody else's.

Anyhow, after the wedding that necklace is going to be delivered to the woman whose husband bought it and, I presume likely, she will be wearing it at her balls and receptions and saloons and all her bosom friends will be jealous and say mean things about her behind her back. And when she is dead and gone—or so Mr. Thornton seems to think—it will probably fetch up in a museum.

Well, she and the museum are welcome to it, for all me. I only hope and pray her and her husband have not bought the curse along with it. There is a curse, I am just as sure of that as ever I was. It killed that one-legged rapscallion Isaac Peters; it killed George Crossley and his first mate and the drowned sailors on board the *Pride of the Fleet;* it killed Freeland Blair—yes, and poor Mr. Gregg. It is my opinion, and I do not hesitate to give it out, that the sole reason it did not kill the rest of us is because it did not stay here long enough, that is all. I look in the newspapers every day, expecting to read that that Mrs. Iron Woman has jumped out of the window or been run over by her eight-syllable automobile or been found dead in her gold-posted bed with a look of frozen horror printed on her face. That is what I expect and what I look for.

I have had, more than once, a mind to sit down and write that woman and tell her what I know and what she must be prepared for. But I do not believe it would do any good. A person who lets her husband spend a quarter of a million of dollars for something to make her neck look like a Christmas tree is not likely to listen to the words of counsel from a well-wisher, especially when that well-wisher earns her living washing other folks's dishes in a place like East Orham.

No. As the Good Book says (Psalm lviii: Verse iv) "They are like the deaf adder that stoppeth her ear." So what is the use?

Whenever I hint even as much as this to the folks here they just laugh at me. Jonas Jones, of course, is the worst one.

"Iantha," says he, "you believe that she who groans first laughs last, don't you?"

I made no answer. I said nothing then, I say nothing more now. I watch and wait, that is all, until the time comes and we see what we shall see.

The End